# WATER,
# SPIDERWEB

Sandorf Passage books are available to the
trade through Independent Publishers Group:
ipgbook.com | (800) 888-4741.

Library of Congress Control Number:
2024935661

ISBN: 978-9-53351-519-9

Also available as an ebook;
ISBN: 978-9-53351-520-5

This book is published with financial support by the
Republic of Croatia's Ministry of Culture and Media.

The European Commission support for the production of
this publication does not constitute an endorsement of the
contents which reflects the views only of the authors, and
the Commission cannot be held responsible for any use
which may be made of the information contained therein.

# WATER, SPIDERWEB

translated by ELLEN ELIAS-BURSAĆ

# NADA GAŠIĆ

SAN-
DORF
PAS-
SAGE

SOUTH PORTLAND | MAINE

The Sava (Latin: *Savus*) is a river 940 kilometers long in south-western Europe. In Slovenia the River Sava has two headwaters:

The Sava Dolinka rises as the Nadiža Creek in Tamar, then goes underground and emerges to the light of day in Zelenci, near Rateče, flowing in a southwesterly direction.

The Sava Bohinjka is formed by the confluence of the Mostnica and Jezernica, and rises from Lake Bohinj, flowing in a northwesterly direction.

—http://sl.wikipedia.org/wiki/Sava

The Sava is one of the three longest rivers in Croatia—the other two are the Danube and the Drava. The Sava has a catchment area of 95,720 kilometers.

The Sava is formed by the confluence of the Sava Dolinka (with its spring in the valley between Triglav and the Slovenian-Austrian border near Kranjska Gora) and the Sava Bohinjka (which has its origin where it springs from Lake Bohinj at the town of Ribčev Laz) near Lancovo in Slovenia, and flows into the Danube at Belgrade.

—http://hr.wikipedia.org/wiki/Sava

The Sava is a river in northern Bosnia and Herzegovina, and it is the longest river in our country. It begins where the rivers Sava Dolinka and Sava Bohinjka flow together near Lancovo in Slovenia. It passes from Slovenia into Croatia, flows through Zagreb and Sisak, and then serves as the border running between Bosnia and Herzegovina and Croatia, and then briefly dips into Bosnia and Herzegovina, before becoming part of the border with Serbia, ultimately entering Serbia, where it flows into the Danube at Belgrade.

In ancient times our River Sava was called the Savus, after the Greek Saovios, while today it is simply known as the Sava.

—http://bs.wikipedia.org/wiki/Sava

The Sava is a river in southeastern Europe, 940 kilometers long. It originates at the point where the rivers Sava Dolinka (with its source on in Kranjska Gora, flowing to the southeast from the Karavanka Alps and the Julian Alps) and Sava Bohinjka (with its source south of Triglav) near Radovljica join and flow to the southeast at Kranj, passing, after 300 kilometers, through Zagreb, the capital city of Croatia. It mainly runs along the border between Croatia and Bosnia and Herzegovina. It flows into the Danube at Belgrade, the capital city of Serbia. The Sava is navigable for riverboat traffic from Sisak to Belgrade.

—http://sr.wikipedia.org/sr-el

# Water as overture

THERE WERE RUMORS that high water was heading toward Zagreb from Slovenia, and those who were naturally vigilant paid closer attention to the older people who warned that *the Sava once nearly washed away half of Zagreb*, and there were those who went to the riverbanks and returned alarmed at the sight of logs sweeping along at lightning speed under the bridge in the churning waters, but as no one takes those who watch rivers seriously, this meant that the residents on the southern edges of town slogged through mud along the unpaved roads for four weeks while, meanwhile, in the city center people anxiously snapped open their umbrellas and fussed over their raincoats.

In the early 1960s, news was generally meant to calm people when it should have been rousing them, and it roused them when it should have been encouraging calm—they knew every last thing about Patrice Lumumba and the fate of the children of Congo; they wept over Kennedy; the sad fate of the hapless dog Laika kept the people of Zagreb up at night. But when it was finally announced that *there was a chance of underground water seeping into cellars on the edge of town*, people were more concerned about a blackout that could keep them from watching episodes of *Bonanza* at the culture centers and those rare households that already had their own TV sets.

This was not the first time Trešnjevka had sunk into darkness—since from the earliest days of the neighborhood it had never fully emerged from its beginnings as a cherry orchard. The unlit streetlamps and flickering kerosene lamps that, luckily, hadn't been discarded only made the shivering from the damp chill worse, so the neighbors pulled up their blankets and duvets to their chins.

Nobody's steps could be heard before midnight. The mud buried all sounds and footprints.

Two hours after midnight, dogs began tugging frantically at their chains, and the dogs that weren't chained lunged at fences. Somebody went out into the rain and wailed into the night; somebody pounded on a neighbor's door; somebody called to their mother; somebody cursed Trešnjevka and the dark. From the highway toward Ljubljana, a blue police beacon flashed through the gloom and a garbled voice could be heard yelling through a megaphone. If the voice had been possible to understand, people would have heard: *As a measure of caution, residents should evacuate all basement and ground-floor areas*; as it was, they noted, in all the confusion, a distant siren raising the alarm, and this prompted a few of the older people to muse briefly on the thought that one tends to forget the purpose and point of this unnatural sound with startling, unwarranted speed.

The only sound missing was the ringing of church bells; ever since time immemorial in Zagreb, the bells had been rung as an alarm before floods. Someone's hand might have reached to pull the rope but then stopped, fearful of the strict regulations limiting the ringing of church bells, or perhaps the hand itself did not believe that a vast flood was about to engulf the city and threaten the lives and property of the entire congregation.

Ana Firman sat up in bed and, lowering her legs, tried to feel her way to her slippers. Even with a light on, she wouldn't have been able to see her feet. And besides, she hadn't even tried to see them for over a month. Her husband wasn't awake and the woman, turning toward him, shook his shoulder. Up he jumped.

"Has it started?"

"What? No. There's something's going on outside. Go see."

Zdravko Firman pulled his pants over his pajamas and in the front hall threw on a coat. He didn't respond to his wife's "Grab the umbrella!"

Ana heard her husband exchanging terse, hurried words with neighbors; she heard a curse that wasn't aimed at anybody and a shout that, though nameless, was meant only for her.

"Up, up, get up!"

Her outer body didn't respond right away, but at the tone of his voice, the other one, inside, precisely gauged the degree of danger.

And the inside body, Katarina, was curled up in her belly.

Her husband shouted to his wife from the doorway, "Ana, put on some clothes, we've got to go! The Sava has breached the embankment! It's headed our way! Hurry . . ."

She dropped her arm and while sitting tried to twist her nightgown around to pull it more easily up over her head.

"Ana, put on whatever you can grab over your nightgown, we don't have time. I'll hold the flashlight so you can see."

Blinded by the glare of the flashlight, she dropped her head, holding the hem of her nightgown. Her feet barely reached the floor; her belly rested on her thighs; her head, seemingly neckless, slumped over her belly, and her husband thought he was chastising a timid, potbellied kid. An unfamiliar feeling of pity welled up in him. He lowered the flashlight and went over and stroked her head.

"Don't be scared. Just your coat . . ."

"I'm not." She looked up. "Shine the light on the bag I have ready for the maternity ward, there by the nightstand."

Sure-footed, she got up and grabbed the bag. She was briefly distracted by the unsteady weaving of the flashlight, and squinting, she peered around the room. Everything she could see, absolutely all of it, was things she needed for the life of the household, especially for the child who, any minute now, would be born, and none of these things should get wet, so as it made no difference what to save, Ana Firman grabbed the glass figurine of an accordion player from the nightstand.

Her husband was already standing on the threshold; somebody yelled to him, *To the left, Zdravko, goddamnit, shine to the left*, and the flashlight beam left the hallway in panicked jerks. Furious voices merged: names were called, *Viiilim, Viilim*, a child's cry arousing not pity but panic, a woman's voice pleading with dear God for help, and the curses of a man who was pounding on a front door, shouting to the Zgorelec family—all deaf and cranky.

Nobody in the neighborhood had exchanged a single word with them for ten years.

Because of the shouting of that name, the panic finally hit Ana, but she did not release her grip on the glass figurine. She moved it to her left hand, in which she held her hospital bag, and in the dark raised the other to the coat hook. She fingered her hanging clothes; her trembling hand no longer had time to check what it was she'd grabbed. She didn't dare set the bag down; whatever she first touched she threw over her shoulder and didn't reach for more. Carefully she switched the glass figurine back to her right hand.

She needed only one step to the threshold. Groping, she reached for her husband. She went to him and dropped her left shoulder so he could bring her in under his overcoat. As if not wanting to frighten her any more, he refrained from hugging her and simply took hold of her soft collar.

"I have sorted everything out. You're going with the Ožbolts. I'll stay to throw a few things up in the attic and I'll be right behind you."

"Don't be long."

She didn't shout, she didn't whisper *I won't leave without you*, she didn't even turn. She was so utterly certain he wouldn't betray her.

Her husband shouted to Ožbolt, "Slavek, forget about the Zgorelecs. I'll take an axe to their door later. Here, take Ana with you!"

She stepped gingerly out of the house and sloshed through the shallow water. If she had been able in the dark to see her feet shod in her house slippers, she would have seen the water swirling, which, like a living creature, encircled her, sniffed at her toes, and began to rinse them off before devouring them.

Down the step she went, the single Trešnjevka step that had never been meant as help for coming into or going out of the small house, but as a sign that, as you raised your foot, you were leaving behind the outside world and entering a refuge, or, as you stepped down, you were going out onto the street, such as it was. The step seemed higher than her foot remembered, broader than it was, and Ana Firman believed the step wouldn't betray her. It would stem the flood.

She didn't know what she was wearing; she left her house wearing not an overcoat but a work smock thrown over her nightgown, clutching the glass accordion-player figurine in her right hand, and in her left the new plaid bag she'd bought at the Trešnjevka Nama department store, and in it, in preparation for the maternity ward: two new nightgowns; a pink nylon topstitched bathrobe smuggled in from Italy, where they'd bought it from a street vendor; soap in a light-blue plastic soap box; a toothbrush with a see-through red handle, in a container of the same color; strawberry-flavored toothpaste; a green comb; a little tin of Sole; two new towels; and the things she needed for the baby.

It's not that the other things left in her room and in the house got a little wet—it's that they vanished without a trace in the Sava River water that flooded the southern part of Zagreb during the night between 25 and 26 October, 1964, where 180,000 people lived, and which destroyed or damaged 8,676 houses and took the lives of seventeen townspeople.

Among them was of Katarina Firman's father, Zdravko. Katarina, married name Horak.

Later, Ana never could remember whether she turned at all to look back at the house and her husband, or simply joined the column of Trešnjevka residents setting off in the darkest night, on foot, with or without umbrellas, pushing overloaded bicycles in front of them and carrying cardboard suitcases and baskets with the items they'd grabbed, or they were empty-handed as they left their homes and the streets and neighborhoods where they'd grown up. The owners of the few private cars that existed in Trešnjevka at the time were attuned and vigilant and had cleared out a few hours earlier, so there was nothing to hear but the shouts and the previously unfamiliar, callous, and insidious noise of the water gushing in from all sides—as if a beast had thrown open its maw and roared and roared and roared.

Ana remembered letting two of her neighbors lead her along the fences of houses through familiar streets they had traversed their whole lives in the dark, so they found it easy to wade through the water, only ankle-deep at first, then shin-deep, and reaching in some places dangerously close to the hips. She knew to obey the voices, *don't look*, when they passed by a gaping pothole on Gvozdanska with the swirling of water gurgling in the terrible darkness. They knew these potholes so well that even then, in the dark, under the wan light from their flashlights, they adeptly avoided them. She knew she'd heard a desperate voice reaching them from Hreljinska, calling to somebody named Joža to climb up on the roof and take hold of their grandmother, and by the panicked squeeze of Ožbolt's hand she felt that he, too, knew the grandmother wouldn't make it. She remembered that on Končarova, which was slightly uphill from Nehajska, the water had dropped back down to ankle-deep, and that they lifted her up onto a truck full of old folks, women, and children, that the mood on the truck was lively, even with some laughter, and this laughter reminded her to call out the name of Katarina's father, though she didn't. As if she'd opened her mouth yet stopped when the truck got going.

Katarina peacefully sucked up the warmth from the body that was shielding her; she couldn't have cared less that her mother's feet and hands were freezing to the point of pain, that she was shivering, her teeth chattering; Katerina didn't care where this belly, her home, would lie down. She clearly signaled that she wanted more room, a place where she could focus for a few hours on herself alone. Ana, Katarina's mother, moaned. The women in the truck were alarmed; they pounded on the cabin and shouted, *Her waters, her waters broke.* The driver of the truck panicked at the very word "waters," and in fear that he wouldn't make it to the Petrova maternity ward, he chose, instead, to swerve onto the driveway to Vinogradska hospital, which was closer. He could hardly wait to get rid of the woman with the belly. And the women in the truck understood him.

Insulted that on this very last day they couldn't leave her in peace to attend to the work of her heart and her birthing mother's heart, Katarina shut out all external stimuli; she ignored the screams and concentrated on using the sudden influx of additional blood that her mother's veins were sending her, the precious oxygen and contractions coming from Ana's body, as Katarina moved centimeter by centimeter toward the outside world. She took care of this good, challenging, and relatively speedy task. She gave a brief cry and quickly dropped off to sleep. Enough for that day.

When Katarina left her mother's body, the day was already dawning, so those who had the chance to climb up onto one of the few five-story buildings, or onto the still-unfinished *Vjesnik* newspaper building, could look across Trešnjevka and Trnje and see for themselves this lake with no name and the wet roofs protruding from it. The watery expanse looked as if it had been there forever. The radio, which nobody in Trešnjevka or Trnje could hear, announced that a catastrophic flood had inundated the capital city of Croatia; that the army, police, fire brigades, and volunteers were making superhuman efforts to save people and property; that representatives of the City and the Republic had gone to the site of the disaster; that the material damages were only now being assessed; that the first who offered to help Zagreb were its fraternal cities from the other socialist republics; that the Red Cross had already been delivering first aid; that hotels opened their doors to provide accommodation, as did all the schools and gymnastics halls; that hospitals were ready to welcome and care for the injured, and vaccinations of all kinds were in adequate supply; that an extraordinary session of the Government was expected, as well as help from abroad; and, finally, that the first Trešnjevka baby had been born at Vinogradska hospital, as a symbol of renewal and the indestructibility of life, and the mother and daughter were doing well. It was also reported that telegrams of sympathy and support were arriving from all sides, and the Yugoslav national soccer team had lost a friendly match with Hungary at Nép Stadium in Budapest, 2 to 1.

Ana saw her little girl and was amazed that she could ever have wanted a son.

They wheeled her from the birthing room to one of the hospital rooms, where they put her on a temporary cot.

She waited.

Sleep lured her, but she fended it off.

She waited.

She finally mustered the courage and did what she could to explain to the nurse that they'd brought her to Vinogradska because her labor pains had come on so suddenly. They'd been supposed to take her to the Petrova maternity ward, and now her husband was probably looking for her there, and did the nurse know if he'd called.

The nurse did not.

Ana couldn't bring herself to talk with the women in the room.

A few more times she asked the nurse in passing whether anyone had asked after her, because they must be looking for her. Then she stopped asking.

They brought breakfast. She couldn't eat.

She waited.

The sounds of the hospital became ordinary, mundane. The women in the room were already mothers and were having the usual conversations about their births. They gossiped about the on-duty nurse. None of them were from Trnje or Trešnjevka, so their curiosity and interest for the extent of the flood were fleeting.

At about eleven o'clock, a proper hospital bed was rolled into the room for Ana. She settled down.

She waited.

A bit before, noon a doctor came in and asked how she was feeling. He took her blood pressure. The women stopped talking.

When the on-duty nurse stepped around the doctor and served her—and only her—an orange on a plate, Katarina's mother realized there was no need to wait any longer. She didn't shed a tear, she just threw back her head and howled as she hadn't howled even once while giving birth. They all shrieked and sobbed.

At that very moment:

A helicopter flew over the intersection of Savska Road and the highway; people waved to it gaily from the roof of the student dormitory in Cvjetno naselje and the still-unfinished *Vjesnik* newspaper building.

The deaf Zgorelecs were up on a beam in the attic of their house, tied in place to keep from falling. With axes in hand, they were poised to attack looters and protect their property.

On Modruška Street, a red patent-leather pump floated by, and its perfect tip bumped up against a green kitchen cabinet. Lying on a mat on the gym floor of the Upper Town high school, a girl, who had been evacuated from Trešnjevka and had just finished high school, wept.

In the concert hall of the Trešnjevka high school on Dobojska Street, the black, shiny body of a piano could be seen under the turbid water.

On Drežnička Street, on a fence that had withstood the torrent, tidily perched was a bedraggled family of chickens, dejectedly watching the water that was coursing through the ruins of their coop.

In a five-story building on Savska, running from numbers 95 to 101A, the news got out among the pupils of the Kata Dumbović Elementary School that the grading registers for their class had been washed away, and two of the seventh graders burst into song, singing: *Youuuu aaare myyyy destinyyyy* . . .

At a shelter set up by the Red Cross, an old man wept for his dog, which had disappeared.

On one of the roofs of the single-story buildings, among the people still awaiting evacuation, a fourteen-year-old girl shivered while watching a door float by, on which rats were nervously scampering. Her blue lips no longer had the strength to purse, and she didn't cry out, or yell, or scream; she just gave a throaty grunt. A man crouching beside her straightened up, and with his stick he pushed the rat raft away. The people were later picked up off the roof and accommodated in the corridors of the Vinogradska hospital.

A boat made its way along Savska Road. In it sat a solemn man, rowing.

At the Student Center, the deluge had begun to lose momentum, but the water had lapped its prey and licked the tram tracks all the way to the Mladost bookstore on Marshal Tito Square. The sandbag levee behind the overpass at Crnatkova, near Vodnikova, held back most of the water. Along that slender sandbag boundary, where the world of the outlying neighborhoods and their poverty ended and the city began, people stood and watched the water. They were smiling. Someone took their picture.

Not far from them stood a hunched seven-year-old boy with his pockets full of stones, and at regular intervals he tossed them, one by one, into the water. Where the water was already still, he could watch the ripples fan out, the ripples and waves that spread and spread . . .

NADA GAŠIĆ

*There were places where a mark was left on the water.*
*Because we couldn't see it does not mean it wasn't there.*

Century: 21st
Year: 2009
Month: October
Night/day: 25th/26th
Time: 8:48 PM

# First stone, first wave

## *Murky plastic sheeting*

HE STOPPED SHAKING and slapping the woman, but he was still holding her body—her head dangling at an unnatural angle. The man thought the skin on the woman's neck might tear at any moment, so, disgusted, he dropped the body, which made an ugly sound as it hit the leather couch. He wiped his hands on his thighs, and then, feeling his own hairy and wet naked body, he moved his hands away and, like a sleepwalker, hands outstretched, went to the bathroom. He turned on the faucet over the washbasin and put his left arm under the stream of water. Leaning his body over the sink, he propped his right arm on the mirror, covering his face. Then he shifted position and rinsed his right arm. He put both hands under the faucet and watched the water eddy in the cup he'd formed with his palms. He bent over and inserted his lowered head into the tight space between the sink and the faucet. The stream hit his ear and, other than the powerful slap of the water, all sounds from the outside world went away. This began to hurt, so the man pulled out his head, gingerly, as if withdrawing it from a fissure. He didn't towel himself off, just shook off the drops. For a time, he stood there, still. Then he returned to the room, went over to the couch, and watched the woman's naked body. Her head, as if sewn onto a body it didn't belong to, lay there somehow independently and to the side. He no longer had any doubt that the body was dead. This was no longer a woman. It was a body. He went over to the table where his phone was. He switched it on. He stared at the thumb with which he sent the message. Then he opened his hand, and the screen showed him that the time was precisely 8:55 PM. His hand, like his thumb, was still. He felt everything would be fine. It had to be.

Twenty-five minutes later:
—Don't ask.
—I won't.
—It was an accident.
—We aren't calling anyone, agreed?
—You know best.
—I'm off to the garage for the plastic sheeting.
—Need my help?
—No. Get dressed.
—Look at me, naked . . . I totally lost it.
—Don't leave the room. I left someone out in my car.
—Are you crazy?
—Don't come out. I know what I'm doing.

He left the naked man. He walked out of the house, leaving the naked man in the room, went to the car, opened the door, and told the person in the back seat not to move and not to look around. He lifted the trunk lid, took out leather gloves, and pulled them on. Then he opened the garage door, went into the garage, and picked up a roll of heavy-duty plastic sheeting. He didn't have to look for it; he knew this garage well. He went through the inside garage door to a staircase that he took up to the room with the open fireplace, the leather couch, the naked body on it, and the man, now dressed, sitting in an armchair. He set the roll of plastic on the couch by the man's feet. He picked up the women's scattered clothing, and, holding it wadded in his left hand, he stirred the fire in the grate with a poker before tossing in the clothes. They must have smelled bad, but the man didn't turn his head away. He waited for the last bit of cloth to burn. Then he went over to the couch. He unrolled the sheeting and slid it adeptly under the body, then with both hands he rolled the body over on its side to make the wrapping easier. After a turn, the body resembled a rolled-up rug, but it was trickier to handle. The huge man panted. He was barely able to hoist the cylindrical burden over his shoulder. He came to the doorway and stopped. He didn't turn to the motionless, clothed man, but his words could be clearly heard.

—Are we even?

The man nodded.

—We are. Where . . . with that?

—Better you don't know.

He needed a little more time to make his way down the stairs. The burden wasn't too heavy for him to manage, but it was cumbersome. He left the same way he'd come in, through the garage, then went over to the open trunk, the trunk lid, like a huge screen, blocking the rear window of the car. Inside the car, nobody moved. Huffing with relief, he lowered the body into the trunk as if dumping a dead animal into a pit. It thudded heavily. The car only shook a little. This was a powerful beast of a car.

The lid of the trunk responded to his command, closing silently, as advertised.

The man closed the garage door with the remote, walked around to the driver's side with a steady step, sat in the driver's seat, fastened his seat belt, turned the key in the ignition, and started the engine. He did not turn to look at the back seat, where there was somebody curled up, nor at the house, surrounded by woods, that was slowly receding in the rearview mirror.

Twenty-three minutes later:
—Why are you driving toward the school?
—Hush.

\*     \*     \*

The number of people at the tram stop had dwindled; the intervals between arriving trams was getting longer, and the boy was, actually, beginning to feel bored. He was no longer sure what he was waiting for. Definitely not the tram. He stood by the sidewalk curb, twisted his head to the side, stretched his neck, and saw the street clock declaring to all four corners of the world that the time was 9:58 PM. The seconds didn't matter. It was time for him to be going home. But slowly, as slowly as possible . . . Mustn't get there too soon. He pulled his hood up so he couldn't see a thing on either side, but he could look straight ahead or down at his feet. If he were to run into anyone he knew looking like this, they definitely wouldn't recognize him. Or so he felt.

He turned onto Nehajska, going in the opposite direction from the tram, leaving behind the sickly light of the pharmacy by the tram stop right next to the Trešnjevka farmers market. He walked by the dark grotto someone had long since identified as a street, Maglajska, left behind the houses leading up to Dobojska, and squeezed by the walls of the buildings that ended along the access road to the Trešnjevka playing fields. He stopped. He'd wait. A little longer. He must not get home too early. Let her wait, yes, let her wait . . .

The area around the school was different looking at night; even the building didn't much resemble itself, and he eyed it with deep-rooted animosity. He leaned with his backpack against the wall. By the last house, he leaned with his backpack against the wall that separated the neighborhood from the playing fields. He dropped his gaze, and only then did he realize he was standing in a puddle; he felt his sneakers soaking up water, and his feet were frozen to the bone. He stuck his tongue out at his own stupidity and then decided to look for a dry spot. He was surrounded by muddy scum that had smeared all over the sidewalk, and the only things that seemed a little less wet were scraps of posters that had peeled off the wall he'd been leaning against. One of them, almost intact, looked a little less trampled, so the boy moved onto its relatively dry surface, though by then an off-putting darkness had already taken hold. He checked once again whether he was standing on a dry spot. He carefully scraped his mud-caked sneaker. The greasy smear on his sneaker left an interesting mark on the poster, and he grinned. He saw he was standing on a photo-graph of a merry group of people, whose good mood infected him, so he decided to make the photograph cheerier yet. There wasn't much light, but it was enough for scribbling over the bright poster surface. With the rest of the mud on his sneaker, he gave everybody mustaches, then he carefully blacked in ev-ery other tooth, and to the face of a perky musician he added Asterix's helmet with the wings. Well, the wings on the hel-met did look more like hairy horns, but still . . . It came out so brilliantly that he was sorry the embellished poster wasn't in a more visible place. He checked out the wall and spotted two clean posters on it, two faces without splotches or the cheery accompaniment, which, being without wrinkles, smooth and pink, opened a whole series of possibilities for ornament. Al-though one poster was mounted quite low, he couldn't reach it with his sneaker, so he began looking around for something he could use to scoop up the mud and fix the faces on the posters. He spun around. He spotted a chunk of wood, stone, whatever, leaned over, and concluded it would do nicely. A decent rock. He dipped it into the mud and went to work. He filled in one of the lenses of the glasses on one of the faces, added a bandage across the forehead, and made one of the teeth quite black. He stepped back, pleased, to inspect the new look of the poster; tomorrow morning, passersby would have something to see. Then he moved over onto a face with a determined expression that wore no glasses, and he decided to blacken those eyes. The person turned into a blind man, a dense jack-o'-lantern. What he'd drawn was terrific. An excellent task. He laughed, hiding the sound of something approaching. He didn't hear it in time.

NADA GAŠIĆ

How could he have failed to hear it? He'd been distracted. Idiot. The car, its headlights off, was already inching up over the curb where the access road ran down to the school. He was horrified. He knew drawing on posters was forbidden, and he knew that occasional police patrols drive slowly, with their lights off, and the only thing he had time to do was to drop the muddy rock and duck behind the wall. Had they seen him? They must have. But maybe not? Their lights were off, and he was standing in the dark. He hugged the wall. It didn't occur to him to budge. Then the car stopped. Nothing happened. Maybe they really hadn't seen him. Were they here for some other reason? He also knew that couples pulled into empty passageways to kiss and wiggle around on the seats. Yuck. But at least people doing that couldn't care less about him drawing on posters. He couldn't resist, and he moved cautiously, enough so he could see the car. The windows were tinted, and he couldn't tell whether the driver was alone or was with somebody. A man, a woman, two men, two women, a man and a woman, more than two?

The car door opened. The boy froze. A very large man stepped out. The boy closed his eyes. That way he felt less scared. But he shouldn't ... He should watch the man so he'd be poised to run in time if the man came after him. He opened his eyes. He saw a huge man with a shaved head, bent over the trunk as it slowly opened. The man was not looking in the direction of the boy. So he hadn't seen him. The boy relaxed. Whoever this was hadn't pulled over because of his drawing. No, not the drawing. Very quietly, he stood there. Now it would be weird to come forward. The man dragged something huge out of the trunk, wrapped. He struggled. With his giant body he blocked the view, and the boy strained to see what the man would do with his long, heavy package. Probably he'd move it onto the back seat?

Then the man suddenly hoisted whatever it was up with both arms and dumped it over into the dark space beyond the wall. It thudded dully on the ground, rolled only once, and came to a reluctant stop. Almost at the boy's feet. Danger, danger. The boy stared as the heavy plastic unwound unnaturally slowly.

From it fell a hand.

If the boy had been certain that he'd seen what he saw, he might have fainted, he might have screamed, and maybe he'd have screamed again and again until finally his nocturnal child's voice would move something in one of the nearby houses, but as it was he only whimpered, then took off, like he'd never run in his life, toward the school fence where he knew there was a hole, which he had slipped through many times. He didn't have to look for it; he ran straight to it and bent down, but not quite low enough. His backpack snagged, and for an agonizingly long three or four seconds, it snared him like an insect on the chain-link fence. The boy yanked for all he was worth; the plastic on the outside pocket of the backpack snarled, released, and the boy wriggled free. He knew he could hear steps, but he didn't turn, he just ran, ran with all his might, till he only heard his footsteps. He stopped. The silence behind the boy was brief; the car started up. The boy panted. He had time to catch his breath; this way, over the playing fields, a car couldn't reach him.

He went quite still; his breathing steadied. He had a look behind, around. Nobody there; nothing moved. The lights of the car weren't visible, but he heard the quiet purr of the engine.

He had to move. It wasn't good that he was wasting time; the car and the man were too close.

He didn't dare cross the open ground of the playing fields. There would be no point in heading toward Sokolgradska down the edge of the schoolyard. And maybe the car was headed for Sokolgradska?

No, not Sokolgradska.

Slowly, seeking darker spots, the boy set off toward Dobojska.

No, not Dobojska! He'd have to go back, he'd have to return to the road, to people. But he couldn't bear passing *that place*. Yet he'd have to. Maybe they're waiting for him at Dobojska?

No, not Dobojska!

But maybe, maybe they left? They're scared of the person who *saw*. Everybody's scared of someone who *sees*.

He has to go back, but how will he pass *that place*?

Fuck it. He started off toward Dobojska. When he came to the little house right by the main entrance to the high school, he knew there was no dog there, and this emboldened him. He grabbed the fence with both hands and vaulted into someone's backyard. He peeked out but didn't straighten up. He knew he was essentially invisible, crouching like this. Dobojska was deserted.

Now!

He hopped the fence, dashed across the street, and scrambled up the fence of another yard. A neighbor's dog barked angrily, and he could hear it pulling at its chain. He sprinted across the yard; lights went on in the house, and a voice shouted, *It's a thief, a thief's out in the yard*. The boy was already on the other side, and he flew out onto Maglajska.

He turned right. Nothing. Not a soul. He turned left. His breath choked, gurgled; he gasped and screamed with an unfamiliar scream. He was standing there before the gaping jaws of the beast, but he didn't move. He froze.

As did the car, black, in the dark of Maglajska.

On went the terrifying headlights. Squinting from the glare, the boy began to move after all and took off at a run. To the right.

The car rolled after him.

Then suddenly it slammed on the brakes.

Maglajska became too narrow for such a big beast to maneuver. It could go no farther, and its doors couldn't even open far enough for the driver to get out and chase the boy.

The mysterious driver was not very familiar with the streets of Trešnjevka.

While the man was cursing behind the wheel, the boy ran like crazy; with a spring he cleared the last fence and came out onto an abandoned lot of land next to the farmers market. Equipped with the same breadth of knowledge as a real secret agent, he understood what lay ahead—he knew the old streets like the back of his hand; he knew which backyards had dogs and which did not, the gardens that were overgrown and the ones that had been abandoned, the houses in ruins on sites awaiting new owners, the sturdy walls around the new buildings, the alarms and bulwarks he couldn't sneak past, the passageways he could scramble down, the building sites that were dangerous to walk through even during the day, and the new streets he didn't even know the names of. But he knew he would make it home. He'd get home.

Just a little, a little more . . .

## Smoking kills, and so does not smoking

—You pricked me with that pin. Where were your eyes?

Katarina looked up from the dress, now and then, glanced over at the door of the little backyard shack they called the Zadruga, and, indeed, she was to blame. She had pricked her sister.

—Oops, sorry. There, I'll be more careful.

She tried to focus on a job she was not good at; a portion of the train for the wedding gown—into which, as if into a big white marshmallow, her youngest sister had wriggled—was snaking around too much on the floor, and Katarina had been trying to grab it and pin it up with straight pins.

—What's wrong? You pricked me again! There will be blood-stains on my wedding gown. What's wrong?

—I didn't mean to. It's tricky pushing through the silk.

—I don't care about whether you meant to or not, you pricked me twice. Stop staring at the door. If she comes, she comes; if she doesn't, she doesn't.

*Now he'd come to a tricky spot along Dobojska. He wouldn't turn left toward Ljubljanska Avenue; the old highway was open and a vulnerable area. He shivered there by the broken fence and watched. Dobojska was deserted. Nearby, a dog he didn't know was barking. A new fear engulfed the boy, but different from the one that had shaken him ever since he'd seen the thing. Any dog he wasn't familiar with was a dangerous dog. The boy took a breath, rebounded off the fence, and dashed across to Ključka. From Bočačka to Čapljinska wasn't far. Those little streets are short.*

*So close, so close to his front door . . .*

Katarina turned so she was no longer facing the door, but that didn't make her feel more relaxed. She'd stop what she was doing now and then and puff on her fingers as if to rest them, and when her sister wasn't watching, she'd glance at the wall clock. From the top of the wedding-dress-marshmallow, she heard a grumpy tsk-tsk. Her sister pulled the dress toward her stomach, lowered and then raised the bizarre, ballooning puff sleeves, and finally pulled the train over to her, yanking out all the straight pins Katarina had been dedicating herself to for over half an hour.

They both started yelling, their voices bouncing off the half-empty room's walls. *You are a nutcase, you are absolutely nuts.* The bride burst into tears. Alarmed, Katarina took her sister by the elbow, shook her a little, and tried to calm her down.

—Ita, don't cry. I'll fix it, don't you worry! I'll be careful, don't worry! I'll go slow now, slow, so slow.

It was easier for her to calm herself than her sister, and, as she was determined to wrap up the job, she bent over to pick up the scattered pins. Then she stopped and straightened. She remembered that the pins she'd already used might possibly stain the white, white satin, so she pried a few clean ones from the box. Like a seasoned seamstress, she held two of them between her teeth, to keep them at the ready and to shut herself up.

The door flew open just when nobody was watching.

—Hey, hey! Hey, girls, mie sorelle, sisters, hey! Jesus, are you gorgeous! Jesus Christ, it looks brilliant on you!

Both of them, Ita and Katarina, turned to the voice.

—Wow, fits you like a glove! You started without me? Okay, okay. I brought everything. Christ, what time is it? Is it already that late?

NADA GAŠIĆ

Katarina took the pins from her mouth.

—It's not *that* late. It's exactly 10:25 PM.

The woman who had just come in moved a few things over on the two-seater and, without a glance at Katarina, calmly said:

—Shut up.

They'd been waiting for her. The third sister.

*Not far to go, not far before he'd be home.*

*At Čapljinska he knew which yard he'd creep through to Bužimska and how he'd take Udbinska to the wall behind the Cultural Center, right by the park. He'd catch his breath there.*

*A little, a little more . . .*

Katarina knit her fingers over her chest.

—You know full well what time it is.

Ita was bothered by Katarina's edgy tone and the old-person stance with her hands.

—Cut it out, Katja, stop! Irma, do you really like it? You're kidding. You really like it? I'm not too fat?

—Of course not; your hips don't show at all.

The two of them chattered on; enthusiastic invocations to Jesus were heard, along with the rustling of silk and the tapping of high heels.

What with the twisting and fidgeting, the marshmallow lost some of its straight pins, but Katarina was no longer paying attention. She said nothing and shot provocative glances at the clock.

—Yes, Irma, my dear, you did see the time. Your eyesight is fine.

The marshmallow swayed and raised a rebellion.

—Katja, stop it already or I'm leaving. So, she was a little late, so what?

Katarina shut up.

Number three set her bags and purse on the two-seater, and from her purse she took her cigarettes; then she plunked down by her packages, next to the armrest, in the shadow of a wax lampshade. She licked her cigarette but didn't have the chance to light it.

—Irma, lay off the cigarettes; you'll make her wedding gown stink.

—Cut it out, Katarina, what's with the hysterics . . .

—I'm not hysterical. The Zadruga has a low ceiling; the dress will soak up all the smoke smell.

*He stepped on something smelly and yucky, but he didn't turn or stop until he reached the hedge behind the Cultural Center. He held the wet branches and, beat, sank to the ground. He panted quickly and too loudly. It felt like his hard breathing made his padded jacket puff up. Any more and he'd take off and fly. For a moment, he could see himself flying, and the thought of it relaxed him. He caught his breath and got going again. Moving along close to the building and hedge, he reached a place where he could see clear across the park. No, he's no idiot, he won't go across the park. He ran to the left in a burst of strength and made it to the Health Center. No more stops to rest. This is a danger zone. Nehajska is too close.*

*And he had so little left to go, so little before he'd be home . . .*

Irma put away her cigarettes.

—Fine, so what, if anything, is allowed here?

She was complaining, but her tone was actually conciliatory.

Nobody answered her as Irma rustled with her plastic bags.

—Might you care to see a little present for my baby sister?

The sisters watched her. She wasn't rummaging through her bags; she knew exactly what she was looking for. She pulled out several wrapped things. She didn't get up, just leaned over and placed gold and silver packages on the dressing table with the mirror that multiplied the reflection of the white silk.

—Gold, for my most beautiful bride, silver for my older sis who has a biiirthdaaay tomorrow.

The way she stretched out the syllables was not nice.

While she withdrew again into the shadow—half-sitting, hunched over, well planted on her high heels—her long red hair swayed under Katarina's hand, brushed her bared lower arm, and left an unpleasant odor of alcohol deliberately masked with perfume.

The little gifts in boxes softened Katarina's tone, but still she wasn't relenting.

—Irma, sit up, I can't see you very well.

Irma did move, but only to retreat even more deeply into the shadow.

—I'm swell right here. Girls, aren't you dying to know what's in these packages? Or are you sick of presents?

—Nooo, I'll open it right away. Let me take off the gloves.

The bride tried to peel the left glove off with the fingers of her right hand, but the hard, synthetically reinforced silk wouldn't release. She brought her fingers to her mouth to peel it with her teeth.

Katarina grabbed her hand.

—Not with your teeth, are you crazy, you'll ruin them. Wait, I'll do the left! Irma, you can do the right.

Irma didn't move.

Katarina glanced over at the two-seater. She said nothing more as she slowly peeled the long gloves back toward her sister's fingers. The left and then the right. Success.

Marshmallow girl raised her arms and waved them around like a child.

—I feel like I can fly now. What a relief. Wow, this wedding-gown thing is torture.

—Hey, Katarina, quit the nagging!

The younger sisters said this in unison and laughed at the sentence they'd been repeating for years, ever since the death of their mother, Ana Firman—who took the name Žiger when she remarried—when the oldest sister assumed the role of nagger in chief.

*Nearly there, nearly home ...*

Katarina didn't react to their laughter.

—You can call it nagging, a pain in the neck, whatever you like, but I cannot understand why you needed to go and borrow a wedding gown. You could have had one made for you or bought something simpler.

—Wow, Katarina, it's like you're a hundred years old. Wedding gowns are borrowed.

—People do borrow, but you don't need to. Why go to your wedding in a borrowed gown?

NADA GAŠIĆ

—Girls, open the presents so we can make a toast! Is this a shower or what?

The *girls* did what she said. The rustling of gold and silver wrapping paper was heard.

—Jesus and Mary! Irma, you're completely crazy. What? A necklace? Real gold?

—Of course it's real, silly girl.

—Where did you get the money? You're crazy!

Nobody expected an answer to the question, just as nobody had any doubts about the sanity of the sister who came bearing gifts.

Katarina opened her box; her lips quivered.

—A pin. An accordion. Iiirma . . . Is this genuine Swarovski?

—No, it's from a Dubrava street vendor. Of course it's Swarovski. It reminded me of that figurine of Mama's that I broke. That's why I picked it. Like it?

—Yes, it reminds me of that too . . . I really like it.

More rustling on the two-seater. Irma produced a bottle, and, using the moment while her sisters were admiring their jewelry, she handily opened it and poured the beverage into glasses that were neatly lined up in rows of twelve on one of the overcrowded tables.

She set two of the glasses on the old Bagat sewing machine cabinet.

—A little cognac to perk up our spirits! Cheers to the bride!

Before her sisters had even taken up their glasses, Irma drained hers, and, with bottle in hand, she returned to the two-seater. Into the shadow.

—Oh look, silly me, I drank mine before you did. Let's have another. Cheers to the bride!

She poured herself another.

Katarina set the box with the brooch down on the sewing machine cabinet, took her glass, and leaned over toward Irma.

—Wait, and a kiss?

Irma turned her head, and her kiss flew by her sister's face. Katarina winced suddenly at the empty space her pursed lips had passed through. Her voice forgot about the present she'd been given. It darkened.

—Irma, you've been drinking.

—Well, you saw me drink first. Get off my case.

Katarina pulled away.

—You've had more than that one sip.

They watched each other. Irma smiled. A not-nice smile.

—Where's your son, dear older, nagging sister? Where's your little boy? Worry about him, why don't you, not me.

Katarina's lips vanished from her face. She leaned over and glared hard into Irma's eyes, into the face she wanted to fling things at. But she didn't. She stopped herself.

With that face there was something off-kilter. It wasn't just the alcohol.

*And there, by the side of the Health Center building, almost right at Nehajska, he found a hedge. He crouched and almost crawled right in. He didn't move. Although the Trešnjevka police station was nearby, it didn't occur to him to ask for help. What would he tell them? Who would believe him? Who would protect him? Better to keep an eye on the streets. The thinned autumn branches of the hedge were not such great shelter, but without it he'd have been visible a kilometer away. All he had to move were his eyeballs to watch the street without turning his head. He spotted it; the black car turned from Ozaljska onto Nehajska. He didn't doubt for a second that this was the car driven by the giant man. He nestled farther into the hedge. His hood was pulled down low; he was very still, and all he had to do was wait quietly, quietly. And not think that he was coming. Through his squinting eyelids he saw lights coming closer. Slowly. Don't be scared. It'll keep driving, keep driving . . . He squeezed the slits tight too. They'll keep driving, keep driving . . .*

*If he hadn't been squinting, he'd have seen that, crouching as he was, he barely reached up to the rim of the huge tire. The car slid by. It passed slowly, the way danger passes: slowly.*

*The boy didn't open his eyes until he began to feel scared of his inner darkness. The sound of the street had changed; other cars were driving by, and the black beast was gone. Loud passersby appeared on the sidewalk, and the boy was relieved to see them.*

*Then he wisely waited for the street to empty out completely, and, without looking left or right, he sprinted across. Now he was certain he wouldn't get caught.*

*He was so near, so near to home . . .*


—Oh my God, take this thing off me, gotta pee.

Katarina was happy to turn away from Irma. She was glad that something in the room had become momentarily more important than the boozy breath and frozen face of her middle sister. Irma was the first to laugh, and she suggested they leave the bride in her trap of silk, sequins, seed pearls, and lace, but in the end, they took mercy on frantic Ita and helped her emerge from the petticoats. The dress was carefully hung on a hanger. Ita, half-dressed, covered in goose bumps, fled to the bathroom. Her emptied, anxious marshmallow was left behind in a deflated heap.

Katarina was feeling good just then, and she didn't stop to think about her son.

*He knew exactly which entranceway to the building on Nehajska was never locked and how he'd have no problem zipping through it to the miniature substation building by Crikvenička. Then he had to be super, super careful. Behind every wall something, or someone, might be standing. He knew that here, just meters from his house, he must be the most careful of all. It was so, so close. His good, quiet house.*

The two of them were left alone, and the room suddenly filled with emptiness, as if they were standing on a bare stage, and as if around them, on the tables, there hadn't been set out rows and rows of glasses, boxes of balloons, boxes of confetti, armfuls of white and pink paper garlands, dozens of white paper bows the size of largish heads of cabbage, plastic transparent cupids, packages of neatly arranged pink napkins, gold plastic platters, pink dinner plates . . .

They exchanged glances.

—Irma, clearly you can't be bothered as far as behavior is concerned.

—Shut up, Katarina, I'm in no mood for your nagging.

—My nagging? You should be ashamed of yourself—your sister is getting married. You could have stayed away from your crowd at least for today.

—You have no idea, so why don't you shut up.

—You look awful. When Ita's done, go tidy up in the bathroom before Cilika gets here.

—I am not one to tidy up in bathrooms.

—Watch it, or I'll have my say about where you tidy up and with whom, in bathrooms, if necessary.

—Go to hell!

—Teacher, dear teacher, your vocabulary is not what they taught us in school, or at home, for that matter.

—Like I said, go to hell!

—You're trash, Irma. Trash. They'll sweep you up off the street, if there's anything left for them to sweep.

—So maybe I am trash, but I'm not treated like trash. While you're a hoity-toity lady, yet you are treated like trash. For instance, your ex and his current wife, right? Odd, isn't it?

—To you he's the father of my child.

Katarina felt there was a hollow ring to her answer, and this unnerved her. She was in the mood for more of a fight, but didn't know how. Once more she spat out:

—Piece of trash. I am still your older sister, and I am telling you to go clean yourself up. You look like . . . better I don't say what.

She looked down and happened to notice Irma's wrist. Her concern about her sister's behavior abruptly shifted to concern about her well-being.

—What's up with your hands?

Irma got up, pulling at the sleeves of her turtleneck. She took a step toward the door and into the shadow cast by the wardrobe.

—Oh, nothing, scratched on the car door . . .

Katarina had the impression that this wasn't her sister's usual voice. Too contrite.

The intonation was infectious. And her own voice had a similar ring.

—Go wash your hands. There's rubbing alcohol in the medicine cabinet over the toilet.

Irma did not respond.

Ita came back, beaming with glee in her jeans and a T-shirt.

—Girls, we should celebrate that I didn't pee in my pants. Let's have another round.

—Ita, that's enough. Irma has already had too much.

—Katja, stop the nagging, can't she have a drink in peace today? What's up with you?

Irma rose to her feet, took the bottle, stood in front of Katarina, and threw back a brazen swig.

Ita was applauding at a moment when someone, only once, knocked and, without waiting to be invited in, opened the door. Katarina winced. She almost hated Cilika because it was she, not Katarina's son, who was standing in the doorway.

Him, she was waiting for him.

*Nearly home . . .*

—Cilika, hey, come right on in! Katarina is giving us a hard time. Tell her she needs a drink.

—My maid of honor! Thank goodness you're here—Katarina is killing us with her nagging. She's on a tear. Where are your boys?

—Vilim is dozing in front of the TV, Gramps is asleep in his room, and Big Boy probably is too.

Irma gave Cilika a glass.

Cilika took it, tugged her T-shirt over her belly, and licked the corners of her mouth while waiting for everybody to be served. She didn't take her eyes off Katarina.

—Katarina, have some! You're all wooden, like this is a funeral, not a wedding.

They drank.

The first for the bride; then for *their dear mother, Ana, who died too young*; then for Katarina's *poor father*, whose death they didn't speak of because, sadly, it coincided with Katarina's birthday; then for Ita and Irma's father, who was *very, very sweet and good to all of them*; and, finally, for Katarina's forty-fifth birthday, the next day. The toasts grew increasingly impassioned. There were toasts to the Zadruga and their good, old house.

*If he could just make it up the slope at Gvozdanska, he'd be there. So, so close . . .*

Shaken by the toasts, the women were emotional and stopped talking. Little drunken crystals glistened in the corners of their eyes.

It seemed as if silence was best suited to this momentary mood of remembrance as it settled over the low-ceilinged room.

They heard a tapping at the only window in the shack. Three times. With pauses between.

They didn't move.

They all looked at the window, but only Katarina had the impression that a woman's pale face peeled away from the outer windowpane. The hand holding her glass went numb.

The silence lasted a few seconds.

They turned, unnerved, when there was knocking at the door. Three times. With pauses between.

For no obvious reason, the women gestured, just in case, to keep quiet.

They still didn't know whether they'd allow their uneasiness to change to alarm or, boosted by the alcohol, spill over into wild hilarity. Katarina cut through the silence.

—Come in!

The door did not open.

Again, they heard three spaced knocks on the door. Now all four called in unison to the unknown person to enter.

The door stayed closed.

—Oh, it's just the boy teasing us.

Katarina wagged her finger at Irma to hush.

—He wouldn't dare. He knows what he's done.

Irma tried.

—Ita, must be your Lovro sent someone to scare us.

—He wouldn't dare.

Irma wouldn't let it go. Her voice was oddly jolly.

—Must be your Vilim, then, Cilika.

This was so unlikely that none of them responded. Ita got up, seeking safety with Katarina as she had as a kid, and held her timidly by the shoulder. The oldest sister understood this as a sign that she would be the first to move.

Boldly, she went to the door and turned the knob. The lock clicked; the door didn't open. Ita invoked their mother as Katarina yanked again angrily at the knob and finally managed to open the door. Not a soul. A gust of cold air instead.

Katarina's head spun at the sudden chill; a greenish wave swirled before her eyes, and she gulped air to block the panic that sometimes swept her before an attack of nausea. She breathed in and out a few times. The frosty air in her nostrils revived her. She turned back to the room; the interior was suddenly thick with cigarette smoke. Both Irma and Ita had lighted up.

—Girls, there's nobody out there. Either it's the booze tricking us into hearing sounds, or someone's harassing us. Maybe it really is my boy . . . I'm going to walk around the yard and wait for him over at the house. I'll be back later. Irma, watch it with the cognac. Ita, at least you don't have to smoke. Smoking kills.

Their laughter saw her out.

*Now he needed only two, three more minutes.*

She stood outside for a bit and breathed deeply by the closed door to the glorified garden shed they called the Zadruga. They'd long since stopped giggling about the shed's moniker, Zadruga—those who had so named it were long gone. Nowadays this vestige of 1950s socialist-era nomenclature had to be explained to the youngest member of the household so he could understand why it was funny: it was a word that had been used to describe collective farms or communal business enterprises in the old days of socialism.

The Zadruga was one of several garden sheds that had been added, one after another, around the main house, but there was no real logic to their arrangement. Maybe a member of the household had been moved by imagination and had squirreled away a little extra cash or had taken out a small loan for building a dubious wing. Katarina was right—it was indeed a low-slung building, and all it took was two or three cigarettes going at the same time for the whole inside to be deep in smoke.

The main house, a small dwelling with two windows facing the street, was now well below street level after all the paving and filling over the years. On both sides it was hemmed in by two brand-new five-story buildings, and a random passerby might think the windows on the little house were bug-eyed with amazement at how its residents had walked out and left it squeezed in between the bulging concrete behemoths. Whoever then walked into the house would see it in a completely new dimension, with a kitchen and two small rooms and a hallway leading to stairs that went up to the remodeled attic; in fact, the little house had two separate apartments. And when all was said and done, even the garden sheds and shacks played a role. In them you could stow trash, fatten a hog for winter, and, in the old days, before the arrival of Chinese goods, you could set up a machine there and crank out on short notice whatever merchandise was needed. Finally, the first of the shacks was dubbed the Zadruga, used for storing broken pieces of furniture, the still usable parts of cupboards, chairs, tables, and the two-seater on which Irma, the smoker, had been nestling and where, now and then, for various lively events, the householders and their guests gathered.

Katarina Horak, née Firman, was waiting for this youngest member of the household, and he had only *a few more steps to get home*. Her brief exposure to fresh air revived her; her gut stopped churning, the swirling of the greenish waves ebbed, and she mustered the strength to march resolutely around the yard. Her courage was back now. Her unease at the suspicious knocking disappeared. *The drinking, must have been the drinking.* Without fear she made her rounds so she could reassure the girls. What could there possibly be for a person to fear in their *own* house where they'd lived since they were born? Nothing. She went toward the part they still called the garden. Garden? The abandoned patch of land had long since ceased playing the role of a garden or the role of a backyard. And even there, on this remnant of a remnant of a garden, a scrap of some 50 square meters of abandoned land had long been under the threat of yet another shed or shack. The plan was abandoned when Irma and Ita's father died, partly because the house had lost the sure hand of a man who could oversee the construction, and partly because the probate process they went through showed them that there were complications with the sharing of property rights among the three sisters. They made their peace with this and began to dream of investors, of the sale of both house and land, of building a new three-story house that would be wedged in among the new buildings. For such an undertaking they'd need more than dreams. The forsaken garden in autumn was extremely unpleasant, and the household avoided it. *But, with the boy you never know. Maybe he was the one who knocked, maybe he was trying to tease us? He's been gone all day, the jackass. Probably he's fine. This isn't his first time.* She was the eldest in this household, after all. The light from the neighboring houses lit the backyard a little and the half-rotted fence that surrounded the garden. She even checked the bushes growing along the wall. Nothing. Nobody. Beyond the fence, the garden was in total darkness; bare autumn branches could be discerned in the gloom. A heavy mist was drizzling, fog, a light rain, whatever; her sweater was getting damp, and Katarina stepped back from the fence. She went over to the Zadruga, opened the door, and from the threshold told the girls nobody was out here; just a little fun. Maybe they'd been mistaken? Maybe the knocking never happened? Alcohol is tricky. She'd be back in a minute.

The bottle was empty and they didn't care. Cilika was *telling them all about what Vilim did on the first night they were married,* and the girls were gasping with laughter.

Katarina went over to the door of the main house, went up the step to the door, and stopped. When they spent time in the shacks and sheds in the yard, they never locked the house, and Katarina didn't know why she paused and why she thought about the unlocked space. A chill of uneasiness licked her neck. She opened the door, reached for the light switch, and then nervously pulled back her hand. She'd felt as if she'd touched someone's moist, hairy lower arm. She even wiped her hand on her pants. *Nerves, Katarina, nerves.* She took a deep breath so it could be heard and, finally, bravely flicked on the light in the hall. Empty. She took her phone out of her pocket and checked the time.

10:45 PM. She scrolled to the number for *Boris* and stopped. She'd wait a little longer before calling his father. So as not to provoke him pointlessly. That is how things went last time: she called, everything came down to a few nasty sentences, and the boy showed up anyway, ten minutes later. No, she wouldn't call him. *Soon. As long as nothing happened ... It has to be that nothing happened. Nothing happened. This isn't the first time. What a little jackass. Jackass, he's doing this to my nerves on purpose.*

NADA GAŠIĆ

The sudden surge of rage chased away her stupid fear of the empty space and her queasiness about her child not being home. She warmed up, her saving fury. *That snot-nosed creep, he'll get his when he comes home. Today he'll get his like he never has before.*

*Will you hit him, Katarina? I will hit him, I'll slap him so he remembers it for the rest of his life, David, my son.*

*Will he be the one who remembers the slap, or will you, Katarina? I'll give it to him, a slap, so he remembers it forever, David, my son.*

David scrambled along the wall around the Zadruga's new blue building and jumped over it, pleased with himself when the alarm went off. Let them all hear, let them hear! He ran through the yard and made it to the passageway between the blue building and his garden. He hopped over what was left of the fence and didn't stop in the garden or by the lit windows from behind which came gales of laughter and singers breaking out in drunken songs. He had no time to listen, or hear, or make fun of them. He stopped by the front door to the house so he could turn the knob, and the door flew open into the hall; he burst into the familiar space, opened his mouth to breathe some air and call his mother—to moan, to sob, to tell her everything, to tell her what he'd seen, but his head, totally unprepared, flew to the left and then to the right, and he had no idea what was going on. He didn't cry out, he didn't scream; it didn't actually hurt, he just had ringing in his left ear. Clueless that his mother had given him the first slap of his life, he staggered and called out for her, probably to help him, to save him from her.

Katarina was appalled by her own blow, seriously frightened. To hide her fear she began shouting, blustering, swearing out of control. The feeling of irreparable disgrace compelled her to grab David roughly by the arm with one hand, while with her other she opened the door to his little room, and while he was howling *I hate you, I hate you*, she pushed him in and locked the door behind him.

She went into the kitchen, sat, and listened to David kicking the door.

For a while she kept hearing *I hate you, I hate you*, but then the kicking slowed and the sound died down.

In the end everything was quiet.

She got up. Her tears had dried on their own and were forgotten.

She stood by the stove, lifted the lid from the pot with the cold soup, and set it back down, musing. *He won't want soup*. She set a frying pan on the gas burner, picked up the bottle with cooking oil from the counter, gave it a brief glance, then put it back on the counter.

She wiped her hands on a kitchen towel and, taking care not to make much sound, went to David's door. She tilted her head but didn't press her ear right to the door. That sufficed. Slowly she turned the key, even slower she opened the door, and through the crack between the doorframe and the door she slipped her head. The blinds were not all the way down, so the streetlight lit David's bed. Enough to see David on it. Quiet, coiled up, unassuming, wearing his jacket with the hood pulled up, still in sneakers. Fast asleep.

She knew his sleep after excitement and exhaustion. Without worrying about waking him, she stepped toward her son with the intention of taking off his sneakers. With both hands she reached down to take the right one off first.

David suddenly shot up to sit, tucking his feet under him.

—Go away, I hate you!

She jumped back. Incredible, but she feared her own child.

—Get out!

She needed a few seconds to pull herself together.

—You are not going to use that tone with me!

—I'll tell Dad you hit me.

—Be my guest.

—I'm going to Dad's.

—He can hardly wait.

Somehow they reverted instantaneously to their usual squabbles, everything relaxed, and Katarina finally said what she'd come in to say.

—Are you hungry?

—I am, but I won't eat anything you made.

—How about palačinkas?

—I'd rather die.

She decided to hold her ground.

—Fine. Sleep hungry if you like, or eat something from the fridge. You can lie around fully dressed, I don't care. I'm going to the Zadruga to help Aunt Ita with her wedding gown. I'll be there with the girls. We're having a little party.

She started toward the door. Then stopped. She'd recovered the serious intonation and reprimand she'd lost and slowly said:

—We're all at the Zadruga. And Cilika is there too; she's Ita's maid of honor. No more spoiling the mood before the wedding. We'll talk tomorrow about why you were gone all day. I've been summoned to speak with the school counselor because of your behavior, and I'll tell her everything.

—Like how you hit me?

—Only because you provoked me so badly.

She didn't move any closer to the door.

—I'll tell her everything.

*Will you, Katarina, will you? I don't know, I don't know, I don't know anything.*

She shut the door behind her, but she didn't lock it.

For him this was a sign that she was relenting and had lost the battle.

He knew how much *she* hated it when he flung himself onto his bed, fully dressed, in his sneakers, so he immediately decided to go on lying there. He wasn't even hot. And besides, maybe he'd slip out of the house tonight and go farther away than even *she* could imagine. Maybe. But could that wait till morning? What happened tonight was bad. Really bad. He was sure nobody had been following him; he was sure he'd been pretty much invisible, but then again . . . From the movies he knew you must never let down your guard; they can find you when you least expect them to. *And, actually, I didn't see a thing and I wouldn't recognize anybody anyway. I didn't see a thing. I wouldn't recognize anybody.*

He curled up on the bed, drew in his feet, and looked over at the window. Through a crack in the lowered blinds, the streetlamp shone in. Nothing was moving. That was good. Then he remembered the unlocked door and the key on the other side, and although he didn't really feel like moving, he felt a surge of courage. He jumped up and quickly reached for the doorknob. But his courage sapped. He'd seen that in the movies. The door would open, and someone would be standing there, standing there quietly in the doorway. *But I didn't see a thing. I wouldn't recognize anybody.*

His lips pressed together; he felt tears coming on, he felt like calling his crazy mother, those dumbass aunts, his father ...

*I am a secret agent—I am not stupid old David!*

That's what he shouted, and, yelling a long and loud *aaaaah*, to fill the silent space, he suddenly opened the door, and, without peering into the gaping maw of the hallway, he pulled the key from the lock, and, without stopping his *aaaaah*, he slammed the door behind him, blocked it with the weight of his body, shoved the key into the lock, and finally locked it from the inside.

Then back into bed.

Done, he's safe.

He did not turn on the light. He knew he'd be visible in a lit room through those narrow gaps in the blinds, so he pressed up against the wall. The sisters would be coming back into the house soon. Even out on the street, the ninnies could be heard guffawing. It was warm in the locked room. He took off his jacket, but not his sneakers. Well, okay, the sneakers too ... *I didn't see a thing. I wouldn't recognize anybody. I didn't see a thing. I wouldn't recognize anybody.*

David fell asleep, drained to the point of pain.

He did not hear the drunken women shouting *lirum, lirum, laricu*—though Cilika didn't know what it meant. He didn't see the cigarette smoke wafting out of the Zadruga through the drafty window and sliding down the walls, or the confetti that they flung from the torn bags over the white marshmallow.

He didn't hear a late-season, earnest butterfly pass through a gap in the blinds in its attempt to find warmer shelter, knocking the windowpane three times.

He didn't hear the drunken women laughing in the backyard late at night, as they dispersed, singing *mi smo dečki kaj pijemo stoječki*, and neither did he hear his mother try to open the door to his room and give up, nor his aunts who stumbled over the threshold, roaring with laughter, peeling off their clothes and crawling into bed, with Ita repeating *It's all good, all good, as long as I don't puke*, nor Irma who sat there on the bed, drunk, but wide, sick, awake.

He didn't hear the black car drive onto the street with only its low lights on, slow to a stop near the house, and turn off the engine.

It was so quiet, so quiet in the house . . . Just as it was in the neighboring houses.

The houses of Trešnjevka couldn't have said how they'd survived. But they did. Not all of them, of course, not every last one, but those that made it through the flood dried out from the Sava water, shook off the crust of mud, replaced the broken windowpanes and waterlogged wooden flooring with nice parquet floors and new siding, so, at some point in the late 1970s, the houses began to see themselves as sprightly in their old age. Without shame they'd admit that they watched with fear as the nearby Ljubljana highway began looming over them, rising by another meter with each surfacing project, while in comparison their roofs sank below the level of dignity. They'd agree that they listened in horror to the machines gradually doing away with the old neighborhood of Knežija. They'd also agree that they hadn't realized how their own residents could possibly seek their demise. They'd admit this made them feel bad. Betrayed. Indeed, a true desire for revenge

NADA GAŠIĆ

was born within their walls when they overheard their residents complaining; now those who had been living in the very same little houses until just the other day barely even gave them the time of day, and even if they did, they did so from on high, only because they were now living on higher floors. And along with the new apartments, they boasted that they'd been paid *oodles of cash, oodles of cash* as compensation. But even after that, some houses survived. They were overjoyed like little girls when they heard that the city had run out of funds for tearing down the old neighborhoods and building new ones; they clapped their shutters with joy when the news got out that all the building projects would be postponed. Until the 1980s they listened to, and picked up on, all sorts of things. Middle age was well behind them by then, and old age was creeping in. They stoically bore the little indignities: the occasional gutter repair, a new door, a window. The early 1990s found them in relatively robust shape. The very beginning of the 1990s introduced to their walls a chilling fear of wailing sirens that took them back to the autumn of 1964, the sirens warning of an impending general catastrophe that might mow them all down. They were themselves surprised now by the fact that houses, like people, tend to forget the purpose and point of sirens with such startling, unwarranted speed. Despite the fact that the word *war*, which arrived with the sirens, had a more frightening sound than the word *water*, they flourished. Splendidly. Aside from the fear and the humiliating tape used to protect the glass from detonations, nothing bad happened to them. Then the sirens stopped wailing but a new danger arose, unrelated to war or water—a danger never announced as such, but for many houses it meant the end. Blueprints paved the way, and foreign currency paid for it. Teardowns. But not all. Not all. Luckily, not all. Though this isn't usually the case, it so happened that the humblest among them were the ones that escaped this worst possible fate. The owners of the bigger houses had been more adept; they found the investors, came up with loans and the powerful connections in city hall, so their old houses ended tragically in a pile of rubble that trucks carted away for days to unknown burial grounds. No weeping, no tears. They were first replaced by gigantic earthmovers, and after them came the cement mixers, the air hammers, and the masons, plumbers, electricians, roofers, painters, decorators. And, finally, the new buildings rose up and became the new neighbors—vast, immense, painted to the point of indecency, the sluts, harlots, hussies, floozies, bimbos, vamps, as the old guard referred to them—these sluts of houses, but not actually houses, know-nothings and naked out there on the street, no gardens, not a single tree, no fruit trees, no flowers, and, worst of all, no cherries.

The bristling, surviving old-lady houses had kept going until this evening, the night between 25 and 26 October, 2009, when they were slumbering and waiting in their usual posture. They knew they looked like hens resigned to the slaughter, and they knew the whole street from afar looked like a flattened jack-o'-lantern whose carved grin indecently displayed the false canine teeth of the new buildings and the decaying stumps of the old ones.

They had no oomph left to feel ashamed. Most of them had dropped off to sleep early, and the ones keeping vigil thought of the upcoming winter, their shabby roofs waiting for the snow to set in like finely ground mother-of-pearl or confectioners' sugar.

# Second stone, second wave

—VIIILIM, VIIILIM!

A woman's voice could be heard calling from a neighboring house, and then was lost to the rumbling of cranes from a nearby construction site.

The little house was only just stirring. It felt groggy, bleary, sheepish. And the members of the household woke up with a bad taste in their mouths: first, Ita puked up in the attic; then Irma, puffy from mixing alcohol and pills, was barely able to crawl to the refrigerator, where she drank a can of beer. She still didn't know whether she'd be able to recover by the third period at school, when she was scheduled to hold her first class for the day, or cook up an excuse for not coming in. Whatever, she'd pour a half bottle of eau de cologne straight down her gullet. On the ground floor, Katarina showered, and though there was too much alcohol from the night before in her system and too much stress after the scene with David, she did manage to make palačinkas. *That's something he'll eat.* She wasn't sure about anything else, especially not whether she'd follow through on her decision to respond to the summons from David's school counselor.

She knocked on the door to his room, and a moment later she was already pounding, and after another minute she'd left the house, and with no fear from gossiping neighbors she ran a lath noisily over the blinds. David winced. He thought this was the ordinary morning noise from the nearby construction site; he was about to turn over and sleep a little longer, but at the repeated racket he stood up with an unfamiliar sense that something irreparable and definitive had happened in his life.

He padded barefoot to the bathroom. While he was washing his hands over the sink, he was glad that most of his face wasn't reflected in the mirror. He turned to go back to his bedroom to get dressed, but then she peered out of the kitchen.

—Shower time, David!

David? Not Dadek? Not Dado? She has not relented. Well, fine. He knows how to pay her back.

He said nothing, ate, and counted the things that were on the table. He paid no attention to what she was saying. Something reached him, but the counting helped him avoid hearing everything. What did come through, he drowned out with his chewing and swallowing. He was already good at this. All of it was, in a way, exercising, studying, and the beginning of his painstaking work on a decision he had made a few days before, during a breakfast much like this one. A secret agent, yes, that's what he'd be, a secret agent. So, fine, even if he didn't become one, at least he'd practice the techniques of self-mastery. He was familiar with this grandiose term, self-mastery, from the computer games he'd played. And here he was, again, mastering himself, when he'd rather have been silencing his mother, telling her to shut up. But that would be a mistake. Next it would be threats, punishments. In any case, he decided to wait for *her* to say what she had to say. She kept doggedly repeating what he already knew: if he wandered off like that once more and if he didn't start doing better at school, she wouldn't take him for a vacation to the seaside and she'd ask social services to place him in his father's care. For a minute, only a minute, something tearful seemed to tug at his throat, but he pulled himself together and choked it down with a palačinka. The size of the mouthful was what hurt, not the choking back of tears. Yes, he was determined to become a secret agent. Cool, calm, and collected, he let her rattle on, forcing himself to drink the milk, and then he got up from the table, only when her voice was reaching him from the hallway, when she came back into the kitchen to add something. Then she went back to the hallway to look for her keys, then her purse, then her earrings, then the keys again, then her phone, then her tissues, and then her keys again. Shoving her hands into the sleeves of her jacket at the same time, she got herself twisted up in a tangle and flapped with her pinioned arms like a little duck flapping its amputated wings, and he laughed at her. For a moment this confused her. She finally managed to get the jacket on, made him another threat, and finally she left.

Silence reigned, which he usually enjoyed, but now, suddenly, he felt bad. He had to give his head a shake to shed the gruesome picture of that murky plastic sheeting. *I didn't see a thing. I wouldn't recognize anybody.*

He pulled on his sneakers, his jacket, and then grabbed his backpack. He froze. The outside pocket on the pack was torn, torn almost completely off. This flooded him with the same feeling of helplessness that had choked him while he dangled, snagged on the chain-link fence by the high school. He shook his head. *I didn't see a thing.*

Back he went to the kitchen, opened the drawer where the scissors were kept, and quite neatly snipped away the rest of the pocket. The backpack looked messy, but at least the torn pocket wasn't hanging there. He finally swung it onto his shoulder, ran down the hall, carefully locked the front door, and bounded across the yard to the wall. Only then did he survey the street. Nothing suspicious there. With a sideways glance he checked the monotonous gray sky; no whiff of rain, and he was pleased. Someone nearby was calling their cat, *Kitty, kitty, yummy yum, yummy yum yum;* someone over at Cilika's was dragging a foot along the wall; four houses away, the construction site was free of its usual clatter; a few cars were parked along the sidewalk. He eyed the cars: unfamiliar cheap cars, harmless, probably belonging to the construction site workers. He turned toward Cilika's house. There, with his left hand on the wall, Big Boy Damir waved to him. David was glad to see him and waved back. He went out onto the street, locked the gate behind him, waved once more to Big Boy Damir, and set off for Julija Klović School. It was some distance away, so he hurried.

He almost always walked along the old highway to the point where Nova Road joined Ljubljanska; from there he could see his school. He wasn't worried about anything as he strode along the noisy avenue and turned in his thoughts to new, faraway places. After some twenty minutes, he began hearing the voices that ever since first grade had let him know he was almost there. Never the sight of the building, never; it was the yelling and discomfort those voices made. He stopped. Should he hurry? Why hurry? It would be enough to get there by the second period. Or third. Who cares? He walked calmly right past the school and didn't give Kovačić a wide berth when he walked by him, even though he knew Kovačić would shove him. He shoved Kovačić back, a bit too hard, which Kovačić usually responded to with blows. Today they made do with *asshole* and *faggot*. For the rest they didn't have time.

He had decided he'd go toward Savska, along Gagarinov Way, but for no particular reason he turned, and a few minutes later he was pushing his way through the Trešnjevka farmers market. He picked up voices feeding, swallowing, chewing, smacking, clucking, gulping, and the voices were offering, asking, refusing, praising, agreeing, bargaining, complaining, lying, promising, consoling, gossiping, doubting, accusing, selling, buying. He caught the sounds of money: expensive, cheap, smuggled, big, small, the rustling of paper; feathers and the scraping of fish scales; the banging of crates, barrels, vats, carts, wheels, hampers, baskets; the smells of ripe, unripe, overripe, rotten, fresh, stale, fried, baked, boiled, deep-fried, smoked, dried, grilled, rare, fatty tasting, dry, sour, sweet, bitter, acrid, rancid, too salty; a hint of things pale, gooey, sticky, raw, slaughtered, skinned, killed, dead. All this gradually transitioned into something about the police who *had already come, about the poor dead woman who was stabbed all over, you don't say, strangled with a belt, come on—there was no belt, someone strangled her with their hands,*

*I saw her, naked, wrapped in a blanket, no she's not, she's wrapped in a plastic tarp, someone butchered her like a chicken, poor woman, and the police are there, the police are there, Holy Mother of God, Holy Mother of God, the church of St. Joseph is right there, a few steps away, what is happening to this world of ours, Holy Mother of God...*

He fled the voices. But why not go into town? Instead, like a crazed moth drawn to a lamp, he went straight to the place taken over by the police. Why? He couldn't say.

At first, he didn't see a thing. Too short. People were standing, shifting from foot to foot, or changing places, looking for a better vantage point from which they could follow what was going on by the playground. Even the trams went slower; the passengers crowded at the windows so they could see.

David started circling around the throng, and then he used his shortness. He bent over and, creeping by people's legs, moved closer to a place from where he could see what the police were doing. Someone almost grabbed him by the jacket, someone warned him this was not for children, but nobody really paid much attention. Nobody wanted to lose their place, so they let the kid through to a point where everything was visible. He crouched.

The white tape with the word POLICIJA written across it blocked access to the high school's playing fields. Between the strips of white tape and the parked police cars stood uniformed officers who were keeping an eye on the crowd and teams of reporters with cameras at the ready, waiting for something interesting to happen. David recognized one of the reporters from TV news. First he watched the guy from TV

NADA GAŠIĆ

and then the police and their weapons. Finally, he summoned the courage to have a look at *the place*. His gaze did not drop to the ground. He looked at the people who were wearing rubber gloves, who were bent over, measuring something, collecting things and putting them in plastic bags marked with numbers. This interested him. In the crowd he felt no fear. The mood was somehow ordinary, and if the people around him hadn't been speaking in tones more hushed than usual, David would have thought this was all just like every day. Normal. Then he saw two officers moving away from the crowd and taking with them four boys. He watched them talk and how the kids were gesturing intensely with their hands, how they bent over, straightened, fidgeted, talked over one another, how the two officers quieted them, and finally he heard someone ask, *Who are those kids?* and the answer *High school students; they're the ones who first found her this morning.* He heard someone say begrudgingly, *No they didn't, a lady from the farmers market who sells cottage cheese and cream went to take a piss behind the building, and that's how she found her.* The crowd shushed him, trying to hear what the reporters were saying when they talked into their furry microphones. No matter how hard the people in the crowd tried, they couldn't make out a single word. They'd have to wait until they were sitting in front of their TV sets.

The reporters would later embellish the story with all sorts of details, but that day, from the first to the last newscast, viewers across Croatia were given only the following official statement from the Zagreb Police Administration's spokesperson:

After the police were informed by members of the community on 26 October, 2009, at around 7 AM, that the dead body of a woman had been found near Trešnjevka Square, officers came out to conduct an on-site investigation. The identity of the victim is currently being ascertained, as is the cause of death.

According to the evidence already collected, the death was violent, so the police are conducting a criminal investigation with the objective of discovering the perpetrator and establishing other circumstances.

The criminal investigation went on for quite some time; people tired of watching and gradually wandered off. The trams returned to their routine speed. On the building wall, someone came along and put up a nice new, clean poster with the group photograph of the merry people. The city was back to breathing.

David's feet were going numb from crouching. He straightened up. The police officer, who had been standing by the house where David had rested his backpack on the wall the night before, stepped away. David went over to the wall, leaned on it, and looked over at the place where he had drawn on the posters. He turned to the man who had put up the new poster with the same musician he'd drawn the winged helmet on. He felt a chill come over him.

—Hey, kid!

David shrank.

—Hey, kid, don't cross that line!

A uniformed police officer strode over to David. Instead of stepping away and reassuring the officer, all he could do was slide down the wall and crouch. Who knew whether this looked like he was deliberately being provocative, or the officer was upset by someone else's rudeness. Within three steps the officer was looming over David and lifted him up with one hand. He made David stand on his tiptoes.

—Hey, what's going on? What's this about? Who's the kid?

The officer was thrown off by this; he didn't know how to respond, so, confused, he went on holding David. He even gripped him harder.

The man asking questions was not wearing a uniform; he was one of the two men who had spoken with the high school boys. Touching one of them on the elbow, signaling he'd be back in a minute, he went over to the officer who wouldn't let David go.

—Let him go. What's wrong?

—Oh, nothing, the kid was rude.

The officer finally released his grip, and the plainclothes officer crouched down. Later, much later, when he thought back on this, he could have sworn that he'd smiled at David. But he didn't.

—So, kid, what are you doing here? Eh?

—I didn't see a thing and I wouldn't recognize anybody.

—Pardon?

—I didn't see a thing and I wouldn't recognize anybody. And I wasn't here.

Instantly, David realized he'd said something incredibly stupid, but there was no way back. He'd said the words.

The man turned to his colleague, who was still talking with the four high school kids.

He wasn't far away, and the plainclothes officer didn't have to shout.

—Hey, Boss! This kid here says he didn't see a thing, he wouldn't recognize anybody, and he wasn't here. What should we do with him?

—Pressure him, Kasumić, and take him on as a protected witness. Your textbook example of an average Croatian witness.

Everybody laughed. Even the author of the witticism. Then, without a smile, he added:

—Come on, get rid of the kid; this is no place for children.

He turned to the four teenagers.

—And it's a bit much for you too, but that's how it happened. What can we do? You can go; we'll see you in the teachers' lounge.

The boss, Inspector Vidošić, turned to speak to his staff.

—Zdilar, let the technicians do their thing. Be sure to collect and secure all the evidentiary material, anything relevant to the investigation. Understand?

Then he dropped his head and had a look at his shoes, which had picked up a lot of mud. He moved over onto a peeled-off piece of poster. He looked over, disgruntled, at the man who had been putting up the new posters.

—Who let that man in?

Seeing that the man was by then quite far away from the roped-off area, he muttered to himself.

—Too late now, anyway.

He angrily kicked a muddy rock, then loudly announced to Detective Kasumić:

—Off to the lounge. We need interviews that are a little more to the point than this average Croatian witness of yours here.

They were laughing at him, and David hated them from the bottom of his heart. He turned; while running, he fixed his jacket, which had come unbuttoned when *that ape* manhandled him; he ran with all his might to the tram stop and flew in through the last door of a tram headed for Dubrava.

Detective Kasumić smiled as he watched the boy go. The last thing Detective Kasumić saw was a jagged shred of plastic from the ripped-off pocket on the boy's backpack.

*　　*　　*

TRAM #12 RUNS FROM THE LJUBLJANICA TERMINUS TO THE DUBRAVA TERMINUS. WHILE TAKING IT THAT DAY, 26 OCTOBER, 2009, DAVID LISTENED AND HEARD:

PHONE, POLICE SIREN:

You don't know how to write? What do you mean, for god's sake? Can you read? Damn it! You're kidding, right? I read, of course I read. Okay, not superfast, but I manage. How can you work your phone? Ah, so you know your letters, you're just not as good at newspapers and books. Well, say that, then. Like all normal people. What adults read these days? That's for schoolkids. You need to know enough, like for the ads, your cell, all that. Right. Who? Klikota doesn't know how to read? But he does numbers like he finished three universities. Yes, and Bogdanušin didn't even need school. They fucked him up over that house on Vir, screwed him royally. Who gives a shit about his universities.

PHONE, "O SOLE MIO":

Oh, no, no, that's not pašticada, pašticada has to be made with blade steak, only blade steak. No. My granny's recipe used prošek, that's a must, and she used homemade pancetta in it, not the store-bought kind, homemade ... If she didn't have any, she'd use store-bought, but that wouldn't be pašticada, would it? No. The gnocchi she made herself ... Oh yes, with the grater, and my God, is it a lot of work. But in the end it is finger-licking good.

PHONE, DINAMO TEAM ANTHEM:
I fucked myself up something awful. Goes without saying I was high as a kite. Yes, thanks for asking, they breathalyzed my teeny-weeny BAC level and only came up with .130 percent. The bike? The bike was totaled. So now I'm on the tram, trundling along like some old loser. The leg is fucked in three places, but the noggin's still in one piece. I'm on my way for, whatcha call it, what the fuck's it called, you know ... Right, the medical board. It always takes forever there. Coming with? Hey, come with, you'll keep me company on the stairs. Right, we'll sit there on the stairs and mess around. Have a hell of a time. I've got to tell you how this guy on Ribnjak told us last night how to make some quick cash. You find yourself a cunt, but she has to be a looker, you know, a model ... How? How do I find her? There's a shitload of them running around. Wait. Hey, wait, damn it, you're talking like you're on TV. Whatsis ... Right. A model. Exactly. So, you find her and then you give her a loaf of dark rye, right, that's how people talk these days, are you living under a rock? Dark rye, meaning dark bread, so dark rye, meaning Black guy. You slip her dark rye, and he's the one who puts up the cash. Sure, if he wants to he can always tip her a little something on the side. What've you got to give her?

NADA GAŠIĆ

Fine, so you give her pocket money for pizza, lipstick. Clothes? Let her have her clothes made at the tailor's. She can always give the tailor cunt. Forget that. So, you take the cash, and if dark rye complains, you don't kick him in the balls like before, you tell him to cut the shit because otherwise you'll report to the cops that he's whoring around town, and the guy will be kicked out of the country in no time flat. I don't give a fuck what that's called, I don't give a fuck, I'm a biker, not a pimp. There's dark rye out there aplenty—Zagreb's crammed with it. Come with me and I'll fill you in on the whole deal. People are checking us out here. You losers, riding with me on this tram, fuck yourselves, I'd send them all packing from Zagreb.

TWO MEN WITHOUT PHONES:
Screw Ronald, what's wrong, nothing works in Pro Evolution. You can't get a goal no matter how hard you try. What do I play? I put together my custom team. Look, I know FIFA is way better with multiplayer, but where the fuck am I to get the money for that, man? Where?

ANOTHER PHONE, POLICE SIREN:
What do you mean, they have no money? Saturdays, I go to Billa. Whatever, I buy yogurt. Not the diet kind, the real thing. And I watch them. You should see how they fill their shopping carts. The wheels are literally falling off. Always the same thing; by now I know them. Okay, so I don't know them for real, but I've seen them so many times. I get it that they've got money, sure, that I get, but how on earth do they eat all that food? That's the part that mystifies me. So much

food! Again, I am back there picking up the same yogurt, and, again, they've overloaded their cart. The same ones. Well, I don't know, maybe it's that they have a whole slew of kids, I didn't ask, but again, those who have a whole slew of kids generally aren't rich. And for me . . . I can't imagine how they eat all that. I'm ashamed to ask, but still . . .

PHONE THAT MOOS:
Fuck me, and who gives a fuck anyway. Fuck. Fuck it. He can sit on it and spin. Moron. Fuck him. Fuck his mother. I'm getting off at the next stop. The next one. Oh, you don't even know where I am? I'm going to that Konzum, the one you know, go to hell if you're that stupid, you don't get it, do you. And bring cash, faggot.

A WOMAN IN HER 70S TO A WOMAN IN HER 80S, NO PHONES:
This is outrageous—nobody has ever used language like this on public transportation before. It's horrifying—this doesn't feel like Zagreb anymore. But a person has to get around. How would I get to the doctor otherwise? What are the police doing about this? I ask you, what are the Zagreb police doing, anyway?


*So what are the Zagreb police doing, anyway?*

They separated: one part of the police team remained on the investigation site, while others went back to Heinzelova, and Inspector Vidošić and Detective Kasumić left for the teachers' lounge at the high school.

NADA GAŠIĆ

By then a lot was already known: the senior boys had a PE class first thing in the morning, so before 7 AM they were about to enter the sports hall through a side door on Ozaljska, and one of them kicked at a pile of plastic sheeting that was in his way, and then they saw what they saw—a woman's hand with rings and polished nails. The rest of the body stayed wrapped up and they didn't touch anything else; they all had phones, and one of them immediately called the police.

When the custodian brought Vidošić and Kasumić to the teachers' lounge, the first things they heard were the voices of frightened women, interspersed only occasionally by a male baritone. They knocked and entered without waiting to be invited. The large room smelled of the herbal teas the teachers were drinking to calm themselves and the boys. As soon as the police entered, a hush came over the room.

Helpful, but not ingratiating, a man came over to them who introduced himself as the principal; he proffered his hand and waited for one of the two to accept his handshake.

Vidošić was the first to shake his hand.

They sat at a table where the four boys were sipping tea. They politely declined the offered cups. Vidošić started right in:

—Boys, let's sum up what you've already told us. We noted the time, we know where you were coming from, where you were going, why you were there, and who first saw the wrapped—shall we call it—package, who kicked the package, who first saw what you all later saw, and we know you called the police. That is what's most important, and we've written it all down. Let's take it slow now. Do any of you think something was left out that you should have mentioned, that might be important for the investigation?

The three spoke all at once; they mentioned someone peeking over the balcony of the house right next to the playing fields, but then that person hid when they shouted; they said someone stopped on the street and then ran away; there was something they heard from the tram stop; a dog barked at them from one of the balconies . . .

They said what they had to say, and all stopped talking at once.

The fourth, whom Kasumić remembered by his earring, and by the fact that he hadn't said much at the site of the investigation, now used the moment of silence.

—The dead woman, she's the Spanish teacher. I recognized her by the rings.

Someone's pencil dropped, and, through the gaping maw of silence, they could hear how it rolled endlessly over the polished floor.

Vidošić didn't know whether he ought to say this, but he asked anyway:

—Are you sure?

The boy shot him a penetrating look.

—No, of course I'm not sure, but I think I recognized the rings and nails. The longest nails of all the women who teach here.

Someone's chair scraped, unhappily.

Kasumić pulled out his notepad, turned to the principal— who, in a state of extreme disarray, was dictating the teacher's first and last name—then turned to the secretary who had helpfully run off to her office and come back with all the information about the Spanish teacher.

Someone invisible, with a voice that no longer had a recognizable age, suggested they call the Spanish teacher first, and if she didn't pick up . . . Kasumić jotted down her phone number.

—We'll do that in a minute.

Vidošić stood, and Kasumić followed him.

Vidošić spoke only to the principal.

—We'll keep you in the loop, and we would like to ask you, and especially these four young men, to remain available. We'll need more information.

Kasumić turned to one of the younger women.

—Could you please tell me who the Spanish teacher socialized with? That will be important, of course, if these suspicions are confirmed . . .

The woman said nothing. Instead of her, the young man with the earring answered.

—With Irma Žiger, who teaches descriptive geometry.

Kasumić wrote down the name in his notepad. He turned to look around the room.

—Is Irma Žiger here?

The young teacher he'd spoken with smiled.

—No, she doesn't have any classes until the fourth period.

Then Kasumić spoke in a quieter voice to the secretary:

—Could I please have her contact information?

As if he were feeling neglected by Kasumić, the principal turned to Vidošić:

—Excuse me, but how was the victim killed?

Already at the door, Vidošić turned to avoid being rude.

—At this phase in the investigation, we still don't know that. For God's sake, we still aren't even sure of the murdered woman's identity.

He already had his hand on the door handle when he added, more for himself than for those in the lounge:

—This may be rape, a sexual crime. Or not. We don't know. We'll find out.

All the women, without a glance at each other, began buttoning up their blouses.

The ageless voice was heard from the corner:

—Oh no. No! I'm retiring, I cannot bear this anymore. Better hungry than dead.

None of the teachers were in their classrooms yet, and most of the students were in the corridors. The windowpanes vibrated from their voices: someone shouted *the cops, the cops are coming,* someone else began baying like a police siren, and the officers could barely stop themselves from breaking into a run. On the steps it was quieter, and Vidošić called the Spanish teacher's number. He got a recorded message about her not being available.

In the car when they were on their way to Heinzelova, Kasumić tried to light a cigarette. Vidošić wouldn't let him, so until they reached Heinzelova they exchanged only terse sentences, like quarreling children.

Out in front of the police department, Kasumić gulped the smoke of his cigarette, walking behind Vidošić, full of hate. Vidošić told him:

—Get rid of that, we have work to do!

Kasumić tapped his shoulder.

—Wait, there's something I need to tell you. I have a feeling about these two, the murdered woman and her friend—I think I know them.

Vidošić looked at him.

—I didn't hear you.

—I said that I think I know the woman who was killed.

—And when did this occur to you?

—Right away, as soon they unwrapped her. But I wasn't certain. The face of a dead person is not like the face of someone who is living. And I didn't remember those rings.

—Why didn't you say something right away?

—I wasn't sure.

Vidošić was colder than usual. He didn't even look at Kasumić.

—Whatever it is that you know, you'll tell the men upstairs. At the meeting. In front of everybody.

—Do you want us to wait for the identification to be confirmed?

Vidošić didn't answer. They didn't talk in the elevator. They parted ways in the hallway: Kasumić went to the men's room to finally finish his cigarette; Vidošić went to his office, called the secretary, and quickly dictated a brief memo. Twenty minutes later, he called a meeting.

The meeting was no different from any other. There was a little more fidgeting and squirming in seats, and fewer wry remarks, because the case was new. Everything else was as usual.

Vidošić said:

—The Scholastic Case—that's the official name we'll be using for this case.

Then he read:

—The report came in at 6:58 AM. We were notified by four fourth-year boys from the Trešnjevka high school, where Trpimir Delić, Domagoj Rozman, Mislav Šoštar, and Branimir Švojić found the female body. The time and cause of death and the victim's identity are yet to be confirmed. In the information interviews, we heard that this may be the body of S.F., a Spanish language teacher at the Trešnjevka high school, so the following has been undertaken: a visit to the address, and S.F. was not found there; identification and check of the phone number for both the cell phone and the landline, and nobody responded to either. According to testimony from work colleagues, S.F. lived in a rented apartment. We are checking to see who owns it. Once the identity of the victim is confirmed, family, friends, neighbors, fellow teachers, and acquaintances will be contacted. All the tasks that can be handled over the computer will be managed by Vjekoslav Zdilar. The rest of you will be assigned your tasks during the course of the investigation.

He stopped talking and looked over at Kasumić.

—Officer Kasumić has something to tell us.

Kasumić looked down at his feet, then at the socks on Vidošić's feet, and, finally, at his colleagues.

—I think I was the first to recognize the victim. When they unrolled the plastic sheeting, I wasn't sure right away. Just as I said to the boss, we all know that the face of someone who is dead looks different from a living person's face. But because the school was so close and because I remembered that the victim worked at that school, I recognized her as someone I met twice. I'm not sure when exactly.

—What were the circumstances?

NADA GAŠIĆ

Kasumić was startled by Vidošić's interruption.

—The circumstances? I wasn't working here in violent crimes yet. We ran a raid because of drugs and suspicious escorting at the Intercontinental Hotel. She was with another teacher and a man… he was not important. They said they'd come to check on the hotel's offerings and prices for organizing the senior prom.

This provoked a spark of amusement in Vidošić's office, and the tension relaxed a little for the boss.

Kasumić turned, a little confused, and continued:

—That was the first time. The second time we were running an operation in Opatija. We were going through the yachts in Ičići, pursuing the same activities, and I saw them there too. Supposedly they were in Opatija to organize a trip for the senior class.

This provoked a burst of laughter, the slapping of thighs, and a testosterone-driven squirm on the chairs, and Kasumić himself chuckled.

Vidošić pounded the desk to quiet them.

—As soon as identification has been taken care of, interview the friend. Kasumić, it would be best for you to take care of that; it will be more relaxed.

They stood. Vidošić stopped.

—Kasumić, you might follow the girlfriend even before the identity is confirmed, as a protection measure for her as a possible witness. What do you say? It would be good to make sure she's alive.

—No need—I called her and hung up. She's alive.

Kasumić looked right by Vidošić, who didn't respond to what he'd said.

The photographs of the crime scene arrived quickly. They were available to everybody over the computer. Most lingered over the photographs of the body of the naked woman, stripped of all body hair; the body looked like a prostrate store window mannequin.

The crime scene photographs actually displayed a disgusting collection of city and school garbage, an assemblage of everything children and adults use, eat, and throw away, all that the wind can blow off of balconies and, from these same balconies, what the residents are capable of tossing.

Kasumić clicked through the images and spent some time on a photograph of holes in the chain-link fence. He magnified the photograph to have a closer look at a piece of plastic that was hanging off the wire, and which had been taken from the scene.

He clicked the button on his internal phone line.

—Boss, may I have a word?

In Vidošić's office, he waited until his boss looked over from his computer screen. Vidošić rotated in his chair, stretched his legs out, straightened his back, and linked his fingers behind his head.

—Yes, Kasumić?

—Listen, I know that what I'm going to say may not sound smart, but I can't get that kid from this morning out of my head.

—What kid?

—The little boy, the one the officer picked up by the scruff of the neck. You joked about him being good as a protected witness.

—Yes, that does not sound smart. It sounds ridiculous. What could that kid have to do with anything?

—Probably nothing. I'd even say it's 99.9 percent likely that he has nothing at all to do with this. But I can't shake off the fear in his voice and what he said.

—Listen, you screwed up this morning because you didn't say right away that you recognized the woman. The high school kid sounded more capable than we are, and now you're cooking up some totally useless story about a kid who was watching along with everybody else. Of course he was scared—the cop had him by the scruff of the neck.

Vidošić didn't change his position, but he slowly spun his desk chair left and right.

Kasumić felt that he wouldn't be able to control his face flushing. Or the pursing of his lips.

—First of all, I didn't screw up, because in the teachers' lounge nobody could know that I recognized the woman. I told you later. Secondly, you could give me a minute to finish telling you why it is that I think the kid wasn't talking nonsense.

Vidošić laughed.

—Go ahead, I'm not stopping you. Who knows, maybe this is the moment when a new theory in the Lika branch of criminal science is born.

Kasumić let him stop spinning in his chair. He no longer worried about how red his face was.

—I noticed that the kid had a torn pocket on his backpack. I don't know why, but I noticed. Now, when I was looking at the crime scene photos, I saw that on a hole in the chain-link fence, a hole a child could crawl through with no trouble, a piece of plastic had snagged. It's the same color as the kid's backpack.

—Oh, Kasumić! I'd say you're fast becoming one of those TV detectives. You don't recall the rings but you remember the color of the backpack? What do you want with the kid? And how are you going to find him?

Kasumić already had his hand on the doorknob.

—As to what I'm becoming, no need to worry about that. The kid I can find, because I'm sure someone from the neighborhood, from the local stores, will know a kid like him who had the time to stand there for an hour and watch what the police are doing. The kid buys either Fornetti pastry or pizza. I'd find him. And what would I do with him? I'd ask him a lot of questions, and most of all, I'd make sure he doesn't get himself into serious trouble.

Vidošić clapped.

—Bravo, bravo, why those TV detectives are nothing compared to you. And what about the 99.9 percent? Let's keep our feet on the ground. Leave the kid to enjoy his life.

The phone rang, and Vidošić gestured to Kasumić to wait. He hung up.

—The identification has been confirmed. It's the Spanish teacher. Go find the girlfriend and pressure her so we can find out what she knows. We can't wait for the autopsy; we'll provide an approximation for the time of death. At night probably. The only time when there's nobody there to see whoever disposed of the body. Those are our basic facts. The rest you know: with whom, where, when.

Kasumić closed the door, seen out with the words:

—Forget the kid!

And time was passing slowly for the boy. He got off the tram at one stop or another when he got tired of the passengers, lingered in front of toy-store windows, leaned on the glass, looked like the other kids did, bought pizza slices at bakeries, Fornettis with chocolate, ice cream, wandered into the bookstores where they were selling computer games, walked along the walls of houses, stayed away from places where he might run into anyone who knew him, hung out at Avenue Mall, invisible like all the people who went there, and then went back to riding the trams, at the mercy of the voices. He waited for the time to come when his dad might be home. In the hustle and bustle of the city, he didn't stop to think about the murky plastic sheeting, or the black car, or the huge man, or the chain-link fence, or his fear on Maglajska, or the slap. From time to time, he'd think of how much it had hurt that morning when he forced himself to choke down the chunk of cold palačinka, but that was the only thing that reminded him of the little house on Mala Street.

*     *     *

Kasumić called the high school secretary and heard from her that Irma, the teacher of the descriptive geometry class, hadn't come in to teach that day. She'd called in sick; the news of her murdered colleague had hit her hard, though everybody was aware that the identity had still not been confirmed. He didn't tell the secretary that the identity was no longer unconfirmed.

He parked in front of the small house on Mala Street, rang, and waited for someone to come to the door. Nobody did. He called Irma. A few minutes later she came down, her face puffy, gaunt. Apparently, she had been crying for a long time.

They didn't speak while they were standing outside. She let him into the house but she didn't go upstairs; she took him into Katarina's kitchen.

—Sorry, I'm alone. My sister's at work, and my other sister is caught up with preparations for her wedding. She left a few minutes ago, and my sister's boy is the one who left this mess of dishes.

They sat down. Kasumić was silent, and Irma began to sob.

—I'm so sorry, I know why you've come, the secretary let me know, I'm sorry, I'm having trouble dealing with this.

—You'll have to, because I need to ask you some questions.

Irma quieted down.

—You were a friend of the victim. The murder victim.

—Yes, we were friends.

—Tell me about your friendship. How close were you? What do you know about her?

—I knew a lot. Everything that matters. She came from Vinkovci as a student. Here, she earned her degrees in Spanish and Portuguese; she got the job at the Trešnjevka high school, where I was already working, and we were younger than our other colleagues, so that's how we started spending time together.

—When was that?

—Back, back . . . six years ago. She is a little younger than me.

Irma started crying again. Kasumić watched the locks of her long red hair tremble. He waited.

—Do you have any friends in common?

She didn't look up. She just shook her head. Then she pulled herself together.

—More acquaintances, in passing. I know some of her friends, and she knows some of mine, but no, I wouldn't say we shared friends.

—The information we have on her says she is unmarried, which doesn't mean she lived alone.

—She did live alone. In Travno.

—Yes, I saw the address. What has her behavior been like lately?

—Same as usual. I didn't notice any changes. But we didn't see each other every day.

Kasumić paused. Irma didn't move. This rattled him, so he quickly asked:

—Do you know anyone from her family?

—Not well. Her father's not in the picture; her mother lives in Vinkovci. She has a sister and brother there. They have their families. That much I know about her.

—When did you last see her?

—Three days ago. We taught at the same time.

—After that?

—After that, no.

—Did you speak over the phone, send emails or text messages?

She didn't say anything for a second.

—I don't know, I can't remember. Everything is a blur. I took some sedatives.

She smiled. Her smile was ugly.

—And a little alcohol, after the secretary called with this terrible news.

Now Kasumić's smile was ugly.

—Did the secretary call you, or did you call the secretary?

Her face momentarily went dry. Kasumić was familiar with this sort of change.

Then she smiled again.

—There, you can see that I don't know what I'm saying. I called, I wasn't feeling well, I couldn't come in to teach, and then the secretary told me what had happened.

Kasumić waited to see whether she'd start to cry again. She didn't.

—Where were you yesterday?

Irma relaxed.

—My sister, my younger sister, is getting married, so I went out to buy a few gifts—I was looking for something pretty, something to surprise her. A blue garter, that's the custom.

—Didn't used to be.

She smiled at his comment, but her solemn expression soon returned.

—That's all, I spent some time at the shopping malls, all of them far away from here; it was Sunday, they don't all work... until you find a place to park... the time passes. We had ourselves a little house party last night, just us sisters and the maid of honor, who is also our neighbor. We had a little to drink; maybe that is part of why I was feeling so bad. I smoked too much. Sorry, I should have told you, you're free to smoke if you smoke.

—No, I don't smoke.

Kasumić had never lied about that before. He tapped the table with his fingers and thought of Vidošić.

—Fine, we'll be in touch; there are things we'll need to corroborate, but it's all normal, purely routine. Don't leave Zagreb.

He started for the door. When he was out in the yard, after having said his polite goodbyes, he bent forward a little.

—And be careful.

NADA GAŠIĆ

He smiled and added:

—Especially with your friends.

She also smiled.

—My sisters, actually my older sister, who is more like a mother to me, can provide confirmation of all I've told you.

She waved to him as he got into his car. He didn't wave back.

He looked at her in his rearview mirror and started the car. She didn't watch him leave.

Both were thinking about how they hadn't spoken of their earlier encounter. Nor that then, a full two years before, they had been on more intimate terms.

\*     \*     \*

Big Boy Damir, who hadn't been a boy for decades, also waved to Kasumić, just as he waved to each person who left. Kasumić didn't wave back, and Damir dragged his foot along the wall.

—Big Boy, time for you to come in, you'll catch cold, and I'll end up having to deal with it. All you do is give me more work.

Big Boy did what Cilika said, and, running the little finger of his left hand along the wall of the house, he came to the entrance; holding the short banister with both hands, he climbed up, passed through the front hall, and went to his room. He took off his shoes and socks.

He sat on his bed all afternoon and tried touching the floor with his bare feet. He rocked. The rocking helped him feel better, but not better enough, so he needed to find his serenity point. He tucked his legs under him, perched on them, and this allowed him to rock quietly and seek his focus. The point on the wall, that had been dug with a needle and colored in black with a pencil, was, actually, well chosen: some 40 centimeters from the head of his bed, but not too low or too high, and again, he could see it from every corner of the room. It soothed him. Now he watched it closely, and within ten minutes he no longer needed to rock or stare at it.

Serenity. He looked away from the point on the wall and stared out through the curtain, counting, out of habit, the crocheted little circles that the eye had to overcome before it could see through the glass pane. He did it. On the cast-iron railing he noticed a pigeon resting its red legs, first one, then the other. Finding its balance, it rocked as he did, and this coaxed a smile from Big Boy Damir. It even seemed to him that it was thinking about the winter to come and the winter pigeons that would be sitting on this same railing, alternating pulling in and stretching out their little legs to warm them on their bellies.

His thoughts were wintry; he began to feel chilled and pulled up the blanket over his legs.

Out on the street, the sound of Cilika banging away with pots and pans and invoking the mother of god could be heard, along with a man who getting on in the years coughing ripely, and someone was threatening strangers in an elderly voice:

—I will tie myself up while the water washes all of you away. Damned bastards, the Sava will wash you all away!

Nobody responded to the threat, and nobody felt the house shiver with a chill.

\*     \*     \*

NADA GAŠIĆ

David's mother kept checking the time on her computer screen. They had inundated her today with work. That's what happens in banks. At exactly noon, when she thought she might be able to slip out, use her break, and ask for a little extra time so she could finally go to see David's counselor, her colleagues came in with a birthday cake, flowers, and cookies; *happy birthday to you, happy birthday to you* was sung, she pulled out her already prepared bottle of bubbly, and then she realized that today, again, she'd miss the appointment. She knew she'd come home later than planned, because her closest colleagues would want to take her out for more drinks after work. But it was important, it really was important to be more with David today, so they could make peace and celebrate her birthday in their own way. She decided she'd use her birthday to give him the new phone they'd fought over two days before. *Stubborn jackass, he's already lost two of them.* She always relented.

She'd come home to Mala Street after 7 PM and wouldn't find anybody there. Not Ita, or Irma, or David.

*   *   *

At the apartment of her fiancé, Lovro Slaviček, Ita was wrapping up the preparations for the wedding.

—Lovro, dear, come on, quit the fussing with the numbers. I really don't care how much it costs. We'll only be getting married once. Take the list and first cross off what we've already bought and paid for: the petits fours, the roses, the sugar-and-marzipan leaves, the sugar deer, mushrooms, and fruit, the silver, gold, and colored sugar beads, the lace and tuille for under the plates, the paper napkins, the tablecloth overlays, the invitations, the numbers for the tables, the ring pillows, the floral bracelets for the bridesmaids and groomsmen, the slipcovers for the chairs, the bows for the church, the garlands and balloons for entering the yard, the house, and the Zadruga, and the crystalware for the table. Now go to the other list for the clothing! First mine: we borrowed the wedding gown, the veil, the fur bolero, the long gloves, the sandals with crystals, and the jewelry for my hair, décolletage, and hands. We bought: the lace thongs, the silk stockings, and the garters. Now on to you! We borrowed: only the tux. We bought: the shirts, the tie, the boxers, the socks, and the shoes. Then, we bought and paid for: the rings and the wine and liquor for the house party at my place and your place. Now, write below! Still unpaid: the cake, the arrangements for the cars, the decoration of the church, the floral arrangements for the hall and tables, the cleaning of the yard and house, the menus with the embossed names of the bride and groom, the CD cases, the makeup artist, the hairdresser, the manicurist with the design for my ring-finger nail, and the church, plus the reverend who'll come to bless the dinner. We haven't made a down payment yet because we'll be using our credit card. Next: using the lighting to color the rooms and the walls, special light effects, and sound. Your parents are paying for the band, and I don't care what that costs. The best man is paying for the photographs and the DVD.

Lovro entered the costs into his calculator, and it turned out that they had already spent more than two thousand euros, that they'd need to spend over three thousand more, and that there were a lot of guests and they'd need to come up with about seven thousand to cover everything, and have enough left over for their honeymoon and remodeling the bathroom at his place, where Ita would be moving right after the wedding. With a smart move, he came up with the money they needed to make up the difference. Ita sold Irma her part of the house that she would have had no use for anyway. The price was below market, but that is how it goes when you sell a tenant-occupied property that nobody else wants to buy. They were relatively pleased.

*  *  *

Irma didn't teach her classes, but she did leave the house.
—No, I'm not calling from my cell phone. I know what I'm doing. Ah, so you already know that the cop came by? He asked me all the things they probably ask in cases like this. I didn't say anything, because I don't know anything and because I didn't see anything or anybody. I know, no need to threaten, I know I'd lose my job and no school would hire me after that. I know. Where was I last night? At home all night. How do you know? You were parked in front of the house? Well if you know, then why ask. Yes, yes. I'll sign it for you; we can go to the notary tomorrow. Wherever you like. Fine. I have to teach my classes tomorrow. No, nobody followed me.

*  *  *

He knew what time his dad usually came home from work. To get to his dad's house, he chose Tram #14 on Ban Jelačić Square.
  The #14 was always packed with students; sometimes they talked about interesting things, and he liked to listen in on

their conversations. But this tram was silent. He couldn't sit; there were too many people and all the seats were taken. He made his way to a window, glued himself to it, and counted the number of shop windows displaying *closed for renovation* signs. Then he felt someone pressing him awkwardly from behind and touching his leg in a nasty way. It didn't feel random, and David quickly turned. Above him stood uninterested faces, staring out of the window. His stop was coming up. The passengers stirred and quite a few got off. David pulled away from the unpleasant crush and sat on a freed seat, his back to the direction the tram was headed in. Now he could freely watch faces; he didn't care whom he'd see and who would see him. He watched a man who was sleeping, his head wedged between the headrest and the window, so his face wouldn't be seen. David was already very familiar with passengers like this man. By their breath. Their breath smelled bad, and it was different from the breath of drunks. They smelled of filth, and he realized the man wasn't sleeping like that because he'd nodded off, but because he had come prepared to sleep on the tram. He knew they never show their faces; he knew they were called homeless. He didn't like the word and averted his eyes. He looked up and saw that the man who'd tried to press him in that ugly way into the window was coming over to him again. He sought the man's face, and the man looked back at him with a dead gaze. David jumped up, pushed the man with all his strength, again felt the disgusting hand, and barely managed to wriggle free of the trap. He made it up to the door, and out of the corner of his eye he still followed

NADA GAŠIĆ

the man's gaze. He could hardly wait to get off. One more stop. The man, luckily, went to a different exit, and David could see a boy over there also beginning to fidget. Shivers went down his back. He shook his head. *I didn't see a thing. I wouldn't recognize anybody.*

While they were passing by the grand Croatian National Theatre, he thought about how stupid it was that he'd never been to a performance there. Once, when his class went, he was sick. His grandfather, in his time, never knew how to choose which play to go to, and his mother and father were forever promising and then apologizing for breaking their promises. On his secret list of things he hadn't done yet in life was going to the theater. He wasn't impressed by the bright lights around the Westin Hotel, but he brightened up when the tram finally rolled by the Museum of Technology. He knew by heart where everything was in the museum courtyard. Everybody knew about the locomotive, but he wasn't sure they knew about the anchor. And the anchor was what he loved most of all.

He hopped off the tram, checking to see whether the man was following him. Nope. He ran across Savska Road. He needed another few minutes to get to his dad's place on Vodnikova. It might be fun today; around now, his dad was never up to much, just passing the time.

He didn't see the black car parked illegally in front of the building right by the main stairs toward the Cibona Tower, and he didn't know that the driver had been circling all day long through the neighborhood. On the lookout. He didn't hear the sound of the engine when it started.

## How David's dad spends his time

David's dad's wife leaned over the kitchen counter, holding an open book. Her quiet poise showed that her hands were waiting to take action, following the instructions she was reading.

RAW FAMILY WILD BANANGO:
Blend well:
2 cups lamb's-quarter (plantain, chickweed, or other weed)
1 banana
1 mango
2 cups water
Yield : 1 liter juice

The hands obeyed and forced the juicer to make the juice. The short, skinny woman poured the beverage into tall glasses, and with a long-handled spoon she began evenly mixing. She stepped back from the counter and set the glasses on the table.

—Sweetie, this is healthy, very, very healthy. We're going to drink this today and tomorrow.

Her husband looked at the unsightly green glop still swirling in the glass.

—I request to be allowed to skip the healthy food today and tomorrow. My nerves can't take it.

—Well, your nerves won't be able to take healthy food, or any other food, if you continue poisoning yourself with all that coffee.

He didn't pick up the glass, but with the fingernails of both hands he tapped at it.

—I am poisoning myself, dearest, at my own expense, so don't criticize me. I'm not criticizing you.

The sound of his tapping nails irritated her.

—You? You don't criticize? You do nothing but criticize.

—You're wrong. I am quite calm compared to the amount of madness you hurl at me.

He stopped tapping, but he smoothed the glass with his thumbs, and she watched his fingers leaving an unsightly streak on the glass.

—What madness? What kind of a tone is that? You must have eaten meat somewhere today, and now you're turning on me with this aggression for no reason at all.

—My, my, you're right. Forgive me. I am the personification of meat madness, and you are the personification of reason. Forgive me.

She was still standing with her glass in her hand.

—That's so like you. An apology as an insult, and an insult as an apology. Boris Horak in a nutshell.

—So shall we take a stab at defining you and your like-minded pals? You mean to change the world, if I understand you correctly. Am I right? In short: my wife, the grand reformer!

—Well, the world is not much good as it stands, and it's unlikely to change on its own, is it? Yes, indeed, we're out to change the world.

—Oh yes! You mean to change the world. And what are you starting with? What you eat, dearest, your food?

She turned her back to the table and returned to the counter. She drank down the smoothie with gusto and set the glass aside.

—Unlike you, who aren't capable of changing even your diet. Even the menu. But you are full of comments about what other people do.

—You are the ideal culture for comments. You're the perfect agar culture for cultivating my comments.

—And you think you aren't? It's easier to comment on you than on me. But I don't waste my breath.

—Oh, I see, you're a lady. Because you eat weeds, you're a lady. A talking herbivore. An interesting species.

—And you're a carnivore who barks and growls to be heard.

—If you hate carnivores so much, why pat every four-legged fur ball? Why do you adore dogs? They eat meat, my dear, they eat meat.

—I pat every furry creature, surprised that it's still alive. Uneaten.

—You pat it because it's meat. Furry and smelly, ah yes, but meat.

—I pat a two-legged furry beast, but that one, unlike the four-legged ones, is not grateful.

—Yes, that one doesn't lick your hand.

She left the counter and sat across from him at the table. She smoothed the tablecloth. There was nothing on the table needing to be cut, and she stared at a knife that was lying in the middle, but she didn't touch it or move it.

She returned to the conversation.

—Dearest, you aren't capable of changing anything. Your development stopped at refusing to eat raw meat. That much you learned from your ancestors: to kill and cook. And this is not because you couldn't eat raw, God forbid, but because what is cooked is easier to digest and allows you to throw yourself on a new piece of meat.

—Such imprecision! Why, we are still capable of eating raw. There is nothing more delicious than steak tartare.

—I see no reason why to mix all those spices into the unhappy meat. Wouldn't it be even tastier for you to gorge yourself on it, all bloody, with a spoon?

—No, that would not be tastier. If it were tastier, that's how we'd eat it, with no twinge of conscience.

—With the meat diet, one thing that is left unsaid troubles me. Why do you prefer it dead? Why not grab a live chicken, pluck off a few feathers, cleave out as much flesh as you need to satisfy your hunger, and then let it go? Or a fawn, for instance? I hear that venison is tasty. Why take all the trouble of butchering it?

She waited for him to answer. The conversation had started well; he was more tired than usual, his rejoinders were tepid, and it looked as if she might be able to come out victorious. He was silent. She tried again.

—So tell me, why give up on live prey?

He looked up, he waited for her eyes to quiet, and he calmly said:

—Because killing is fun.

She saw his hand slowly approach the handle of the knife, but she watched him only as much as she needed to gauge how much time she'd need to reach the kitchen door.

Holding the knife at eye level, he got up before she did. It was terrible that he wasn't hurrying, and she froze. She could hardly move. Finally, she screamed, leaped back, shoved the chair away, and ran for the door. She didn't have time to turn around.

She heard his growling, closer and closer, too close, and in her panic she missed the doorknob. She scrabbled with her nails on the glass that magnified the reflection of the knife. When he bit her neck, it tickled; she laughed, choked, coughed, and she didn't stop laughing.

He couldn't carry her in his teeth, but at least he bit her while he steered her toward the bedroom. She took the knife from his hand. While he was taking off his clothes, she laid the knife along the edge of her pillow. He eyed the blade.

The doorbell rang, and for a moment he was quiet.

—Forget the doorbell. Shhhh. It's those people distributing ads. Shhhhh. Don't you dare get up, don't you dare get up. It's just ads. Shhhhh.

She breathed into his ear, and he didn't get up.

—Shhhh, hush, shhhhh . . .

The doorbell rang again, but they no longer paid any attention.

He panted and inhaled the fragrances of the essential oils his wife used to enliven their bedroom. Had he cared, Boris Horak would have recognized, in the way she flung her head back, in her breathing—too loud and too quick—that she'd picked her moves up from movies. But he was not acting, and he didn't care. The only thing he did care about was the naked fact that the powerful male had strangled his own fear of knives.

David rang once more, but not long. He waited and then gave up. He figured he must have come too early, and it would be better to come back later. He'd spend the night at his dad's. He walked out of the entranceway. There was still a little daylight outside, but the evening moisture had begun to seep into his jeans, and

David decided to go into the bakery on the corner. He still had a little money, twelve kunas. He bought a slice of pizza, but he chewed on it without being fully aware of what he was eating. All he wanted was for the time to pass.

It was cold; he had no other choice but to hop onto a tram. He saw that if he ran, he'd catch the tram that was just passing through the intersection. He dashed; he didn't turn and didn't see the black car that had been stopped at the traffic light accelerating before it turned green; he didn't hear the shouts of frightened pedestrians, *he could have hit someone, idiot, asshole.* He was pleased when he managed to jump onto the tram just as the doors were starting to close. At the corner of Frankopanska and Ilica, he got off and got onto the #11.

### TRAM #11, THE ČRNOMEREC–DUBEC LINE

PHONE, *GODFATHER* THEME SONG:
Why won't you pick up when I call? I've called you at least ten times since this morning. What are you saying? Is that why you're not picking up? Very funny. When did you get home? At 3:15 AM? I was awake, but not in my apartment. I was out in front of your house. Yes, in my car, parked at your house. Yes, in the car. You didn't come home. No, I'm not asking. Just, if you have something to tell me, tell me. I'm obsessive? I am not obsessive, it's that I hate sleaze. I hate sleaze. Did I call her? Her? Well, who is she that I'd call her? A slut and an imbecile. So I say. Yes, so I say. Just you try. There are police in this city, you know. I can report you too. And her, yes, and her. You fucking piece of shit!

PHONE, LIKE A CUCKOO CLOCK:

Ah, you know I had in mind to call you, but I got to thinking the poor woman is probably napping and I didn't want to disturb you. You weren't? How's the gentleman? It didn't help? Then it must be, this really must be about a curse. He stumbled onto a curse. You think he couldn't have stumbled onto a curse? How long has it been since he left the house? Two years? Oh, that's nothing. A curse can hit you retroactively. No, for sure we'll find the right therapy. For sure. Patience. They worked with you with a divining rod, over television? Who was doing the divining? He was? Look, he's no expert diviner, he reads tarot cards. No, the gentleman is a friend of mine, and Mrs. Vesnica. Yes. They are pretty good, but my clients of many years say I am a miracle worker compared to them. How much did you pay for the phone? Two thousand seven hundred? Yes, that's expensive, but it's worth trying. Yes. Look, call me exactly at midnight. Not a second before, not a second after. We'll work together. We'll rouse him. You'll see. Be careful, cytostatics do more harm than good. Cytostatics are what led to this. Exactly at midnight.

Takes another call:

Yes, yes, yes, I'm listening closely. How old? Sixty? You need to concentrate now and lay your hand across the place that hurts. Yes, the pendulum is showing me that your head is hurting, problems are arising for you in your abdomen, near your hip, actually closer to the knee. Yes, your spine is very questionable. So I got it right? No, it's not that I got it right, the pendulum got it right. Yes, more therapy will be needed. Just call, please do, yes, bye-bye.

TWO MEN WITHOUT PHONES:

Listen, no matter what I put in my mouth, it goes right to fat. I hardly eat a thing, yet look at me. I was on Montignac. I'm on a moon diet every month. I went on that one that separates out the foods. I was on a purely protein diet. I was on miracle soup, on a seven-day fast, on pineapple and detox teas. What helped you? Enterovirus? You're so right, getting sick is the best. That does the trick.

PHONE, OUTGOING CALL:

Hey, cousin, it's me. Yes, me, Ante. Yes, it's been a couple of years since we saw each other. There's news, Ante my man, big news. First of all, I have two boys—ah, you heard. You don't say, and you? Well, congratulations are in order—congratulations. Yes, thanks, and back at you. So what's up? Anđa died? You're kidding. I had no idea. Mother sends news along but I don't hear half of it, I'm so busy with work. Yes, the people from our part of the woods are only getting older. Hardly anyone left. Well ... so people are building vacation homes, ugh, listen to me, they're building, nobody's building anything anymore. Whatever was built, is what is there. Yes, that's the thing. You're right about that. Listen, I have this little company, a business, and it used to be doing well, in fact really well until the shitshow with the recession hit. Now everything is standing there, all my building materials are just sitting there. I deal as well as I can. No, not drugs! What's gotten into you? Building materials. Nobody is paying anything. Nobody. Some faggot dumped radiators on me instead of what he owed; he went down and I knew I'd never get a cent from him, so I said, give me whatever you've got, I'll find a way to turn it around somehow for chump change. Chump, chump change. Roca told me you have good building materials, that you are on great terms with the guys in the city, scaffolding, that kind of thing, so he told me to ask you, we're cousins, after all. Can you find a way to take these miserable radiators off me? Fuck the radiators and me for taking them. You're out of the game too? So when did that happen? Roca said you were, like ... solid. I was hoping. Sure, if you can't, you can't ... Two boys, you said. What are their names? My boys are Dominik and Patrik. What? Your boys are Dominik and Patrik too? Well, sure, nice Catholic names. I wasn't too keen at first, but then my wife put the pressure on. Why should everybody be Ante, Ivan, Josip? No matter what, at least one grandfather will be insulted, so I agreed. Now I'm used to them. But still, I'm sorry, they're in pre-school now, and when I call their names, half the kids turn around. Right. So, like you say, no way with the radiators. And your boys are Dominik and Patrik too ... well, nothing then, say hi to everybody—we'll probably bump into each other one of these days.

He hangs up and talks to the window.

Fuck you, lying motherfucker. Roca knows who you are in with at Holding. I sure hope he fucks you over.

ANOTHER ON HIS PHONE:
How can you not get it, you ape, how can't you see? Zap him with the pyroblaster, the pyroblaster!

TWO FORTY-YEAR-OLD WOMEN WITHOUT PHONES:
Listen, it's too expensive for me; even if he gave it to me at
half price, it would still cost too much. Did you get paid last
month? You neither? They haven't paid us for two months.
We are afraid the worst is coming. The worst. And you? I don't
know where this is headed. I don't understand anything anymore. You and your husband lost your jobs? Mother of god.

He'd never been this far from home. The tram passed the terminus in Dubrava and went clanking on its way: one stop, the
next stop, one more stop, one more. Nothing interesting out
the window: tall buildings, low buildings, tall buildings, low
buildings. Red light, green light, red light, green light, red light.
They stopped.

In the distance, to the right of the tram tracks, beyond a
narrow strip of sidewalk and a wet field, stretched a row of
new buildings painted pink. The city was entering twilight;
the colors were fading, and the pink buildings took on shades
of gray. The lights in the apartments hadn't gone on yet, so
David wondered whether there was anyone living behind the
black windowpanes. The tram creaked, swayed, and started up.
They trundled along for only a short stretch. Then the tram
slammed on its brakes; the roadway was blocked by a pickup
truck that had entered from a side street. The rows of buildings stopped at the same time as the tram. The twilit meadow
narrowed and looked to him as if it were coming closer to the
tram. The windowpane on the right side flickered in the reddish
glow. He stood, pressed up against the window, then stepped

back, seeking a vantage point from which he would be able to see where the glow was coming from. He leaned way over, and into his field of vision finally came a garland of brightly colored lightbulbs, swinging back and forth over a little fairground with small bumper cars. He was delighted.

The bumper cars were linked by a chain, and David puzzled over whether the daytime rides were already over or the evening rides still hadn't begun. Along the very edge of the miniature amusement park stood a trampoline, a taut rubber square, and somebody was jumping on it. He focused on the figure who was now flying quite high. No sound reached the tram; he could tell there was no music playing. There was nobody standing near the trampoline, just a wet meadow and, a little farther on, a line of buildings with a row of empty balconies. He plugged his ears with his fingers, and now he could no longer hear the passengers talking or the short-tempered tram driver. Nothing from the street, nothing from the place he was watching. Just the silhouette on the trampoline bouncing high then dropping low, bouncing high then dropping low, slowly, as if flying through a vacuum. He unplugged his ears, turned his head, and the flying silhouette was gone. The tram finally began moving, but he no longer had any real reason to look out the window. New neighborhoods followed one after another, interspersed with fields full of discarded construction detritus—spools of rusted wire, mounds of rubble, scattered broken boards—all the way to the last stop. Billboards occasionally appeared with the outsized faces of smiling people. The women on them weren't young, or attractive, or naked, though they were smiling, and David knew

NADA GAŠIĆ

these were not ordinary ads and that a very serious product was being advertised here. The men on the billboards were mostly wearing suits and ties, and this showed they were advertising more serious things than the women. The poster, identical to the one he'd drawn on the night before, briefly returned him to the image of the black car and the awful plastic sheeting. *I didn't see a thing. I wouldn't recognize anybody.* He stopped looking at the posters, and up until he reached the last stop he entertained himself by counting the trams that were coming from the opposite direction. They finally stopped and he got off, polite and unassuming, with all the other passengers.

*Katarina exchanged birthday kisses with Ita, who had come back from Lovro's and right away started to discuss with her oldest sister the current state of what had been paid for and the expenses still outstanding on the wedding list. Katarina didn't hear any of it, not even Ita's question of whether she'd dye her hair. She was getting more and more upset; this was the second day in a row that he was missing. The second day in a row.*

He shivered once he'd stepped outside, surprised by how cold the night was; if he hadn't been embarrassed about being such a wimp, he would have done up his jacket. He decided to move on with most of the passengers to the bus stop. That way he didn't stand out. He let pass the ones who were in the biggest hurry, ran around two buses with motors already running, and then, with his head down, went back to the tram stop. He boarded the first tram that had an open door and sat on a seat roughly in the middle of the car.

This was, actually, a poor choice. He had already taken the #11 along the full length of the Črnomerec–Dubec line once, and now he felt silly getting onto the same tram, at the mercy of the same driver. Sometimes they pestered you with questions. He panicked. He was becoming suspicious even to himself. He sank a few centimeters deeper in his seat and, feeling smaller that way, he felt protected from the driver's gaze.

His panic subsided and he managed to remember that earlier, out of caution, he'd gone the route without his hood on, so wearing the hood now wouldn't draw attention. He was pleased that now his hood would have its turn. He slipped his hand under the collar of his jacket and felt the softness of his skin. His tracksuit was keeping him warm. Pleased, he worked the hood out, pulled it up over his head, and, with a practiced move, smoothed and fixed it so he could turn his head while the hood stayed still. He felt protected, and for a while he turned his head and amused himself thinking about the empty, motionless hood. If something were to happen in the tram, the newspaper would publish the headline: *Who is the mysterious witness in the hoodie? Who is the phantom figure in the tram?* For several stops, he was the mysterious witness who remembered, just in case, everything the passengers were saying into their phones. He tried to memorize this:

—Look, I'm telling you, the location is terrific. It's fifteen, twenty minutes max, to the bus, if you need it. There's enough room for a small garden. There'll be running water any day now; the water utility people came by. What with the elections coming up, it's time to push. Yes, the parish priest said push for water, but be careful. So they don't promise and then fail to deliver. I'm saying, the grandmother is old. What really matters is that she's sick. Keep after her about it, and she'll sign. I wouldn't recommend one of those assets-for-care-type things. Much better for you is to move in right away, and she can sell it to you. Gee, I don't know, fifteen or twenty thousand. Sign that, and you'll have everything you need to apply for the deed. Euros, of course, euros, nobody in their right mind would sell for kunas. Listen, you won't end up paying anything, no kunas, no euros, what are you thinking, it's all just on paper. No, no need to kick her out, all she needs is a little maid's room off the kitchen—she won't last long anyway. But see to it tout suite. So what's up with Stipan? You don't say . . .

That bit was too complicated for him to memorize, so he looked over, hopefully, at another passenger.

—You could see her pussy. She was standing that way on purpose, bro, to show off her pussy. Anyone who wasn't paying attention wouldn't have noticed. I looked where I was supposed to. I don't give a fuck about her singing voice. No way, she wasn't drunk, she stood there on purpose just to show off her pussy.

This began to irritate David, and in disgust he stuck his tongue out at the pussy guy and Stipan and the grandmother and the owners of the phones; then he stopped listening to the voices around him. He pressed up against the window.

*Katarina told herself she'd give him another half hour. Then she'd call his father. She didn't even turn to greet Irma, who had just walked in, or to follow the conversation between her two younger sisters. She couldn't follow them. They were saying something about the house, Ita was leaving, Irma ... She couldn't keep track of them. Okay, another forty-five minutes.*

It was only by the stretch of darkness that went on and on outside the window that he sensed they were passing the city zoo. He thought about the boundless amount of sleep the elephant needed and he yawned, grandly and slowly, just like an elephant. He saw his reflection in the glass, and his gaping mouth reminded him of a monkey, not an elephant. He grinned at the monkey and wished him good monkey night. For a while he sat there quietly and breathed onto the windowpane. Soon, a circle of breath steam appeared. He let down his guard for a moment and pursed his mouth in an O, but then he remembered he'd only attract attention that way, so he wiped away the drawing with his sleeve.

—No, sweetie, not with your sleeve. What will your mama say?

He shrank into himself and didn't answer.

—So late to be coming home from school?

He didn't dare stay silent anymore.

—Sports.

Usually after this sentence a third person would make a comment, most often a man, and the boy impatiently eyed the passengers. Nobody reacted. The old woman wasn't joined by anyone.

—So what's your sport?

He didn't answer.

—Did you hear my question? What's your sport?

He had an answer ready for that too, but he could already see he'd have to be getting off at the next stop. When these *hundred-year-old* types start in with the questions, all sorts of things can happen—at that age they're fond of the police.

He tossed his backpack over his shoulder, and as the tram was slowing to a stop, he was already at the door. Just in case, he didn't turn, so the woman wouldn't be able to remember his face.

He got off at the stop by the intersection of Maksimirska and Jordanovac. He only liked this stop in daytime. At night, because of the pastry shop by the stop, it had a hungry feeling about it; the locked display cases with no cakes and the empty dishes without ice cream looked as if someone had run away and would never come back. He stepped back from the display and went over to the next building, covered in graffiti up to the ground-floor windows. He tried reading what it said, but he was too close and all he could recognize was an ear-shaped letter U and inside it a cross. He grimaced and growled, grrrr ... Then he stood by the curb, and from there he read that someone had added nO paNTiEs. He laughed, rocked from side to side, and doubted his sanity. A tram was speeding toward him. It braked to a stop too close to the traffic light. The boy stepped back in time. He didn't even look to read its number; he got on and decided he wouldn't sit for at least two or three stops. That is all he needed to get to Kvaternik Square, where, while having a look at the little glass houses of the flower vendors and the flat granite surface, he was reminded of his grandfather and the funeral at the Crematorium. He looked away and squinched his eyelids.

*Katarina was getting frantic. Now she'd call his father. Never had this happened before, that he was gone day after day.*

He opened his eyes at the stop in front of St. Peter's and got off.

The door to the church was closed, and the boy turned toward the street. The only cars were a Honda Civic and a Renault Scenic that were waiting for the light to change. He knew all the different makes of cars. Their light turned green, and he watched to see how fast the cars would go. He was missing the proper sound, so David made it himself, as if dubbing the soundtrack of a cartoon. Vroom, vroooom . . . The cars left. Then he stood right next to the edge of the tram tracks and looked in the direction that the tram would be coming from. It was late and fewer trams were running. There was nothing all the way to the place where the street curved and kept him from seeing any farther. With a sideways glance, he took the measure of the stop. There were several people waiting for the tram, but David avoided making eye contact. Again, he had to shake his head. *I didn't see a thing. I wouldn't recognize anybody . . .*

He turned around toward the display window of a clothing store, but instead of the plastic mannequins, he stared at a man who was rummaging through a nearby trash bin. The glow from the display window lit the man, and David was interested to see that the man was holding the handle of an umbrella from which he'd torn off the cloth, and the lower end of the tip was sharpened so he could spear whatever he wanted. David envied the man's cane. By the man's tense posture, David could see that he'd found what he was looking for, and that, as if he were reeling in the prey he'd caught, he was focused on retrieving his quarry. A

NADA GAŠIĆ

huge fish? A carp? A catfish? *Green, five points—white, zero,* David gambled with himself. If he guessed right, he'd give himself those five points. As it was, zero. The man pulled out a clear plastic bottle and stuffed it into a sack. The boy eyed the sack and concluded that the man was making good money. He himself sometimes sold empty plastic bottles, and by the bulges in the sack he could already gauge the earnings. The man moved away; clearly someone else had already been through that bin. Then David had a look at the kiosk where popcorn and peanuts were sold. He was hungry and even had a few kunas in change, but the kiosk was already closed, and the lowered shutters only sharpened his hunger. He heard the sound of a tram coming and was pleased. It was a #12 and he decided he'd take it all the way, with no getting off or changing lines, to the stop nearest to his father's street. With a glance at the big clock in a watchmaker's shop window when the tram passed it, he saw that nine o'clock had already passed. This meant that all, every last one of them, knew he wasn't home, and now Mama's anxiety had reached tears and panic. So be it. Now she was calling his dad. He smiled. They're all scared. So be it, let them die of fear.

*The black car circled through the neighborhood once more, then around the Cibona Tower and the intersection with Vodnikova, and then it came to a stop by the Museum of Technology. Its engine off, it waited. The driver was patient.*

The window was his friend again, for a time.

*Katarina could no longer bear it. She got up and left her sisters at the Zadruga to freely add, multiply, divide. And subtract.*

The shop windows thinned to the right, but the strong lights of the tall Importanne building let him know they were near Draškovićeva. The cathedral spires were well lit, and the boy kept an eye on them until they disappeared from view. On Draškovićeva, his tram lined up behind the #14 and moved through the stop and the street quite slowly. He waited for the fountain on Bourse Square. He got up and stood on his tiptoes, but even without that it was clear that the fountain had been turned off for whatever reason. Insulted, he looked away and sat back down. On Jurišićeva, he waited for the post office building to appear. He always felt a little solemn when they passed by it. He didn't stand this time, but he sat up straighter in his seat. They approached Ban Jelačić Square, and David knew that after counting to four he'd see the cathedral spires again. He was right and lorded his superiority over the other passengers. The tram stopped, but the door didn't open; they hadn't pulled into the stop. He saw a light rain pock the water in the Manduševac fountain. He shivered, suddenly remembering the drizzle the night before. *I didn't see a thing. I wouldn't recognize anybody.*

He hid in the dark of his hoodie and watched the passengers: two drunk men were already on the tram, and he checked to see whether a third, swaying there by the stop, would join them. No, he stayed at the stop. The tram pulled away from the well-lit square, so he entertained himself by counting posters: how many men, how many women, how many group photos. Shop windows were lit along Ilica, and he managed to find the ones that didn't have the *closed for renovation* sign on them. The display for the Kraš chocolate store was better to look at when the tram was going in the other direction, but even from this angle the rich brown color of the chocolate had him salivating.

This finally began to bore him. He waited for the tram to pull into his stop. When it did, he did not look out the window and instead just swung his feet. And that's why he missed it.

He didn't know how he could have been so stupid: instead of getting off at the Westin, he stayed on the tram for one more stop for no particular reason. What could he have thought to see on the grounds of the Museum of Technology? It was nighttime. Nitwit. He got off the tram at the Cibona stop.

*Out in front of the Zadruga, she glanced at her phone, then ran across the yard and into the house. While still in the hallway, she called David's father. She let it ring, but when the voicemail came on she didn't leave a message. She decided she wouldn't call him again that evening. He'd see her number and know she never called him for no reason. And she wouldn't wait for David anymore; soon he'd come. Soon he'd come.*

He glanced up at the traffic light; it was silly to wait for the green on Savska, so he started crossing at the green for Tratinska. He'd cross Tratinska to Savska, and then he'd walk in front of the Student Center to Vodnikova.

The cars waiting to turn from Savksa onto Tratinska were lined up there. He clearly heard the hum of their motors. David was the first to cross, and he stopped on the traffic-light island.

He saw the lights, heard the cars start. He didn't see *that car.* But he did recognize the powerful surge of its motor charging forward.

Terrified, he didn't turn. He sprinted. The #12 was free to make the right turn from Savska onto Tratinska, but he didn't have time to wait for the traffic light.

He ran like crazy.

He didn't feel a thing, nothing hurt, he didn't hear a thing. Not the women screaming, or the people invoking God and the Mother of god, or the curses, or the ambulance sirens, or the doctors, or those who carried him, or Tomica, the ambulance driver, when he said, *Look at these motherfuckers, how are they driving, we're just picking kids up these days on the streets*, or the police, or the voices that kept saying *a black car, a black* suv, *no, not an* suv, *it was a Golf, come off it, no way was it a Golf, a Jeep, no, it was, it wasn't, it . . . It was driving the wrong way, not the wrong way, but from the right, it came in from Savska, it didn't, it was parked in front of the Cibona, it came from there, don't be ridiculous when you didn't see . . . He took off, the creep ran away, what garbage, the kid was scared, what a piece of trash, he took off, a hit-and-run.*

Through a drop of blood that was dribbling down his forehead and over his eye, he saw a light that was moving away, and in that light Big Boy Damir was waving to him. He couldn't wave back, and this worried him. Then the light, too, went out.

# Third stone, third wave

### A *small light*

Weird . . . Actually, I don't know why I'm here. I know I'm lying down, and I know nothing hurts. This makes me suspicious, because usually I'm only in bed when something hurts. Or when I have a fever. I think I'm in a hospital; in fact, I'm pretty sure I'm in a hospital, because it smells exactly like a hospital, and I can hear Mama crying. The light bothers me. It is always on, and that's why I don't know whether it's day or night, and I don't even know which day. Tuesday, Wednesday, Sunday? Although it should be all the same to me. When I feel like it, I'll ask someone, and that's that. The light really is strange. It's as if there's a curtain in front of me, but a thin one, a very, very thin curtain, though it isn't see-through or opaque. Whatever . . . Through it I can't see very clearly who is near me and around me, but still I can see them. In a way. I know exactly when Mama is with me, when Dad came, when the nurse came in, and when there's somebody in the room I don't know. And I have a feeling that I've caught on to the doctors. Actually, I hear all of them just fine, and, what's funniest of all, I can smell all of them. Mama is always by my side, but it really gets on my nerves that she's always crying and calling my name and asking like an idiot whether I can hear her. Of course I can hear her when she's wailing right here by my ear. The funniest thing is that she keeps saying *wake up, wake up,* but it's wild exactly how awake I am, because of all her tears and questions. She won't let me sleep, though I am really, really, really sleepy. Why won't Mama let me sleep, when she's always after me at home to go to bed? Idiotic. I'd like to tell her to give me a break. Or actually it's like this: I'd like her to stop crying so I can fall asleep, but . . . hm, well yes. Now I guess I'd like to pretend, but better that I admit it up front. There, I admit it: I'd like her to stay here with me. No need to lie about it. When secret agents don't have their wife yet, sometimes they need their mother, but nobody needs to know. At least at first. If she'd just stop crying—I can't bear to listen to that anymore. Now I'm going to sleep, no matter how hard she cries. If only someone would turn out the light. It bothers me. The light bothers me something awful.

*   *   *

Katarina understood the nurse's wink, and she moved away from David's bed and discreetly left the room; the doctors had just come in on their rounds. She leaned on the wall in the

NADA GAŠIĆ

corridor, right by the doorway, to be as close as possible when the rounds were done, so she could ask the head doctor about her child's condition right away. This was when the hospital was busiest: the glassware jangled on the carts the nurses were pushing around; they were removing piles of dirty linen and bringing in the clean bedding; the little patients who could walk were up and about in their pajamas and little bathrobes. It occurred to Katarina that she should buy David a bathrobe, and then she immediately realized she'd be wasting her money —he'd never agree to wear it. She heard laughter from a neighboring room; the nurse went by carrying a portable urinal, the stench mixing with vapors from powerful disinfectants and brewed coffee, and from somewhere came the smell of burnt cooking oil, and in a panic Katarina tightened her solar plexus to hold back a wave of nausea. She needed air, but she didn't dare move, aware that the doctors' rounds might wrap up at any moment.

—Are they inside?

She turned at the sound of David's father's voice.

Her nausea retreated.

—Yes. They'll be out soon.

—I can see you've been here the whole time. Right now it's unnecessary, and you're wasting energy you're going to need when David wakes up.

—Talk with your wife about energy. I'm here because David needs me and because they let me.

Boris looked at her, surprised by the new tone in her voice.

—David needs me too, but I'm not acting like a fool over it, and I'm letting people do their jobs.

She didn't have the chance to respond. The door opened and someone held it to let the head of the ward come through. Katarina and Boris Horak stepped forward at the same moment, but the doctor spoke directly to Boris.

—You're the parents?

—Yes, his father.

Katarina said nothing.

—Come see me in my office in half an hour.

Surrounded by his colleagues and nurses, the doctor proceeded down the corridor.

A nurse stepped into the room to check on the IV line over David's bed. Katarina and Boris followed her in and went over to David's bed, each on one side.

He looked different, not because his head was bandaged, and not because he was wearing a hospital gown with little flowers on it, and not because he was hooked up to equipment that lit up and hummed, and not because he was sleeping. He was different because he was sleeping with a sleep they couldn't reach.

Boris's lips trembled; his chin wobbled in an ugly and painful way, but he didn't shed a tear. At least that was what he hoped. Katarina found a little patch of free skin, skin that wasn't under bandages or other dressings, or poked with needles, and slowly, so it wouldn't hurt David, she pressed her lips to that patch. She whispered something and tensed with the effort to hold back her own tears.

The nurse warned them that it would be better to go and wait out in front of the head doctor's office; if they didn't catch him now, it could happen that he'd be called away for something urgent: an operation, a meeting, a consultation.

They did what she said, like children.

The doctor:

—Yes, come in, have a seat. Your child is stable, and for the moment all his vital organs are functional. Everything else we could tell you would be premature. The child suffered a serious concussion, contusion; injuries to the head are never harmless, so we are watching for any swelling on his brain. And if he weren't in a coma, we would have to induce one to let his body recover. Everything urgent was done last night—they treated the fractures of his right shin and his pelvis. There was trauma to his kidneys, but we aren't panicking about that for now. The injuries to his sternum aren't threatening his lungs. Your son is receiving medication, of course, through the iv, and I won't burden you with that; for laypeople such as yourselves, it is all a lot of Latin. Pardon me, are either of you medical professionals? No? So, I think what's needed now is patience. This condition may continue for a very long time. It's totally unpredictable, but precisely because it is unpredictable, it could end at any moment and your boy could wake up. We are monitoring his condition constantly, both with monitors and examinations. What can you do? Well, it's very important that you maintain contact with the child. I personally granted unlimited access to the child. Yes, Horak, Mr. Horak, if I'm not mistaken? Your director called at the break of dawn this morning. We are tennis partners and fierce adversaries. Do you play? No? A shame, so relaxing. There, that's all for now. You can always come to me with questions, but it's best to ask the on-duty doctor. You're most welcome, goodbye, we've done everything we could, but, I repeat, there still is a risk; the injuries are serious. Have faith. Children have powerful bodies.

They left the office, smiling. Katarina was looking for support for her little surge of optimism.

—What do you think about what he said?

—I don't think anything. We need to wait and see. David still hasn't pulled through.

She was sorry she'd asked. She picked up her pace and was sitting by David's bed before he even entered the room.

\*      \*      \*

These were the morning hours in Zagreb, when some are already working, some are driving, some are sleeping, and some are just waking up.

\*      \*      \*

Big Boy Damir was already dressed when Cilika came in.

—Wait here, I'll bring it in to you. Let Gramps eat first, then Vilim and me, and then I'll bring your doughnut and your tea. Did you wet your bed?

Big Boy said nothing. She left.

Late that night, maybe before dawn, Big Boy Damir was the first to hear the cars, one after another, that parked in front of David's house; he heard the commotion start, the crying and slamming of doors, the groans, the sound of running footsteps, the shriek.

Then he curled up in bed.

He heard someone opening the gate of his yard; he heard Cilika pacing up and down, moaning; she began wailing, calling on the Mother of god and repeating, *A tram, a tram hit our David, our sweet Dadek was hit by a tram.*

Front doors opened then closed, then the car door, then the motor started up; Katarina, Ita, and Irma went to the hospital. That is how it was the night before too.

Big Boy Damir would sit out the day in his little room, on his bed; he wouldn't go out in the yard, he wouldn't wait for anyone, he wouldn't wave to anyone. Until the night.

He found his serenity point and gently rocked. Until night.

*   *   *

They gathered in Vidošić's office; it was morning, and the officers were moving sluggishly. There was coughing, a few words exchanged, the scraping of chairs.

—Close the door, Kasumić, we are not aboard ship.

Vidošić snarled at the last one to arrive, looked over all his subordinates, and spoke loudly, louder than usual; he was afraid of having to repeat himself.

—Listen up. As you know, the victim's identity has been confirmed, and that's already a lot since yesterday morning. What we have to work with now is based on the realization that the victim was not murdered where her body was found. Where she was murdered, we don't know. So, the location of where the crime was committed is unknown. We don't know why she was dumped in a place that was so visible, along a busy street, at the entrance to the school where she worked. On that, please, I'd appreciate your thoughts. We know nothing about the motive for the murder. Every theory is of interest until it is proved wrong by the truth.

Somebody was heard saying *oho* and then shut up. Vidošić looked them over, but he was not in the mood for wisecracks, and nobody laughed.

—What we're missing is the autopsy report that still, no surprise, isn't ready, but it should be here today. When it comes, we'll know the time of death and what sort of murder it was, the injuries, and the cause of death. From the Center for Criminal Forensics we'll be sent a finding on any biological traces. Only then will we be better informed. For now, we can only speculate about those things, but until we receive the autopsy we won't know what kind of a crime this was. So, Zdilar, to Travno to see the neighbor; Komšić, to the school and the neighborhood around the school; Kasumić, to her good friend after you submit your report from yesterday. I didn't see it on my desk. How we do these things, I hope I don't need to instruct anyone on the basics. Okay? As soon as I get the reports, I'll send everything to you and will call for a meeting. Okay? We're done.

The room emptied. Kasumić remained. They exchanged looks.

—So? What did her friend say? Were there heartfelt greetings?

—Not particularly. She said the usual, that they spent time together because they were close in age, that she knew a little about the family, that she didn't see her on the day when it happened. She bungled a few things. She fumbled over whether she'd called the school secretary or the secretary called her, but clearly she'd taken a shitload of sedatives, and alcohol to boot, so her bungling was almost to be expected.

—Friends? Acquaintances?

—She said she had met them, but they weren't mutual friends.

—We'll see about that. We'll learn more about what sort of organizing of senior proms and travels these dear teacher friends were up to. That night?

—She was with her sisters and a maid of honor; their youngest sister is getting married, so . . .

—Go for another interview, either at home or at school. Push her until she falls apart. If either of the sisters is at home, interview one of them as well. If they aren't, ask where you'll find them. Okay?

Kasumić was already at the door.

—Okay. Bye.

As soon as he'd closed the door, someone thumped him on the shoulder.

—Tesla, it looks like you're serious about this. Eh? A copy, no two ways about it.

Kasumić turned.

—Josina, what are you doing here? How did they let you in?

—The camo scares them, that's how.

A tall, muscular man in a camouflage jacket was grinning from ear to ear; he pulled his hands out of his pockets to shake Kasumić's hand.

—Time for coffee, Tesla, or are you up to your nose in work?

—Up to my nose. We're dealing with a murder.

—What's that to you? It's not your first.

—What brings you to Zagreb, work?

—Well, I came up to see if they'd return a rifle of mine, and then I was thinking, you're a big shot here. If you nudge it along, it will go faster. Eh?

—Bullshit, I'm no big shot. Why don't you go over to the Petrin-jska police station and fill out all the forms by the book, and then we'll see what we can do.

—And coffee? A drink?

—Drinking during the workday? Ancient history.

—This afternoon?

—We'll see. Give me a buzz.

Kasumić backed away; the man raised his hand to see him off.

—Hey, Tesla, nobody knows you here by that name.

—Josina, cut the shit, that's not a name, it's a nickname. You had to go trumpeting it around?

—Ha ha. Your office buddies are laughing at you.

—You sure are a true-blue Lika pal. You screw me whenever you have the chance. And don't come barging in here like this with no advance warning.

—As long as I'm wearing these colors, I'll barge in wherever the fuck I please. See ya!

\*       \*       \*

—Drive more slowly, I'm not in great shape today.

—Whatever you say.

—How are you?

—Fine, thanks.

—Everything taken care of?

—Yes.

—Spick-and-span

—Yes.

—We won't speak of it again.

—No need.

—I am not asking who was with you, or how it went down. I saw something on the news.

—No need to speak of it.

—Watch how you drive up Mesnička Street on our way up to my office in the legislature. I'm not feeling so hot.

—Whatever you say.

\*     \*     \*

Ita came to the door. Irma wasn't there, and Kasumić had to show her his police ID. She brought him into the kitchen. She repeated Irma's apologies, but skipped the part about the nephew making the mess. Even professional curiosity hadn't convinced Kasumić to take a good look around rooms when he came to interview someone. He felt this would be far too intrusive. What you learn in childhood is difficult to forget. But this? The house looked even worse than it had the day before. Ita offered him a place to sit, then she saw that the chair was piled up with David's clothes they'd brought from the hospital, and, finally, she started to cry.

She lifted up the folded clothes and with them in her arms, she stopped.

—I'm sorry, we have had a terrible tragedy. Terrible. My sister's son was hit by a tram last night.

—Is he alive?

Kasumić said this; Ita stopped sobbing and looked at him in surprise.

—Yes, he's alive.

Kasumić was staring at the blue backpack swinging in her arms and the jagged shred of plastic from the ripped-off pocket.

Within ten minutes he'd had a good look at the photograph of the boy, which he'd asked Ita for; he took down all the information about David, his parents, the hospital, and the spot where he'd been hit by the tram.

He raced to Klaićeva Children's Hospital.

He'd completely forgotten about Irma.

\*     \*     \*

Irma slept briefly before morning. She was with Katarina for a long time and only left the hospital when David was placed in intensive care after he came out of the operating room. She couldn't follow him there; she kissed Katarina goodbye and barely made it home. Over the last two days, she'd been drained to the maximum and no longer even had it in her to cry. She had to take a sedative. She thought of taking something else, but didn't have anything in her room. Her brief sleep was more like delirium, and she woke up to the alarm clock, shaking, groggy, and, in fact, feeling very ill. She had to go to school that day, she knew she did; she had to see to everything Katja couldn't manage. Ita would bite off her head if she skipped her obligations for the wedding. And, worst of all, today she could forget driving; she wasn't capable of holding the steering wheel.

Water was always her friend, but this morning there was nothing she could do to refresh herself. She left the house, ill. She spent the whole day riding trams from one place to another around town.

# TRAM #9, TOWARD THE TRAIN STATION

IRMA, ON HER PHONE:

No, I'm not using my phone. I'm calling when you asked me to call. I'll sign. I told you I'd sign. Where should I come? Can we make it a little later, I am teaching this afternoon. Because of All Saint's Day, they switched the schedule around. Sure. Yes. You can hear the voices and people because I'm on the tram. I told you I'm off to teach. At the Trešnjevka Nama department store, 6 PM. I'll sign.

PHONE LIKE THUNDER:

Wow, what a load of crap that bitch ranted about me to the police. That I knocked her around. I tell the police, look, if I'd hit her right and proper she wouldn't have gotten up. The cop just laughed—he's a man after all, fuck it, and he knew what I was on about. That big fat bitch, if she opens her blubber mouth once more, they'll be out looking for her dentures up on Sljeme. Fuck her. She's forever chattering away with your wife on her phone, so I'd watch it if I were you, keep an eye on what your wife is up to. Listen, enough about that. Are you all in for the whole November hog slaughter thing this year? We'd join in with a hog and smoke it and do the sausages and everything. The store-bought kind are a waste of space. Homemade sausages rule. I give them more heat and then I wash them down with spritzers. If you want to come by and lend a hand, you'd be welcome. So long as her jaw is healing by then, so she doesn't scare you with it. Heh, heh, well sure, I did her one, you know, gave her a little work over. Bye, see ya. Wait, wait, so how much does the guy want for the cracklings?

A GROUP OF SCHOOL CHILDREN WHO GOT ON THE TRAM AT THE CIBONA TOWER, SURROUNDING A CLASSMATE:
Kill, kill the Serb, kill, kill the Serb!
    They giggle.
    The teacher escorting them:
    Quieter, children, we aren't alone here!

PHONE, OUTGOING CALL:
Hi, it's me. Why'd you take so long to pick up? Sleeping? Did I wake you? Why sleeping so late? You have the night shift, so you wanted to rest up before work? Look, I forgot, no need to get all worked up about it. Go back to sleep. Why am I a pain? Turn over and go back to sleep.
    To the lady sitting next to her:
    My daughter. She's so worried about me, she's forever calling me.

PHONE, NINTH SYMPHONY:
The concert was magnificent. The conductor held them from beginning to end. From beginning to end. I was a little anxious about the second movement, but they pulled it off. Can you believe not a single phone rang last night? True-blue concertgoers. Yes, Saturday is the worst; that's when the people who have no clue about music come. You're right, you can feel the difference now from a few years ago. It's getting better.

Ita, it's me. Who? A cop? Ah, the same guy as before. David was all he asked about? No, I can't imagine why. Did Katja call? I can't get through to her; she's probably with Dadek at the hospital, so she turned off her phone. I can't go to the hospital, Ita, I've got to go to work, I didn't go in yesterday. What's gotten into you? They'll kick me out of school. Lighten up. I don't know whether his dad is at the hospital with Katarina. He stayed on last night after I left, but I think he took off right after that. I didn't wake you up, because that would be a shame. You need your sleep. Where's Lovro? Are the two of you going to check on the hall? Ita, chill, I'm taking care of the flowers and that's all set. Look, don't say anything more to Katja today. When things quiet down, I'll tell her. Or Cilika. Of course Dadek will be fine, medicine makes miracles happen today. Everything will be okay with Dadica. My David, Auntie's little sweetheart.

\*　　\*　　\*

Right, I'm at the hospital. Quite a scene: I'm lying there, pretending I can't hear a thing, surrounded by this throng of stinky people. The head doctor or whatever he's called, then some professor guy, then a colleague, then Mr. Doctor again—I didn't get it quite right, maybe that's not how it's said. His condition is cerevral cabbage, no, not cabbage, but a little like that and only silly things like that, better I shut up. Communication with his surroundings, out from his uvinal tact, and other stuff. In any case, I figured out that they have no idea I can hear them, and, of course, it doesn't occur to them that I can even see them. Like that, from inside. But I smell them; this they don't realize at all. If they think they can come barging in here all the time, pester me, and then say this stuff about me, as soon as I am able, and that will be way faster than they're thinking, I'll hoof it out of here. That is what worries me the most right now—I don't know where my sneakers are and all the rest of my clothes. Will I have to go walking around town in my pj's? If I'm even wearing pj's. You heard right. I don't even want to say this, but I believe these morons dressed me up in a n-i-ght-ie. Exactly—a n-i-ght-ie. There's a nurse who is constantly poking me where she shouldn't. It's her fault. And Mama's no better, not to speak of the old man. He lets them do everything. He could stand up to them. But he doesn't say a word. Traitor. If my grandpa were here, he would have put his foot down. Then they all vanished somewhere, and I was left listening to myself breathe. Afterward they all came back. Mama cried more, but then this doctor came in—he was called the on-duty something—and he said a bunch of things too. I heard Mama repeating like a parrot what the doctor said, that *of course, communication is the most important now, we'll do everything, we won't capitulate.* Clearly, she was listening in behind the door the whole time the doctors were saying all kinds of stuff about me. She only uses words like *capitulate* when she's upset. Otherwise, she's normal. And she's saying *we.* Who is this *we* she's talking about? If she means her and Dad, there's gonna be a nasty mess when all this is over.

When I say *all this*, I mean all the fuss they're making over me. Then she cried again, then she finally stopped crying and rolled up her sleeves, like my grandpa used to say, and started saying over and over again how much she loves me, and stuff like that. She wore me down. And she kept going on about how we'd go down to the seaside. I don't mind the seaside, don't get me wrong, but she loves it five times more than me, though she sinks like a stone and nobody alive knows why she loves being at the seaside so much. If she really wants to convince me to get up, it would be way better to promise Gardaland. I've never been to a big amusement park, but lots of the kids from my class have gone, some even twice. Kovačić three times. And in the end she even promised she'd read me stories tomorrow. Now that's a real nightmare. My mom doesn't have a clue. It would be better for me to get some sleep. I'll need rest if I'm to survive her reading.

*The on-duty doctor shone a light in David's eye and turned to the nurse: Everybody out, only his mother was given permission to be here; what is this circus now, and what is this gentleman doing here?*

I was away for a while, and then I looked through that curtain of mine to see who all was in the room. Mama of course was sitting right next to me. And I recognized Dad, though he was standing a little farther off. The nurse was poking around on me. I sure hope they all turned around and looked somewhere else, because I think I was, I'm still, buck naked, and the nurse was up to some kind of nonsense on

me. Better I don't talk about that. Then by smell, or rather stink, and by the fact that he was whiter than the others,
and because everybody got quiet when he came in, and
by the way he behaved as if he were at home, I recognized
the doctor and I heard just fine when he told everybody
they had to leave the room. Actually, he was chasing away
some guy, and I'm not sure who that is. But he didn't send
out Mama. I don't know if he tried sending out Dad. Then I
heard Mama when she told the man I don't recognize, and
who the doctor chased out of the room, *It would be better for
you to leave, while we can still control ourselves.* Who is this *we*?
Me and her, she and Dad, all three of us? I doubt it. I think
she's not in her right mind if she's saying *we* for herself and
Dad. The man said something, and I could swear I've heard
that voice before, but I can't remember where. Dunno, but
I'll remember. The nurse is pulling and pushing on all sorts
of tubes, and Mama's crying. The doctor is shining a light in
my eye. He's crazy. I'm going deeper in behind the curtain. I
feel better in there. I'm sleepy . . . I'm scared of the light . . .

Kasumić didn't give up easily, though he knew it was extremely impolite for him to barge into a hospital room and harass
the parents of a badly injured boy. He could see that the kid's
mother could barely stand, and he, walking backward, left, but
he stayed with the on-duty doctor, who was nervously leaving
the room, and walked by him. He flashed his badge.
—Police.
—We don't provide information about patients.
—Today you will.

The doctor stopped to say something, to resist, to protest, but Kasumić's face looked so twisted and primal that he backed off.

—Yes, what would you like to know?

—I would like to know how the kid was hurt.

The doctor sneered.

—For that you've come to the wrong address. Ask your colleagues. We deal with the results of the care you take of the people of this city.

—I'll ask you once again: How was the kid hurt? A tram? A car? A motorbike?

—A tram, but luckily it was turning, at a slow speed; the kid was knocked over, his body, but more dangerous was that he smashed his head on the pavement. He wasn't run over, he was hit and thrown to the side.

—So this wasn't intentional?

—I do hope this question is coming from your professional obsessiveness.

—Hope as you like, and thank you.

Kasumić started down the corridor.

—Officer, one moment.

Kasumić waited for the doctor.

—This is not my department, but I did hear from the guys in the ambulance that the police recorded some statements that there was a car, supposedly, that frightened the kid, and it disappeared from the scene of the accident. Check in with your folks.

Kasumić stood there and listened to the wheels on the cart that was bringing tea to the quiet little patients.

\*     \*     \*

Vidošić's day was dragging on. His officers had gone off to take statements from neighbors in Travno, tenants whose balconies looked over the high school playing fields, and the staff at the high school, who certainly had to know more about the murdered woman. The autopsy report still hadn't come in, and Vidošić was bothered that no matter how much he magnified the photographs of the victim's body, he could not determine what the circles were on her neck and chest, though, of course, he had his assumptions.

During the early afternoon his team began drifting back in, calling to one another before they came to his office with their brief reports, which, mostly, all came down to the same thing: nobody heard anything, or if they did hear something, they thought it was the normal sound of a car; nobody saw anything, because one doesn't usually go out on the balcony at that time of night; nobody in Travno knew the murdered woman, because the faces of renters are not memorable. Her fellow teachers did not want to get involved and were tight-lipped in their attitude toward the woman.

Kasumić waved to Simčić and Zdilar when they invited him to join them for coffee, and he went straight in to see Vidošić.

—Last night the kid fell under a tram, and it looks like some car that vanished from the scene of the accident forced him to.

Vidošić stood, shoved his hands into his pockets, and turned to the window.

—How did you find the kid, and where does this story come from?

Kasumić dropped into a chair.

—I went to Irma Žiger's house, like you said I should, but only her younger sister was there. She said their nephew, the son of their oldest sister, had been in an accident last night. She swept up a big pile of things to free up a chair, and I saw the backpack I'd seen on the kid yesterday. I asked for a picture of the kid, and I had something to see. It was him.

Vidošić turned, saying nothing.

—Look, Boss, I went to the hospital without your go-ahead. The parents were with the kid; it was awkward, but still I heard from the doctor about the car that caused the accident.

Vidošić took his hands from his pockets.

—In a case like this there's no doing things on your own. This might all be pure coincidence, and if it isn't, you've already made a few serious blunders that could upend the investigation. You should not have gone to the hospital.

—I know, but things are heating up. The kid's aunt, Irma Žiger, is the murdered woman's best friend; the kid was prowling around the crime scene yesterday; last night he was seriously injured under suspicious circumstances. We have no time to waste.

—What time to waste? Who is wasting time? I, who am holding everything in my hands, or you, who happened to forget to mention that you know the murdered woman? Ha? You went to the hospital before we'd put two and two together. When she goes home, the first thing the kid's mother will tell her sister is that a cop showed up at the hospital. If this Irma of yours knows something, she'll keep all four eyes wide open. Do you see what you've done?

Vidošić's tone was gradually rising, until his last sentence could be heard in the corridor.

—Kasumić, this is your last time, last time! If you do anything else on your own, you'll be saying goodbye to the department!

Kasumić was already standing. Now he had his hands in his pockets so his boss wouldn't see him clenching his trembling fists.

—It may be my last, but it would be better for you to assign protection to the kid at the hospital. Somebody from the car will find out he survived.

—This is not an American TV show. Cool it before you push me too far.

Vidošić had already sat back down and was leafing through some papers when he added:

—Maybe you'd be better off back home in Lika, watching those TV shows of yours and guarding kids in the hospital there. Enjoying the fresh air.

Kasumić had not expected this. As he stood there facing Vidošić, he'd been considering telling off his boss, but he didn't; he shoved Vidošić hard, along with his chair. When the chair slammed into the wall, Simčić and Zdilar, who had been eavesdropping out in the corridor, burst into the room, threw themselves on Kasumić, and dragged him out.

Vidošić pulled out a bottle of grappa from the lowest drawer in his desk and took a swig. For a long time, he trembled. For the first time in two years, he regretted stopping smoking. When he calmed down, he picked up his phone and called: It's me. Where are the kids? Have them come in immediately, and until I get home they are not to go out. Don't ask why. Get the kids off the street.

Kasumić had already walked out of police headquarters on Heinzelova.

*　　*　　*

　　　　　　　　　　　　　　　　　　　NADA GAŠIĆ

Katarina and Boris Horak left the hospital once it had become abundantly clear that Katarina was on the verge of collapse and Boris might lose control. They walked in silence to the tram stop by the theater; finally, they were breathing air not thickened with hospital smells. They said not a word about who had called whom the night before, who hadn't picked up the phone, where she, he, and David had been.

—Katarina, are you going to wait for the #12?

—Yes.

—I'll take whichever comes first; it's only the one stop. Don't spend all of tomorrow at the hospital. You're burdening the boy.

—I won't be there all day, but you heard him—the doctor said communication is now what matters most.

—I've got to go to work, but I'll be by.

—I'm requesting sick leave.

—Don't allow that gorilla from the police or any of his colleagues into David's room.

—I won't.

—Here's my tram. Don't pass your panic on to Dado, everything is going to work out.

—I know it will. I feel it with my whole body.

—Goodbye, Katarina.

—Goodbye, Boris.

He got onto the tram and stood by the door; he'd be getting off at the next stop anyway. He looked out and saw Katarina following the tram with her eyes, searching for him among the faces behind the glass. He recognized her worried look and felt the precise moment when she spotted him among the passengers. With even more precision he determined the fraction of a second during which their gazes locked, when her face transformed from worried to smiling, when her hand moved, but then she changed her mind and suppressed her impulse to wave to him. He knew, then, that no matter how his life proceeded from this moment on and how long it lasted—despite the more significant days and moments to come—this image of the woman resisting her urge to wave at the overcrowded #14 took first place, by some unknown pathway, among the images that would always fill him with grief.

Two students talked about what was on the menu at the Student Center and reminisced about grilled meat and octopus roasted under a bell lid. One said, *Even heavy drinking is no help with choking down the shit they cook up here.* They agreed that *the weather sucks* and that today was *one helluva boring day.*

*　　*　　*

Only when she was left standing there alone did Katarina realize she wouldn't even have the oomph to get onto the tram, let alone take it along a route that would pass by the place where David had been hit. She called a cab; waited for it, leaning on the tram stop sign; and asked the taxi driver to take her home the long way. The driver didn't mind.

This allowed her to avoid the scene of the accident, and maybe it also helped her avoid seeing Irma, who was on her way from the Trešnjevka Nama, a little after 6 PM, to one of the notary offices on Tratinska, where she'd sign documents that were several pages in length. She was accompanied by two men, one of them very large and with a shaved head; he was dressed in a pristine custom-made suit and shoes so large that they weren't sold in stores.

Katarina entered the house and saw a light on in the attic. She heard Ita and Lovro laughing, and without calling out to them, she went to David's room. She lay down on his bed and shook so hard that she thought the house itself must be shaking.

And the house was, indeed, shaking, with sobs. Her oldest neighbors weren't there to hold or console her. Between them towered mighty, powerful high-rises done up in bright, pretty colors.

*　　*　　*

His serenity point no longer sufficed for Big Boy Damir, nor did the window, or his musings about pigeon feet. Time to turn on the light.

He didn't get up; instead, as if he were a huge cone, he rocked back and forth and tried with his right hand to reach the light switch. At first, he couldn't, but then by wriggling the muscles on his bottom and his bent knees, he wormed his way toward the nightstand and the lamp and finally reached the switch.

The waxen lampshade encased the sudden flash of the bulb, and dense light flooded the little room as if warming it. Damir went back to his pose, waiting for the lampshade to heat up enough that it would spread the smell of singed dust.

He was quiet.

The open palm of his left hand lay forgotten on his thigh; it piped up with tiny tingles, and Damir balled his hand into a fist.

Now his closed palm became terribly itchy, and he had to fully extend his middle finger so he could scratch at the spot that felt as if he'd caught an insect there. His finger did not obey him, so he tried to use the finger of his right hand to persuade it to free him of the tickles that, oddly, were not making him laugh. But his right hand, for whatever reason, also disobeyed. He raised his left fist toward the lamp and the whole hand, including the fingers, acquired a ruddy glow along the edges. It seemed that with a slight effort and some patience, his fingers and fist had become as translucent as a gecko. Beneath the edges of taut skin there was something he could see that was dark. Had a butterfly landed on his left hand while he was busy switching on the lamp with his right? He fingered the velvety little body and gave his hand a shake to get it to move. The being was still, and finally he dared to open his hand. Though his fingers, with that translucent edge, looked as if they weren't capable of harming anything, anything at all, he opened them gingerly, taking care not to touch the soft wings. Something made his heart begin to flutter and his neck to sweat profusely. His hands, oddly, didn't sweat. He spread his fingers and saw wings. He melted with tenderness. He could not understand why he was so girlishly thrilled by his little guest. Finally, with force and speed, he moved his finger and stopped breathing. He did not see a butterfly. He saw and now stared, astonished, at a butterfly-like creature. *Unknown butterfly*, his reason told him, and it also whispered that there are such changes in nature and that it wasn't at all weird that he had the impression that, instead of a butterfly on his palm, there perched a filigree human dressed in a purplish-blue velvet cape that rose a little toward ears that were hidden behind black hair. The little

NADA GAŠIĆ

head of black, curly hair, combed with a part, had a strong copper sheen that cast light on a tiny tanned face and, or so it seemed to him, even above the teensy head. Though incredibly small, the eyes on that face seemed wide and slightly goggly. They watched him closely, and Damir was filled with a feeling from head to toe that this little creature, this magical Tinkerbell, knew him well, and now she was studying him closely. The wee little girl smiled, doing what she could to reassure Damir with her smile; meanwhile, he would have been happiest fainting dead away. He did not succeed in fainting, nor in making any movement that would free him of the tiny apparition. If it was an apparition. His excitement subsided, his heart quieted, and a feeling of unfamiliar ease replaced his initial astonishment. He smiled at the little creature. The little girl nodded and shifted her legs. Damir noticed sandals made of tiny woven strips on her feet. He smiled, and the girl greeted him with a nod. He nodded back readily. He didn't open his mouth for fear of injuring her with his breath, but he knew that if he were to ask her anything, the little thing would understand him. What was left of his reason told him he was behaving foolishly—nothing he was seeing could be real. Nonetheless, Big Boy reconciled himself to the notion that a dainty little girl was sitting on the palm of his hand. He struggled to ask her a question, but he couldn't decide whether to ask her who she was or what she was. He hesitated. The little girl didn't open her mouth, but Big Boy Damir wasn't altogether surprised when he heard her speak:

—You know who I am.

He wanted to explain that no, he did not, but his lips wouldn't move. His voice had disappeared somewhere. Luckily, after a moment, his mind, politely and gently, despite Damir's will, voicelessly addressed the little girl:

—I know, you're our Blessed Virgin.

It didn't occur to him to feel the slightest bit concerned about how she'd heard what he thought.

The dainty little girl moved, twisted her neck; clearly she was seeking to draw Big Boy's gaze. He didn't dare blink and return or not return her gaze. He waited. Finally she spoke:

—What will I call you?

Now, he had no trouble responding.

—They call me Big Boy.

—No, I prefer your real name. I'll call you Damir.

He blushed with delight. He even grew brave.

—And what will I call you?

—Why not: Our Little Lady?

He mustered the strength to ask a real question. One of the first he had ever asked in his life.

—How long will you stay here?

—Can't say. It's not up to me.

—I see.

He felt he had uttered a mature sentence, though actually he hadn't understood what it was he had said or what she had said. But he felt he could proceed.

—Will it be comfortable for you here with me?

—It will, don't you worry. But we will have to agree on something.

He nodded.

—Damir, you must promise me that you won't let anybody know about me.

NADA GAŠIĆ

Being asked to make such a promise filled him with pride. If he hadn't been afraid of disturbing her, he'd have stood up. As it was, he made do with a solemn tremble in his voice.

—I promise that I won't let anybody know about you.

It seemed to him that her taut dress sagged with relief, and he heard a soft sound as the velvet relaxed. Both of them smiled.

—Where will you sleep?

She didn't answer right away. She was a little distracted, probably because of the new space.

—Me? I never sleep. Don't you worry about me. And in general, act naturally. Like every day. As soon as I feel you're getting sleepy, I'll go. Don't worry.

Damir breathed such a sigh of relief that it felt as if the whole room released its air. His grief and his daylong anxiety left him.

—Damir, we don't have to be quiet because it's nighttime.

—I'm afraid of Cilika.

—Uh? This woman who is your . . . What's it called?

—Guardian.

—Yes, guardian, I couldn't remember. No need to worry, she can't hear us; we're conversing on the inside. Are you afraid of anyone else?

—No, Vilim is good, and old Gramps can't see me anymore.

—He sees you, but he doesn't notice you.

Damir said nothing, but he slowly started to rock, and Our Little Lady asked him not to.

—Don't rock, it isn't comfortable for me when I'm swaying like that. I see you need to ask me something. Please feel free.

—Do you know what happened to David?

—I do. A nasty story. He had an accident.

—That's what I heard, the tram, but how did it happen?

—There was something black, terrible, in the dark. David was frightened, he ran, he couldn't avoid the tram, and it happened.

—What was the terrible thing, in the dark?

She raised a finger, as if to warn him.

—You'll learn when the time comes.

He didn't want to be impolite, but he had to say what he said:

—Couldn't you have stopped this black terrible thing, or stop the tram?

—Damir, don't be a baby. My powers aren't such that I can stop a tram. When a tram gets going, it's difficult to stop.

He was briefly confused and fell silent. When he spoke again, his voice was shaking, full of anxiety.

—Where is David now?

—At the hospital.

—Is he alone?

Our Little Lady's voice also changed. She became emotional.

—When they're sleeping, all people are alone. David is asleep.

He closed his eyes; he didn't have the strength to look at her. And that inward voice grew quieter with boundless worry and dread.

—Our Little Lady, will David be okay?

He felt that she tickled him with her hand. He opened his eyes to see her smiling at him.

—Don't you worry, everything will be okay. As it must be.

Damir took a deep breath in; his shoulders rose into the air, his hands jerked, and Our Little Lady pinched his hand, quite assertively. His involuntary movements scared her.

—Forgive me.

—You're forgiven. But you must be careful.

Damir felt he could talk away until morning.

—Tell me, may I tell Katarina tomorrow that David will be okay?

—No, she'll know herself how he'll be. When the time comes.

Disappointed, he said nothing.

Our Little Lady was the next to speak.

—Tell me, when did you fall in love with Katarina?

—Immediately, as soon as she was born.

—Lucky you.

Now they both enjoyed the silence, until she spoke up again.

—Will you sleep? Should I go?

—No, stay a little longer. I really, really like it that we don't open our mouths while we speak.

—It's practical.

—Well yes, anyone who likes can come into the room, Cilika, Vilim, Gramps, while I, as usual, never speak with anyone. So nobody will ever know.

—With them, you never speak, yet with me you're a chatterbox.

Damir was a little insulted.

—I am no chatterbox.

—Yes you are. I'm a chatterbox too. You can see how much we're talking.

—Are you a chatterbox with everybody?

—No.

—Was your son a chatterer when he was little?

He was alarmed by his own impudence, but there was no going back. The words had been spoken. Now it was Our Little Lady's turn to be a little insulted.

—Damir!

He shook his head. For him this was a sign that he hadn't meant to and felt sorry. Our Little Lady understood.

—Well, okay, you have the right to ask questions like that too, but I can't answer everything.

He waited. Had there been more light in the room, he would have seen her furrow her eyebrows in dissatisfaction.

—Well, okay, if you want to know, he was a chatterer, always asking something. And later he talked too much, and that ended up costing him . . .

She stopped halfway through the sentence.

—No, I prefer not to answer questions like this.

—Do you come to everybody who calls for you?

—No.

—Who do you come to, then?

—What do you think?

—Well, I think you come . . . to those who pray the most, who call for you the most.

—You think wrong.

—How, *wrong*?

—Like I said. According to your *who calls for you the most*, that would mean I give in to the troublemakers and ignore the decent, quiet types. Were you calling for me all the time?

—No, I was not.

—When did you start to call for me?

—Well, seems to me, um . . . I didn't call for you at all.

—There, you see.

—Maybe it's just that I thought a lot about you. Fine, maybe not exactly about you, but about somebody who could help me. Who wanted to.

—So that means you might have been thinking about me?

—Yes, I thought of you. And I could no longer do without you.

—Wait, wait. Without me?

—You sure are picky.

—You asked.

—Okay, I could no longer be alone.

—There's your answer.

—So you come to everybody who is alone?

—No.

He started rocking left, right, right, left, right, mustering the courage to say:

—So, you don't come to everybody, even if that person is alone, but if you do come to a person, you come to someone who is alone.

—More or less.

—And you don't go to troublemakers.

Our Little Lady laughed. He heard laughter, as if a child were tapping its fingernail on glass.

Damir spoke up with a voice that was unlike his own. Our Little Lady knew such voices well.

—So, tell me, are you really the Blessed Virgin?

Our Little Lady said nothing.

—Why won't you answer?

Our Little Lady said nothing.

He fidgeted; his back hurt from sitting still. Whether he stretched or for some other reason, his voice reverted to its usual sound. His childish persistence also came back.

—How do I know David will be okay?

—You'll know.

—I'll know . . . I'll know . . . But how?

—I don't know.

He became restless, squirmed, and carelessly flipped his hand over. Our Little Lady barely was able to keep from falling off.

—Please, be a little more careful.

—Forgive me. But I don't like hearing you say *I don't know*. It scares me. Who will know if you don't? You really frighten me.

—Don't be afraid, everything will be as it should be. And besides, do we always have to keep talking about what troubles you?

He took a deep breath, and his breath came with a smile. He was in a fix. He felt as if his smile served as a kind of flattery, and he changed the subject.

—No, we don't always have to be talking about my troubles. We can talk about ordinary things.

Now it was Our Little Lady's turn to give a flattering smile.

—Sure, let's talk about ordinary things!

With a graceful move to assume a more comfortable position, she held the hem of her long dress, carefully making sure that no accidents happened when she shifted from place to place. The way women do.

—Wait while I lean on your Mount of Saturn.

She leaned on the fleshy pad between Damir's index and middle fingers.

—Forgive me, what you said is funny. Do you actually believe in those things, in the Mount of Mars and that . . . all on the palm of the hand?

NADA GAŠIĆ

—Yes and no. When I need to, I believe it. When I don't need to, I don't believe it. Like everybody else.

—But it's not exactly *like everybody else*. I would think for you everything should be obvious. And if everything is obvious, you don't need to look at what is written on the palm. But you are . . . somehow . . . among the stars and planets. You have to know. Know everything.

—No, I don't. Maybe I could. I haven't checked, but I like it better, not knowing.

He opened his mouth with a smile, but he didn't laugh out loud, or shake. He was afraid of endangering her with sudden movement.

—Now, if you tell me that you believe in the horoscope, I'll really start to laugh.

—Why? Because, according to you, I'm different.

—Well, you're not different just *according to me.*

—I'm not?

—Fine, we don't have to talk about you. But why do we *ordinary* people believe in . . . those things?

—That's what we're like. Or, if you'd rather, that's what you're like. It isn't enough for people just to see the stars. They want to get closer to them, and, if they can't touch them, they need to yoke them into their service, in their minds.

Damir felt her sigh; it even seemed to him that her little gown tightened over her chest.

—Yes, Damir, people have an irresistible need to be served.

—Does everything have to serve them?

Our Little Lady brushed this away bitterly with a wave of her little hand.

—Please, let's not go there. I know best of all what it means *to serve.*

—There you go again, starting in about something I don't get.

—I know, my fault. Where were we?

—I tell you everything. I confess to everything you ask, but you don't. You always avoid answering. I'm not going to tell you anything more.

He stopped smiling and looked away.

—Damir, where are you looking?

—Why do you care? You know everything, so since you know everything, then you probably know where I'm looking.

—Those are not things I know or am aware of. Where you are looking isn't important to you, or to me, so I don't need to know.

—Actually, I happen to be looking at something important right now, but I won't tell you.

—Damir, how old are you?

—They treat me like I'm seven, but I'm not. I'm over fifty. I'm pretty sure. Nobody celebrates my birthday, so I'm not altogether certain.

—Thanks for telling me.

Damir was first a little upset, then he smiled.

—You knew, but you wanted me to tell you.

—I did know. I wanted you to tell me.

Our Little Lady smiled.

He felt better.

—So, tell me, how old are you?

—That depends. Sometimes I am not quite sixteen, and sometimes I'm much, much older.

For a moment, the copper sheen of her hair seemed to fade.

—And why are you so small? On paintings you look so much bigger. And when people have visions of you, you're bigger there too.

—Visions? People see what they want to see. I am always the same to myself. I don't care how I look to others.

—I know, but that way doesn't work. Now, if I were to say that you were visiting me, nobody would believe me. Everybody would think I'm lying, especially if I said you can fit inside the palm of my hand.

—Then don't tell a soul. You promised. It wouldn't do you any good, and I would have to leave.

—Don't leave.

They were silent. The alliance had been formed, and for this night that was enough.

# Fourth stone, fourth wave

—VIIILIM, VILLLIM!

Big Boy Damir jolted awake. He worried that Cilika might come in before he was fully dressed, so, very quickly, as quickly as he could, he stood up and—stirred to waking by the cold parquet floor—he thought of his guest from the night before. He glanced at his hand, empty, and turned to look around the room; she was nowhere to be found. He thought about how in a moment, he would be awash in sorrow and bleakness, because it had only been a dream after all, but nothing ugly happened in his soul. He waited.

—Viiilim, Viiilim! I'm off to bring our Katica a few doughnuts. The poor thing needs to eat, otherwise she'll collapse. She needs strength to carry her through all of this, may our dear God and the Blessed Virgin Mary protect her. I'll give Big Boy his when I get back.

A moment later, the door to the yard could be heard closing, and Big Boy no longer had any reason to hurry getting dressed.

—Damir, Damir! I'm here.

Damir smiled, sat up, forgot he wasn't properly dressed yet, and started searching for the little voice of the invisible butterfly girl.

—Here, by the picture!

He spotted her peering from behind the framed image of the Blessed Virgin Mary that was always on his table.

Remembering that he was only partly dressed, he jumped back in bed and pulled up the covers. She noticed his awkwardness and reassured him.

—Damir, I'll be back later, once you get dressed and have your breakfast. When the others busy themselves with their tasks, we can talk in peace.

He heard her so well, so clearly, that he almost wept for joy.

*Here, yes, she's here! It wasn't a dream after all—it wasn't a dream!*

He even felt it difficult to breathe; his elation choked him, and without fearing Cilika, he decided to lie back down.

Carrying her dish covered with an embroidered white napkin, Cilika strode across to the neighboring house and entered through the unlocked door. There was nobody on the first floor, but Cilika went into the kitchen and gently set the dish on the table. *They can stay here. If I take them upstairs, the others will eat them all before she has the chance, poor thing.*

Up she went.

Irma was already dressed, neatening her room, and Cilika was pleased to see that. Ita, her phone glued to her ear, was puttering around in her nightgown between the bathroom and the kitchen. Irma called to Cilika.

—Dear, come over here, we need your advice.

This was an invitation Cilika could not resist.

—For my goddaughter Katarina's family I am always here. And for my neighbors. If I can, I'm glad to advise. But please tell me, how is the boy doing?

She started to cry.

—Cilika, don't cry, the worst is behind us. Katja called the hospital this morning before six. They said they couldn't give her information without the doctor, then the on-duty doc got hold of the phone and said the child is stable. David's dad called on a few of his connections, and now it's easier for us to get information.

Cilika crossed herself.

—Thank you, dear God. At least some good from the man.

The problem was a serious one and, without thinking, Irma gave up on the playful way she usually talked with Cilika.

—Listen, Cilika, I've got to ask you this. It's impossible to talk with Katarina, understandably. David's her only child. I can't decide on such a thing alone, and Ita is beyond hysterical. The wedding is coming up on Saturday, as you know. Everything has been organized, vast sums of money have been spent, the invitations have been sent, and people have already started sending gifts.

Cilika said nothing.

—The church has been reserved; they've seen to all the preparations, the premarital seminar and confessions; rehearsals, the whole shebang.

At the mention of the church, Cilika stood a little taller, and in a solemn voice she declared:

—The wedding must go on. First of all, it's my thinking that dear God and the Blessed Virgin Mary will help us and David will come to and be on his feet by the wedding. Second, the marriage has been publicly announced in the church, and this is no joke. The wedding must go on. If it were postponed, it would all end up being Katarina's fault.

—Cilika, you are a wise woman. Will you tell Katarina this evening? She and I have not been on the best of terms of late. See if you can do better.

—Fine, I will, but promise me you'll make your peace with your older sister.

Cilika scowled and wagged her finger at Irma.

—And clean up your act. Are you regularly going to confession?

—I'm confessing, don't you worry.

—Good. The only thing is that Ita shouldn't invite her guests to the house; they should gather at the church. That's a very nice custom when the groom waits for his bride in front of the church and he's afraid she might not come.

—Fine, fine, Cilika. Don't be mad, I have so many things to do, don't be mad.

Getting up first, Irma saw out Cilika, who tiptoed into the kitchen and took the covered plate with the doughnuts. *The poor thing will come home too late, and they'll have eaten them all before she gets home anyway. I'll make fresh ones for her tomorrow.*

Meanwhile, Ita had dressed and was off to tell Lovro the joyous news. The wedding would not be delayed. Cilika had had her say.

\*　　\*　　\*

Josip Vidošić was a tidy man, but that morning, on his well-showered and deodorized body, he put on not only clean clothes, but brand-new clothes—a new shirt and suit he had only worn a few times. He had shaved, and his short, orderly haircut, with only a few gray hairs, was obedient this morning. From Lanište to Heinzelova he drove at a leisurely pace, but without mercy for those who tried to pass ahead of him into his lane.

He was the first to say good morning to everybody by the entrance, and on the faces and in the eyes of the officers at the front desk and the guards, he could see that everybody in the entire police headquarters knew about his confrontation the day before with Kasumić. The only one to give him a friendly glance was a new officer—that man was clearly clueless.

The corridor in front of his office was empty and Vidošić walked in, determined not to give way even a millimeter. He called his secretary before he summoned his team to a meeting, and he dictated to her his proposal about Kasumić's suspension. He gestured to the secretary that she could go; he read what he'd had written and put it in a drawer. Then he called the forensic unit, and when he heard that the autopsy results would be delivered after 1 PM, he scheduled a team meeting for the collegium at 2 PM and expected a detailed report from each of them on *the actions that had been taken relating to the new murder investigation, the Scholastic Case.*

He logged on to his computer and briefly dwelled on the suspicious circles on the body of the murdered woman, although he was already quite certain as to their source. He got up, opened the file cabinet with the paperwork for solved cases, checked the register, shut the cabinet, went to the window, and paused a moment to ponder. Then he went back to his desk, entered the database of Zagreb residential addresses, copied what he found, and then quickly grabbed his jacket and told the secretary he'd be out of the office for at least two hours.

Before he turned onto Mala Street, he was already driving very slowly so he wouldn't miss the street sign. At the intersection where he was about to turn, he stopped to let pedestrians cross. He smiled, honked briefly, and lowered his window.

—What are you up to, Švojić?

He was pleased he remembered the boy's last name.

The boy with the earring leaned toward the window.

—Hello. I live near here.

—And you're in no hurry to get to school?

Vidošić grinned, waved off the boy who had been the first to identify the murdered teacher, and continued on his way.

On Mala Street, he stopped as Cilika was on her way back with the dish of doughnuts. This moved him. He'd already forgotten how things used to be, not so very long ago, when people went around the neighborhood with baked goods, and if he'd been a little bolder he would have asked the good neighbor what she was carrying. But he didn't. He sat in the car and waited for his thoughts to sort themselves out. He wasn't entirely sure what it was he wanted to ask Irma Žiger. He didn't know all the details of her conversation with Kasumić, and that made him hesitant. He'd improvise; this wasn't a first for him.

Waiting after he rang the doorbell, he turned to check the street. So ordinary and so average. Something old, something new, something whole, something in ruins, something appealing, something ugly—a typical Trešnjevka street. Oh yes, and something blue. Out of the corner of his eye stood a new blue building he could see through the thinning branches. Vidošić smiled. He rang once more.

NADA GAŠIĆ

As if he'd been hoping no one would be home, he was genuinely surprised when a pretty young woman with long red hair opened the door and invited him in, very politely, introducing herself as Irma Žiger. This wasn't how he'd imagined her. There was nothing vulgar about her. She took him to a room in the attic, which, like its owner, was neat and clearly had been cleaned that morning.

—Welcome, Inspector. You are standing in for your colleague?

—No, I'm his boss. I have a few more questions.

—So that means you know the basics, and I don't have to repeat them?

—No, you don't. Tell me, is this your first time speaking with the police?

She didn't frown, did not grimace, but at that moment she was no longer a beautiful woman.

—Perhaps something random, along the way… an officer checking my car registration, that sort of thing. I met your colleague a few years ago at the Intercontinental Hotel. And a little after that in Opatija. We were organizing the senior prom and a trip for the senior class. Those were chance encounters with the police.

She smiled.

—Just like everybody else.

Vidošić straightened up in his chair.

—Something else. I know your nephew had an accident. I am a father; I can only imagine what that must mean for the family, but I do need to ask you a few questions about that.

She watched him. She didn't move. And she said nothing.

—You told my colleague that you were at a family gathering the night before last. All night.

She smiled.

—Tell me, where was the boy? Your sister's son?

Irma looked down, as if thinking back to pictures of the night before last.

—He was probably in his room. I didn't ask my sister; our party was in another shack in the yard, precisely so we wouldn't bother the child. Just us ladies.

—I see. Forgive me, I will need, regardless of the situation, to contact your sister. The child's mother.

—My sister went to the hospital early this morning. She will be there all day.

Irma watched him very closely and very politely asked:

—Now, please forgive me, but if I may ask . . . What does my nephew have to do with the case? Why are you interested in him?

The inspector, taking care not to bump his head on the slanted ceiling, stood up.

—Probably nothing at all, but apparently the boy was scared by a car, so we need to look into that.

Irma smiled.

—I see. Thank you for your concern for him.

He thanked her and told her she needn't see him out.

*He knows something.* Irma opened a bottle of cognac and took a long swig before she left Mala Street.

*She knows something.* Josip Vidošić looked in his rearview mirror before he left Mala Street.

\* \* \*

Already from the door to his room, Katarina had the feeling that David was doing better, and her exhaustion melted away

NADA GAŠIĆ

instantly. That morning, when she'd looked out the window and saw the sky clearing, she had taken it as an auspicious omen.

She took off her jacket in the corridor, stood by the bed, watched the child for a few minutes, and didn't even burst into tears. She felt so, so powerful. She leaned over him. She didn't search for a patch of bare skin to kiss; instead she glued her lips to the bandages and, truly, felt good. She now fully understood what the doctor had said the day before: communication and only nice, appealing stories, the kind David liked. Even time watching TV, the shows he liked, would be helpful.

The on-duty nurse came in; she was kind, and with a smile and a nod she listened to Katarina, who explained what she was planning to talk about today with the boy and the surprise she had in store for him.

—Energy, we need to infuse him with energy.

The nurse agreed. Katarina opened her bag, and from it she pulled out a well-thumbed, colorful book. She drew up a chair and sat by the bed.

I hear just fine. My mother. She has totally lost it, and it's a lucky thing there are doctors here. Maybe they can help her? She has convinced herself I'll feel better if she reads to me. And what would she like to read? Wait for it, folks: fairy tales. The very oldest ones, the ones she read to me when I was little. My mother has no clue about what is modern, what computer games are, iPods, nothing that is *in*. She has no clue who is interesting today, and what is *cool* and what isn't. She thinks a computer is only useful for calculating, and she's constantly gossiping about her colleagues at work who are forever playing games on their computers while she is the only one who gets any real work done. Her lack of cognizance of the world is the result of this, as my grandpa used to say. So now she is going to read me fairy tales that I, you know, used to love so much. I think ... I hear her tell the nurse about some sort of energy she's going to infuse me with. With this reading? She's not in her right mind. If she were a little more on the ball, she'd realize that energy is in the protagonists, as they're called, in computer games. And besides, what's up with her all of a sudden? If Dad's new wife were to say something like this, the *positive energy* thing, that would be completely normal, because she is always going around saying stupid stuff. But Mama? Now, all of a sudden, she's babbling on about this energy thing—like I'm supposed to get it from fairy tales. Oh please ... I bet she's telling everybody around, the nurses and the doctors, that I love these. Mama tells people random things. This story about how I love fairy tales. Stories for *little* kids. She is crazy. Now I bet she'll say, *David, fairy tales require an attentive listener,* but I can't answer like I usually do, *and a good reader.* Maybe she'll give up. Nope, here she goes.

## A TALE ABOUT CAKES, PASTRY CHEFS, BLACKSMITHS, AND A STEEL SPIDER

Once, long, long ago, in a distant and faraway time, in a vast and luxurious castle, lived a chubby king. All the other kings were known for their victories in battles, their hunts and fancy balls, while the fat king was known only for the pastries served at his court. His tables were known for immense cakes baked in the most unusual forms, with enticing flavors—filled with fruits brought from distant lands, fillings nobody had ever tasted before—and fragrant decorations the likes of which nobody had ever smelled. There were strudels so crispy and delicious that no one could resist them; there were cookies in a wide array of colors, so nobody could eat their fill of them. The tables groaned under this abundance: mounds of sweets, cakes, cookies, soufflés, scrolls, gingerbread, and tortes. Everybody, absolutely everybody, loved visiting the fat king; they'd stay for a long time and would only leave when they could no longer button up a single dress or suit, they'd put on so much weight.

Oh yes! There were days when one might hear a young princess at dawn, wailing:

—Horrors! I have turned into such a cream puff, I can no longer do up any of my clothes!

Of course, the king did not bake all of these delicacies, but all the glory for them went to him, and to him alone. All the princes, princesses, kings, queens, counts, and countesses who loved to accept the invitations the fat king sent them praised the cakes and said:

—These are royal cakes indeed! This king certainly knows how to delight us with pastries! This king knows his cakes!

But the secret to making all these marvelous royal sweets was known by one man only: the royal pastry chef.

He was a puny, scrappy little man, which is very unusual for good pastry chefs, who are most often rotund, as round as a nicely raised loaf of bread. He was a man with a fine palate and agile fingers, who spent days and nights mixing eggs and sugar, sifting fine flour, foaming butter, and working with the choicest walnuts, the best hazelnuts, luscious cream, thick chocolates, unusual fruits, enticing vanillas, and even more enticing cinnamon. Truth be told, he used some of the secret spices whose names and scents have since been forgotten, and can no longer be found anywhere in the world. He had many assistants, but everything he could do himself he did, and he even came up with the designs of the molds that the court blacksmith made for him every day at his behest. And so it was that almost every day, the pastry chef went to the court blacksmith and ordered a new mold.

—Make me a mold in the shape of a rose. I wish for my new torte, which the king will serve to his guests, to be in the shape of a rose.

Or:

—Make me a hundred tiny molds of steel shaped like raindrops, into which I'll pour my batter and serve little cakes as fine as a summer downpour!

Or:

—Make me a mold in which my soufflé will rise to at least a meter tall, to tower over all the world's soufflés!

The court pastry chef made the cakes and designed the shapes, and the court blacksmith made the molds, but only the king garnered the glory from the cakes that were served.

This went on and on. Countless guests happily gorged themselves, and the king served his sweets and basked in their glory.

But as such things tend to go, one evening the court pastry chef could not fall asleep. He wasn't obsessed about a new mold—the mold was ready and waiting. He wasn't worrying about a new recipe—it was already set to go. He wasn't fussing over his oven—others would stoke it. But, nevertheless, for the life of him he could not get to sleep. He wondered:

—What's troubling me?

Then he jumped a full meter up into the air.

—I know, I know what's wrong! I would like to be famous!

He admitted the truth to himself and did not sleep at all that night. He imagined walking down corridors and through grand halls while queens and kings, princes and princesses, and counts and countesses prostrated themselves before him and exclaimed:

—Long live the very finest pastry chef in the world! Praise be to him! Praise be to him!

In the morning he rose, angry, sleepy, and grouchy, and off he went to his pastry chambers to mix up a new torte. Alas! The torte, on its stand, was off-kilter, the icing lackluster, the decorations too soft, and when the surprised guests went ahead and tasted it, they rudely spat it right out.

—Yuck! This tastes terrible!

The torte truly did taste terrible; the pastry chef had forgotten to stir in the confectioners' sugar.

Frightful!

Many of them dressed their fat bodies in their travel clothes and departed, barely stopping to say goodbye.

Frightful!

The king was sorely distressed! He bounced around on his throne in anguish and fury, and had he been a little thinner, he surely would have dashed off to tweak the pastry chef's ears.

Instead, he shouted, threatened, and promised, publicly, before the remaining queens and kings, princes and princesses, and counts and countesses, that this very evening he would order the pastry chef himself to be baked in his own bread oven if, by the next day at breakfast, the chef hadn't made the tastiest cake he'd ever served the court.

The servants spread the word that the pastry chef had committed a grievous error and had been threatened with death.

The pastry chef himself heard this news and hurried to the blacksmith to order the marvelous mold he'd use to bake the marvelous cake and save himself from certain death. But . . .

The only thing the pastry chef did not know was that the court blacksmith also hadn't been sleeping at night. He, too, had been passing his nights plotting how he might become the most celebrated blacksmith of royal molds, before whom all the mighty of the world would kneel. The court blacksmith fancied himself walking down corridors and through grand halls while queens and kings, princes and princesses, and counts and countesses prostrated themselves before him and exclaimed:

—Long live the very finest blacksmith of molds in the world! Praise be to him! Praise be to him!

And it was precisely at the moment when the blacksmith was giddy with his fanciful dreams that the court pastry chef came in, and instead of asking the blacksmith nicely, he ordered him, brusquely:

—By tonight, make me the most beautiful torte molds, such that my torte will be decorated with sugar threads as fine as spiderwebs, with little balls of sugar like crystals, and when I sprinkle confectioners' sugar on them, they'll shine like finely ground mother-of-pearl. This must be a cake above all cakes, a delicacy above all delicacies, that no one will ever forget. By evening it must be done, because otherwise I'll have you roasted over your smithy embers.

He said this and went off to his chamber.

In the late afternoon, the pastry chef went to the blacksmith again, angry, frightened, and anxious. There sat the happy blacksmith next to his new molds, shining, gleaming, and unusual. He stood and with a bow said:

—Good evening, pastry chef! I have made you shining and gleaming molds through which the melted sugar will flow and create threads as fine as spiderwebs, molds in which the little balls of sugar will glisten like crystals, and when you sprinkle confectioners' sugar on them, they'll shine like finely ground mother-of-pearl. With your skilled hand, this will be a treat that nobody will ever forget.

Overjoyed, the pastry chef took the molds, even forgetting to say thank you, and off he hurried to bake the torte and prepare the sugar icing.

In the morning, the king dispatched his guards to find out what the pastry chef had created. When they reported that the torte was baked and decorated, and they'd never seen anything so splendid, the king bounced for joy on his throne and had all the remaining guests awakened.

Breakfast was served in the largest, most magnificent hall. Everybody was dressed in their finest finery, which had already become too tight for them, but in their excitement at the prospect of biting into another never-before-seen delicacy, nobody noticed that they themselves closely resembled cream puffs.

The king arrived, clothed in his finest morning golden robes, and when he clapped his hands, the assistant pastry chefs wheeled in the gigantic torte on a platter the size of a bed, covered in sugar threads as fine as a spiderweb, on which sugar dust glistened.

Cries of wonderment rang out; the queens and kings and princes and princesses and counts and countesses clapped their hands.

The king brandished his royal knife and sliced the torte, first serving himself and then giving each guest a slice. With a rattling of forks, they all took a bite. The fat king and guests began chewing away greedily.

Then, suddenly, instead of elation, there were painful moans:

—Ouch, my tooth! Ouch, ouch!

—Ouch, my tongue! Ouch, ouch!

If the king hadn't been so overeager, he surely would have heard that something had been crackling and snapping when he carved the torte. But in his ravenous greed, he didn't feel anything until the moment when his teeth began to fall out.

The vengeful blacksmith had poured ground glass into the molds, and so it was that many of the high and mighty lost their teeth.

And before the king was able to send for the pastry chef and put him to death, the terrible news reached the chef, and he hurried to find the blacksmith to kill him, of course. He knew that something had been slipped into the molds, something that the guests and the king himself had cracked their teeth on.

But he found nobody there. Nobody, not a soul, except for one shiny, steel spider that in the empty, sooty smithy was crouching in the corner and spinning its web. It was busy with its task

NADA GAŠIĆ

and didn't stop even to glance over at the furious pastry chef. The pastry chef burst into sobs and fled as fast as his legs could carry him. He was terrified of the steel spider and its dreadful spiderweb.

All the guests abandoned the fat king, thereby disgracing him for all time. Those same guests had their teeth fixed and later claimed they had never been to that court and had never so much as tasted the crumbs from those lavish tortes.

They say the pastry chef wanders the world to this day, offering his services, and they say the castle still smells of his fragrant cakes, and that someone can be heard at night groaning because of their broken teeth. And they also say that the steel spider is diligently spinning its web.

Only you and I and that industrious spider know the story.

Well, okay, I can't say I wasn't listening, but was I infused with energy by *The Tale of the Pastry Chef and the Steel Spider*? No. I was not. I am not hungry, I don't feel up to eating cakes, and I am not overjoyed that she read me this entire story.

I admit, when I was little, it's not that I hated fairy tales, but why go around telling everybody now, *He absolutely adored this story*. She's blabbering on. It's amazing what a blabbermouth she is. When I'm ready to, I'll tell her to zip it. This really bugs me, and I'm embarrassed, and I'm scared someone might hear that she's been reading me fairy tales and let everybody know at school, and then I'm done for. Kovačić will crush me. Or maybe it's not that I actually mind so much that she's reading to me, but I'd really like it if she didn't tell anyone! Actually, there is an upside to all this reading, because while she's reading, she's not crying, and then that helps me feel better. Because of these little tales, I feel like I never even started school, that I'm still in preschool. A little silly, but it's not a bad feeling. It's sort of comfortable, like when I was small. Mama reads the fairy tale—I can't tell whether she's reading to me or to herself. I think she likes them more than I do. Like with the seaside. Like, she tells everyone, *David loves being by the sea*, but it's not true; she is the one who loves it. That's what she's like. The same thing with the stories. I remember thinking a while ago that she was always reading those stories to herself. She loves them. And it was always peaceful in the house while she was reading. While stories are being read, nobody fights. So here she is again, reading, and we are listening to the story, she and I, but I'm listening less, because I'm sniffing a little. Mama, not the story. Mama has her own smell between her shoulder and her ear, where she always sprays a little perfume. At first, and I mean ever since I've been here, I'd noticed the fragrance a little, but not anymore. Not so much. Clearly at least two days have passed since I've been here. She's worried sick if she forgot to spray herself with the perfume. Dumb. She shouldn't be so worried. At least not that much. I'm fine.

My mama . . .

*What would David's mom have said*
*about herself if she'd kept the appointment*
*with the school counselor?*

Well, I don't know what I can tell you about myself. I don't have much to say. Dunno, maybe there's not much because I think of myself, if I think of myself at all, as an ordinary, average sort of person. Yes, I do believe I'm average.

Really, I don't know. Maybe it would be better if you were to help me with questions. Maybe then I'd relax a little. I'm not so good at talking about myself.

My childhood . . . Childhood? Well, childhood . . . I don't know, maybe others might think my childhood wasn't ordinary because I didn't have a dad. Well, I mean I had a dad, but he died the day I was born.

How did my dad die? No, I don't know much about that. I know what my mother told me, what I heard from neighbors, but I don't know much. There was this flood in Zagreb, and he drowned. Nobody knows how. Some say he was saving neighbors, but that's just a guess. As a child I imagined that must have been how he died. But I didn't think about him *a lot*. People just imagine, because that's what happens in movies and novels . . . that you always are thinking *a lot* about the parents you never met or lost early. But actually, no. As a kid you live the life you came into. No, I didn't think of him often. Only now and then, when I looked at the photograph from my parents' wedding that Mama was given by her sister-in-law. You know, during that flood, the pictures were all destroyed, so the photograph was a precious gift . . . Forgive me, I've lost the thread again. There. When I looked at that picture, I remember wondering what he would have been like as a dad. A child grows up too fast; the man in the picture never ages, and soon I stopped wondering about that. But I never used the word "Dad," not even to myself. That's all I can say about my father. I didn't think of him often. Hardly ever.

My mother? Mama and I lived alone in our house in Trešnjevka . . . Until I was eight. Afterward she remarried and had my two sisters. One of them is ten years younger than me, and the other is thirteen years younger. The youngest is just now getting married. All of us are thrilled. The wedding. Forgive me. I lost the thread . . .

Stepfather? Well, he was, you know . . . also ordinary. A precision mechanic; he had his vocation. He wasn't much different from others in the neighborhood. I think he was . . . normal. Ordinary. Like others around us. He didn't drink; that's something people always know in Trešnjevka . . . Trešnjevka. At least we did before. Now things are changing. Actually, they've already changed. New buildings, almost the whole neighborhood is new. Everything has gotten bigger. Full of new people. Now people don't know what they used to know about their neighbors. All they know is what they can see. What car the neighbors drive, how many kids they have, but other things? No . . . We don't know. We don't even know how they've furnished their apartments. When the furniture is delivered it's all wrapped up.

Yes, I lost the thread again. Sorry. No, I didn't love him, didn't *not* love him. My stepfather. My sisters I loved. Although I remember that, at first, I was ashamed in front of the kids from the street and at school that my mother was pregnant. That's normal. We don't think about our parents as someone who ... who is physical. Who does ... everything you have to do to make a baby. You understand, right? But my sister who was born first, I loved her loads. Right away. And the other one too, but a little later.

No, I didn't skip over my stepfather too quickly. Why say that? Today it's probably normal to think about a stepfather as a person who ... abuses his stepdaughter. It wasn't like that then.

I'm not evasive, why say that? No, he was ordinary, he worked a lot; Mama got really sick after my second sister was born and she stopped working. She couldn't clean anymore. She was one of the cleaning ladies at the school. She had a pension of some kind. It used to be easy to get a pension ... It's different today. But there was never enough money. He, of course, loved his two daughters, and me, so-so. The way that sort of thing usually goes. Today I'd say distanced, but at the time they didn't use words like that, so I won't use them either to describe my feelings then. We were reserved with our feelings, yes, that's just the right word: reserved. But you know, now that I'm a mother, I understand it. I absolutely understand it. I think they're lying when people say someone loves another person's child like their own, such as a child from their husband's first marriage. That's a lie. It's possible to love another person's child, but never like your own. Or they don't know how they love their own. I know.

Sisters? What is my relationship like with my sisters? I don't like the term half sister. It's ugly. I think of them as my sisters. My relationship with them is, how can I put this? A positive one. That, too, is an ugly word for feelings, but at the moment

I can't come up with a better one. Our mother died young, actually young for *them*; I was already old enough that I could deal with it more easily, so I looked after them. And my stepfather, their father, died from cancer a few years after our mother. He had a painful death ... That was harder for them to bear than it was for me, though I looked after him, tended to him once he was bedridden.

No, there was nowhere I could have sent him. And my sisters, I looked after them too.

Sorry? What do you mean, *like a mother?* That I took their mother's place? No, that's another one of those, how to say this, collective untruths. I did not replace their mother. That's impossible. When I had my own child, then I learned what it is to be a mother. To my sisters I was an older, caring sister and nothing more. But there, it turned out well. The older one even earned her university degree. While the younger one wasn't so enamored of books. But we are not all of us born with the same capabilities. No need to fuss over that. Maybe she'll fare better in life for that very reason.

Do we clash? Sometimes. With the younger one, no. With the middle sister, only now, recently. I don't approve of the way she's living her life, but each of us has the right to choose.

How is she living? What do you mean, *how is she living?* I don't approve that she is out of the house all the time, and I don't like the people she hangs out with. What does she do? She's a teacher, teaches in a high school.

No, they all think well of her, at least I think they do, but now there's this fashion among young people like her ... Fine, she's not so young, but somehow she's snatching at life; she hasn't been in a steady relationship, and yet she's almost never around over the weekends. I don't know, I don't approve and that's that. Her circle of friends is the problem.

Why do I think I can't forgive my sisters for spending a part of my young years shut up in the house because of them? I didn't get out enough? I went out plenty. You forget the war arrived right when I was a young woman. I sure did go out. Unlike others, I was involved in charity work. I believe I was a big help to displaced people, but later I didn't take advantage of that. What's the word? Exploited. Others, they did.

And my husband, I don't know what I could tell you about him. It would be good if he were to tell you something about himself. Though I bet he'd prefer writing it. (Laughs.)


*What would David's dad have written about himself?*


*Dear Doctor,*

*Thank you for allowing me to address you in writing to describe everything that might be of use to you in conducting your challenging job. This will allow me to concentrate more productively on the details that may, in my opinion, be salient to describe everything that went on before what happened happened, though I cannot imagine what good can come of anyone dealing with me. But since you were kind, you didn't treat me badly, and you didn't force me to respond verbally to questions which, even if I'd wanted to, I wouldn't have been able to answer, I will try to help by writing. Please forgive me in advance for occasionally getting sidetracked by details that are too petty. Feel free to ignore them, because I don't* believe they are worth anyone's attention, let alone yours. I also hope you will not burden yourself with my ornate style, which is in part the consequence of the medications which, as you know, I am now taking against my will.

Here:

The secret of the eternal longing for travel is the subconscious desire of people looking for a change of identity.

I remembered this, something I wrote on my calendar on Christmas Eve 1999, amid the millennial fervor as we tried to leave behind something sage and unique in that century, which had spent itself. I truly don't know what it was that I was expecting with the advent of the next thousand years, but evidently I did expect something. Computer bugs? Political upheaval? The end of the world? I don't know. We all know now that no upheaval of any kind happened, though, as you may remember, the government of the past ten years was replaced by a new one, with which I had no particular connection, just as I have none with this current government or any that will follow it. I say this because I believe it is important to explain that external factors haven't had anything to do with me, nor do they have anything to do with me now; they don't influence my thinking and especially not my actions. At least that is how I see it. Or am I flattering myself? I don't know. Quite some time ago, my attitude toward what is called social movements developed into a lethargy of sorts and is a question of upbringing, but not intellectual distancing, as someone well-intentioned might think.

As I recall, others also expected something from the turn of the century, but I can't remember whether anyone but me felt so terribly let down when nothing dramatic happened. I remember feeling

NADA GAŠIĆ

deceived, alone, and unjustly deserted. I know this sounds crazy; this is why we are communicating, after all, but, I admit, I felt as if the universe changed its mind and abandoned earth to fend for itself as best as it could, and, along with the planet, me, so puny and unimportant. This feeling of emptiness at the moment of transitioning to something intangible, such as entering a new millennium, seemed only to be the culmination of my pervasive sense of discontent and alienation, not only within my family but with everything surrounding me. Simply put, I felt as if I'd died, yet by some miracle was still breathing. I drank my share, of course, of the toasts to the new year and new millennium, and even the new government, but in fact I was coolly indifferent. Please forgive me for this trite simile, but I was as indifferent as a gambler who has lost a huge sum of money at roulette, gambling with someone else's money, easily earned, so in a certain way this was nonexistent money, and this indifference was a necessary and normal outcome. There, like that.

What engendered my discontent and when it started, that I can't tell you. Sometimes I have the feeling this is a long-lasting—better said—permanent state of discontent for me, in a way a primeval discontent and alienation I've carried since childhood, of course, not out of my own will, but through some inherited discontent and inherited alienation from the environment in which I live and which I was handed, and I think this still holds true today, by my ancestors who moved here. The family is always, especially in terms of your profession, the be-all and end-all, so I will try to start with it. After all, you advised me to do so. We'll start there, but I will need more focus. Today I'm not up to it. Forgive me.

There's Dad. Who was he saying hi to? Mama? Me? Probably me, then Mama.

My dad smells of the cold. He came in wearing a jacket, unlike Mama. Mama takes hers off in the corridor so she can throw herself on me immediately. Not Dad. He stands; he stands there a long time, a really long time, and the whole time he is fully dressed. Only when he's stood there a long time does he come over to me. Funny, because someone watching from the side might think it's a wolf in bed, not me, and Dad is afraid of that wolf. I can smell him clearly too. I know the smell of his jacket and coat. Before, while we lived together, my dad smelled of cigarettes. This bothered everybody but me. The hall and hall closet still smelled of his coat until last semester. Dad stopped smoking when he married that she-goat, and I was pretty sad because his coat changed its smell. It became weird for me when he kissed me, as if someone I didn't know was kissing me. I pushed him away a little when he tried to kiss me. For some reason, it bugged me that he'd changed his smell, so in the end we stopped kissing, and I think we would have stopped kissing anyway, because that's not for kids my age. So that's how it all turned out that in the end we stopped kissing because Dad stopped smoking. Today, Dad smells of tobacco again, as my grandpa used to say. Not of cigarettes, of tobacco. That's old-fashioned. Today Dad smells like my dad from before. The way he's supposed to smell. He must be worried, if he's started smoking again. And I bet he's smoking secretly, because he doesn't dare do it

NADA GAŠIĆ

openly in front of his beloved she-goat. He doesn't stay as long as Mama does, but even so, I'm tired when he goes. He doesn't call to me madly the way Mama does, more like he's mumbling to himself, but he pats my hand for such a long time, I wish I could pop him one. But I can't lift my hand. I don't know why, but I can't. Not yet. Seems to me they've already managed to fight, maybe yesterday, I don't know when, and now they're continuing on with their fight. They think nobody can hear them because they're not shouting, but hissing at each other, like ganders, as my grandpa used to say: Mama at Dad, Dad at Mama. I'd love to see what a real gander looks like, though that's a silly wish. What am I, six? But, still, I'd like to see one. The kind that's in a village, not at the zoo. I must write that down on my to-do list. And one more decision, which is a little more important. I'll smoke when I'm a little older. In seventh grade. Maybe in sixth. Kovačić said he smoked at Gardaland. And drank beer.

I also know the nurse by her smell and by how quick she is. And that nurse! You guys, she can't stop giving me shots. She also does other things to me, which I won't mention. Better that nobody at school ever finds out. When she changes these tubes and needles, I hear her talking to Mama to keep an eye on the iffusion. Think of all the stupid words I'll learn before I get out of here. But maybe I'll need them for my job. Secret agents have to know all kinds of things.

I also know the doctor, or rather doctors. They come in here like they live here. A whole bunch of them congregate, like my grandpa used to say. My grandpa used all sorts of words and phrases nobody says anymore, and he didn't know the words everybody usually says. For instance, he didn't know what a CD player was, and not only that, but he wasn't even willing to try and say it. And he drank raspberry syrup and soda and hated cola. That's what he was like. So there's this bunch of doctors, and one of them will peel back my eyelids and try to wake me up with this flashlight. Then I deliberately retreat farther back behind the curtain. Idiots. If they only knew of the advantage I have. Their stupid flashlights are not helping them. I'll come out from behind the curtain when I'm good and ready and when I want to, not when they want me to. Idiots. And they reek, they don't smell. Again, idiots.

It's weird that I'm not hungry. I have no idea why I'm not hungry. I can't even bear the thought of ice cream; the very idea makes my stomach hurt. And cakes? Yuck. I'm not even particularly thirsty. Sort of, medium. It's as if I'm not thirsty in my stomach but more in my head. Something like that. That's weird, and it's also weird that my head drops somehow, while my legs fly up into the air before I go in deeper behind the curtain. I need to write this down once I get up on my feet. Or better yet, I'll memorize it—secret agents memorize stuff. Just in case, I'll hide behind the curtain, so Mama doesn't think of reading anything more to me and so they can fight in peace. As if I can't hear them!

\*　　\*　　\*

NADA GAŠIĆ

—Katarina, I told you, your constant presence will harm the boy.

—I don't give you my advice, so please don't give me yours. I know what the doctor said.

—I have requested a second opinion from Professor Liznjek from Rebro Hospital, and he thinks David needs peace and quiet. Good god, woman, it's his brain we're talking about.

—Are you jealous of me spending more time with him than you are? Nobody says you can't. You can be here as much as you like.

—As much as I am able. Don't push me.

—Lower you voice, David can hear us.

—David cannot hear us.

Inspector Vidošić cautiously pushed open the door, and the two of them stopped talking. He introduced himself and asked David's stunned father to step outside for a moment.

Horak could not help himself.

—Pardon me, but this is an outrage. Do you even care about the boy? First, your colleague yesterday . . .

Vidošić interrupted him.

—I understand. I have two boys his age.

He nodded toward David's room.

—You don't understand, your boys are healthy.

—What I meant to say is that it is completely understandable to me that I'm the last person you'd like to see here, but I came as head of the police department to apologize for yesterday's, shall we say, outburst.

Horak softened.

—Well, fine. It wasn't exactly an outburst, but my child is in critical condition, and his mother and I are on the verge of collapse. Please make sure that nobody else comes.

—I'll do all I can. None of my subordinates will come. But, please, hear me out. We are conducting an investigation on a completely different case, a murder case, and your son probably, I'd even say most likely, has nothing to do with it. But we must check everything. The team of investigators at his accident says he was spooked by a car, and there are indications that the car itself may have had something to do with the case we are investigating.

—Yes, someone did frighten Dado, and the piece of shit fled the scene. And hasn't been apprehended.

—For now nothing is known, but we would like to make sure your child is safe.

—And, of course, when he wakes up, you'll want to assail him with questions.

Vidošić didn't answer. He spread his hands in a gesture of apology, said goodbye, and turned to go down the corridor. He only turned back when Horak shouted:

—Who is the other person? Was he also run over?

—He wasn't run over. And it isn't a *he* but a *she*.

Horak stood for a few minutes more out in the corridor and then went back to say goodbye to David. He told Katarina once more to leave the child in peace, she answered something, and at that moment the on-duty doctor came in with unpleasant news. After the doctor left, Katarina couldn't stop herself and got in another jab at Boris before he left. He had just enough time at the doorway to say:

—Your thinking is currently functioning at the level of Big Boy. Must be that mental illness is contagious on Mala Street.

## The game of Go

Of the doughnuts Cilika had intended for Katarina, she set two aside and brought them to Big Boy Damir. He was quiet and did nothing to provoke her. He waited for her to close the door.

Our Little Lady sat down on the table edge, and with a gesture of her hand and a slight tip of her head, she showed him he should go ahead and eat.

—And you?

—Thank you, not hungry.

Damir was hungry and he bit into a doughnut. When he ate, he always looked only at his plate. That was how Cilika had taught him. The only thing he allowed himself was steadily rapping a glass bowl on the table.

—What is this?

He saw the feeler-hand that seemed to be pointing impolitely at his bowl.

—My bowl.

—I see it's a bowl. What is in it?

—Those are my sugar packets. They are given to me as gifts.

—From whom?

—From Katarina, and from the others too.

—Do you eat the sugar?

—No.

—Will you ever eat it?

—Dunno. Maybe.

He went back to eating, and only after his last bite did he ask:

—Aren't you hungry sometimes?

—Actually, no, but there are times when I get a yen for something. For instance, sometimes I'd love to have a little sugar.

There was slyness in her voice, which Damir missed.

He relaxed in his chair and was quiet. He had said more the night before than he had his whole life. He wasn't in the mood for conversation; he felt as if he'd already asked everything he had to ask. The only thing he really did care about was her presence.

Our Little Lady fidgeted, slid both hands under her dress, and began swinging her legs over the edge, as if she were bored.

—Don't sit there, you could fall.

She laughed.

—Don't you worry—unlike others who rise, I can't fall.

They were quiet. And the house was quiet. Cilika was busy with her work, Gramps was fiddling with ropes up in the attic, and he couldn't hear Vilim. Our Little Lady could no longer keep quiet.

—How do you spend your time? Do you play games? It can't be that you sit here all day long doing nothing.

—I know chess, but I've never played it against anyone. Nobody has any idea that I know how to play.

—How did you learn it?

—I watched the pensioners at the park. They didn't chase me off the bench.

—Would you like me to teach you to play Go?

—Go? What is Go?

—An ancient game. They say it was invented more than four thousand years ago.

—Well, that really is ancient! Did people play things back then?

—Yes, of course. When they can't fight wars, people play games. Games are a lot like wars, but not dangerous.

—Who invented this Go game of yours?

—They say a princess invented it. In China. A mighty empire.

Damir smirked behind his hand.

—A princess invented the game? A woman?

—You think I can't see you laughing?

There was a rebuke in her voice.

—Are you making fun of women, Damir?

—No.

—Go ahead and say it. I am so used to women being despised in all those places where they glorify me the most and supposedly revere me. Phooey!

It looked to him as if she shuddered.

—Forgive me, Our Little Lady!

—Don't apologize to me, apologize to all woman, at least in your heart of hearts.

Damir froze. He didn't know how to do that, or how not to do it. He was scared. It looked to him as if Our Little Lady intentionally stopped talking and was thinking about his behavior.

But she wasn't. She was thinking about something else.

—I love the game of Go because it is even older than me.

—I am not sure I understand why.

—Why? Because what is older than me extends the limit of responsibility.

—I don't understand what you're saying. I don't know all the words.

—Oh yes, you do. It's like in . . . ordinary life. You know how younger people are forgiven for many things. The same is true of younger creatures. The younger ones. Even the animals. So it is with me. When I know that something is older than me, which makes me the younger one, I have the feeling that perhaps some of my failures, my errors, might be forgiven. And besides, all sorts of things, anyone and anything, are forgiven.

She laughed.

—Even whole countries.

—I'm not following you. A minute ago we were in the ancient Chinese empire, and now we're in . . . young countries.

Our Little Lady clapped her hands, delighted.

—Oh, let that go. Let me teach you how to play Go. It's a wonderful game for thinking.

—I don't believe I'm capable of learning anything new. You know yourself that I'm not . . . a quick thinker. You know that I'm . . . different.

He turned to look at the wall and found the point that didn't move.

—Nonsense. You can do whatever you want.

She paused and then whispered, alarmed:

—Damir, Damir! Is somebody standing by the window?

Unnerved, he turned toward the window, and even got up.

—Where? I don't see anyone.

He heard her teensy laughter. Now he wasn't comparing it to anything. He knew it.

—Oh, Damir, nobody's there. But I know from experience that people protest when something appears suddenly . . . out of nowhere. That's why I made you look over at the window. Now look over here, on the bed.

Damir was a little miffed.

—Now hold on.

He wanted to scold her. He didn't have the chance. He saw a board on the bed, with a grid of lines crisscrossing it.

—How can a game start with an empty board?

—Like everything else in life. Everything starts from an empty board.

—And what now?

—You put your stone on a certain place, and after that it remains on that place until the end of the game. Or it is captured. They say, *losing the liberties.*

—That's not any sort of game.

—Ha! And does it look like life to you?

—I didn't say that.

He noticed he was starting to repeat Our Little Lady's phrases. He could no longer follow Our Little Lady or the game of Go. He turned away. She understood, and the game board vanished. Our Little Lady waited; she saw he was preparing to ask her something.

—Do you know how David is doing now? Right now? What is he thinking about while he sleeps?

She smiled, but not happily.

—I know what he's thinking about.

*     *     *

They argued right by my bed... Actually they were asking themselves questions. Mostly. They were also blaming each other: you, you, you, and you, and you. They really got on my nerves. I could no longer bear it, so I retreated deep down behind this curtain of mine, so I wouldn't have to listen to them or smell them. When I pull away like that, I see a white light; nothing, absolutely nothing, hurts. I don't hear a thing, I can't smell a thing, and it's as if all I can see is my forehead from the inside. And how about this: I can hear myself breathing, as if I'm breathing inside a big pot. Or something like that. It's as if my head swells big and light, and round like the world globe in a classroom, and somehow it's as if my head is all there is, no neck, no arms, no legs, no belly. Then I'm all my big, round head, breathing inside a pot. It looks as if the others have noticed that I've become a head, and someone was shaking me and the doctor was shining a light in my eye, and I got scared. I had to come back, so I heard it when the doctor said to my folks that if they intended to keep this up right next to the child's bed, it would be better for him if they didn't come at all. And the child and the him he referred to, that's me. Even my old man clammed up. Then he patted my hand for the millionth time and said something stupid like *Son, please forgive your father*. Oof, I was so embarrassed! What is he doing, asking for forgiveness? He didn't get me hit by the tram. I hate it when my old man apologizes to me, I hate it something awful. Then he left, and Mama whimpered until the nurse came in and said it would be better for her to leave too. Then she pleaded with the nurse about something, and, finally, in the end, she stopped crying. She didn't read to me. When she left I began thinking I'd actually have liked it if she'd read me another fairy tale. I'd have liked that a lot more than them fighting and her sniveling away. If I were to start whimpering and wailing and crying, they'd see what crying can be. But I am not interested. Although I have become a little ... soft. Yes, soft. My folks sure do have a knack for ruining a person's life. Nobody else in the world can do it like they do. I decided on purpose that, for a time, I'd stay all the way behind my curtain. The doctors call this a worsening of the overall condition. When I'm near the edge of the curtain, they call that stable, or something similar. It sounds like a weather forecast, but it isn't. It's about me. Stupid David. Now and then I tell myself that I'm stupid and that makes me feel better. I can't bear it when someone else tells me I'm stupid, but I can tell myself whatever I like. Hey, Mama again. Oh no, she's so stubborn; boy, it's amazing how stubborn she is. She's calling my name again and fussing over me. Ah ha, her conscience is prickling about her fight with Dad. She's all bumbly. If she gets the idea of reading me more fairy tales, I hope she doesn't trip up and read one that's really meant for girls. When I was a really little boy, I could listen to ones like that too, but I liked the ones best that were more for boys. I don't know what makes me feel that a story is for boys and not for girls, but I do feel it, no mistake. For instance: "Sleeping Beauty" is for girls and "The Bremen Town Musicians" is for boys, a hundred percent, and "Cinderella" is for girls a hundred percent. But "Snow White" is for girls and for boys, because there are stupid parts about how some old lady stares into a mirror, which is definitely the part for girls, but the rest of the story could be for boys too, because there are dwarfs in it who are doing something and can be funny and all over the place. And the stories that are definitely for boys are the ones that have dragons, swords, lots of flying. And for girls it's when they get married happily ever after, when they have golden gowns, all that stuff. That's the idea. Sometimes my mom gets this all wrong and then she reads me things I don't like, but last time she did pretty well. And I'd be interested to know whether the same fairy tales for girls could be retold a little differently and be for boys, and vice versa: the ones for boys could be retold so they can be for girls. I'm talking nonsense, like the Horvat girl who sits in the second row—I like to call her Horvatica. I'm a little restless, aren't I? I don't know why I'm restless. Am I scared of something? What? Nothing hurts, and once the curtain is pulled back, everything will be fine . . . I don't know, but I am a little afraid; it's just that I don't know what of. Maybe it'd be better if Mama doesn't read to me. Somehow all of it bugs me, and it's as if I'm scared of the stories. Have I gotten that sick? Maybe it would be better for you to finally make the effort and come out from behind the curtain, stupid David! If I keep this up, I'll get behind in my preparations for being a secret agent. I have to make a serious effort to come out from behind this curtain. But I can't, there's no way I can do that. I'm scared of the light from the flashlight.

*     *     *

Damir wouldn't give up.
—You know what David is thinking. Why won't you tell me?
Our Little Lady gave her hair a shake.

NADA GAŠIĆ

—Damir, it's not good to know everything. What matters for you is that you firmly believe David is doing well and you hope he'll get better soon.

He began to rock. She saw he was seeking his serenity point. She had to draw him over to a different subject.

—Damir, are you always in the house?

—No, I go out in the yard, and sometimes I go out to the street, and there are times, but only in secret, that I go all the way to the farmers market.

—They don't let you go any farther?

—That's what they're used to. And I'm used to it.

—Aren't you bored?

—No.

They stopped talking. Our Little Lady fiddled with her feet, and with a quick move she tightened the clasps on her sandals. Damir looked away. He felt it was impolite to be watching her while she was behaving in such an ordinary way. Like a person. Then he felt anxious.

—Aren't you chilly in those sandals?

—No, I've gotten used to them, the same as you are used to being shut up inside.

He pursed his lips. He didn't like her thinking he was, actually, shut up.

—Tell me, would you like us to take a little walk? Say, to the farmers market?

Our Little Lady perked up. Her hair flashed with a blazing, copper sheen. For a moment, Damir had the impression he'd seen the reflection of a golden aureole above her head.

—I would like to. I'd really like for us to take a little walk.

—Maybe tomorrow. Cilika and Vilim go to tend to the grave; All Saints' Day is coming up. And I'm not afraid of Gramps. What will the weather be like tomorrow?

—It will be a lovely, sunny day.

Both of them clapped, he with his hands, she with her teensy little hands.

*     *     *

Irma had no time for a walk. She had taken it upon herself to order the floral arrangements her sister wanted for decorating the church, the wedding hall, the cars, and her house. Today she had a key meeting with the arranger, to whom she had to explain why they wouldn't be decorating the house. Of course, there would be some flowers there, but much, much more modest than what they'd originally planned. Cilika was right; Ita wouldn't be inviting her guests back to the house, but she would have to host the closest circle: the bridesmaids, groomsmen, and immediate family, and they all had plus-ones. There'd be too many people. But they would have to spruce up the house a little. No garlands or balloons. Fine. And certainly there wouldn't be the sixty-odd guests they'd planned for, with all the glasses, napkins, platters, forks, spoons, cognac, rakija, whisky, amaro for the women, wine, and beer. She'd cancel the catering, fine, not all of it; there was still time, people would understand, the situation was hardly ordinary. People would understand.

Some understood, others didn't. No matter what, they all pocketed the deposit.

NADA GAŠIĆ

She did her share of driving that day and managed to see to everything. All Saints' Day was coming up, so there had been changes in the teaching schedule and that helped. She made it on time to her fourth and fifth period classes, and later she'd have just enough time to zip up to the cemetery. Their parents' grave had to be cleaned before All Saints'. She couldn't count on Katarina and Ita.

Irma Žiger was the one to see to that.

\*     \*     \*

At 2 PM at the police headquarters on Heinzelova, officers were conversing in hushed tones about ordinary things. They all seemed relaxed, but the atmosphere of ease was strained. They were careful to avoid mentioning Kasumić. They waited for the boss to start the meeting. And he sat there, relaxed, at his desk and had his eyes on his computer screen.

—All here?

The question was the usual one, and usually there'd be a group response of *yes*, or we're waiting for so-and-so, but now it was met with silence, and nobody even laughed.

—So we're all here. I'll read it, that will be quicker. I'll hit the key points. You can go through the rest later.

### Autopsy report

—External examination of the female corpse; height: 1 meter and 71 centimeters; weight: 59 kilos; age; about 30; rigor mortis fully evident. Also evident is livor mortis on the back of the body. The skin, pale gray. Hairs removed from the entire body. On the skin of the neck, characteristic thin stripes and spots of laceration, which indicate choking. Strangulatio colli manualis. I hope I pronounced that right.

Thinking he'd be witty, Zdilar blurted out:

—Kasumić isn't here to tell us. He studies Latin.

Vidošić didn't even look at him.

—In the areas of the shoulder, neck, and breasts, and on the inside of the thighs, there are several bruises and lacerations of the skin, which by their appearance and features suggest these are due to bites by human teeth. On both wrists and around the ankles, there are bruises arising from objects used as constraints, probably handcuffs, but it is possible the bruising on the wrists came about by physical constraint by a very strong male. An examination of the sexual organs and tests of specimens taken did not confirm the presence of sperm. Internal examination of the body established heavy bleeding and swelling of the mucous membranes at the entrance to the larynx, and extensive bleeding to the membrane at the opening of the windpipe. The cartilage of the larynx and windpipe has been crushed. The pathologist is of the opinion that death is the result of a deficient supply of oxygen, as a consequence of physical *asphyxie*.

Again a Latin word, but this time nobody said anything.

—We have also received the findings of the criminal investigation center; the entire report has been emailed separately. Most important: on the nails of the victim, traces of a man's blood, and skin and hair of human origin, have been found, sufficient for DNA analysis.

Vidošić looked up.

NADA GAŠIĆ

—There, that is what we have. Things are clearer today. We already knew the identity, but today we know that the woman was killed by asphyxiation. Probably a sexual crime. I say probably, because there are no traces of violent penetration, or traces of sperm. I repeat, no traces of sperm. One thing we still don't know: where the crime was committed. But the time of death has been established: around 9 PM. So she was killed earlier than what we'd assumed, but we were right in assuming that she was not killed where the body was found. Everything else is still in question.

They gave their reports on interviews with neighbors, fellow teachers, and the owner of the apartment where the murdered woman lived. Komšić reported that the Vinkovci police had already sent a report about conversations with the family of the victim.

—Good. And now, let's move on to yesterday's question: Why was the woman dropped behind the school, which is near a busy street and a residential area?

Zdilar raised his hand.

—Maybe she was killed nearby, and the murderer didn't have time to transport her to a more secure location, to throw her, for instance, into the Sava.

The officers began talking, and Vidošić hushed them and pointed to Simčić.

—Maybe she was killed by accident, maybe the man who killed her wanted her to be found right away.

Zdilar smirked.

—So why not take her home with him?

Two of them said, in unison:

—Or throw her into the Sava.

They didn't have the chance to laugh, because Vidošić lost his temper.

—Enough. We haven't made any progress in three days, and the newspapers have been writing about nothing else. Take a look at what's on television—they're raking us over the coals. How long can our spokesperson keep repeating that there are no new developments? Ha! Is this preschool? Anyone who's in this for the laughs can go home right now.

They all remembered how Kasumić left, and silence settled over the room.

Vidošić lowered his voice.

—There is one more possibility. By discarding the body behind the school where the victim worked, the murderer was signaling to someone that he could do anything. Maybe there, in the school, he wanted to caution somebody about something. And besides, this is no ordinary murder, as I'm sure we'll see when we receive reports from the forensic psychologists. According to the forensic findings, this cannot be considered a usual case of rape, but rape cannot be ruled out. Every rape is not the same, but it is always a sign of the rapist's need to prove his power. We've learned this. The murder is so unusual that there is even the possibility that we may be dealing with a serial killer.

They fidgeted a little; there was discomfort in the air, but nobody said a word.

Vidošić went on.

—Today, we interviewed the victim's colleague. We will start to follow her. Komšić, Zdilar, you have her address, you know where she works. You've been emailed her photo. Start to tail her tomorrow morning. Her nephew was injured in an accident.

There are various indications that lead us to believe the child is linked to this crime. I'll be in touch with his parents. Dive into your work.

He signaled to them that they were free to go. He didn't say a word about why he'd fought with Kasumić and that this suggestion about the involvement of the boy came from him. He didn't even stop to think about it.

It was time for him to go home. The children were waiting for him.

*     *     *

It was not yet time for Irma to go home. She'd finished teaching for the day but was barely able to get rid of her fellow teachers, who were assailing her with questions since she was the victim's closest friend. She barely managed to take care of everything she'd planned, and now she was hurrying to get up to the Mirogoj Cemetery before dark. She wasn't afraid of being at the cemetery after dark. Her parents' graves were in the old section, where many people would be visiting and cleaning graves for the holiday. But the cemetery was not lit well enough to allow for arranging graves properly. Even during twilight it was tricky. She was really rushing.

She glanced at her watch, 3:40 PM. She'd make it. She was already looking for a parking space near the cemetery arcades when her phone rang.

—I'm by the arcades, up at Mirogoj. Good, I'll wait. Yes, I'm waiting for you in my car, somewhere near the arcades.

In Irma's car at 4:15 PM.

—The police don't know much. They were sent an autopsy report. Their boss came to see you today.

—I first thought to let you know, but you'd said I should only call you if it's urgent.

—This is urgent. What did he ask you about?

—Nothing much. Whether I'd had any earlier contact with police. I mentioned Kasumić. He asked me where the kid was that night.

—What did you tell him?

—That we were having a party in the little house in the yard, and the kid was probably asleep.

—And nothing more?

—Nothing more.

—Keep it that way.

The man had already opened the car door. She stopped him.

—May I ask you something?

—Ask away.

—The kid was spooked by a black car. He ran to get away from it, and a tram hit him. Do you know anything about that?

The man turned to her and smiled.

—There are plenty of black cars in Zagreb. Most of them are black.

—My nephew is in critical condition. If anything happens to him, I'm not sure I'll have any reason to keep my mouth shut. As it is, I no longer know what I'm doing. What did I even sign at the notary? Both of you were so hurried.

The man closed the door again, moved restlessly in his seat—it was all too cramped.

—Listen! You won't breathe a word. You were in the car that moved the body. You were right there the whole time, from the house all the way to the school. Do you know, my dear teacher, what that's called? An accessory to the crime. That's what it's called. Besides, it might happen that you won't even have the time to say anything. And it could happen that the kid suddenly takes a turn for the worse. He might not get better. Go ahead, open your big mouth.

—You didn't used to take that tone with me.

The man laughed.

—You didn't used to be thirty-five years old, my dear teacher.

He got out.

\*       \*       \*

She finally arrived at her parents' graveside when dusk was already dangerously on its way to night. The lights were lit, and people were hastily finishing their scrubbing, polishing gravestones, and arranging flowers and candles.

Irma had everything with her: the bucket of water she'd filled up on her way there, and the little broom and cleaning rags and rolls of paper towels and trash bags and new grave candleholders and gloves so she wouldn't chip a fingernail. First, she dumped all the dried flowers into the trash bags; she collected the leaves that had fallen from a nearby horse chestnut, then swept the gravestone and brushed the mournful statue of the Blessed Virgin. She poured water over the gravestone and scrubbed it with a cleaning rag, then with paper towels. Finally, she collected the trash and supplies she'd brought. Only then did she stop to look around. Far away, almost to the arcades, she saw a couple moving through the colonnade. There was nobody anywhere near her. She went closer to the Blessed Virgin and reached out to touch the head. She spun around.

He was standing there quietly, watching her. She shuddered, feeling that she had heard herself let fly a wracking sob.

—You startled me. Why scare me like that?

—To check and make sure you are acquainted with fear.

He laughed, turned, and walked away at a steady pace.

\*     \*     \*

Ita and Lovro were happy that the wedding wasn't going to be called off. Ita was a little upset that everybody who was supposed to accompany her to the church wasn't going to come to the house before the ceremony; Lovro didn't care about that, but he was sorry he'd spent so much money on the decorations for Ita's house. They decided to move the white balloons, the white garlands, the glasses, and the golden plates to Lovro's place. The rest was pink and would stay at Ita's, for what would be now a smaller gathering of some twenty people.

Lovro took his car to his mechanic to have it checked so there'd be no car troubles on their wedding day, and Ita went home on the tram. In the #3, from Ljubljanica to the corner of Nehajska and Ozaljska, Ita mulled over how she'd pull it off to gather her best friends at the house without insulting Katarina and coming across as insensitive to David's illness.

Preoccupied as she was, she didn't hear anything.

Hey, I think it's hilarious that he has no idea what kind of a woman she is. I mean, look, he can like her as much as he wants, not for me to say, but to be frank, she is one helluva bitch. No, it's just awful that he is the only one who can't see it. I'm not going to be the one to tell him. Can't he see that all her little ploys around adrenaline sports are, like, so transparent? Oh, you know, let me tell you, and besides everybody knows who she goes with and what happens there and what boosts her adrenaline. I'm not saying. And he, to be frank, I don't get it. I don't care, I don't like him at all anyway. I'm totally cool as far as he's concerned. No, honest. Her? You're kidding! I can't believe it. Horrible. Wow, I'd completely forgotten what it's like to take a tram. They told me the course will end tomorrow. If it doesn't, I'm making a huge fuss. That would totally ruin my weekend. How can I take my suitcase with me to wellness? No, I'm bringing my own towels. Aha, I bought some new ones. Fendi Collection, to die for. The bomb. Totally sexy, black, they have this gold stripe across them, you know, you'll see them anyway. No need, I know you'd come pick me up, but why, you get it that they have to. Okay, kisses, see you, I'll send you an email. Bye. Listen, listen, hey, come pick me up after all.

TWO MEN:
Way too expensive, my kids would have to forgo their university studies, I can't pay that. But anyway, what's the point

of driving if there are no jobs if all you've got is a high school diploma? True, the kids with degrees don't have work either. No, I don't know, I don't know, I'm not up to speed.

PHONE, ALLA TURCA:
Agency here, hello. Ah, it's you. I'm on a tram, I'm going to notarize my signature. Listen, that old lady gave us a price as if she has, I don't know, a palace. Yes, it does have an attic above, but the price is too steep. Listen, if I were you, I'd go for it. Start building, let them sue you. You can raise a roof in three days. I'm not kidding. Change the lock while they're away for the weekend and go for it. SMS me, that's the only way. I have to give that presentation. You know the one, I told you about it. Čović will be there, that's why I'm going. I need to grab him. It's best at the presentation. A relaxed atmosphere. If he can't, I don't know who can. C'mon, SMS me. Bye.

PHONE LIKE A CHIMING BELL:
Who said it? That's outrageous. I mean... C'mon... I cannot believe it. Um... see, that's the thing. See. Tell me, is that normal? Is that normal? What? Jesus! No, me neither, me neither. But, again... C'mon. Will you? You will. Ha, no, super, super ... super, agreed. Jesus. No, that friend of his. Christ, are you dense, the guy with the motorbike. Yes. He did. Me too. He blows me away, totally blows me away. It's killing me. Aha, right. Absolutely. You will? Okay. Bye, bye. Aha, bye, kisses.
　　Super, super, super super-duper. All set, all set. Right, bye.

# Green magma

Most days Boris Horak came home around 4:30 PM. But the traffic was dismal today; a tram broke down somewhere, there was a fender bender, nothing major, but bad enough that he only made it home around six. He was utterly exhausted. His wife even had to help him take off his jacket.

He could hardly wait to sit at the table.

—I'm dead tired, please don't bug me with stories about healthy food.

—It's not that I'm bugging you, but if you pile all sorts of poisons into your system right now in this situation, your body will succumb. Your heart is not in great shape, your triglycerides are going wild. You may feel young, but the state of your body says otherwise. Stress will kill you.

—I'm not up for a fight.

—Oops, sorry, I didn't ask how things went at the hospital.

—They didn't. That woman throws me off. Her violent worrying will drive me crazy. She doesn't think about the kid at all. Her pain is front and center.

—Don't be that way, she's a mother. Will you give this a taste? Pure energy, the very essence of energy.

She handed him a glass filled with a thick greenish-brown mass.

—If it tastes anything like it looks, then better bring me a basin, just in case.

But he did reach for the glass and sipped a little.

—What is magical in this glass?

—Energy. Green magma. Young barley leaves, plus an extract of shiitake and maitake mushrooms in ideal proportions. It raises whoever drinks it from the dead.

She sat across from her husband. Their dinner wasn't ready yet, and they had some time to talk till the food was ready to put on the table. The woman massaged her neck and closed her eyes in a desire to appear relaxed so as to have a soothing effect on her husband.

—Energy, my dear husband, energy. We must enjoy it while there is still some left. Soon our Mother Earth will be squeezed dry and bare if we don't turn this around, if we don't wise up and find something new. We've squeezed her to the max. We don't know how to preserve ourselves, and we don't know how to preserve the planet.

Boris looked into the glass.

—Why take care of sources of energy?

—Probably because we need to leave something behind us after we're gone.

—Absolutely wrong. No need to leave anything at all. Let those who come along after us come up with new sources of energy.

Her eyes opened wide; she dropped her hand, and she no longer looked relaxed. Far from it.

—Oh please, stop being so maddening.

—Maddening?

—Maddening and spouting nonsense.

Horak began feeling better. He sprawled in his chair.

—Why nonsense? Everything having to do with the exploitation of energy has already been invented. Over the last one hundred fifty years. Our fellow countryman Nikola Tesla invented electricity only yesterday. Yes, yesterday. Why are you looking at me like that? Oil was unheard of until a century ago. We are essentially the generation that came up with the whole energy story. Why should we leave anything behind? Let them invent new energy. For themselves.

—What you're saying is totally nuts.

—Can't you see? If they live off of our inventions, their brains will shrivel up. They'll gradually regress to the primate stage, and then, bit by bit, to the amoeba stage. The brain develops because it is compelled to come up with something new. And only the things that are nearly impossible to find motivate it. That is why the brain develops, my dear, and not from tofu, my beloved little wifey.

He smiled. His wife stood up.

—Really? If we fed the brain with tofu, it would develop more easily and quickly. And more quickly come up with new sources of energy. The Japanese are smarter than we are because they don't poison themselves with fats. We poison our brains with deadly fats and produce sclerosis instead of health.

—Totally wrong. Everything that has been invented, and which means progress, was invented during times of peace, through the joyous nourishing of the brain with saturated fatty acids. Now that you've declared war on meat and fats, we've begun recycling ideas. All forward movement has stopped. We're stuck. The peak of new ideas and inventions stopped with diapers that don't leak. And as for the Japanese, if we were to slave away eighteen hours a day, maybe we'd be more successful than they are.

—Not true. Besides, how do you know we wouldn't have made miracles if we hadn't been eating meat? Maybe we'd already be on Mars.

—A hungry person, my dear, is not up to travel to Mars. A hungry person sits at home and dreams about food. Meat.

Now she was huffing.

—So that's what you tell yourself?

—Don't you go thinking that I'll contradict you. I despise myself for having knuckled under to your arguments about healthy food. I despise myself for starting to fear illness and death. And meat.

She no longer kept her voice in check, and she stood up to say:

—You despise yourself? You, my dear man, adore yourself.

Horak pretended not to notice the change in her mood. It amused him.

—Nowhere near as much as you adore yourselves, you health nuts. This quantity of self-infatuation and scorn for everything and everybody around you is immeasurable compared to my scorn and self-disdain. It defies measurement with anyone's scorn for anything. There is nobody as infatuated with themselves as you are. You have made your bodies into a religion. In this you are unsurpassed.

The woman tried to find a conciliatory tone. Again she sat.

—All God's children are obliged to respect their body. It is a gift.

He laughed. There was genuine, green malice in his voice.

—Respect their body? You have replaced God with your own body. You lick it and kiss it like iconoclasts. And who is this God of yours? You New Agers have mixed God with the gods. You've mixed the philosophies of others, none of which you understand, with the juice of mangoes and papayas, to which you've added star anise, powdered golden lentils, and bingo, a new God is born. You drink it and gobble it up like natives. Like cannibals. Which

God are you talking about? The Christian God is only your B team, sitting on the bench.

—Pardon? You are not in your right mind.

—Would you like me to say this again? The bench. If the A team of Eastern religions succumbs, which you totally adore like total ignoramuses because you don't have to know anything about them, you can fall back on your reserve bench. Here we are— Jesus runs out onto the court, he's rested and ready to go!

She threw up her hands. She couldn't look at him anymore.

—Cut that out. You're not even funny.

—Yes, it's not funny. It's pathetic. But that doesn't mean it's wrong.

—I'm not longer a good audience here.

—I don't need a better one. You are ideal because you'll put up with it, even when I tell you that your relationship with your metabolism and digestive tract is far more spiritual than your relationship with God. You are merely genuflecting to your intestines. You're bowing down low. The toilet is your altar. There, you'll put up with that too. You have spiritualized the product of your digestion. At the recommendation of your gurus, you bow down every morning over the toilet bowl to your product. You examine it to see what you have produced with your health food and admire it as if you've seen the Almighty. You have produced a new religion: the intestinal religion.

She stood up.

—You are wrong. This is not bearable. What you are saying is repulsive. If you think I'm like your ex, who, poor woman, suffered from your outbursts and attacks of sarcasm and conceit, then you are oh so wrong. I have my way of thinking, and you'll either respect it or we'll find a different form of communication.

—And what would that be, do tell, so I have time to adapt. It must have something to do with healthy bodily fluids, which we'll mix with essential oils.

—You're behaving like a total dolt.

—Look, we got angry. And that poisons the blood. Don't retreat from the field of battle, this is only now starting to get interesting.

He listened as she furiously forced the door to make a sound that would let him know she would not be back anytime soon. He thought he heard the word *idiot*. He smiled. He was pleased. He got up and from the door he called:

—Off to the hospital, no telling when I'll be back.

Dad came in. Mama's not here yet. Aha, looks like the two of them are angling to be the first to come see me. Now we have his quick peck, then *pat the cat*, then a little *Daddy's little boy*, then a little eyeballing the humming and beeping medical equipment flanking my bed. My old man has no clue what's going on with any of it, because he's an economist, an economic analyst, as he calls it. Those are the first difficult words I learned, and Dad was hugely proud of me. That I knew how to say what he did. He's always proud about that sort of thing. Like, *David has no problems turning on a computer; he is on friendly terms with his computer*. I let him think this is very important, and I don't tell him that nobody in my class has any problem turning on a computer, and all of us, except Horvatica, are on friendly terms with our computers. Once she figures out that she can find new hairstyles and everything about makeup on her computer, she'll catch on fast enough. And he's proud and tells everybody how *David was able to be left on his own at home at four and a half,* and now *at age ten, he looks after his own mother.* That's him forgetting how when I was four and a half, the two of them had a fight, and Mama stormed out of the apartment first, and Dad after her. Grandpa came over to take me to the park and found me there alone, and he got so upset about it that he had to take a double dose of his heart medicine. After that he yelled at my dad, his son, and scared me, so he stopped. And he told Mama she was not a mother, and then there was some kind of huge fight, and now they're suddenly all proud that I can be on my own at four and a half. If they'd started fighting when I was two, I easily would have stayed alone, because they easily would have left the apartment. To be fair, Dad has his advantages. He's mainly in a good mood when we're together, he takes me everywhere with him, we eat out, which I like, and he is pretty fair when it comes to his new wife. He doesn't talk about her much and doesn't expect me to spend loads of time with her. This is actually pretty funny, because it seems to me that he doesn't like being with her much and he'd rather be with me, not even because of me but because he loves eating. Dad went completely overboard, as my grandpa used to say, when he got to know this new woman. She talked about the healthy life she loves, as if everybody else loves a sick life, and this healthy life of hers is her being a terrible cook. She eats no meat and doesn't let anyone else eat it either, and she's always off to work out at the gym as if she'll get a reprimand and be marked absent if she doesn't. She calls it yoga in everyday life, and Dad and I laugh and call it yoga in everyday death. Now the way things stand, it seems to me that Dad can hardly wait to go out to eat with me so he can order meat. Worst of all is that he seems a little anxious while he's ordering the meat, and he's even more anxious while he eats it, and most anxious of all after he has gorged himself. Once, when I was angry at him, because he'd bought me the totally wrong, totally hick sneakers, I intentionally ordered a pizza without ham and with that yucky Swiss chard stuff, that otherwise nobody normal would ever eat, and then I waited to see what he'd do. He ordered the best kind, with the sausages, and then after that he totally, but totally freaked out. He kept muttering that I'd made such a better choice than him. But first he ate it all. Later he was sorry, and ever since I have always gone first and ordered some kind of meat when we're at a restaurant. I order pizza with ham or sausage, and then he looks at me, looks, looks, and finally says, *I'll join you*. It's like he's keeping me company, along with the the the ham and the sausage. He sees that I can see it, but so far we haven't talked about it. Once I part this curtain of mine that I'm lurking behind for now and get up off this bed, I think I'll try to sort out a few things with him. He'll probably want to hear me out, at least at first, because that's how it was when I broke my arm when I fell off my bike. It's as if something has to happen to me for them

NADA GAŠIĆ

to listen to me. And, besides, it is about time for us to have a little talk. I'd really like to know what my dad would have to say for himself. And what he'd have to say about my grandpa. I bet that would be a laugh riot.

## David's father—on himself and his father

*I think we're best off taking this one thing at a time.*

*The family I was born into is, at its roots, an interesting mixture of all sorts of things that washed ashore in this part of the world during the Austro-Hungarian reign. I'm not sure it makes much sense, for your needs, to get tangled up in my distant past, though I definitely picked up a little something from the Czechs, the Slovenes, and even a bit from the Russians. I assume what you're interested in is to hear about my parents. I wouldn't say I had a different relationship with my parents than most kids my age did. I got along fine with my mother. She died while I was still in high school, and premature deaths and partings are virtually a guarantee of eternal love. Dad was widowed early, but I can't remember if he found it difficult to deal with his status. I think he behaved decently; he didn't bug me with his loneliness, he had his friends for cards, the occasional coffee at the Splendid restaurant. We mostly didn't get in each other's way while we lived in the same apartment on Vodnikova. We weren't close, but we weren't enemies. I think we showed more interest in each other when he got sick and I started spending more time at his place than with my ex-wife. But did I really get to know him? Know him well? That's a big question. Before he died, I already knew I was going to leave my first wife. I didn't have the strength yet to break things off completely, so using the excuse that my father needed me, I moved into his apartment on Vodnikova Street. She watched me meekly when I left with my suitcases. And when she asked, after he died, why all of us weren't moving in there together, she acquiesced to my let's not go there now, I can't talk about that now, there's time. I never went back, and she never moved into Vodnikova. When I was left alone in the apartment where my father had ruled, I was surprised by how the feel of the space remained intact, despite the flood of new things without which I could no longer imagine living. It wasn't about furniture, and, of course, it wasn't the television or the radio, and I could live without a DVD player, but it was all the pointless odds and ends, the household items. Dad had no paper towels, but he had five kinds of laundry detergent and fabric softener; air fresheners; oven mitts; the Zepter pots, juicers, and mixers; the universal dicers and magic graters; the sets of knives; the plastic containers for leftovers; a supply of salt tablets to reduce scaling; the toilet fresheners; the body lotion, body oil, and deodorants; a set of nail files; the cuticle cream; the fragrant candles with essential oils. Basically, nothing that I had begun to consider necessary and essential for leading a household and keeping one's body alive. Amazingly, the apartment was clean, as was my father. He somehow kept it in decent shape, with the assistance of a lady who came in once a month to help him out. The apartment smelled as it always had; it smelled of the place where I'd grown up, and not of orange blossom, eucalyptus, or bitter almond.*

*As one usually does after someone's death, whether people admit to it or not, I set out to dig through the boxes, stacks of papers, and hidden nooks and crannies. I found this was awkward yet irresistible. I felt one really ought to take trash bags, stuff everything into them, and throw them away, but I didn't have the strength. I'd say I was looking for something.*

　　　　　　　　　　　　　　NADA GAŠIĆ

*I found incredible things. I found shoeboxes with countless bills and receipts for all sorts of things, and heaps of photographs, but nobody had written the names of the people in the pictures, which, unmarked as they were, no longer belonged to anyone and referred to no one. I found a drawing for someone's dentures from 1936; million-Yugoslav-dinar banknotes; federal bonds for building the railroad lines; unused summonses for elections; medical records from Golnik; someone's letters from the Yugoslav People's Army; boxes full of Christmas and Easter cards from Ljubljana and New Year's cards from Belgrade; prewar postcards from Essek and Abatie addressed to my grandfather, the esteemed gentleman trader in hops; letters dated 1972 from a distant Czech cousin who, as I managed to decipher, was requesting a letter of guarantee for a visa to travel to Yugoslavia and see the Adriatic; all my school report cards and commendations; the certificate that I had learned how to swim; my Pioneer cap; an extraordinary number of lung X-rays; a collection of metal toys; brand-new heel and toe protectors for shoes; hairnets; something called a lizeze—a healing shawl for ill women to drape over their nightgown; an alum block that could still be used after shaving. I found crocheted slipper socks for cold nights, a boots "servant" for pulling off boots, and a cruet that was missing its corks.*

*But there wasn't a single word written by my father's hand. Then I realized that this is what I'd been looking for: something in his handwriting that would disclose to me a person different from the man I knew and didn't know. He left everything behind, absolutely everything that could serve as a portrait of the second half of the twentieth century, but about him, this heap of things said not a word, except that he found it difficult to throw away things. Intentionally, he erased everything that had been written by his hand, and in a way,*

*this was how he bid farewell to this world. What you don't write with*
*your hand is merely a part of the general thinking; it doesn't oblige*
*anyone, least of all you, and, in a way, I think this was the true testa-*
*ment my father left quite deliberately behind. Intended for me.*

*Forgive me, this writing project is wearing me out. I'll contin-*
*ue and finally dedicate more to my ex-wife. I believe you are more*
*interested in my relationship with her. But this, about my father, I*
*had to write.*

*   *   *

One of these days, I'll ask Mama what she thinks of Dad.
But not so she says, you know, something useless like *he is
your father, no matter what*, but so she says what she really
thinks of him. Now and before, while they were what they
were. Married to each other.

### *What David's mother would have said
about David's dad to the school counselor
if she had attended her appointment*

My husband? Well, first he was a fellow student, then my boyfriend, and only then my husband. Now he's nothing to me at
all. Except David's father. And that is a lot. That's most of all.

What was our relationship like? Well, I feel as if it wasn't
exactly as I've said. I mean, we were enrolled in the same year
at the university, but in a way we weren't exactly collegiate as
students. It's strange, but in university classes, just like in high

school, you feel the differences between people in a particular way. You can spend twelve years with someone in the same classroom, yet you feel this someone has no connection to you at all. It's the same at university. You feel like you're not studying the same subjects, that nothing connects you except the hallways and walls. At first my future husband, David's father, didn't notice me at all. I noticed him, but I wasn't a colleague of his. Others, who were more like him, were his colleagues.

You find this interesting? How I felt about this? How I knew we weren't colleagues? By the way, he and his colleagues sauntered around the building as if they owned it. Seems to me, especially judging by the things they all laughed about together. In unison. I don't know. Maybe I'm off on a tangent here. But laughter—that's what seems to show the differences among colleagues the most. And among people in general. Other things, like clothes for instance, may look similar at first, but I don't think we laugh at the same things. Something along those lines. Or is it that we don't make fun of the same things? Yes, this seems closer to the truth. We don't make fun of the same things. Maybe that's it.

Him? He always appealed to me. He was different. Sure, everybody is different. That's true. But he was appealing. I think he knew it, but at first he didn't care. Though later, while we were still getting along, he said that what he liked best was that I found him appealing. I don't know.

And me to him? No. Maybe for a short while. It's more that he didn't know what to do with himself. Yes, he could have had others, but, well, I don't know... as if he were defying his father. I think his father didn't like me. No, it's not that he hated me, he was polite enough, but you can feel that. Always.

Friends? Were we ever friends? Good call. I did skip over that part. To be honest, he and I skipped friendship. I don't think we ever were friends. And we aren't now.

Maybe this will sound funny to you, but it seems to me that my attitudes toward people have something to do with poverty, not my character. I'll try to explain. Why not? Something stupid to do with poverty. Fine, not real poverty, but doing without. And people who do without always remember gifts. For St. Nicholas's Day, Christmas, whatever. But they remember. I remember that I could never open a present straightaway. It would attract me intensely. I'd circle around it—I know this sounds stupid—but, as if I were sniffing it out. Taking its measure. I didn't even take my own child in my arms the same second they brought him to me. I waited, waited so the magnificent moment of receiving a gift would last longer. It's probably that I always put off that moment when something nice begins to happen, so it lasts as long as possible. I unwrap everything slowly. And I unwrap people slowly. Human relations. I think I expect others to do the same. Him always watching me, not opening up to me fully, that attracted me at first, it was seductive, alluring. I wanted to be something wrapped and precious. For him to discover. Then it lasted, lasted. In the end it turned out that I felt like an unopened package, which he stepped around and ultimately left behind. Unopened. That happens.

*   *   *

Katarina opened the door as Boris was saying goodbye to David.
—I just went home to change. He wasn't alone for long.
—I'm not criticizing you.

Now I'll go deeper behind the curtain. I can't listen to them anymore.

Boris left and Katarina took the book of fairy tales from her purse. She looked at David and had the feeling he seemed to be breathing differently. More slowly. Panicked, she rang the buzzer next to the bed and held it down while she listened to footsteps that weren't stopping at the door to David's room. Finally, two on-duty doctors came in and several nurses. Katarina left, leaned on the wall, closed her eyes, clenched her fists, and covered her eyes. She wanted—sincerely wanted—to pray, but she couldn't muster the words. Over and over again, she just kept saying, *It's nothing, it's nothing, it's nothing.*

A few minutes later the doctors came out. Katarina heard what they had to say, and, reassured, back she went into David's room.

I've figured out that it's not good for me to retreat too far behind the curtain while the doctors are around. I'm onto that now. For a time I manage to keep it up, but then they wear me down so badly with those flashlights that in the end I have to come closer, but then after that I'm completely worn out for a long, long time. And what's worse, then Mama gets all upset, and she cries so hard that I can't listen to her anymore and I feel as if I'm crying on the inside too, but not because of myself or because of her, but, like, in general, I'm crying. All of a sudden, like a girl, for no reason. That is why I held out for so long while the bad-smellers tormented me with all their hands on me, their examining, and their stupid words. Mama, who was off by the door, of course, came in full of cheer, so I know the doctors told her I'm getting way better. How can they know how I'm doing, when I haven't said a single word to them? But it's good they said that to her. At least she won't cry. She started with that *Mama's little sunshine, my golden boy*, but soon she was telling me all the people who'd asked her to say hi. Big Boy Damir. Fine, I'm betting he didn't say *please convey my warm regards to David*, but mumbled something, drooled, bleated, though I don't doubt it was a greeting. Mama said Damir has always thought of me as his best friend, ever since I was a baby in dipes. He is okay, but I find it hard to say we're really friends. Then Arijen, which is also fine because he really is my best friend. But my teacher? Please, I'm hardly her favorite pupil. Heršak, he sits in the row in front of me, and Kovačić, who also sits in that row, because he sits with Heršak, but how stupid that he's sending his regards, because he and I can't stand each other. Then Horvatica, nooooooo, not Horvatica, and, finally, Mama said Mirna from 5C. There is no way I'll tell Mama that she isn't Mirna but Mirta, and actually she's my girlfriend, though even Mirta doesn't know that, because I haven't told her yet. Mirta doesn't know, nor does anybody else but Arijen, and not totally. Until you tell, it's only sort of, like, an idea, but nothing real yet. And then Mama adds that the entire class said to say hello. You're kidding. How? They stood up and in unison said, *Say hi to David*? No way. I bet it was the teacher who told Mama that they all say hi, and Mama is famous as a parrot, so she repeated. She wants to believe it's true. She does

NADA GAŠIĆ

have a thing about believing stuff. My mom is sometimes a little odd. I mean she's good, she's not bad. You know, she's not the worst. But she worries over nothing. She worries not only when I'm out of the house, but it's like she's always worrying. If it rains, she worries the trams won't run; if there's no rain, she worries there won't be enough water; when it snows, she worries about the slush; when there is no snow, she worries I won't be able to go sledding. I got used to all the worrying and crying a long time ago. But suddenly, I don't know what got into her, she wasn't crying in front of me, and I don't think it was because of me, I really don't know what was going on with her, but here's the thing: I went into the bathroom, and there she was, sitting on the bathtub and crying, and when she saw me, I saw she was ashamed that she was crying, but she couldn't stop right away. Then I got all confused because I could see she wanted to stop but she couldn't, and totally, but totally weirdly, I said, *Don't cry, everything will be okay*, or something even stupider. And later I locked myself in my room, and I remember that I cried inside then for the first time, because it is totally weird when a person has to comfort their own mother. Parents. That sucks, because it isn't the way things ought to go, the way my grandpa would organize things. That's why I was crying, because something had gone all wrong, and I couldn't fix it. Not right away. Later things got fixed by themselves when I pulled off another one of my shitstorms and she slapped me one. Well, no, it's not that she slapped me, but she swung to slap me and I ran around the table and teased her. That's something that we, Mama and I, call *doing the runaround*. And there are ways that I'm like Mama: by the way I can stare out the window for no reason, yes, that, and by the way I get all awkward when I really like someone. Mama is always at first confused, and I, too, get all confused when I first like someone. And when I add my being confused and staring out the window for no reason, and then add that I'm smarter on the inside than I am on the outside, and that I talk a lot inside myself but on the outside hardly anything at all, it turns out that at first glance I'm a first-class idiot. Big Boy Damir is sheer genius compared to me. Maybe that will be my main gig when I train to be a secret agent. Everybody will assume: he's an idiot. But I'll know what I know. Maybe Big Boy Damir isn't as clueless as everybody thinks.

I watch her looking for the book to read to me, and the book is either right there in front of her nose or on the nightstand. But my mama will *believe* she found it, as if the book was off somewhere in a forest. My mama . . .

My dad calls Mama *the little miss collector of empty bottles*. This is not entirely inaccurate. She holds on to empty bottles and all these little containers. She puts them on the glass shelf under the mirror in the bathroom, so in our house we're full of empty things, but we're generally short on things that are full. She keeps the empty little boxes from her lotions, and she's always scraping away on something that isn't there, and when she does that she's always mulling. That's how all the little bottles and containers and—wait for this, folks—all those corks have multiplied.

NADA GAŠIĆ

At first, I liked the way Dad called her that; it was said with all sorts of nice sounds, from the "tt" and "ss," and then I added in an "l" and it became *little miss collector of empty blottles*. Mama was really insulted and asked me why I was insulting her, and she added what she always adds, *You're just like your father*. That turns out to be their kind of insult: *you're just like your father, you're just like your mother*. As if I was the one who married my mother, and, stupider yet, as if I married my dad. But, actually, if I had a way to choose my parents, I'm not so sure I'd have chosen them. Well, probably I would've. Ever since I've known them, they've always been fighting over the same things. When Dad was living with us, they fought. How can I put this? While they were husband and wife, they fought . . . as if they were divorced. But back then I couldn't see that, because I was too young. Now I know, because ever since I've known them, they've been the same. Divorced. In any case, they don't much like each other. It's cute that they expect me to think well of each of them. I mean, Mama wants me to think well of her, but poorly of Dad, and vice versa for Dad: good about him, and bad about Mama. Although that's harder and a little bit messed up.

And my grandpa used to be a little odd sometimes, at least as far as this kind of thing went. He really liked it when I was a little angry at Dad and I'd tell Grandpa, *Your son is weird*. Then he'd laugh and laugh, and often he'd say, *My son has a good father, that father has a good grandson, and that grandson does not have much of a father*. That was how we were always messing around and laughing, but when my mama told him once, *Your son is not a good person*, Grandpa was very insulted and told me, *Your mother is a stupid woman*. Then I got insulted, and it was all so ridiculous that in the end I thought it was funny. Grandpa did too. There. Finally, she found her "misplaced" book. I hope she won't start in with the golden slippers and fairy hair. Right, I knew it. *David, fairy tales require an attentive listener*, and I answered, *Mama, and a good reader*, but she didn't hear it.


## THE FAIRY TALE ABOUT
## THE LITTLE CATERPILLAR

Once, long, long ago, in a distant and faraway time, there lived a gardener. The gardener grew potatoes and carrots and parsley and peas and turnips, but he was proudest of his cabbage beds. Everybody praised him, everybody bought vegetables from him, and when he looked over his dew-laden crops at dawn, his heart would happily pound, and he'd lift his face to the sky and give thanks to the rain and sun for helping him raise such beautiful vegetables.

—Ah, nobody else, from one end of this land to the other, has such carrots, nobody in this land has such parsley, nobody in this land has such peas, and nobody in the whole wide world has such cabbage!

The gardener began to sing his own praises, not only at dawn by his vegetable beds, but in city squares and at farmers markets and county fairs where he offered his goods for sale. And people listened to him. The gardener liked this, and he began touring the market towns and county fairs and traveling to places as soon as he heard that there would be people gathering. Little by little, he spent less time working on his vegetable beds. Yes, these were times when there were rain and sun in abundance, but vegetables don't become tasty all by themselves; they need to be cultivated and cleaned of all sorts of pests—butterflies and caterpillars, insects and bugs, shrews. Rabbits would show up now and then and, emboldened, would stay for breakfast, lunch, and dinner in the cabbage patch.

The gardener knew all this, but he'd grown so fond of shouting and boasting in the farmers markets that he didn't notice how his potatoes were getting smaller, his onions thinning, the carrots and parsley wrinkling, the kale moping, and the cabbage shrinking. And while he praised his produce to all and sundry, people began guffawing and pointing at his pitiful wares. In the end, he realized he no longer had much to boast about, but he simply could not stop. Was he concerned? Yes, he was. He was so worried, he couldn't sleep at night.

But during that time, as worries ate away at him, a rollicking banquet was going on in his cabbage patch. A whole host of caterpillars came wriggling out of their cocoons, and, thrilled that there was nobody to stop them, they began diligently nibbling and munching on the cabbage. In a flash, they'd gobbled up the tastiest leaves and were just about to proceed to the very heart of the cabbage head, when the voice of a tiny little caterpillar piped up, shining like mother-of-pearl in the moonlight. —My darling sisters, is what we're doing wise? We'll devour the whole cabbage patch, and then there will be nothing left for us to eat tomorrow, and the gardener won't have his pride and joy.

Wouldn't it be better for us to limit ourselves to what we've already eaten?

The rest of the caterpillars exchanged looks of surprise. They wriggled, rocking the cabbage leaves with their plump, hairy little bodies, and went right on chewing. A few insults and ugly, sarcastic remarks were directed at the little caterpillar.

Crestfallen, she saw that her sisters were none too smart and that within the next two or three nights, they would devour the remaining cabbage, destroying themselves and the gardener.

The little caterpillar decided to find a way to warn the gardener. She puzzled and puzzled over this, but could not think of a way to bring him back to his right mind.

Meanwhile, the gardener, anxious about the fate of his garden, tossed and turned at night, while by day he attended fairs, boasting and bragging to the point of exhaustion, although he knew full well that the day would soon come when he'd have nothing to sell or eat.

He pondered and he fretted and he mulled and despaired— all the while neglecting his garden.

The little caterpillar nibbled a leaf here and there, then she hid and thought about how to save the gardener and her greedy sisters from their downfall. The cabbage patch was vanishing before their very eyes. What was still cabbage in the evening would be nothing by the dawn of the new day but an ugly, gnawed stalk poking out of the ground. She tried to shout. She couldn't. An arrogant person hears no voice but their own. She tried stomping on her invisible tiny feet. A conceited person does not see what everybody else sees, let alone notice the invisible things. She tried rocking the cabbage in hopes that the gardener would finally see her. Her body was minute, and the cabbage leaf did not budge.

All this time, the other caterpillars were eating and eating, nibbling and smacking their lips, stretching and curling their plump little bodies, and starting their preparations for the major change soon to come.

The little caterpillar gave no thought to that. Wracked by despair, she looked down at her unimpressive body. When she crawled, her body first curled and then stretched in bends, then curled again, then stretched. Once more she looked carefully, then she breathed in and breathed out, then breathed in again, and her body began to squinch and spread, squinch and spread. Suddenly the little caterpillar began to play.

Midnight had just passed. A great moon hung over the cabbage patch, and had anyone stopped there, they would have thought that the moonlight was pouring down like confectioners' sugar, like finely ground mother-of-pearl.

The gardener leapt from his bed.

What was it he'd heard?

He left the house, and now he clearly heard music being played. This was an entirely unfamiliar sound to him. He turned toward the bright and cheery melody. Slowly, he approached the source of this song and found himself out among his garden beds. He stood and gasped. He saw the gnawed leaves of the cabbage, and when he leaned over, he saw the fat caterpillars munching away greedily. Smack, smack . . . But the music didn't stop. He leaned even closer, then knelt on the ground, and strained his eyes and ears, and finally he saw the tiny, little caterpillar that was squinching and spreading, squinching and spreading, and he could clearly hear her playing, playing, playing.

He saw and he understood: the little caterpillar was summoning him to his right mind with her music. He raised his eyes and arms to the sky and prayed, prayed with a full heart for the caterpillars to go away. Let them all disappear, except the little, shiny caterpillar that is playing. She had summoned and warned him. He immediately resolved to return to his garden, that every day he'd diligently clean and tend to his vegetables, that he'd stop with his arrogance, his vending, and his boasting at the farmers markets, market towns, county fairs, and bazaars. He promised this and wished he could reward the caterpillar in some way.

He returned to his little house, and for the first time in a long time he fell sound asleep. He dreamed that the big, fat caterpillars were wrapping themselves in cocoons, and that the big cocoons were opening, and from them were flying white butterflies heading to distant cabbage patches tended by other lazy and arrogant gardeners to lay their eggs there, eggs that would hatch into new caterpillars set on devouring those other, lazy gardeners' cabbage crops. And furthermore, he dreamt that the little caterpillar did not do as the others did, but began to swell, to spread and glisten, gleam and blaze, and play louder and louder.

At dawn, he splashed his face, picked up his tools, and went to the garden. The cabbage was quite gnawed, the cabbage patch quite ravaged, but the caterpillars were gone. Right by the edge of the field, he caught sight of something beautiful, large, and shiny, full of mother-of-pearl buttons and polished keys. When he bent over and lifted the shiny thing, it stretched, then contracted, and finally there was the sound of a sigh, as if someone who was tired after working hard had finally caught their breath.

The gardener pressed the buttons, the gardener fingered the keys, the gardener drew open the broad bellows, but aside from the sigh, there was nothing to hear. For a long time, he puzzled over the strange thing, mused and pondered, and then swung it onto his back, and off he went to the county fair. But when he got there, he didn't shout or brag about his cabbage. Instead, he roamed around until he heard the strains of a violin. He followed the sound and came to a small, swarthy fiddler. He placed the shiny thing in the man's hands. The little fiddler set aside his violin and touched the strange, shiny thing with his little dark fingers. He drew open the bellows, pressed the buttons with one hand and the keys with the other, and the strange thing began to play. Joyfully, joyfully . . .

Ever since then, at county fairs, on the streets, and in squares, you can hear the accordion, the very one the little mother-of-pearl caterpillar had changed herself into, playing gaily.

Only the gardener, you, and I know how the accordion came into being, and why it plays such lively tunes that sometimes sound like someone is sprinkling confectioners' sugar in the mother-of-pearl moonlight.

\*     \*     \*

Vidošić got into his car and headed for his apartment in Lanište. But something happened on the way. When he found himself in front of the children's hospital on Klaićeva Street, he told himself he'd ended up there by chance. *Random traffic patterns.*

Nobody stopped him at the front desk, and he went down the corridors that had an evening-ish feel to them; they were wheeling the same carts they'd wheeled that morning—loaded with glasses, teas, bedding, and meals—and nurses and visitors were passing by; there wasn't the bustle of daytime. It felt softer.

He came to David's door and entered right as Katarina finished reading the fairy tale. Her eyebrows shot up. She put the book down and signaled for him to wait for her in the corridor.

—Ma'am, I apologize; I was on my way home and thought I'd stop by to see how the boy is doing and to apologize to you once more.

Katarina's expression softened; her chin trembled.

—Thank you, things are going well. I was the one who had the crisis, not David. I had the impression he was breathing differently. My nerves are shot.

—No, you're a true hero. I admire you. I am moved by what happened. I told your husband, I have two sons myself, one is six, the other nine; I don't know how I'd manage.

—He is David's dad, but he is no longer my husband. I hope for your sake that you never learn *how you'd manage* something like this.

She had warmed up to him a little, and let slip a barely visible smile.

—Thank you for coming.

Vidošić touched her elbow. Both of them were unsettled by that.

—Save your strength for when he comes around.

She pressed the door handle; Vidošić looked at her hand and almost placed his over hers, but he quickly busied his hand with fixing his jacket.

—Ma'am, I promise we'll catch the monster who scared the boy. He won't get away with this. I'd give anything in the world if we had been able to protect your son.

She didn't say a word. Vidošić felt his last sentence scratching his throat.

Who is this man? I can't remember, but I know I've already heard his voice. I think he isn't the same guy who was here before. When was that? I can't tell; I've tangled up time. Stupid David, get some sleep.

That night the little house also slept. Tearstained, scared, tired, inconsolable. When Irma, Ita, and Katarina came in, and when Cilika finally joined them, the house no longer had the strength to listen to how first Cilika, then Irma, then Ita explained to Katarina that everything would be done with dignity, *there will be no circuses in the house, or at the wedding. All the guests know what happened to Dado, nobody would think of doing something unbefitting, but the wedding cannot be put off; everything is ready to go, and they have already had a rehearsal at the church.*

—Do whatever you like, I don't care.

That's what Katarina said.

The little house didn't have the strength to wait for Katarina's answer; it drooped with all its windows, roof beams, and tiles. Its good old neighbors heard.

# Fifth stone, fifth wave

—VIIILIIIM, VIILIM!

They were already on their way out the door when Cilika lost Vilim for the third time that morning. Who knows why he went back in: to see whether they'd shut off the gas, if the attic door was locked so Gramps wouldn't climb up there again, or if Big Boy was in his room?

Cilika was standing by the back door, fussing and fixing her scarf. *Up at Mirogoj Cemetery, it's always chilly for All Saints' Day. No matter what you wear, it's never enough. This is a sunny day, but this sunshine has teeth, it can fool you.*

—Viliilim, Viiiliim!

He finally came out of the house. They closed the back door behind them and, arm in arm, went down Mala Street, carrying bags with brushes and pails and polish for the gravestones, poured into a little beer bottle so it would be easier to carry.

Big Boy Damir woke up earlier than usual. He was impatient, excited. He could hardly wait to do everything he was supposed to do at breakfast time and see Vilim and Cilika leave the house. Gramps was fast asleep up in his room.

He didn't look at the framed picture of the Virgin Mary; he knew Our Little Lady was probably already there, but he didn't want to talk until the family had left.

As soon as the back door closed and the key clicked in the lock, Our Little Lady came to the edge of the table.

—Hey, sleepyhead, slugabed, are we going for that walk, or were you leading me on yesterday?

Usually, people didn't joke around with Damir, and if they did, then there was always something ugly and dangerous in it, so for a minute he was scared. But only for a minute. Then he remembered that this was jaunty humor, real humor, the way people joke with ordinary boys.

—You're the sleepyhead, slugabed—I'm all dressed and ready!

—Then let's go!

—Yes, but first we need to figure out where you'll be, so you can see everything without being seen.

—You have pockets on your shirt. Put me in a shirt pocket, and I'll hold on to the edge.

They both were flustered. Nicely flustered.

—Will you be able to climb up?

—It's a bit tricky for me.

Damir carefully set his right hand down by the table edge, and Our Little Lady gingerly climbed onto his palm. Damir held his breath as he brought his hand up to his left shirt pocket. He waited for the pocket to stop shifting. He turned to look away while Our Little Lady raised her little leg to hop over the pocket hem.

—Damir, Damir!

He wasn't used to this agitation in her voice, and he even thought she was shouting. He quickly looked down. Our Little Lady was covering her ears with her teensy hands.

—What happened?

—Nothing terrible, but I can't hear you because your heart is pounding. Move me to your pocket on the right.

He took a paper napkin from the table and used it as a ramp to the right pocket. Full of concern, breathless, he waited for her to hop over the topstitched edge. He no longer looked away, as he saw this was a joint task. Her safety mattered more than his shyness.

—Wow, I can't hear a thing. Your heart really does pound like crazy. I can hear it on the right side too.

Damir smiled, pleased.

—I had no idea it's so loud. I guess I must have a very big heart.

—Everybody learns sooner or later how big their heart is.

Damir felt like she was showing off a little. Our Little Lady finally settled in and held the top of the pocket with her left hand, while with her right she fluffed out her hair.

—Do you have a mirror? I can't go out into a crowd looking like this.

—Why not? First you didn't want anybody to notice you, and now you're fixing your hair.

He didn't even smile at her. She had really perplexed him.

—Well, there are things we do for ourselves. And the *crowd*, that's, how can I put this? That's a word about exercising control over ourselves when faced with what doesn't exist.

And now it was his turn, finally, to brush this off with a man's typical wave of the hand.

—Women.

He wasn't scared by the gesture or the word. He was proud. She wasn't watching him or listening; she was fixing her untamable curls. He relented.

—Oh, don't worry, there's a mirror in the hallway. We can look at ourselves on our way through.

Just in case, Our Little Lady turned up her dress collar, and with it, like a hood, she covered her hair. Although he knew there was nobody but them in the house, because Gramps couldn't be counted among the living, Damir took off his slippers so he'd be as quiet as possible. But he couldn't contain his curiosity.

—How can you bear all those prayers when you're even bothered by the sound of my heart?

—They make a different sound. Prayers, prayers are . . . Prayers are a constant noise. I'm used to it.

He couldn't see, but Our Little Lady puckered her lips and nose.

—But sometimes they really go overboard with all the singing, that's for sure. Singing can really irritate and wear me out.

He laughed so hard that he shook, and Our Little Lady had to grab hold of the pocket.

—Hey! Hey! A little concern here for your fellow travelers!

She was bright and cheerful. She didn't seem vexed, and he felt her mood had changed thanks to him. He turned manfully, looked around the room, and solemnly warned her:

—Now we have to be careful and quiet.

She withdrew farther under her hood. Damir went to the door, cracked it open, then tilted his head to hear better. The house was quiet. Empty. The stuffy smell of the room had changed, but not for the better; the dark hallway smelled of the autumn damp. He closed the door to his room behind him. Still in his socks, he took another long step and stopped in front of the mirror. He had the impression that the reflection wasn't like usual, that it was casting a long shadow which, fracturing on the edge of the opposite wall and floor, climbed up toward the ceiling. He froze. He bowed his head. He had never looked directly into a mirror. He always had the feeling of being cheated; another creature was watching him from there, and now he wasn't particularly surprised when, out of the corner of his eye, he noticed that instead of seeing himself with Our Little Lady in his shirt pocket, he saw an elderly woman in a tattered black robe who, in misery, was wringing her hands over someone's limp, pale form. He didn't recognize anybody; he didn't see himself, or Our Little Lady, or the hallway, nobody—nothing. Before he retreated from the ugly reflection in the mirror, Our Little Lady tugged at the edge of his pocket.

—Let's go out!

He slipped on his shoes and quickly pulled on his jacket. There was very little light outside, but compared to Damir's little room, the day was bright white. Both of them breathed a sigh of relief. Audible.

Damir didn't follow the path through the yard and out to the street, but instead went the other way, slowly, by the garage that, with a shed, created a passage to the walled-in garden. There they were met by a low, latchless wooden gate, which he opened. With a sideways glance, he watched his passenger and saw how she was carefully following his every movement. He was proud. He addressed her, his tone a little jaunty:

—Now we can speak freely.

—We have been able to the whole time, even without opening our mouths.

—I know, but . . .

—I understand, you mustn't be distracted.

He didn't answer. With his left hand, in a proprietorial sweep, as if sowing seeds, he gestured in a half circle, and in a solemn voice he introduced Our Little Lady to the chrysanthemums.

—Thank you, Damir, I know chrysanthemums well. This is the time of their lives and the time of their violent demise. They will die, as cut flowers, on tombstones everywhere.

The solemn tone of her voice bothered her, so she quickly added:

—Where are you taking us? What route will we take? All I can see ahead of us is this high-rise, a wall, I don't dare even look at it.

—Don't be afraid.

This was the most beautiful sentence Damir had ever uttered. It made him straighten up and stand taller. Our Little Lady noticed the change.

—Ah yes, a person is the most powerful when defending another from fear.

Damir was no longer thrown off by her speedy reactions to his mood changes. Again, he said:

—Don't be afraid.

NADA GAŠIĆ

The sentence, when repeated, no longer had such power, and Damir felt himself hunch over again. With a flood of words, he tried to mask his sudden clumsiness.

—Another passageway remains. There's trash in it and it's a little overgrown with weeds, but I can squeeze through. I know everything around here really well.

Between the blue wall of the new five-story building and the half-rotten fence around the autumn garden they were leaving behind, there was a pathway that didn't belong to anybody or anything: not the garden, or the wall, or the local residents. The pathway was cluttered with rubble, dried branches, leaves, a rotten cement sack, chunks of plastic, and rusty wires, and Damir progressed through it very, very carefully, taking slow steps and watching where to place his feet. He finally managed to reach the place where the multicolored concrete paving stones began.

—Now we're on someone else's property, but nobody stops me here. Only once did a man chase me. Later he moved away. To an even nicer house, Cilika said so.

He looked down at his pocket. Our Little Lady wasn't paying attention.

—Aren't you listening?

She lay her finger over her lips as a sign for him to stop talking. He did. Our Little Lady pulled her collar-hood even more over her head and signaled that he could proceed.

—Nothing. A voice stood out with a prayer. I had to attend to it.

—And?

—And nothing. I checked, and nothing more can be done.

—Where did you check? With whom?

Our Little Lady was distant and quiet, and he could tell she had no intention of responding.

They went through several paved yards without a single blade of grass, with no leaves, bounded by a cast-iron fence. The fence gate opened easily from the inside, and Damir went out onto the street, which ran parallel to the street where he lived.

—Now we'll turn, and then a little farther, and we'll come out on the main street, Ozaljska, and then in a few minutes we'll get to the farmers market.

—I know, I remember.

—You do?

—I've been here a few times.

He didn't hear her; he was concentrating on his steps. As he'd been taught, he walked along the inner edge of the sidewalk. He always felt more secure when the wall of a building was on one side of him, close to his shoulder. He didn't show her anything. He felt there was nothing to show. Indeed, there was nothing except buildings that followed one after another at regular intervals: a multistory building, a single-story dwelling, a multistory building, a single-story dwelling. Our Little Lady looked straight ahead, as if bothered by the tunnellike impression created by the high-rises towering over the low-slung houses.

They turned and came out on Nehajska.

She turned toward Ozaljska and pointed at Okićka, a little farther off.

—There, on that little street, there used to be a movie theater. The word *kino* was written on it . . . and something else.

—It said Triglav. I was there once.

—When, when were you? What color were the seats?

—I don't remember. I was awfully excited. I was afraid they'd throw me out. But I remember how the whole row shook when one person laughed.

—Ah, so the seats were connected. Right, the seats used to be connected in movie theaters, but they had moving parts. What movie did you watch?

—I don't remember. Just that I was scared they'd throw me out.

Our Little Lady was intrigued.

—Let's go see what's there now.

—They sell detergent there now.

—Detergent? At a movie theater? Odd.

—No. The movie theater is gone. And so is Triglav. That used to be a hill, the tallest mountain of all.

—What do you mean Triglav is gone?

—It's gone, I know it's gone; I looked through David's schoolbooks about nature and society.

He worried Our Little Lady might think poorly of him, so he added:

—David let me have a look.

—Oh, I know you'd never touch anything without permission. I wasn't thinking that. I was just puzzled about Triglav.

She closed her eyes and fell silent. Damir was also quiet. Our Little Lady breathed a sigh of relief.

—Let's keep going, everything is fine with Triglav. The mountain is right where it always was in Slovenia. I checked. It's the schoolbooks that have changed, not Triglav.

He, too, was relieved. They finally came out into the open area of the park, and Damir, for no particular reason, proudly crossed the street and set off down a gravel path.

—Damir, why are we going this way?

—It's nicer.

—Not for me; I'm interested in people, not some empty park.

—It's not empty. Look, there!

He pointed.

—Look at those ladies over there tossing corn to the pigeons.

—Ladies tossing corn to pigeons are the same all over the world. I don't need them, and they don't need me. They have the pigeons. And the pigeons have them.

He was hurt by this and trudged on toward Ozaljska.

—Well, now you'll see all sorts of people!

They had just stepped up onto the sidewalk when Damir leaped back; a racing bicycle swerved around them, and Our Little Lady clapped her hands.

—Cycling on the sidewalk—I know that's against the rules. Now that poor boy will have to deal with the police.

—Oh, no he won't. Cyclists mostly ride on the sidewalks here.

He kept to the right side along the walls of buildings. He felt that she was safer too, in his right-side pocket. Sheltered.

Our Little Lady tilted her head and looked toward the tram lines and roadway.

—When I was last here, a river was coursing down this street, and you couldn't see the tram tracks. Trucks crammed with people passed by.

Then, after a pause:

NADA GAŠIĆ

—You aren't aware, you people who live in Zagreb, that you're living on streams and ponds. You're living on the water. Zagreb is one large, buried lake.

Damir protested.

—That's not true. Zagreb is the most beautiful city.

Our Little Lady tried not to laugh, but her little voice snorted.

—Damir, besides Zagreb, how many cities have you seen?

—Not a one.

She didn't say anything more, but she felt his shoulders sink and she was sorry she'd gone too far. She stopped talking about the most beautiful cities. And the buried lake. But she couldn't shake the story about the water.

—Back then, when the river flooded this street, there were many prayers.

—Did you answer any of them?

She said nothing. Damir was already used to her not responding to questions like that, so he focused his attention on his feet.

—Look, Damir! A brand-new street, not a single old house.

—That's Sokolgradska.

—Now I remember. It was full of small houses, yards, gardens, and old water pumps. I remember, I remember.

Damir couldn't see it, but Our Little Lady had closed her eyes.

—I remember a boy who ran out to the water pump in the middle of winter without wearing a hat or sweater. He was never cold.

She opened her eyes, and without knowing why she was saying this to Damir, she grumbled:

—Just the other day I saw him on the street. He's old, gray-haired, he doesn't live here anymore, but he roams around these streets and never does up his jacket. He's too hot. And he's on the lookout for an old water pump. He suffers from an incurable disease: nostalgia.

Damir wasn't listening. He slowed, then went even slower, then stopped altogether.

Our Little Lady was dismayed.

—Something happened here. I feel it. I know why you stopped.

Both of them were swallowed up by the silence of fear, recognizably distinct from all other kinds of silence in the world by the vacuum of its aura. Our Little Lady knew it well, and she interrupted it with a deliberately loud and well-articulated sentence:

—Not too far from here, the body of a dead woman was dumped.

—I know. I heard.

Damir could feel Our Little Lady fidgeting; clearly, she was moving her teensy feet. Her voice sounded nervous and scolding and angry all at the same time.

—Ah, poor woman, what she got herself into . . . It is always like that. They have learned nothing. They have learned nothing.

—Who?

—Why, these young Magdalenas. But my son too. He, too, got involved in all sorts of things.

She waved her hand.

Damir didn't understand, but he didn't have the will to draw out the conversation. He had taken the walk for other reasons—to show her his part of the city, which belonged to him by squatter's rights. His pulse quickened. He decided to hurry as fast as his legs would allow, alongside the yards and the high school playing field.

NADA GAŠIĆ

As if she could hear him, Our Little Lady said:

—I'll help you; just keep your eyes on your feet, and I'll follow so nobody bumps into us. No cyclists.

How did she know what was making him anxious?

They moved along by little Maglajska Street, where David had been so frightened by the headlights of the big beast. Our Little Lady retreated deeper inside her collar-hood, as if an icy gust of wind had blown their way.

As he was taking the last step to the spot where the building with the pharmacy ended, they were plashed by the sound of the farmers market, and Damir stopped. There were all sorts of voices mingling—shouting, calling out, sputtering, drawling, whispering, expressing surprise, lack of recognition.

Our Little Lady exulted.

—Aha! Aha! People!

She was really shouting, and Damir stopped, alarmed, because out of the corner of his eye he saw she was leaning dangerously over the edge of his pocket.

—Watch it. Don't, you'll fall out!

—Oof, you're such a coward! I won't fall! Look, look at all the umbrellas. Look at all the flowers!

Damir barked.

—Why are you shouting so loud? Such a typical woman. Wait till we are in the middle of the market, and then you can admire it.

She pointed to the wall of a three-story building.

—Wait! Wait! Stop here for a minute, so we can catch our breath. I have to prepare myself for the farmers market.

Damir leaned on the wall of the building that had been a pharmacy for as long as he could remember.

Our Little Lady stretched her neck, trying to see the whole building.

—I remember! Movies were projected on this wall. It was called *kino* too. Even before the big flood.

—No way, there was never a kino here. Why do you care so much about movies? You're wrong.

—No, I'm not, I remember. People brought their own chairs without armrests and watched the movies.

Damir wasn't sure he could believe all she said. So many years were behind her, maybe she'd confused things. Older people forget stuff. He was scared she'd see his doubt, so for no reason he added:

—Chairs without armrests are called folding chairs.

—I remember, I sat by a little girl on her folding chair and we watched a cartoon. I even remember that it was called *Scamp*.

—So this *Scamp* of yours, was it really a cartoon?

—Yes, but the old-fashioned kind.

—What do you mean?

—Well, there weren't too many ugly pictures, scenes, that's what they call them. There was no fighting, smashing, killing, slaughtering, pulling hair, burning, or torturing.

—So that means you don't like the new cartoons?

—There are a few nice ones, which are at least fair.

She leaned back to see his face.

—*Asterix*, for instance, I like it. A story about the great and the small. The just and the unjust. The newer ones I don't like so much, but I'm not saying they don't interest me.

—Really? How can you be drawn to something you don't like?

—Oh, things you really don't like can draw you in big-time. Even a person you don't like can be attractive to you. Especially that.

—I don't want to talk about people. Let's talk about cartoons. What appeals to you?

—What do I like? Well, I don't know . . . Actually, I do know. I like seeing destruction with no consequences. Like that coyote of yours. He carries bombs around; seconds later, he's alive, well, and whole. Jerry zaps Tom with an electric shock and chops off his tail, and seconds later Tom is alive and well and has his tail back. That's exactly what I like. I am deliberately taking part in destruction without a price to pay.

She laughed. Devilishly.

—And resurrections without consequences.

Damir leaned back, arranging his arms against the wall so they became his lever, which effortlessly bounced him rhythmically off the wall. He rocked, forward, back, forward, back . . .

—You're starting to talk with me like . . . like with any old ordinary person.

—You are an ordinary person. Just a little wiser than average.

—Pardon?

—What you heard. You are smarter than most of your fellow citizens.

—No, I'm not. You're consoling me, yet you know there's so much I don't understand.

—You understand. What you don't get right away, you'll get soon enough. And in Go it's the sense of the moment, what is called intuition; that is the art of it. Look, I'll check right away on that, on, on . . . on that lady over there, to see how smart she is.

—Which?

—The lady in the nice clothes. Wait, wait for me to check.

They both stopped talking.

—Just as I thought. She believes her neighbor is a witch. She believes in evil curses, hexes. She believes cards and beans will be able to predict how much she'll earn next year from some apartments in a place called Crikvenica. So, you see, you're smarter than she is.

—No, don't be mad, but you're . . . how do you say it? You're flattering me.

—Flattering? How did you understand immediately what Go was about? No one is able to pick up the skill of playing it at the drop of a hat, but you'll steadily progress in your mastery of it. You move toward your goal, relying on your own wit and intuition.

She dropped her head, and Damir thought she'd snapped off a thread from the corner of the pocket. Her voice was a shade darker.

—Damir, the life of wise people is the game of Go.

—And the life of cartoons?

—The life of cartoons? A miracle of miracles. Not the life of cartoons in and of itself, but that people live their lives in the illusion of cartoons.

—Now I really don't understand anything. Please, let's go into the farmers market. I am baffled.

—Wait, just let me say this. Look, it's like this . . . In simple terms—people live in a cartoon illusion. As if they hope they will always, no matter what happens, wake up without suffering the consequences. That is why they are so alone when something

NADA GAŠIĆ

truly bad happens to them. What they call a tragedy. Their whole world collapses, while meanwhile everybody else is living peacefully, happily, and brightly, as if they're in a cartoon. That is why they are so alone and doubly unhappy, because only then does it hit them that they are alone in their tragedy, and that Tom's singed tail will never grow back. Do you understand now?

—I got the part about Tom's tail, but nothing else.

They laughed as if they'd never stop. She adjusted her hood.

—This hair of mine.

He didn't know what to say about this. He was no good at woman talk.

—Fine, we can move on; probably no one will see me all tangled like this.

He didn't hear her last comment as he boldly strode into the crowd.

—Damir, Damir, look at all the cute mini houses and the smells. It's like the Orient!

—Those aren't mini houses, they're kiosks, and it's not the Orient, those are ćevaps. Sometimes they buy me some.

He passed by the kiosk where meat was roasting and entered the section of flower vendors. With All Saints' Day around the corner, there were too many women elbowing their way to the chrysanthemums, so Our Little Lady signaled to him to move on to the tables piled high with cheeses, eggs, and slaughtered geese. He could have sworn he could feel Our Little Lady hopping from one foot to the other in her excitement.

—This I remember, from even before that big water. I forgot what it's called.

—Cheese and cream.

—Cheesencrim?

—Not like that, separately: cheese and cream.

—And what does this mean, "local"?

—That means it was made here, it's ours.

—Ah, I see. So they're warning people not to buy it?

Damir was a little irritated.

—No, the opposite— it's better quality! If it's ours, that means it's better.

—But it looks worse than the other kind that doesn't say "Local."

—It may look worse, but it's better, healthier. So they say.

—I'm a little confused. The last time I was here, whatever was better was marked with "Imported," or "From Abroad," so that's why I was confused.

—No, now it's the other way around.

—These changes happen so fast.

—Fast for you, maybe, because you have lived for such a long time, but for us they aren't fast.

Our Little Lady didn't hear him; she was pointing in excitement at the center of the farmers market.

—Let's go there—people have gathered around because of something.

He looked at the crowd and said:

—No, I'm scared of crowds.

—I understand. I even remember.

—What do you remember?

He stopped and began rocking, left, right.

—What do you remember?

—I remember some children, I remember a little boy who fell, I remember . . .

—Don't remember, please don't remember. There, I can't remember.

She kept going. With a merciless determination.

—I remember they did something bad. Ugh! Bad, bad. They peed on the boy who fell. They laughed and shouted, *Come on, fly, Peter Pan!*

Damir was rocking quite hard now, and women were anxiously moving away from him. He raised his hands and plugged his ears.

—I can't hear you. I can't hear you!

Still, he heard.

—Yes, crowds are always dangerous. Even when it's a mob of children. Yes, those small, evil mobs are especially dangerous. Do you know, or do only I know, that you were baptized as Petar?

She stopped talking. Damir stopped rocking. He unplugged his ears.

—You are . . . cruel. I am Damir.

—Well, fine, then. And remember, Damir, we are all cruel sometimes. Especially children.

—You aren't listening. You are being cruel now. Do you hear me?

Silence. He got frightened. He bowed his head, and in relief he saw her leaning against the pocket hem and trying to look up at his face, huge as it was. He quieted down.

With a chime-like, girlish voice, she asked:

—Do you want us to make peace?

—I do. We didn't come here to fight, but to go for a nice walk.

Damir was so, so thrilled by his wise sentence and by being willing to forgive.

# *Forgive?*

—Katja, I'm pleading with you, God help me, please find forgiveness deep in your heart. You must forgive everybody before you stand with me in the church. God will judge that maniac in the car, but you, come on Saturday to the church with an open heart.

Ita burst into tears. Katarina's eyes were dry.

They were standing around David's bed. Ita was sincerely shaken to the core. She had so, so many things to take care of before Saturday that she hadn't visited David after that horrible night when she, Lovro, and Irma waited with Katarina for the operation to finish. But today she grabbed some time to see Dado and thank Katarina once again for allowing the wedding to go forward.

—Katarina, I was at the church; you should go yourself and pray. Pray with an open heart; it will help you. Pray to dear God and Mary to help David.

—I won't pray to them. If they'd cared for my David and me, they wouldn't have allowed this to happen.

Ita's mouth dropped open, and so it remained. She could hardly speak.

—Don't talk that way.

—I never talked that way before. I was obedient and good, and now it turns out they don't care. Will they lash out at David again for these words of mine?

—Katarina . . .

—Yes?

—You can't be this way.

—Why can't I be *this way*? And what does my *this way* look like? What have I ever done to anyone? What has my David done that's so terrible that now . . .

—Katarina, love. I'm scared when I hear you talking like this.

—Leave Katarina be. She's fed up with life.

—Don't give up like this. Now David needs you more than ever.

—For the last ten years, two months, and eleven days, David has needed me, and for every single second of these ten years, two months, and eleven days, I have been aware that he needs me. And that is how I live. Don't talk to me about when my child needs me most.

—Katja, please, don't . . . I prayed to the Blessed Virgin Mary, and Cilika is praying constantly. You should pray too.

—Maybe we'll get on her nerves, what with so many of us pestering her with prayers for this one boy?

—Katja.

—Fine. I am not giving up, and I'll get through this. I'll go to church and I'll pray. And I'll confess all that I have to confess. And I'll ask for forgiveness for all the things I've said. I'll pray. Humbly. But never, never again tell me that I must forgive. Please, Ita.

Ita burst into tears again and kissed her sister.

—Thank you, thank you so much. Lovro will come to fetch me now. He wants to thank you for not insisting on putting off the wedding. You know how much he loves Dado. He'll just send a kiss from the doorway.

Ita brushed away her tears.

—You know what that maniac did? He shaved his head. I almost killed him yesterday. You'll see, he looks like a caterpillar. He's not in his right mind.

The conversation about loftier matters was over, and both of them slipped into household talk. Katja laughed for the first time since the accident.

—Whatever got into him?

—I can't imagine. Supposedly the guys were teasing him about having a big head. They'd been drinking, and half of his friends are security guards and have shaved their heads, so he probably wanted to be like them and went and did what he did. Now he'll look like a caterpillar at the wedding. Cilika told me Vilim has some lotion that could make at least a little hair grow in two days. I'll give it a try. I'll pour the whole bottle of it onto his head.

The door opened, and Lovro poked his head in; he blew Dadek a kiss and whispered *thank you* to grinning Katarina. The sisters kissed. Katarina promised once more that she'd come to the church, that she'd go to confession and pray for Ita and Lovro and Irma and Dado. And herself.

\*     \*     \*

The morning was slipping by. Vidošić spoke with a forensic psychologist over the phone and sent him all the relevant information about the murder. This was the first time he'd pursued *offender profiling*, based on the information they sent to the psychologist. He was curious and impatient, but he had to wait at least a day or two for the psychologist to do his job.

He wanted, without getting up, to grab some papers from his side table, so he pushed off with his foot and the chair rolled over. He remembered the speed with which he'd flown in this same chair when Kasumić shoved him. He stopped, shot angrily to his feet, and went over to the window. He stared out at the bright, clear day. Usually, the weather wasn't like this before All Saints' Day, but this year it would be beautiful. Sunny. That morning he'd conducted all the conversations with his men, and he left for himself the conversation with Irma Žiger. The autopsy showed that the murder had happened earlier than they'd assumed, so he was no longer interested in late night, but in a time around 9 PM. He would talk with her about that. And though he knew this would be going overboard, he had to go to the hospital and ask David's mother whether David was with her all afternoon and evening, and when, precisely, the party of the three sisters began in the little house in the yard.

He called the high school secretary; *yes, Ms. Žiger just held her class, yes, she has another class period to go, and then after that she's free.*

He decided he'd see Irma later; first he'd talk with David's mother. To bolster his courage, he took a swig from the bottle he kept in his drawer and then locked the desk. With a lump in his throat, the inspector set off for the hospital.


## Useful bacteria

David's dad decided to use a few days of his annual leave. All of them understood that this was about his child. He didn't hurry to the hospital. He talked with the head doctor in the morning over the phone; he had the impression that the doctor was giving him some sort of sign that the child's condition was improving, though there was caution in the doctor's responses. He knew

David's mother was already at the boy's bedside, so he took a little time for a nice breakfast. His wife taught evening classes at a language school, so, with pleasure, she prepared them a proper meal, including a special drink. She poured the thick substance, which hardly could be deemed liquid, into a glass and added a spoonful of linseed oil and some Brita-filtered water.

—There you go, healthy bacteria.

He reached for what she was offering him and swallowed it down with a gag.

—Repulsive. Repulsive and expensive.

—Repulsive and healthy. Without this we cannot manage. Especially you, now that you're dealing with so much stress.

—Yes, I am dealing with stress, but I am far from demented. Revolting and revoltingly expensive.

She fell silent. Sometimes silence helped and he'd lose his will to gnaw at her. She cleaned a stalk of celery and waited for him to calm down. This time it didn't help.

—Would you like me, in the most precise way currently available on the planet, with a cute little purely economic mathematical analysis, to show just how appallingly expensive this is?

She didn't look up from what she was doing.

—No, I would not.

—You will. I did a quick run of the numbers and converted the kunas to euros. Probiotic, a 5-decaliter container, the requisite treatment of at least four weeks, 1 dl per day, the cost negligible, fifty euros. Noni, 1 liter per month, fifty euros; aloe vera, twenty-five; cleansing tea, warming tea, linseed oil, beet juice, Biobran—too many more to name. So, I figure that for maintaining our physical constitution alone, we ought to be setting aside some two thousand five hundred kunas per month—in other words, nearly four hundred euros.

—In Europe that costs twice as much. The prices here are nothing to speak of.

—Nothing to speak of, but the average income here is also nothing to speak of.

—Well not everybody has to buy it, nobody's making them.

—Nobody is making them, but those with the most limited resources are also the sickest. Is illness pressuring them? If you intend to save someone using green energy, you should be saving the people who are the sickest. Pensioners, for instance. They are the neediest.

—They are, pensioners are the neediest, but that same older generation has exhibited no consciousness about a healthy diet, and that's why they are to blame for half of their complaints.

—They have exhibited no consciousness, because consciousness costs money. How can you and your acolytes claim this can possibly be paid for?

—I don't understand the question.

He stirred his oatmeal sweetened with honey; it was still too hot, so he got up from the table and paced between the door and the window.

—What I'm saying is that this story about a healthy life and healthy food is a bit hyped. I think those who sell healthy food are manipulating people to get their hands on profits.

She didn't tell him to sit down.

—I'd say this conversation is over.

—Why?

—Because you're negative.

—I am negative. You are positive. Positive in terms of euros. And besides, you and your like-minded pals are underhanded.

—Excuse me?

—You're underhanded. You have managed to foist a guilty conscience on people. Nothing glistens more than your marketing, and you've roped in physicians and pharmacists, mainly those wearing white lab coats.

She was grating the celery. She noticed how her movements were getting faster and faster.

—The white-coat wearers do so in keeping with their professional conscience. At least you are now in a situation when you must value those in lab coats.

—I value them, but I'm not blind. Today the white coats have stepped in to replace the black mantles of the clergy. And people believe in them and fear them with a pagan terror, just as they used to fear witch doctors and the inquisitors.

—They needn't fear.

—They needn't, but they do. And suddenly everybody is uncomfortable about eating what they eat. It's almost as if *normal* people have begun apologizing for a slab of meat.

Her hand stopped for a moment and she glared at him, furious.

—What are you saying? Those of us who don't eat meat are the sick ones?

—Oh, no. You couldn't be healthier. Fully conscious and with a healthy mind, you are on top of the numbers. So adept. How much does a kilo of lentils cost, which your shops sell in those little 20 decagram packets? Eh? How much does that little bag of flaxseed cost, imported from China? Eh? A ton of flaxseed there costs like your shitty little decagram sack. Shall we do the numbers together? Why so quiet?

—Your rudeness has made me quiet. The lentils and the flaxseed are farmed in a special, organic way and the cultivation is expensive, hence its high price.

—You don't say. Especially in China, where the wage of the workers who cultivate the flaxseed is incredibly low. And besides, my David knows that China is the most polluted place on earth. And you call this organic farming? How much land do you take up on this planet of ours? These things you sell at such fabulous prices are present in all the health food shops from Vancouver to Australia, from Moscow to Dubrovnik. Eh? Organic farming? Eh?

She didn't wait for him to sit or eat; she got up and collected the plates and cups.

—I am not involved in sales, and don't go prodding me with these primitive *eh*s. We know exactly why it is that the prices for health food, yes, *health* food, are higher than what we'd like.

—Oh, come on, nobody is accusing you of anything, but at least admit that your like-minded pals care about profit.

—About health, and then about profit, of course.

—*About profit*, of course, and then about health. And about disease. Who, healthy, would ever buy Noni juice that has been stored in crates on the outskirts of town in garages rife with rats and cockroaches? Yet they brazenly tout it as the best-selling juice drink in the world. If so, millions would be healthy beyond belief, yet the percentage of the population that is sick remains largely unchanged.

Then she did what she had almost never done. She respected food, and this was a first for her to take a full dish of oatmeal sweetened with honey and sprinkled with flaxseed and dump it into the garbage can.

—The people who want it buy it.

—The people who can afford to, my dear. It costs. And that's the world's biggest problem. The healthy folks who calmly shell out fifty euros for a bottle of a sketchy sour raspberry beverage that was *mysteriously produced on Tahiti* never think about how Tahiti is one of the poorest countries in the world, where people are probably dying from malnutrition. Right in the same place where the mysterious noni fruit is grown. You want to know the biggest problem in the world? It's the healthy people who are dying not from fatty foods, but from hunger.

—Since when have you, the dyed-in-the-wool cynic, become such a valiant protector of the poor and hungry?

—I'm not a protector, but I do have a conscience.

—Are you planning to join the ranks of fighters to protect the planet?

—Heaven forbid. Earth will protect itself.

—Earth will not protect itself. Earth, my dear, doesn't care who lives on it. It is up to us to protect both earth and life, so we can survive.

She tried to calm down. Again, she picked up her knife and went about chopping the celery.

—Wrong, my dear, wrong again. Our beloved mother planet is sick and tired of us. She has had it up to here and will very soon do all she can to rid herself of us.

—Well, unfortunately, she is not selective; if she were selective, she would get rid of people like you first.

—Well, well, and why is that?

—Because the amount of negativity you exude makes life impossible. We can't budge, not the two of us, or humankind.

—My God, I do pity you. Can you possibly believe I am that important? I truly, truly pity you; please accept my sincere condolences, my dear.

She stilled the hand that had been chopping the celery stalk. Raising it some 10 centimeters, she rotated her wrist and froze it at the moment when the light reflected off the steel blade. She was no longer bent over. She looked him straight in the eyes, and he at her motionless eyelids, which showed just how fully she was in control. With both movements and voice.

—Never pity a person who is holding a knife.

There was no grimace of mimicry on her face, and this sentence, pared down and quiet, stood between the two of them. He saw the blade reflected in her eyes, but the image looked cheesy, embarrassingly trivial, and first he smiled, even laughed, to see if he could compel her to fill the silence. She did not respond, and there hung his laugh, lopsided, pathetic, even fawning.

She smiled with the tiniest immeasurable delay, and he was horror-struck by the reaction in his body, his skin, or rather the hairs on it that bristled from the end of his nonexistent tail all the way to the back of his neck. This lesson in atavism was mastered in two or three seconds.

How she laughed at him! She chuckled, guffawed, shrieked, giggled.

—You were scared! Love, we genuinely frightened you!

—I was not afraid of *us*, love, I was not. Your imagination outstrips my fears.

—You were afraid of us, afraid of us!

He saw that she could no longer control her laughter. He turned away, sickened, and walked by her, but intentionally walked right by the hand that was holding the knife.

The kitchen walls and dishes rang with the sound of her cackles, and he intended to leave the room at once. But he didn't. He stopped.

He faced her again and looked at her hair, which shimmied and swayed from her laughter, and her neck, which was bared when, choking with an attack of guffaws, she dropped her chin to her chest. How he would have hungrily bitten her neck under the ears to smother her cackles and forced her to swallow that damned *us*! Instead, he was taken aback by an erection that restored his confidence, and, from behind, with both hands he grabbed her ass. He didn't let her go.

She stopped laughing. Set down the knife.

Boris Horak arrived at the hospital much later than he'd expected, but still in time to find David's mother talking with Inspector Vidošić.

\* \* \*

Vidošić knocked at the door only once, but he knew nobody would invite him in, so he entered very cautiously, his facial expression saying everything: he was sorry for coming and he apologized, but the situation was as it was.

Katarina got up and went over to Vidošić.

—You needn't say a word; I'm sure you wouldn't be here if you didn't have to be.

He was grateful to her for that.

—How's he doing?

—Better, we all think he's better.

She fixed her hair for longer than was necessary and saw that he was watching her hand.

—I am by his side constantly. Sometimes I read fairy tales to him that he used to like. The doctor recommended constant contact and speaking audibly of the things he loves. I feel I'm sending him energy that way. Even with these silly stories, about pastry chefs and caterpillars and accordions.

She was rattled.

—I read to him yesterday.

Vidošić smiled.

—I'm sorry I wasn't here, I haven't heard fairy tales in a long time. My boys are always deep in those computer games. I can't follow their imagination anymore. They don't even watch cartoons, and what they do watch, I don't understand.

—I hear you. David's no different. But now, when he can't play those games, maybe this helps a little. Of course, now and then I enjoy watching a cartoon with him. *Asterix*, for instance. I don't understand the other ones.

This lightened her spirits; she resorted to the usual parental grumbling and was grateful to Vidošić.

—Did you choose your brooch based on the story? A nice accordion player . . . Even I noticed it.

Katarina touched her brooch and wrapped her fingers around it.

—Ah, a gift from my sister. It was my birthday and our youngest sister is getting married, so they are all in a gift-giving mood.

Last year I went on a trip to Austria, and we stopped in at the Swarovski Museum. Everything there is crystal and the place is full of kitsch. Dado was bored; he could hardly wait for us to leave, and then we happened upon a surprising item on exhibit. You know, unusual; the accordion had crystal buttons, it gleamed, and, most appealing, it actually played. Dado was delighted, and he laughed and laughed. I'm grateful to my sister for getting me this for my birthday. I'll wear it till Dado recovers.

Vidošić smiled, but he didn't say anything, and, muddling through, Katarina went on.

—But what I liked most of all was a sculpture of a crystal spiderweb. Stunning.

They moved on from the story about the brooch, and Vidošić breathed a sigh of relief. He came back into the conversation.

—I saw plenty of spiderwebs like that when I was a kid. Dew like a glass bead, shimmering. So fleeting. The droplet drips away, the sun comes out, dries it up—the beauty is gone.

She smiled and patted her hair again. Actually, she flicked her bangs over an eyebrow and looked to the side. She was sure he was watching her hand.

Unfortunately, the rest of the conversation had to be dedicated to the matters that had brought the inspector to the hospital. He had to tell her that the murder victim's precise time of death had been established, and he was interested to hear whether Irma was at their house party by 9 PM that night. *Yes, she was.* David? *He was home that whole afternoon and evening.*

Boris Horak came in without knocking.

—Sorry if I interrupted your cozy little chat.

Both Katarina and Vidošić were thrown off-balance. Katarina was the first to collect herself.

—Would you please go out into the corridor and explain to David's dad why you came?

Horak bit his tongue and spent a few minutes with the inspector in the corridor. Everything was explained to him, and that they had *new moments* in their investigation, so he would have to ask the lady a few additional questions.

Horak heard him out and then calmly said:

—Sir, as I understand it, you are not interested in the health or life of my child. All you care about is whether he'll wake up so he can give you the first and last name, address, and, if possible, license plate number of the car that pushed him almost to his death. You are interested in David's mother's sister, so speak with that sister wherever you can find her. You can speak with David's mother wherever you like and as much as you like, but not here, in this hospital. I will personally ask the head doctor to prohibit you from barging into my child's room.

Vidošić had never experienced anything like this, and the only thing he could think of to say was:

—I am here on official business.

If there had been mirrors along the corridor, down which he quickly strode away, he would have spat.

Before he got into his car, he decided he would no longer talk with Irma Žiger in her house, and not even at the school. The police headquarters would soften her up.

*　　*　　*

That must have been Lovro. Yes, it was Lovro. Why was
I so scared of him? I have no idea, but I really was scared.
And it should have been funny, but it wasn't, so I was glad
he left right away, and I was glad when that man came
again. Mama is no longer irritated with him. I don't know
why she became kind all of a sudden, and I can't remember why he comes. Mama even sounded like she was
talking with him today in that way I don't like. Like . . . way
too friendly. Not friendly like with the doctor, but different friendly. This gets on my nerves. But what gets on my
nerves the most is that today she smelled like perfume.
Okay, fine, maybe she's thinking I'm getting a lot better, so
now she can think about her perfume, but I think it is a little because of this man. I can't see her too well, but if she is
flicking her bangs over her eyebrow, that's for his sake, for
sure. When she flicks her bangs over her eyebrow, I don't
like my mother. And Dad is sketchy too. Not because of his
hair, not that way, but it's like he and I know something,
but right now I can't remember what. He is talking with
that man out by the door so I can't hear, and that's why I
don't know what they're talking about. If I could hear, I'd
be able to remember right away who he is and I'd figure
out why he keeps coming. From the conversations he was
having with Mama, you can only learn that both of them
are stupid, and I mean stupid squared. They are just carrying on next to my bed. In that respect my dad is better.
Sometimes I have the impression that Dad is crying, but I

don't want to even think about that. I'm glad I can't see so well. He'd scare me shitless if I saw him crying, I think; I'd really think I'm dying, which, of course, I'm not. I only saw him once with tears in his eyes and I almost hated him—it scared me so badly. That was when my grandpa died, and his crying was almost normal then; after all, my grandpa was his dad, although it seems a little silly for you to have a father when you're already old yourself. It would be better for him not to cry, otherwise I'll really, really run away behind my curtain. Can you say *really run away*? Well, I said it, so I guess you can.

How weird is this? While that man was chatting with my mother, I felt as if there was something I wanted to remember, but right when I'd nearly remembered it, I wanted to go fast, as fast as I could possibly go, meaning *warp* speed, way down deeper behind the curtain, just so I wouldn't have to remember what it is I was about to remember. A little weird. And while Dad was patting my hand, I also wanted to and didn't want to remember something having to do with him. And it is practically the same with Mama. It turns out that there are all sorts of things I want to remember and don't want to remember, things someone else would like me to remember, while someone else maybe wouldn't. Totally weird. And when I don't feel like remembering something, I don't. I think of other things instead. When I was little, when Dad still lived with us, and when they fought, I distracted myself by thinking about all sorts of things: that I was a spider, that I was tickling Dad behind the ear while he was talking to Mama *that way*, or that I was Spider-Man and appeared at the window just to scare them. And once I imagined that I'd turned into a camel, and while they were arguing in the living room, I would, like, wander in there and chew and chew. That made me laugh like crazy and that weirded them out, and then for a while Mama kept always saying to Dad, *You're going to make our boy sick. He'll lose his mind.* Now I'm tired out from all this thinking. Maybe it would better for her to read me something than to fight with Dad.

That one about the caterpillar wasn't bad. When did she read it? Yesterday, I guess. I can't seem to figure out time. Light, the light bothers me. I don't know when it's night and when it's day. The caterpillar is okay, although it would have been better if she'd eaten the cabbage and shut up. She'd have changed into a butterfly, and that's pretty cool. I know that from *National Geographic*. When the teacher talked about it, I didn't remember anything. For whatever reason, I'm not one of those kids who's crazy about butterflies. But that's another story. And in this story, it looks as if those caterpillars who binged on the cabbage got the better deal. They became nice butterflies, while she became an accordion. Can you imagine someone pulling you out like that every day? La la la. But again, it's cool to be in the city and at an amusement park and at fairs. And on top of that, someone loves you like crazy. I was just scared Mama would start in about little dresses and stars. I'm talking nonsense only because I don't want to admit that I was scared of that kooky story about the caterpillar. I know it well, that story. When I was a little kid I listened to it a hundred times and I was never scared of it. But now I'm scared of the caterpillar and the butterflies and the accordion. All of it. When I put all that together, the things that scare me . . . turns out I'm not only stupid David, but totally crackpot David.

Here's my scowling dad. Now we'll do a round of *patting the cat*. But first, they have to go another round at each other.

I'm off behind the curtain to think, but not about caterpillars that play and sing.

Boris Horak didn't spend long at David's bedside. He told Katarina on no uncertain terms that he'd request that the head doctor insist on order in David's room. The processions had gone far beyond what was appropriate. This was not the Marija Bistrica shrine to the Virgin Mary. Not anybody could come tramping through.

## "Hava Nagila"

Damir was getting a little tired, and without saying anything to Our Little Lady, he worked his way out of the crowd, crossed with the traffic light at the intersection where Vukovarska joins Tratinska, and stopped at the concrete island with the clock surrounded by flowers.

Not far from there, a one-man band had set up. The man was waiting for Mass to end in the nearby church. At the moment, the congregation's singing was being broadcast through speakers so the crowd that was standing in the doorways could take part, as could those who were busy with buying and selling on the square.

Damir turned to the one-man band and raised his hand. He gestured toward the church. Rarely did he do something like that.

—This is the Church of St. Joseph.

—I know.

—Right. Of course you know; after all, he was your ... your fiancé.

—No, he *was* my husband.

—What do you mean, *was*.

—Just that. Was.

—His church doesn't interest you?

—He's free to take care of what belongs to him. I have my own worries.

Her voice was edgy.

—But aren't ... up there ... aren't you together?

—Up there it's members of the same generation who meet, not families. Families get together on the holidays, like here. Many are surprised.

—Where is that, up there?

—That's just how we say it. People can't imagine anything beyond their own worlds, so that's how it's said: *up there*. Of course, it isn't.

—Where is it, then?

She looked at him rakishly.

—Up there!

He laughed.

—You don't get along with Saint Joseph?

NADA GAŠIĆ

—With *Saint* Joseph, I get along. But he was not always a *saint*. He used to be my husband. Joseph. Husbands are never saints.

She waved her little hand.

—There are always things between husbands and wives that go unexplained. Better that you don't know.

He saw that she'd dropped her head, signaling she wanted to leave this topic behind. Damir rocked gently, not to disturb her.

He heard something. It wasn't unpleasant, and he quieted down. He waited for the sound to come quite close. As if someone far, far away were singing?

He dropped his head as far down as he could and listened intently. Was that her singing? No, it wasn't his imagination. She really was singing.

—You're singing?

—I am.

—A hymn? Are you following the one we can hear from the church?

—Pardon? No. No way. I'm singing an ordinary one.

—A little louder?

—Sure.

He cocked his ears, held his breath. Finally, he heard the hoarse little voice.

—Hava nagila, hava nagila, hava naglia venis meha . . . Come on, Damir, sing with me!

—I don't know how to sing.

—Everybody knows how to sing.

—I don't.

—Come on, with me. Hava nagila.

—I can't.

—Come on, come on. Hava . . .

He joined in.

—Hava nagila, hava nagila.

—There, see, you do know!

Damir sang. Our Little Lady sang.

Nobody heard, but their song rang out gorgeously under the clock on the main square in Trešnjevka.

*Hava nagila, hava nagila, hava nagila ve-nismecha*
*Hava neranena, hava neranena*

When they reached the end of the verse, they laughed the way people always do when finding themselves in a predicament after a sudden outburst of singing joy.

—What else do you know how to sing?

—*Madame Butterfly.*

She laughed, which sounded like a child tapping its fingernail on glass.

Damir didn't understand what she said or why she was laughing. To find his way out of the predicament, he himself started singing.

—Hava nagila . . .

She joined in. They sang; they sang beautifully.

The passersby moved away; the more polite among them looked down and sped up their pace. There were disturbed to see this older disabled man mumbling and drooling, rocking back and forth by the flowers planted around the old Trešnjevka clock.

They finally had had their fill of singing.

—What were we singing about?

—We were inviting people to enjoy themselves.

—What language were we singing in?

—Hebrew.

—Which?

—Hebrew.

—And in what language did you sing when you were a little . . . girl?

—I can't remember that I sang. And I can't remember ever being a little girl. Childhood was so short back then. Especially for girls.

There was an angry bitterness in her voice.

—Especially for *cute* little girls.

She stressed this, but she wasn't sure whether Damir would understand the sentence.

—What language did you speak?

—Aramaic, I think. But we don't know that for sure, and I can't quite remember. It seems to me that language is always the same. Regardless of what other people call it. That's how language is. You always speak the same way, in your language, regardless of what other people call it.

—I haven't heard of that language. The one you said.

—Many haven't. That church there is full, yet it may be that among them there is nobody who has heard of the language I speak.

—Do you know all the languages of the world?

—Many, but not all. Not all.

—Why?

—Because there are people who have never heard of me. Their languages are the ones I don't know.

She scolded him a little.

—Damir, you want to learn what other people study their whole lives. And never fully master.

Done with talking, she lowered her head and her hair spilled from her hood all down her face.

If anyone were to take a good look at the two of them, they'd see a frowzled old man dressed in threadbare corduroy pants and a faded plaid shirt whose right pocket, poor fellow, was decorated with an odd pencil or a tassel of black silk thread with a ruddy glint.

*    *    *

Done with her classes for the day, Irma went to the restroom to tidy up before she left the school. Brushing her hair required both hands; her red hair had always offered resistance. It was a chore to tame.

She stopped midstroke. An alien face was looking at her from the mirror. It was hers and it wasn't.

*What have you done, Irma, what have you done? There will be a way to fix this, a way to fix this. What have you done, what have you done? There will be a way to fix this, a way to fix this.*

She sighed deeply and retrieved her face. Out she went into the corridor, calm, self-confident, standing tall and aware that all those who were hurrying to go through their already-closed classroom door were looking at her. She came to the stairs.

Leaning on the banister, a young man was rubbing his ear-ring. He said hi to her, but his greeting was intoned in such a way that stopped her.

—I said hi.

She nodded and started to walk by him. He blocked her way with his arm, and she lost her temper.

                                               NADA GAŠIĆ

—Švojić, are you in your right mind?

He smiled but did not lower his arm.

—Oh yes.

She was very familiar with the lascivious smiles of adolescents.

—Drop your arm. I'll send you to the principal.

Now he was sneering.

—I doubt it.

—Švojić, you are going to the principal's office!

—Okay. Should I tell him or should I go straight to the cops and say that I saw you on Sunday evening around 10:30?

Irma got herself under control.

—I'm not interested in what you saw. Drop your arm.

—I saw you when you were getting out of a black suv and getting into your car, which had been parked all day near my house. You drove off toward your place. We aren't exactly neighbors, but we do live nearby. However, if we agree to agree, I can keep my mouth shut.

He licked his upper lip with the tip of his tongue.

Irma watched him closely, and then she, too, smiled lasciviously.

—Better for your health that you don't breathe a word. If you keep your mouth shut, I also won't say a word to anyone. Black suvs can be dangerous.

She took a lock of her hair and brushed him across the face with it.

He dropped his arm.

Her phone rang. Irma answered the call, and with measured steps she went down the stairs. She did not turn around. In the car she took another phone from her purse, checked it quickly, and put it back.

Inspector Vidošić had summoned her to police headquarters for a conversation, and she didn't want to waste time on conversations of any kind.

She waited at the front desk for them to check her ID and sign her in. One of the uniforms took her to Vidošić's office.

He was Vidošić, but he was not the same man she'd spoken with at her house. This man, who was sitting at his desk, greeted her, pointed to the chair across from him, and looked down before he said:

—What are we going to hear today?

Irma raised her shoulders and didn't drop them.

—There have been some changes in the case. The exact time of the murder has been established. We are not only interested in the night now, but also the afternoon and evening. Do tell, where were you on 25 October around 9 PM?

She said nothing.

—Ms. Žiger, I must warn you that this is a conversation that doesn't have to be recorded, but it could be. You are not a suspect.

Irma spoke. She was calm.

—I don't care whether you record it or not. Like I said, I spent the afternoon shopping, and later, with the gifts for my sisters, I drove home and we had a party in our garden shed.

—We have already heard that. More precise.

—I can't be more precise. Maybe, if I were to concentrate, I could remember precisely. Maybe. It seems to me that by 9 PM I was already done with everything and was back home.

Vidošić kept his eyes on his desk.

NADA GAŠIĆ

—Once more, explain your relationship to the victim. When did you spend time together, who did you socialize with, where did you go?

—Nothing special. Movies, the theater, an occasional cup of coffee.

—Private gatherings, parties, anything like that?

She was briefly quiet, and then answered, calmly:

—That too.

—Where? With whom?

—I can't tell you that, because I don't keep track of the addresses. These are usually quick dates, music, conversation. That sort of thing. Like everybody else in this city who has no obligations.

—No obligations?

—I mean those who don't have families of their own.

—If everyone who didn't have a family went out on *quick dates*, there would be quite a crowd, wouldn't you say, Ms. Žiger?

Vidošić tapped his pencil on the desk and did not look at Irma. He paused for a long time.

—Did you go to your friend's place?

—Yes, I did, but not often.

—Did she go to yours?

—The same.

—Summer vacations?

—Well, we did spend vacation time together over the summer. Both of us are single.

Vidošić got up.

—Tell me, how did your friend seem recently? Was she worried, restless? Were there any changes in her behavior?

—I didn't notice anything.

—With whom did she have intimate relations? A boyfriend? Several? Lovers? Friends?

—As far as I know, recently, no.

—And earlier?

—She is younger than I am. I didn't know much about her boyfriends.

—Names?

—No, I don't remember.

—It would be good for you to remember those names. And to remember the names of the friends the two of you had in common. And acquaintances. As soon as possible.

She said nothing.

—Was your friend invited to attend your sister's wedding?

—Yes, she was. She was invited as one of my party, yes.

—Interesting. You are close enough that you'd invite her to your sister's wedding, but not close enough to remember the name of her ex-boyfriend. Or current friends.

She didn't answer. Vidošić went back to his desk.

—When will the funeral be held for the deceased?

Irma now stared, unblinking, at the door. She was quiet for too long.

—I don't know, I found it too hard to call her folks. This has shaken me. I didn't ask anyone at school. I start to cry as soon as I say her name.

—Will you be going to Vinkovci?

—I don't know. Because of my nephew and my sister's wedding, it is possible that I won't go. Vinkovci is far away.

—Well, you don't need to go that far. Here, I'll pass on the information. The deceased will be cremated at Mirogoj. A strange friendship, wouldn't you say, Ms. Žiger?

She said nothing. Vidošić said she could go, but then he stopped her at the door.

—Wait a minute. I keep forgetting to ask you, was your friend worried about anything recently?

—No, I don't think she was. I told you, I didn't notice anything.

—And you, Ms. Žiger, are you afraid of something, or someone?

She shook her head.

As soon as she got into her car, she took out her phone, checked it briefly, and then put it back in her purse.

She held the steering wheel and watched her hands slide and leave a moist trace on the plastic. She had to put on gloves. From the Heinzelova police headquarters, she went straight to the hospital.

*   *   *

Vidošić sat down and spun around on his chair. Then he paced the corridor, went to see the secretary, then went to the restroom. Something was lingering in the air after Irma Žiger's visit. In the corridor he passed by a man whose face seemed familiar, but as the man didn't say hi, Vidošić walked by him and forgot him that instant. He went back to his office.

He had a lot to do, and after a full hour spent on the phone, studying autopsy reports and photographs of the crime scene, and having conversations with his bosses, he summoned Simčić and Zdilar.

—Where did Žigerica go today?

—Nowhere special, stores, the school.

—Don't let her out of your sight even for a minute. You hear me?

The boss stretched.

—She'll be singing soon, Žigerica will sing soon.

On his way out, with a troubled expression, Simčić turned to Vidošić and began to cough.

—Boss, a man was looking for Kasumić today.

Zdilar laughed.

—Not Kasumić, Tesla. He hid his nickname from us.

Vidošić stopped stretching.

—Who asked for him?

Simčić coughed and Zdilar was faster.

—It wasn't the same guy from the other day, the one wearing camo. This one was well-dressed, clearly from around here. Maybe he's a little closer to our profession. That's what he looked like. They probably registered him at the front desk.

—I am the only one giving out information about Kasumić.

While they were on their way out, Vidošić called his secretary.

—Let the front desk know that anyone inquiring about Kasumić is to be sent to me.

Later he buried himself in his paperwork.

*　*　*

—The document she signed, be sure to have it processed immediately.

—No problem there. You won't have to wait even for a single day.

—Let it be entered in whatever books and registers it needs to be entered into, because my blueprints are ready to go. Am I making myself clear?

—Yes. All that matters is that we have her signature now.

*　　*　　*

Irma entered the room just as a smiling nurse was leaving and greeted her courteously.

Katarina was surprised.

—You didn't say you'd be coming. What brings you here?

—I wanted to see Dadek and see how you're doing.

—It's good, thank God, it's good. Everybody is so, so kind here.

—Thank goodness, at least that. Does his father come?

—He comes, but he's always tense.

—Oh, I know, but he has connections. He's probably already in good with the head doctor, that's never a bad thing.

—No, of course not, he's welcome to come. I can handle it.

—Katja, I am only here for a minute; you know how much work Ita has dumped on me. Thank God I cleaned up the grave yesterday. I wouldn't have had time today.

—Well, good.

Irma tied her hair and shrank a little into her jacket.

—Katja, may I ask you for a favor?

—Fire away.

—I doubt the inspector will be so intrusive, but if this Vidošić, I believe his name is Vidošić, comes, and if he asks you what time I came to the party the other night, tell him, please, that I was there already at 9 PM, and maybe even a little earlier. I'm sick from all this, I'm in a state of shock, and I have no strength left to wrangle with a cop.

Katarina said nothing. Irma's eyes filled with tears.

—Katja, I'm begging you, as my sister who looked after me like a mother, please, tell him that.

Katarina looked away.

—I already told him. Exactly that.

Katarina pulled away when Irma came over to kiss her. Irma blew kisses to Dadek and left. Katarina would never forget how Irma didn't go to David's bed, even for a moment.

I'm so glad Irma didn't kiss me. That's all I need right now. When I come out from behind the curtain, the first thing I'll do is write: *Kissing David Horak is banned.*

Ah, at last, stupid David! Stupid, stupid David! Of course—the inspector! Mama was calling that man who was here before Irma *Mr. Inspector.* And now they are talking about him. The inspector. I know him, but I can't quite remember where I know this inspector from and why I know him, and I can't quite picture his face. He knows me and I think he is coming here because of me. After him the room gets this stinky smell from some drink or other, but not something he drank, whatever, but like he drank it before and never in his whole life will he get rid of the smell. Always the same. Like when Dad and I go out to a café, and we smell as if we've been drinking and smoking. That smell is the first thing I remembered, because the guy who was here before him had the same stink.

But, of course, I'm hopeless; I can't remember when I saw them, and even less what we talked about. And it's as if they asked me about something very, very important, but I can't remember what exactly. I'll remember, at some point. But right now, remembering is not working.

If someone were to hear me, they'd probably ask how come I'm talking so much on the inside, when otherwise I mainly don't talk much. This is a little weird, but I think I'm smarter inside than I am outside. Inside, I know all kinds of words; I can talk pretty shrewdly on the inside, and I get everything. But on the outside, I get all flustered and come across like a dimwit. At school everybody sounds smarter than me, just because they are chatterboxes and don't care a bit about what they say. Like that girl, Horvat: she chatters day and night, and the teacher doesn't dare flunk her, except when we do written tests. She talks like a windup doll and always manages to get at least a C, and only on tests do I get some sort of decent grade. But when the teacher calls on me, I sit there silent like a blockhead. And when she tells me to come to the blackboard, I clam up until the day after tomorrow. A pure catastrophe. Basically, that's why I don't talk a lot. Well, actually, that depends on who I'm with. I talked a lot with Grandpa. But everybody talks a lot with their grandpas and grandmas. And then the grandpas and grandmas tell everybody they have smart grandchildren. Right. All of them smart. Fine, but my grandpa wasn't like that. He didn't go around saying he had a smart grandson, though I know he thought so. My grandpa was a special case. He wasn't like the others. One way with their grandchild and another way with everyone else. He was a straight shooter with everybody, but with me he was a little straighter. If he asked me something, he asked because he was interested in my answer and because he listened to what I told him. For instance, when he asked how things were going at school, I told him that we learned about camels, and that Kovačić knocked me down in PE and then I bashed him; then after that my grandpa never would say *so have you eaten*. First, he'd ask me all about camels, and then about how I bashed Kovačić, and then he'd ask whether I'd eaten. But other people would definitely ask *have you eaten*, and Mama would also ask where Kovačić hit me. What I want to say is that my grandpa went somehow straight ahead with questions. He'd have sorted out things here. First, he wouldn't let the nurse show me naked in front of everybody; he wouldn't be calling my name all the time; he wouldn't let Mama keep crying; and I think his son, my dad, would pat me less on the hand. And he would definitely forbid them from fighting and definitely, definitely, very definitely, he'd forbid them from dressing me in a nightgown. But fine, Grandpa was old and it makes sense that he died. I cried a whole lot, but I cried less than I thought I'd cry while Grandpa was still alive and when he got sick. He had taught me that older people die but younger people don't. He always said, *What matters is that everything proceeds in the proper order*, so that's why I think he would have introduced a little order here, and he'd explain to them right away that there's not very much reason to be afraid, because this isn't my turn yet, following the so-called *proper order*. There.

That is what I think about Grandpa, but when I think about my dad and my mom, I never think about them as *my parents*, the way they say it at school. My dad is my dad, and my mom is my mom. It doesn't bug me that they are, like they say, divorced. It bugs me more that everybody thinks I'm sad that they're divorced and that's why I'm not such a good student and that's why I have so many unexcused absences. Half the class, well maybe not half, but a lot of the kids in the class are divorced, I mean their parents are, and it would be total chaos if all of them were crummy students because of that and all had unexcused absences. Arbanić's parents are divorced, and he's the best student in the class; Horvatica's parents aren't divorced, and she's as stupid as a goat. I am not the best student, and sometimes I skip out from school and go off from home because I can't bear to be at home anymore, but actually I don't know why it is that I can't bear it. All I know is that I have to get out. It's as if at home I can't think in peace and quiet, because when I am quiet for a long time and stare, for instance, at the same model car for half an hour, then my mom starts in: *What are you thinking about? Did something happen at school? Something happened while you were with Dad?* And then she's terribly worried while we eat, and she doesn't look at her plate but at me, and then I start getting edgy, and I do something on purpose, like spill my juice. I know that's totally weird, but, still, I spill it. And then she stops being worried and gets angry and starts threatening. Her whole life she has been threatening people, and me most of all. Like, you're not going to get a phone, you can't watch television whenever you like, you're grounded, and things like that. Then I leave. Not always, but often, I leave. And if I'm out a little longer, then she gets scared and she cries for a while, but for a while she stops with the threats and those dumbass bans. And then Dad is better, because he, of course, first hears that I'm not there when I am supposed to be, either at home or at school. She always blabs. But he becomes better, though he doesn't have so much to make up for, because we, my dad and I, aren't together all the time, so he doesn't have as many chances to be bad. We're together every other weekend, so it's like I'm a guest in his house every other week, and when you're a guest in someone's house, then you aren't going to be rude to him. And actually, folks, the funniest thing is that I have the feeling it's not just me being a guest at Dad's but that he is a guest with me, although not in my apartment, but, you know ... How can I say this? It's as if he's my guest in Zagreb. Fine, he pays for everything, but in a way it's me, when we have our weekend together, taking him around town. Before he always took me to the places I liked the most, the zoo and those things, but now, recently, since I noticed him worrying about secretly eating meat, and he's sort of a mess, I suggest watching sports and things like that, which I don't like but he does like. And so it turns out that he is my guest. And he, of course, is alarmed when Mama tells him I'm not around, though he never tells me that, but he has these conversations with me, like, for instance, *tell your daddy everything*. And I don't tell anyone *everything*, especially not Dad. But he tells other people that we're *friends*. Right. I'd rather choose Big Boy Damir as my friend. He, at least, never speaks at all. And I definitely would not choose for a friend someone whose wife is always saying what's healthy and what isn't. Like *beef is death*. Well, it is if a cow is alive, it chases you, you fall, and then it tramples your head. Then beef is death. It's a little silly, but I don't think about her that way only because she's Dad's wife, so it's like normal for me to think of her only in the worst way. No, she isn't even the worst. She's a little wacky, like Horvatica, though Horvatica is younger so it's not so obvious. With Dad's wife you see the wackiness right away. A lot. When she puts a slice of cake on a little plate and immediately says, *This is made with integral whole wheat flour*; that's how I learned the word "integral," and the only thing I can't figure out are what the integrals are doing in math. There. You can imagine what it would look like if everybody in the world, when someone gives them something to eat, immediately said what it's made of. Or someone looks at a tree and you tell them right away what chlorophyll is. I also know about chlorophyll from *National Geographic*. Or, you're taking a tram and over the loudspeaker they explain about the tram's engine—okay, fine, that's a bad example, because that might actually be interesting. I mean it's a little weird that Dad married her, and he's no dummy. He's even smart, but it's as if he's embarrassed about being smart, so he doesn't talk much and says he'd rather be writing than talking. In this, I'm not like him, because I'd rather not be writing or talking. Well, okay, we're kinda similar. He and I are smarter on the inside. He has plenty of good sides. For instance, when I was little, he didn't let anybody scare me. Other kids were scared, but I was only scared when I had a fever, because then I'd think something, not black, exactly, but more purple like ink, was sitting by the door, wrapped in its butterfly wings. I told Mama, and she began to cry and said, *Don't be scared, sweetie, there's nothing there*, so then I got even more scared because I thought Mama didn't see what was really, really visible. And then I said the same thing to Dad, and he went right over to the door and gave such a kick to that purple monstrosity, that gigantic butterfly, or whatever it was, that I never saw it again, even when I had fevers. There, now I've blurted out why it is that I'm not a big fan of butterflies. And for a while, when I was still little, I called him Daddy–Dragon. Like, he was as fearless as a dragon.

Does Dad talk to himself like this on the inside? Dunno. I think I'd be scared if I found out he talks on the inside. But if he does, he doesn't talk in fits and starts like I do, stupid David, but organizes everything in the proper order. Like my grandpa. But not the same.

## *David's father organizes everything in the proper order*

*And now, as I'm writing about my first wife, this brings me back to my father. My father did not accept my ex-wife, and it never occurred to him to permit her to move in with us on Vodnikova. She had her own*

290                                                    NADA GAŠIĆ

reasons for staying put in her house in Trešnjevka—there were issues having to do with the property rights to the house, and she also felt her younger sisters still needed her. So that's how I ended up in Trešnjevka, among people who, though familiar, were so alien, so far from me in every possible way, that I'm amazed I lasted as long as I did among them. Yes. It now seems to me that my father was not the only one who, ever since he met her, could not stand my wife. Now I realize I couldn't stand her myself. From the very start of our relationship. I know it sounds strange, but you probably understand better than I do that the process of falling in love and its duration are metaphysical manifestations that have no tangible explanation and are the result of our hormones, and it is possible from the moment you fall in love to know that you should be fully aware that this person, all of her, completely, in her entirety, with all her habits, her background, her thinking, her inclinations, her relationship to the world, even her looks, all this is intolerable for you. Still, you can't resist her. This is something even those much smarter than I am don't understand, so I won't waste time on it, and I certainly won't look for excuses in flat-footed stories and stolid phrases like: she changed. She did not change.

Believe me, she is who she is and has always been, from the moment I met her, and I have nothing to reproach her for. We met in the early 1990s. Both of us were late in starting our studies, but that was normal then and the war was our blanket excuse for everything. Those were days of wartime euphoria, a sense of community, when hairdressers, doctors, professors, waitresses, journalists, tram conductors, psychiatrists, and police officers all said the same things, thought the same ways, probably felt the same. What do you think? That I was any different? I wasn't. I believed everything other people said. I was for our side, heart and soul; I truly hated the enemies, and

not just hated, I sincerely considered them lesser beings and was root-
ing, genuinely, for every single one of our defenders. The only thing
that separated me from the defenders was my total awareness that
I was not capable of open warfare or beating my chest, so I did my
best to avoid the army and combat. And I succeeded. I waved around
documents about problems with my kidneys and managed to evade
the draft. I admit, both to myself and to you, that I am someone who
is happier admiring fights from the sidelines. I admired our military
successes from the sidelines as well.

She was a breath of fresh air in this whole story. She was one of
those concerned, active types who spent night and day lending a hand
at parish offices, attending meetings where there was emotional talk
and even more emotional singing. She, a student engaged to the max,
stood apart from the rest of us quiet supporters with what I'll call her
volunteer efforts. She stood apart with her direct engagement. It must
be that I subconsciously hoped I'd find it easier to believe my own story
about my ailing kidneys with her at my side—a committed activist in
all possible wartime groups—and that her social standing would rub
off on me because I was intimately involved with her and her sincere
suffering for each and every displaced person, a true activist. I don't
have many illusions about myself from that time. I introduced her to
my circle of friends, who listened to her closely while she spoke about
her work through her parish to help those in the greatest need, as the
phrase goes, and how by night she dug through the old clothes and even
older medicines that came by the ton to our city. They even voiced loud
admiration for her, and from the shadow she cast I picked up a bit of
the undeserved glory of someone who was, if I can call it this, behind
the lines. Suddenly my tale about ailing kidneys seemed more convinc-
ing. I forgave myself for everything I'd been doing to evade military

NADA GAŠIĆ

service. My father was the only one who watched her. He made no effort to pander to her, nor did he admire her. Nothing. It was really a challenge to please him. And what could he have thought of me? That's the man he was.

Both she and I managed to graduate, and our professional titles are the one thing we have in common. There is absolutely nothing before or after that dipl. ecc. that ties us. Though we were both born and bred in Zagreb, I'd gladly swear that we're not from the same city. She was born and raised in Trešnjevka. Since birth she has carried the burden of the grotesque story about the loss of her father in a long-since-forgotten flood, which is mentioned in the media only when there is a round-number anniversary. She grew up with her mother, who remarried and went on to have two more daughters and died when the little ones were still quite young. This meant that my ex-wife took up their care on her own. When her stepfather, the father of her half sisters, died, she really was a parent to the girls. My ex lived in a community where everything came down to petty gossip and schemes for how to get more money. Her interests and her desires had nothing in common with mine, and when I finally outgrew that phase of what I'll call being in love, I began to feel an intense, even physical, repulsion toward her. For a long time, I couldn't even remember what had attracted me; I couldn't remember those special things she surely had. I secretly pored over photographs and saw nothing remarkable: medium height, henna-dyed hair, always flicking her bangs over her eyebrow, blue eyes, a forced smile, as with most people when their picture is being taken—nothing, absolutely nothing. I needed time and time and more time until it became clear to me that I could no longer abide her meekness. This was precisely the rare trait that had drawn me to her in the first place, yet in the end it completely pushed me away. I came to hate what had first attracted me. I hated

*that she was meek. This word, meek, is heard less and less often nowa-*
*days, not for any linguistic reason but because no longer are there meek*
*people around us. I am convinced this is one of the first words to die a*
*natural death. Nobody will brand its use unacceptable, but nobody will*
*stand up for it. It will fade away the way a rare species of insect dies out*
*when the endemic plant on which it feeds is destroyed. Soon enough*
*there will be nobody left who can be described with this word, and by*
*the process of natural selection it will simply disappear. There, I could*
*no longer abide this meek woman. No point in even mentioning men;*
*nobody expects them to be meek, but women, women ... Around me*
*new, interesting women began coming of age, a whole generation of*
*partners, while she remained pinioned by her Trešnjevka family—a*
*forever simpering, fatherless child who courts everybody with a smile*
*and agrees in advance to everything. The child in her sought paternal*
*support from me, but I didn't want to be her father, I didn't want to be*
*a father to my wife. And out of that intolerance toward her as a person*
*who is constantly, in every way, giving ground was born a true, incur-*
*able physical repulsion: first it was her meek smile that bothered me,*
*her retreat at the least conflict; then her idiotic henna hair dye both-*
*ered me, the smell that spread from her head as soon as it got even a*
*little wet; then wearing wired bras that thrust her breasts out unnatu-*
*rally, when I knew her body had only snippets of breasts; then the lock*
*of hair flicked over her eye, through which she'd look at me meekly—all*
*of it, absolutely all of it, repulsed me. Her walk, smile, smell, everything.*
*And what's worse, I began to feel a visceral disgust at the way she ate. In*
*my earliest childhood, my family taught me how to behave at the table,*
*and when I was a teenager, planting my elbows on the table was one of*
*the first acts of defiance against my father, but when I met my future*
*ex-wife, instead of understanding that we were galaxies apart from*

NADA GAŠIĆ

each other with our different backgrounds and upbringings and running away as fast as my feet would carry me, I found it adorable that she didn't break off pieces of bread but chomped straight onto the slice. You know the way, so primitive. And when I finally came to, I was no longer able to sit at the same table with her, and I hated her from the bottom of my heart because she chomped onto her sorry piece of bread. I began to hate the food she made. There was nothing more disgusting to me than the huge roasts that began arriving on the table when the reign of cheap meat began at the shopping mall.

This all culminated at the table. It was all about fingernails. Until the moment when her nails followed the natural ends of her fingers, I could say she had beautiful hands, something relatively rare for people of her background. Yes, her hands were, actually, the only part of her that was beautiful. I didn't even notice the changes in manicure fashion, until one day she shoved under my nose a set of horrifying white shovels on the tips of her fingers. And what's worse, she thought this made her sexier. More appealing. To me? I know I'd jumped on her earlier, I can't deny that, but I said terrible things to her then, mainly about her background, about the dirt from gardens on the edge of town that can never be hidden, no matter how hard she scrubbed or if she glued on fake nails, with the scum of feces lodged under those nails, which she'd end up eating with her bites of bread. After a few days I apologized, and, probably as a gesture toward reconciliation, I performed certain physical activities with her, but, in a way, having seen those fingernails, I was gone. My brain simply walked away. I no longer had control over it. It left on a journey of its own and did what seemed far more natural at the time than living with a person who had white shovels instead of fingernails. It sought someone close. But more about my mental wandering after I get some rest.

*　　*　　*

—Damir, do you have anyone in the world except Cilika? Anyone you're close to?

—No, I have no one, at least that's what I think.

—No cousins?

—No, nobody. First, I was in a home, but I don't remember that. And when I was seven, I was with Gramps, but he was Uncle then, and his wife was Auntie, and later Cilika took me over once Gramps got too old. For money. They take care of me.

Our Little Lady could see he looked dejected.

—Damir, did I hurt your feelings?

—No.

—Do you want us to go home?

—No, I haven't shown you hardly anything.

—Okay. Where to now?

—Would you like us to sit in the park?

Not without pride, Damir showed her a strange pit overgrown with old, gnarled trees and neglected bushes, which the people of Trešnjevka had referred to as their park ever since the beginning of time.

—I'd rather not; I'm not fond of land that dips down into a hollow. It draws the damp.

For no particular reason, she added:

—And I'm not fond of caves either. Also because of the damp. And besides, what kind of a park is this?

—This is a real park, ours, Trešnjevka's. A proper park.

—Fine. A proper park, but I have the right to say that I don't like dips and hollows.

He bristled. She ignored this; she was holding forth as if the main square and the park and everything around them belonged to her, and as if she had taken Damir out for a walk, and not that he had taken her. She fidgeted in his pocket.

—Turn around, turn around toward those tall, white buildings. They used to sell firewood there. A long time ago they brought it in on carts that were pulled by horses, and later by truck. The same with melons.

—Even I remember that. Did you know they also brought in all sorts of animals too? There were birds and hares, rabbits, chickens. Once a gander bit me right through his cage.

—A gander? In the middle of Zagreb?

Our Little Lady's laughter shook Damir's pocket and was infectious. Then the laughter died down, and both of them went quiet. The time had come to be still, until Our Little Lady began to fidget again.

—There used to be a prison near here.

—No, there never was a prison here.

—Yes, there was, there was a prison.

With her teensy hand she gestured toward the intersection of Savska and Vukovarska.

—The prison was over there.

—I don't remember.

—It was a prison. People died so fast inside that I can't remember whether anybody had the time to call me.

She shivered.

—There was a war. I think people called it the *Second*. That's right, it was a war, but it wasn't soldiers dying in the prison. It was civilians. A strange custom you share with the rest of humankind.

Now it was Damir's turn to do the ignoring.

She noticed, so she spoke a little louder:

—Back when there was all that water, your park was a dangerous, murky lake, and a little farther from the farmers market, everything was under water. Terrible water.

Damir ran his hand over his face as if wiping it off. For a time he didn't want to listen to her. Once he calmed down, he asked:

—Why do you always appear in strange places? Or to strange people like me?

Our Little Lady pretended not to hear.

—Why don't you appear in . . . in big cities, on squares?

—It's not I who decides that, but those who see me.

—Okay, fine, you don't decide. But why don't they ever see you in big cities?

—Because of the traffic; there'd be huge traffic jams.

—Aren't there big traffic jams anyway?

—No, no. Those are different sorts of traffic jams. Imagine if columns of thousands and thousands of people were pouring toward your main square. And people crawling on their knees. Ha?

—Ugh!

—Yes, ugh.

—Still, I'd like to be able to show you on Ban Jelačić Square.

—I know, I know. But an agreement is an agreement. Besides, they'd have to put up a church for me on the square, or at least a monument. It would be a problem. And even the name of the square—would it stay the same?

—I don't know. I wouldn't be the one to decide.

—What would we do with the statue of the guy riding the horse? They already moved that once. It caused no end of trouble.

—Oh, I know about that, but it would be nice to show you off right by the horse. Or under the clock. I'd like to show you to everybody on Ban Jelačić Square under the clock.

—Damir, we're not going to talk about this anymore.

—Okay.

He ventured off to wander among the vegetable stands. He jostled with the women; they clucked at him, annoyed, and in the end he was alarmed by all the handcarts they were pulling along behind them, which he stumbled over twice, painfully banging his ankle. This tired him out, and then he remembered that among the kiosks selling clothes there were fewer people. It was also more interesting there. At least for him.

—Our Little Lady, would you like me to take you to where it's even more colorful than here?

She turned to look at him, and he even thought he saw her clapping her teensy hands.

—Yes, take me where there are pretty dresses!

—I'll take you, but I don't know whether they are particularly pretty, or if you'll like them.

—Don't you worry about my tastes. Just take me there.

Damir made his way among the stands selling clothing. Nobody offered him anything, nobody said anything to him. Our Little Lady was silent.

He was the first to speak.

—Well, there you have clothes, as much as you like.

—I don't like it—show me something different. I don't like gray, and I don't like the color black.

He turned and walked, flustered, by the stand selling lingerie. When the woman at the counter called out, *Panties, come right this way, my ladies, panties cheap*, he would have been happiest hiding far away. He turned abruptly and found himself in front of a booth selling toys.

Our Little Lady shrieked:

—How marvelous!

This made him a little angry.

—But those are toys. They're dolls, not clothes.

—Please, take me closer, please, to the one on the right!

—But I'm telling you, they are little dolls . . . clothes for toys, baby dolls.

He saw his little guest literally hanging out of his pocket, and this scared him.

—Watch it—you'll fall!

Cautioned, she dropped back down into the pocket up to her waist, but she didn't give up.

—Look at that see-through one, and the pink one!

Damir came over closer to the booth and waited for the vendor to chase him off. She did give him a look and kept an eye on his hands. Thieving hands. But she did not look at the pockets on his shirt.

Our Little Lady began to moan.

—If only I could touch it. Just for a minute.

— I can't get that close. They'll chase us away.

The woman behind the counter finally decided that the man with the hunched back was not a threat; the child inside him was enjoying looking at the toys and nothing more. Damir, out of terror that Our Little Lady might fall out of his pocket, began to drool, and the woman turned away, disgusted. He took advantage of the moment. They went over to the doll dresses. Our Little Lady stretched out her hand, fingered the cloth, and looked despondent. Damir felt sorry for her.

—Would you like to rest? You probably aren't very comfortable in my pocket. Maybe we could go over to that empty bench over there? I'll take you out.

—I'm not sure.

—Nobody will be taking the seat next to me.

Her gaiety came back.

—You are so thoughtful. I would enjoy a little rest.

The bench was awkwardly placed, facing huge sunshades, so Damir was quite sure nobody would join them, and he sat down. He carefully lifted his hand and didn't turn his head while Our Little Lady clambered out. She found a comfortable perch, lowered her collar, then her hood, and shook out her hair. She sighed. And Damir, moved by her sigh, did the same.

—Tell me, are you still wearing the same dress?

Our Little Lady bowed her head, spread her gown with her little hands, shook her head with a womanish gesture of disappointment, raised her gaze, and looked at Damir.

—Well, yes, I am. I'm always dressed the same. That's how people have become used to me, so I stick with it.

—I'm sorry; there are many fine dresses that would suit you well.

—There was once a little seamstress, and she was a marvelous sewer. Her dresses I'd wear.

She sighed nostalgically.

—What pleats those were!

—Pardon?

—Oh, you know, when a skirt looks like an accordion.

—I, too, almost always wear the same things. But I'm not the one who chooses my clothes. Why do you always wear the same thing? You, at least, could choose.

—No, it is I who can't choose her clothes.

—Why?

—It's one of the rare things that is eternal. As you're remembered, so you remain—for all time.

—What about those who keep changing their clothes?

—They usually aren't remembered. For anything.

They swung their feet.

She spoke up, full of merriment:

—Would you like me to tell you a story?

—What would you tell?

—A fairy tale, "The Tale of the Little Seamstress"; everybody loves it.

He was at a loss. He didn't want to think that she, like others, was beginning to think of him as a child.

—I'm not sure that's right for me.

—Don't worry, everybody likes a good fairy tale now and then. Here, while we see the sun set, while we bask, I'll tell you the tale. But you must know how to listen!

Damir nodded and made himself comfortable. Our Little Lady asked if she could return to his pocket so she could be more comfortable, and so he could better hear her.

# THE TALE OF THE LITTLE SEAMSTRESS

Once upon a time, a long, long time ago in a faraway city that took pride in its lovely squares and church towers, and most of all in the magnificent castle on the hill that towered over the charming houses, there lived a little girl with an unusual name: Harmony. All the other little girls in the town were proud of their ordinary names. They were all Marthas, Marias, Anas, Kristinas, and Katarinas, but so it was that Harmony had been given a very unusual name. And no, she was not happy about this. When she was still very small, other children teased her in their games, and while when she got older they no longer teased her directly, she'd hear malicious laughs as she passed by on the street.

—Harmony, Harmony, ha, ha, ha, Hahaharmony!

So, Harmony began avoiding others her age. She played less and less with other children, and spent hour after hour at home. She picked up whatever there was to do, but she found working with a needle and thread the most appealing, and under her little fingers soon appeared beautiful blouses, dresses, and coats. She was so adept and diligent that she did not allow anyone near the clothes she was working on; she washed and ironed everything herself. The members of her household and neighbors and relatives and her godmother and her aunts began to sing her praises. Little by little, word of the industrious little seamstress began to spread, and in no time, aunties and neighbors and distant relatives began flocking to her, and soon enough it was ladies she'd never met, all hoping the little seamstress would make them beautiful clothing.

The little seamstress was able to fashion a bright and pretty frock from the most ordinary fabric, and the women could not imagine how from the simple broadcloth they had brought was made a splendid gown that shone in all the colors of the rainbow. On Sundays, when the women wore their splendid gowns and went for walks, the square in front of the church was a marvel, like a flower-filled meadow rippling in a spring breeze. These were dresses in a marvelous array of hues and striking designs, and in them there wasn't a single lady who felt ugly or old, but instead they felt beautiful and full of life, as if each were still seventeen. The little seamstress tailored and stitched, laundered and ironed, and did not waver. And so it was, in the little town and all around it almost everybody forgot the name Harmony and called the petite girl the Little Seamstress. Everything in her life was beautiful and bright, like reflections of the vibrant colors that shimmered in her hands when she gave each thrilled woman her new dress.

But in this city, there was one woman for whom nothing was ever good or beautiful or fun, and that woman happened to be a petulant princess who lived in the castle overlooking the town. She dressed in golden gowns, but the princess would look in the mirror, burst into tears, and the gown would instantly become a pitiful, rumpled rag. They'd slip silver shoes onto her toes, but the princess would angrily stomp her feet, and the shoes, before the very eyes of her flummoxed maids, transformed into clunky, peasant clodhoppers. They brought her all sorts of delicacies and tasty dishes from distant southern lands, but a pineapple on a platter turned into a huge turnip when it was set before her, an orange into a lowly potato, and cherries rolled away because they turned into horse chestnuts. They'd lead to her a handsome black steed, and it would begin braying like a donkey, pinning back its huge ears in shock, thereby terrifying the courtiers, who fled as fast as their feet could take them.

The king and queen, the poor parents of the petulant princess, were troubled and worried. Their royal hearts were torn while listening to the daily laments of their darling daughter, and, indeed, they did not know what they could do about it. Until one day they heard tell of the Little Seamstress and sent for her at once.

That morning, blissfully unaware, the Little Seamstress, having finished dresses for her two little sisters, was watching her delighted youngest sister twirl around in front of the mirror in a cyclamen-colored dress, which also had the fragrance of a forest cyclamen. Suddenly, they could hear the thudding of horses' hooves, the squeaking of the courtyard gate, the agitated protests of their parents' voices, and the stern voices of soldiers. The door to the room where the girls were was flung open. The frightened girls quickly became astonished when before them stepped a handsome young courtier who announced to the household that the king himself was inviting the Little Seamstress to the court. The girl was terrified; word had already gotten out in town that the court was having serious problems with the young princess, and people added all sorts of other stories to this. There was talk that with just a glance the princess could turn a head of cabbage into a warty toad, and turn a potato into a chubby mole.

But the Little Seamstress didn't dare oppose the order; a royal command is a royal command. She kissed her parents and her little sisters goodbye, wept and brushed away her tears, and packed her sewing needles and threads, and with her royal escort, off she went to the castle. Her godmother, aunties, grandmothers, and neighbors, and all the other ladies from the town, burst into tears, not so much because they felt sorry for the Little Seamstress, but because they knew that never again would anyone be able to make them such fine dresses.

As soon as she arrived at the door to the court, the Little Seamstress was brought to the king and queen. They were still clutching their golden crowns in despair over their daughter, the petulant princess, but when they laid eyes upon the charming seamstress, their spirits brightened and they began telling her their tale of woe. The king and queen told the Little Seamstress to sew dresses for their beloved daughter that would not turn instantly to rags. They took her to their treasure trove and laid out before the Little Seamstress the most sumptuous fabrics and velvets, silks and brocades interwoven with gold threads and beaded with precious gems. But instead she asked for the plainest cloth, and she shut herself in the little room they'd assigned her and set about immediately cutting and stitching; she worked through the night until the break of dawn.

Early that morning, a courtier summoned her to appear before the king and queen. The Little Seamstress was escorted to the royal hall, where she presented to the king and queen the new gown for the princess. They threw up their hands in amazement: the dress shimmered in all colors and gave off a bouquet of floral fragrances. Depending on the angle from which you looked at it, before your very eyes it opened and gave off the scent of dark violets, or tender cyclamens, or lush, velvety

NADA GAŠIĆ

roses, and these heavy fragrances would totally intoxicate who-ever looked at it.

The king and queen immediately summoned the princess. But they had to wait a goodly amount of time for her! Finally, they heard the door flying open and the nervous scampering of her ladies-in-waiting, and at last the princess's unbearable screeching and wailing. Her woeful parents again clutched their crowns.

And how did the princess look? Although her ladies-in-waiting had dressed her in a silken gown and silver shoes, the princess entered the royal hall in a jute sack and tattered peasant clod-hoppers, and instead of a diamond diadem on her head, there was a cracked saucepan. Her parents began to weep when they saw her looking like that, and the Little Seamstress dropped her gaze and gave a modest bow.

The princess stopped, stared at the dress that the Little Seamstress had humbly laid out on the stone table, and, to the great surprise of all and sundry, instead of her usual dismissive *ugh*, she said, *Hmmm*, and ordered her ladies-in-waiting to fol-low her, bearing the new gown.

As she was on her way out, the cracked pot that had been on her head bumped against the doorway, tumbled to the floor, and turned into a sooty tomcat, which slunk down the dark corridor.

All assembled in the royal hall waited, excited, and finally they heard tiny steps which, to the vast amazement of both the king and queen, were not followed by screeches and wails. They sat bolt upright on their thrones as the door to the roy-al hall opened. There stood the princess, beautiful and smiling, dressed in the gown that shone with all the hues and gave off the fragrance of a flowering meadow. Both the king and queen leapt to their feet, and, overjoyed, showered their daughter with kisses. They forgot all about the Little Seamstress. She watched the work of her hands a little while longer and then quietly withdrew to her room. The young courtier, when no one noticed, secretly kept an eye on her.

Soon the king and queen held the first ball for their princess. Many powerful princes flocked, all of them wealthy suitors, loudly praising the princess and her charms.

Princesses the world over heard that the princess was wearing the most splendid gown ever seen.

The Little Seamstress had been hoping she would be able to return home. But . . .

The princess did not want to wear the same dress more than once, so she demanded new dresses nonstop. One morning, the princess flung yet another dress into the fire and ordered the Little Seamstress to sew her a new one. The poor girl, having not had a moment's rest for quite some time, picked up her needles and stitched and stitched all night long. The new gown was so very beautiful, as beautiful as a spring forest in all its reflections and nuances of green; it glistened like an emerald and gave off the fragrance of a young forest, and under the silken folds that turned into golden leaves there peeked tiny, lively little birds with many-colored feathers which, furthermore, also chirped.

Again, there was a ball where the princess, again, astounded the guests with her new gown. But as soon as the Little Seamstress closed her eyes and laid her tired hands on the coverlet,

NADA GAŠIĆ

they told her that the princess had thrown away the dress and was demanding a new one.

Again, the little girl cut and stitched all night long. The new gown melted in all the hues of the sea, from the deepest dark blue to the lightest light turquoise; a person could barely look, it shone so brightly. From the dress spread the fresh fragrance of a sea breeze, while from the sunlit waves leaped golden fish that then dove back into the blue depths of the dress's folds. Every last one of the guests said there could be no gown more beautiful than this.

Ah, but how this infuriated the capricious princess! She summoned the Little Seamstress.

—How can there not be an even more beautiful gown? Make me a new one! Finer than all of the others.

—Your Royal Highness, my hands are weary, my fingers no longer obey me, my eyelids are closing. Please allow me to rest.

—I wish to have my new dress tomorrow. And I don't want those stupid scents, I want . . . I want . . . I want my dress . . . to play music!

The princess stomped her silver-clad feet, but the silver shoes did not ring out; they merely gave a dull thud, because they had instantly turned into scruffy clodhoppers.

—Make me a dress that plays music by tomorrow, or I'll have your head! And not just yours, but your parents' and your little sisters'!

The princess laughed malevolently and left the hall. Behind her hopped frogs and scampered mice, and if anyone had dared to look more closely, they would have seen a snake slithering silently down the dark hallway.

The Little Seamstress entered her room, sad and frightened. She sat down and shed a tear, and then she remembered that the eyes of the dashing young courtier were following her as she left the hall. She relaxed and smiled.

But then she recalled the threat that the petulant princess had made, and she was frightened for her parents and her little sisters, so she thought and thought and finally commenced with cutting and stitching. She cut and stitched the whole night through, and before daybreak she picked up the heavy, hot iron in her little hands and began ironing and pressing the pleats on the lavish new dress.

Right as she pressed the final pleat, she was summoned to the royal hall, where sat the king and queen and petulant princess. All three had cracked pots on their heads and their garb was in tatters, and when they tried to take tasty morsels from the serving trays, the morsels squealed and went scampering off every which way. The courtiers pretended not to see any of this.

The Little Seamstress proffered to them the lovely, lavish dress with a mother-of-pearl sheen. When the Little Seamstress spread her arms, the pleats spread and the dress played merrily. It played marvelously. Everybody jumped to their feet, crowing and clapping.

The most magnificent ball was held, and many suitors came, thousands of candles were lit, everybody was thrilled, and the musicians were told to stop playing when the princess entered the hall. In the hush that followed, the princess stepped into the hall, firmly gathering up the folds of her marvelous dress. She sized up the guests, especially the suitors, then spread her arms wide amid the lavish pleats. Alas! Instead of merry music, there began a terrible grinding sound, squeaks and bangs, as if there were a hundred lids banging on a hundred saucepans, as if a hundred mice were squeaking and a hundred donkeys braying. The guests clapped their hands over their ears, and the suitors rushed for the door. The king and queen raised their hands to clutch their golden crowns in despair, but their hands found the cracked pots instead. Then suddenly, amid all the terrible clamor and clanking, loud guffaws rang out. They all turned to see where they were coming from. There stood the young courtier, roaring with laughter. After him the rest followed suit, and this made an indescribable noise and brouhaha, with a great deal of dashing about and hissing, while the princess, hoping the dress would play its music, kept gathering and spreading the folds of her marvelous mother-of-pearl gown. The clanking and cacophony, the squeaks and croaks, became more and more unbearable.

The Little Seamstress crouched by the door until she felt someone's hand. When she looked up, she saw the young courtier smiling at her.

The guests and suitors and courtiers, every last one of them, fled as fast as their feet would carry them, and later, of course, most of them claimed they'd never been inside that castle, let alone sought the hand of the petulant princess.

And the princess, king, and queen, banging away on the cracked pots on their cracked heads, stumbling around in the dark, searched all night for the Little Seamstress to exact their vengeance.

As the story goes, one can still hear the banging of pots and lids, the croaking of frogs, the braying of donkeys, and the creaking of old doors at the castle overlooking the town.

And word has it that all trace of the Little Seamstress was lost, that the handsome courtier took her to faraway lands, and that somewhere she is sewing marvelous dresses that give off fragrances and fly, and sometimes she even makes a dress that plays music, but only if the person who wears it is good. In honor of her real name, they called the Little Seamstress: Accordion.

Only you and I and that black cat that jumped out of the cracked pot know how the accordion came about that plays so merrily that it might seem to a person listening that confectioners' sugar has been sprinkled by someone in the mother-of-pearl moonlight.

Our Little Lady finished her story and felt Damir's chest rising and falling in a regular rhythm. This wasn't uncomfortable for her, but it was strange. She twisted her head around and saw he was sleeping.

—Of course, he fell asleep to a story about dresses. A typical man.

She left him alone for a time, and then she tweaked his pocket.

—Damir, Damir, wake up.

He started.

—I wasn't sleeping.

Our Little Lady shook her head, dissatisfied.

—Oof! And he lies too. Typical man!

Then she suddenly went quiet. She was listening intently to something and became quite still.

This frightened Damir.

—Our Little Lady, Our Little Lady, what is it? What happened?

—Nothing. Don't worry. I ought to, no . . . actually I must leave for a time. But I'll be back. Don't worry, I'll be back.

Then she added:

—You'll be faster without me.

He cleared his throat to protest. His voice was gone. He couldn't make a sound. Not a word. His eyes welled up with tears, and for a moment he couldn't see properly; he brushed the tears away with his fingertips. He couldn't reach his handkerchief because she was standing on it. He squinted and cleared the corners of his eyes; his vision sharpened. He looked down. He couldn't see her. And his pocket felt empty. He turned, looking over at the sunshade. The sun had gone down. The shadow of late autumn was somehow definitive on that day. Our Little Lady had gone off somewhere, and Damir, filled with sadness, went slowly off toward home. He'd get there on time, before Cilika and Vilim returned from the cemetery.

## What about Cilika and Vilim?

They, *the poor things*, had a lot to tend to at the cemetery. They had to sweep the leaves, scrape away the old, dried candle wax, clean, scrub, wipe dry, and polish. There was a line at the water pump, and Vilim was late returning with the pail. This flustered Cilika, as it did the lady tidying up the next grave over, whose husband had also gone to fetch water and was late coming back. When they finally finished the job and laid out the fresh, charming flower arrangement on the grave, they were barely able to make it back to the bus and could hardly wait to sit down. There wasn't enough time to catch their breath on the brief bus ride, but they were not bored.

PHONE, "WALTZING MATILDA":

Yes, I called, why didn't you pick up? Tamara, indoor voice, please. I'll call again later, to make sure you got up. Don't you talk back to me. Put on a sweater at least, or, damn it, button up your shirt. Your belly is bare, you'll catch cystitis again. After school, go to the dry cleaners and pick up my suit. I left the receipt on the table. How? How could you throw something away before you even read what it said! Take it out of the garbage, put the pieces back together, and take it to the dry cleaners. Listen, don't be rude, I'm on the bus and we'll talk this evening. No, no you can't go out again tonight. Don't be rude, and don't talk back to me. Hear? Tamara! Hello . . . hello?

TWO WITHOUT PHONES:

I tell you, cemeteries make money hand over fist. We have a grave all the way up in the last section, nearest to the crematorium. It was a very nice plot, green all around it, but now, God help us. Everything has been dug up between the chestnut trees, and now it's grave to grave. Sure, I know there's not enough room when everybody wants to be buried in Zagreb. It's the most lucrative work there is these days. Think of how much money you have to shell out, and, in the end, you don't even own it, you just have the right for a burial. And you pay. No, the city owns it all, and, of course, the mayor is the owner. They rake it in. And there's plenty of space there near the arcades. After all, that whole section there used to be Jewish, and nobody is being buried there anymore, so there's plenty of space. I don't know why it stands there empty, but up where we are among the chestnut trees, everybody's pushing and shoving.

TWO OTHERS WITHOUT PHONES:
No, no, not chrysanthemums. Always, but always, I buy a pussy willow arrangement. They last for ages. Sure, chrysanthemums are everywhere, but pussy willows last. You could only buy them in the spring before. Now everything's different. Absolutely everything. The whole climate, that's why we have the pussy willows. You can see how warm it is. Fine, it's not warm, but it's sunny. Well, fine, tomorrow it won't be, but better that than rain on All Saints'. Used to be. How much did you pay for those shoes? They're really nice. Sure, Ara shoes are comfy, but the way I see it, shoes like that won't do for Lisinski Concert Hall. I guess I'm always happiest wearing pumps.

TWO OTHERS WITHOUT PHONES:
It's going to be warm for All Saints'. Too warm. A breeding ground for disease. Too warm.

A HUSBAND AND WIFE, A LITTLE OLDER THAN CILIKA
AND VILIM:
As soon as we get home, I'm slicing it, and that'll be that. Custom has it that it's served either on All Saints' or earlier. But now the walnut roll happened to be hot, so I didn't put it

out. You know how badly you'd bloat from hot walnut roll? No? Looks like your mother didn't teach you such things. Of course, we first went to my parents' grave. Because my parents were good, decent folks. Not that yours weren't, but I know mine were good and decent.

Cilika and Vilim were so tired, they barely made it home. *Thank God, Gramps is already fast asleep, and thank you, Blessed Virgin Mary, there is not a peep from Big Boy's room.*
There would be peace till morning.

*       *       *

In a shopping mall parking lot:
—I was summoned to the police station, nothing more to report.
—I know you were at the police station. I don't know what you were asked.
—He was just checking the time when I came home that night. And he asked about my nephew.
—Your job is to keep your mouth shut. Remember, you don't know a thing.
—Well, in fact, I don't know anything. I don't know who was at the house. I don't know anything. You were driving.
—Go ahead and tell yourself that. Anything more?
She did her best not to think about Švojić, and her reaction was too slow.
—No, nothing.
—I didn't quite catch that.
—No, nothing more to tell you.

NADA GAŠIĆ

With his right hand he reached for the door handle, but then he stopped. With his left, he grabbed her right fist and began bending her fingers and palm back toward her wrist, until she slumped down on her seat without a sound. The steering wheel stopped her from falling. He released her, then got out, smiling.

She sat for a long time in the car, rubbing her wrist. She could barely use her right hand while she drove, but she was a capable driver and returned home without further incident.

Laughter rang out from the Zadruga. Irma paid no attention; those were Ita's girlfriends, and she left them to have their fun. She climbed up to the attic, went to the kitchenette, put ice cubes in a plastic bag, wrapped the bag around her wrist, and went to her room. She sat at her desk and watched how the bag fogged up from the change in temperature. She didn't cry, she didn't moan. Irma had a high tolerance for pain.

She set the bag of ice aside, took her key from her purse, unlocked the desk drawer, and took out a folder. She slowly leafed through some documents. *What did I sign, what did I sign, oh, Mama, what did I sign? Calm down, calm down, we'll find a way to make this right.*

\*     \*     \*

Ita was in the midst of dry runs for makeup and hair. Nothing must be left to chance—everything had to be perfect on Saturday.

At the Zadruga she served cold cuts, pastries, and champagne; her friends came to advise her on preparations and to run down all the lists so there wouldn't be unbefitting levity in the bride's home because of David's accident, while still keeping the spirit of the wedding. There couldn't be any missteps after so much effort and time had been invested. Not to speak of the money.

Little by little, the women forgot they were guests in a home where laughter, at least for the moment, was not welcome. The champagne, bolstered by the occasional shot of something stronger, relaxed them. Before Katarina got home, they were already tipsy. The conversation was punctuated by bursts of laughter, and, in keeping with recent events, it simply had to turn to stories about men. They avoided the painful experiences. Those are buried deep anyway and never spoken of. But lively stories sparkled and laughter shook the only window of the low-slung shack. *And he, wait, wait for this . . . Ha, ha, ha . . . Oh, that's nothing, listen to this . . . Ha, ha, ha. Listen, this is too awful, wait, wait, but if any of you breathe a word, you're dead, Lovro would kill me, but it happened before he came along. The guy was married, but for God's sake, this happens to everybody—his wife was away on a trip, so he invited me over, and in the living room we got ready as one does. I stripped, but kept my high heels on, because the guy liked that; he stripped, then the two of us went to the bedroom. He led the way, and then he stood on these floor rags, did you hear that? Floor rags. He pushed two of them under my feet. And then he skated over the floor on the rags with his bare ass, and I followed behind him in the high heels! Can you believe it? His wife had taught the guy to take care of the parquet flooring, and so we skated over to the bed. I began giggling before we made it to the bed, and I laughed so hard that he went all soft. The idiot was scared of his wife's floor, even while he was cheating on her. What a creep!*

They howled. The makeup dry run had to be delayed while Ita's tears dried, her flush subsided, and her hiccups stopped.

NADA GAŠIĆ

*     *     *

Katarina kissed Dado goodbye and decided to walk home; she still didn't have it in her to ride a tram by the place where he'd been hit. And a walk could only help. She chose streets that weren't close to the tram tracks, avoiding even the thought of the street where the accident happened. There was still daylight when she reached Old Trešnjevka Park.

Regardless of its name, this was a relatively new park, and it always reminded her of a meadow. The trees and bushes that had been planted did not create dense foliage, and, unlike old parks, you could see across it from one side to the other. And the people and dogs. She crossed it at a leisurely pace and came out onto Nehajska Street, at a point where all she had to do was cross it and enter the tangle of little streets that formed her neighborhood.

Her purse slid off her shoulder, so she stopped for a moment to switch the strap, like a letter carrier, over her head to her opposite shoulder. The hospital on Klaićeva was many blocks away.

She turned to look at the park.

At the start of the pedestrian pathways stood trash bins where two ravens were perched, each on its own bin, happily plucking out bits of garbage. They flew off after each of them found a hefty chunk of discarded bread. Only then did Katarina notice an entire flock of ravens hopping around in the meadow, their heads rhythmically bobbing. The pigeons had cleared out to give them room. Sparrows, and ravens, cared nothing for the company they kept.

She turned away and went into the first little street. Knowing this area so well, there was nothing to distract her from thoughts about David. Looking down at the pavement, she focused on what she'd heard at the hospital. She carefully repeated every-thing the doctor had told her, remembered his pauses while he was speaking, and thought about what those pauses might mean, filling them with her own meanings, with her intelligent, reason-able meanings which would be as they had to be: full of faith that everything was moving toward a quick recovery. Very, very quick.

The late October day was suddenly engulfed by twilight. This didn't unsettle her. There was plenty of light, and the windows of the houses also helped; the lights were on indoors. At the end of the street, which at that block formed an intersection at a crooked angle with her street, she reached a building she didn't know well. This new, three-story edifice—only recently completed—had been painted a garish blue. The white blinds were lowered, and a long banner advertised the sale of the re-maining apartments on the bottom and top floors. Nobody had moved in yet. So full of silence, the building slowed her pace a little. Nothing serious. But something unknown, and her brain no longer allowed her to remain on automatic pilot.

She stopped to take a good look at the building. To remember it, so it wouldn't distract her from her thoughts the next time she passed it. The building's color was losing its vibrancy; the dusk suddenly added the pallor of a sickly gray hue and Katari-na was struck by the resemblance of the lowered window blinds to the eyelids of corpses. On the dead face of the building. She forced herself to drop her head and move on. She shook off the unpleasant image yet, again, she stopped.

She turned, facing the empty ground floor where the win-dow blinds had not been lowered. She stared at the window as if looking into the gaping maw of a corpse. She shivered. She

NADA GAŠIĆ

even took a step back. Was someone standing there in the window? She realized she was no longer in control. Her nerves were jumping, boggled, and they couldn't decide what to do next: warn or soothe. First, they upended the clarity of Katarina's awareness about her surroundings. She needed a few seconds to collect her thoughts. *A street, Katarina, a street, an ordinary building, Katarina, an ordinary building. And yours is close. Almost there.* She smiled at her own heartening words. The kind she'd use for her child. *Fear? Face it. Have a good look at the ground-floor windows!* From one window she was watched by a blind, leering jack-o'-lantern, lifeless, with candles flickering inside it. Katarina laughed aloud. Her laughter, for some reason, rang false, forced. Metallic. She turned. There was nobody nearby, and nobody had heard her. She breathed a sigh of relief. *Katarina, Halloween! Of course, Halloween!* In another day or two, the evening for carved pumpkins, witches, and freaks would be here. David would have joined in too. Earlier he had put a jack-o'-lantern in the window. To defy them for thoroughly banishing all the black masks and orange decorations from the store windows this year. David would have done it out of defiance, your son. Defiant.

She took a step back, dropped her head again, and walked on.

Then she turned. She had to take one more look. An orange monster. A freakish sun. A travesty of summer. This jack-o'-lantern tell-tale heart. A mocker of death? No, a mockery of life.

She stared at it.

Or was it staring at her?

Katarina turned her head away.

And so did the jack-o'-lantern.

Katarina turned, but slowly, slowly, to the point of going rigid.

The jack-o'-lantern turned slowly, without a twitch, and followed Katarina.

Its dead, gouged-out eyes wrinkled in a burst of laughter.

Cackling laughter.

The jack-o'-lantern laughed, turned slowly, and began rising up as if to come down off the window and slowly, inexorably, move toward Katarina.

It cackled like a raven.

Katarina ran, screaming all the way home.

Behind her she heard laughter.

And the cackling of ravens.

She flew into her little house, and without stopping she went straight to David's room and flopped down on his bed. She shoved her head under his pillow and inhaled the boy's smell.

The little house keened. It felt so ashamed that there was drinking going on at the Zadruga— rocking with laughter, giggles, shrieks, and hoots—so much so that long into the night, its old neighbors thought a whole flock of ravens had settled in what was left of the garden, on the Firmans' leafless cherry tree.

Cackling.

And with them, dogs were barking.

Before daybreak, nobody could stand the barking of the dogs. Not the neighbors, the landlords, or the passersby.

# Sixth stone, sixth wave

—VIILIM, VIIILIM! GO ahead, Ita dear, off you go, my sweet bride. Vilim has wandered off somewhere. I'll find you that lotion for Lovro's hair. Whatever was Lovro up to, the knucklehead? Now, right before the wedding? How will he stand at the altar? You'll look like a princess, and what will he look like? A caterpillar! Ah, here's Vilim. Good, Vilim, find Ita the lotion, I'm in a hurry to pick up something at the store. Yesterday we spent all day at the cemetery; it was so crowded on the buses, and I had no time to tend to anything or buy anything. What with All Saints' almost here.

So Cilika left Ita, who was edgy, with Vilim, to find the lotion that was supposed to restore at least a millimeter of Lovro's hair in two days. Vilim first looked in the bathroom, and when he didn't find it, he looked for it in the pantry, and when he did find it he was sorry to give her the whole bottle, so he poked around for a small empty bottle he could use to siphon off half, and pouring out the thick liquid took ages. By the time he'd finished, Cilika was already back. She ran into them at the door.

—Whatever took you so long? Your face is all red, like you got a sunburn.

—Oh, Cilika, he drove me crazy. You know Vilim, he had such trouble finding it. Bye, I'm in a hurry, Lovro's waiting. I swear, I'm going to pour the whole thing on his head.

While he was waiting for Ita to come back with the lotion that would miraculously restore his hair, Lovro was rechecking the lists they'd been over the day before, and out of boredom and curiosity he picked up a menu to see what they'd settled on and was stumped by the appetizers. For the life of him he couldn't imagine what *Dalmatian-style Zagorje štrukli* might be? How in the world could Zagreb local specialties be prepared Dalmatian style? Nor could he imagine having agreed to such a thing. And finally, just as he had literally begun to seethe over the *selection of fresh fruit served on a mirror*, Ita walked in and ordered him:

—Strip off your clothes! I can't bear the sight of you scalped like this.

Lovro protested as he took off his T-shirt.

—Ita, we chose some bullshit dish for our appetizer. What could *Dalmatian-style Zagorje štrukli* possibly be? Our crowd will laugh us out of town.

Ita didn't answer. She led him to the bathroom, ordered him to lean over the bathtub and close his eyes, just in case, and, without further ado, poured half the contents of the bottle over his head.

It smelled a little odd.

—Now rub that in and I'll pour the rest on.

NADA GAŠIĆ

Lovro rubbed it in.

—It's slippery, disgusting.

Ita poured the rest out vengefully onto his head. Then she took paper towels and wiped away the molasses-like goo. It didn't soak in well. She used up half a roll trying to rub it into his head vigorously.

—Now wash your face, but don't touch your head.

She left him in the bathroom and went back to the kitchen. Lovro joined her a few minutes later. At first Ita was dumb-struck. Then she wailed.

—Jesus Christ, you're so shiny! A proper police-car beacon!

Shocked, she heard someone running across the yard.

—Ita, Ita, Ita!

Out of breath, Cilika flew into the kitchen.

—Ita, Vilim gave you our *headstone cleaner* for polishing grave-stones, don't . . .

She looked at Lovro.

—Wash him off immediately!

They washed him, but by evening Lovro Slaviček had developed a serious rash and his face and head had swelled up; he swallowed histamines and, over the phone, called Ita an idiot. Ita sobbed, then quieted down; then she called to see if he was feeling better.

Everything went ahead . . . The wedding will happen tomorrow. Today they can *socialize* a little with the groomsmen and bridesmaids and later with her sisters, have a bit to drink, play some music, chat sentimentally with her best friend who had come to help her hang the garlands, arrange the chairs with their white slipcovers and pink bows, decide where to put the floral arrangements, put out the tablecloths, set the tables with glasses and napkins, and prepare the places for the platters of cold cuts that the caterers would bring the next day. There was no room left in the refrigerators, but luckily the next day was 31 October, the weather was chilly, and all the drinks would chill perfectly just outside the door to their little house.

And the little house, like a woman, enjoyed being dressed up. Jealous, it looked out its window facing the yard at the women decorating the Zadruga, and although the house knew it would remain undecorated because of David's accident, it hoped that at least a little of the festivity would rub off.

At first, Ita didn't dare, because she'd promised Katarina she wouldn't, but then she heeded her friends and agreed they could *liven up the house just a little.*

Ita went into David's room; she changed the sheets, pushed the dirty ones into the washing machine, and then cleaned the room. They hung garlands in his room too. Luckily, not all the white ones had been taken to Lovro's apartment; David would have been embarrassed to find pink ones in his room. Once David's room was done up nicely, they spruced up the rest of the house. Ita's maid of honor's son came over with his friends a little later, and, in the general spirit of merriment and a touch of frivolous amusement, they blew up the balloons, strung lights across the yard, and festooned the fence with decorations. They'd fix things a little the next day and add more. For today, all that was left was to hang the new curtains at the Zadruga. They'd wait for that until Katarina came home from the hospital and Irma was back from school. Cilika would come along, and that way the four of them would finish what they'd started the Sunday before.

Katarina was certain that David's condition was improving. She, too, as much as she was able, had entered the festive mood of the wedding preparations. She knew what she'd be wearing the next day; she knew she'd have to work on her hairdo, take a longer bath, wax her legs, rub herself with exfoliating brushes, slather herself with body oil, and do her nails to perfection. She knew she had beautiful hands, and her fingernails were her only natural feature she took pride in. She remembered the brooch on the lapel of her shirt jacket and decided to wear it on her beige silk suit. She'd be standing next to Ita after all.

Before she went into David's hospital room, she mustered the courage to snag the on-duty doctor. He didn't have the time; he held his hands in the pockets of his white lab coat and only told her in passing that the rounds had gone well. David was stable; there were no changes in his general condition. She had already learned that when doctors didn't take their hands out of their pockets, they had more important things to do than talking with the family of a patient.

David was peaceful, still. The hum of the machines calmed her as well, though she had learned not to look at them, unlike David's dad, who always first checked the screens. She didn't. She believed David's face.

She still hadn't kissed his foot that was sticking out from under the covers, she still hadn't gone over to him, when the door opened and in came Inspector Vidošić.

She smiled, blushed red like a teenager, and didn't even say hello. She was thrown off-balance.

Her blush, like a yawn, was infectious, and Vidošić caught it.

—Forgive me . . .

—Oh, no, please, come in, I was startled. I thought you were David's dad. *Katarina, you're lying.*

—I happened to be driving by and thought I'd pop in to let you know I have been in touch with the traffic police. They are searching for the driver of the car who brought David to this. There are reasons to believe that they are onto him. And that will be a boon for us as well. *Vidošić, you're lying.*

—Thank you, but somehow, I'm not thinking about what happened, and who did what. *Katarina, you're lying.*

—I understand. *Vidošić, you're lying.*

He smiled at her.

—You look more chipper today. David does seem better, and that's why the color has come back in your face. *Vidošić, you're not lying.*

—Ah, no, that's all because of my sister's wedding tomorrow. *Katarina, you're lying.*

—The brooch also gives you some color. So, tomorrow is Saturday, and then there are the two days off for All Saints'. I won't be able to come by the hospital. I have family obligations; our family graves are far away. I'm not from Zagreb.

She didn't ask Vidošić where he was from, and he, for whatever reason, ascribed this to her good manners. He went on:

—But, of course, I will be in regular touch with my on-duty colleagues, and the investigation will not be back-burnered at any time. There are no holidays for us. *Vidošić, you're lying.*

—Now, don't you go troubling yourself with visits to the hospital. I don't think it's necessary anymore. *Katarina, you're lying.*

NADA GAŠIĆ

He apologized that he hadn't given her his personal phone number yet. With gratitude Katarina entered it into her phone, looked over at the inspector, and blushed, and again her blush crossed over onto Vidošić.

Without knocking, Boris Horak came in. He said something; Vidošić turned to the bed, said, *Hold on there, David,* and said his goodbyes to David's mother and David's father.

*     *     *

What would Grandpa have had to say about all this? Grandpa would have said *this has gone far beyond what is appropriate.* My mom is flirting with the inspector, not him with her. Well, fine, he is flirting a little with her too, but she seems to be the main one. That's obvious, because she was overdoing it when she talked with him. I know her. Wow, was I mortified! And then my dad came in right as things were the most interesting, and he told the inspector, and probably Mama as well, *I don't want to interfere with your fun; I hope David's enjoying it too.* Then the inspector left, because even though he's a cop, he's not stupid, and after that my parents fought, of course. But not, you know, like usual. I know my mom; she suspects something, and accuses my dad of something, but I guess it's like I don't want to hear what she tells him, so I didn't listen all the way to the end. All I caught was that Dad was really pissed off, because he told her he would ask the doctor to limit who could come to visit and at what time, and then Mama told him, *Well, so then you'll come every other weekend.*

That's when I switched off my ears. First, when I was still little, I practiced that with my folks, and now I can do it with everybody. I switch off my ears neatly, like I have a remote. Anybody who wants to can say whatever they like, but if I don't want to, I won't hear them. And now, when I switched off my ears, I thought about something altogether different. I thought about how weird it was that Mirta said to say hi. Last year that would have been absolutely normal, because even the boys in middle school didn't know us kids in the lower grades, let alone the girls. But now that she's a fifth grader. Impossible. It would be normal in a movie for her to come see me and stand by my bed and hold my hand, and buy me, say, a balloon. But our school is way different. Forget the hand-holding thing if you're in fourth and she's in fifth. Eh, now imagine that she comes, and my dear mother is reading me fairy tales! It would be better for me to go deep behind the curtain while I still have time. I don't dare think about it. But now I'm a little tired. Though my parents sure aren't. They'll keep on fighting, unless the doctor comes in and really forbids them from coming to see me.

*    *    *

—I warned you, Katarina. I do not wish to see this man in this room. Where you choose to meet with him is your business, but here, with David, you will not be holding your coy little chats. Clear?
—We were not holding a coy little chat. He came to say . . .

NADA GAŠIĆ

—Please, don't treat me like a fool. I have been holding back for a full five days from telling you what I have to say: had *you* taken adequate care of David when he needed it, he would not have been out on the street at night, when no child who has a mother is out on the street.

—And *child who has a father*. And that father did not answer his phone when I called him to tell him that *his* child wasn't at home.

—You didn't leave a message.

—You didn't call back. You saw I was calling.

—Where was your child?

—Maybe he was going to his father, who did not listen to his messages.

—Katarina, this conversation is over. I will not allow talk like this in this room, at his bedside.

—Well, well, now why is that? You're the one who doesn't believe he can hear us.

—When all this passes, I'm going to request custody.

—Ah, and your little wifey can hardly wait to welcome him. What will she feed him? Nettles?

Horak fell silent and looked at Katarina, who was not looking like the person he'd known. There was nothing meek about her.

He kissed David and promised he'd be back the next day, when nobody else would be there.

They left, first Dad, and then Mama. I should be glad, I guess, that they're gone. But I'm not. It would be better if they could agree to split the time when they'll be with me. They can say what they like to me and read me fairy tales, they can even pat me, but each on their own time. Weird, after all this lying around, and I've been lying around here for a hundred years already, I should have gotten smarter and a little stronger, but instead I've turned into a softie. A real tadpole. I'm constantly feeling sorry about something, scared of something. But I can't remember anything. Kovačić can set off fireworks above the school at this point. When I get back, I'll be worse than Soblić, who went off into special needs. I'll cry when I'm up at the blackboard; I'll be a scaredy cat; I'll hide behind those grimy classroom curtains and run like crazy as soon as I see Kovačić. And this is me we're talking about, David Horak, secret agent. Luckily, nobody knows about this, so it's not so disgraceful.

If someone asks me what I want to be when I grow up, I definitely won't say secret agent. If someone does ask me, and there aren't many who would, I'll say what most people say, either *I'm not sure yet*, or *computers*, or *builder*, which is just as ridiculous and unlikely as becoming a test driver for Formula 1, or a secret agent, because I can barely pass my math classes, but people fall for it anyway. Whatever, I'm obsessed with becoming a secret agent. Why? Because I want my life to be interesting. For something to happen in this life of mine. Take my mom, for example: she has this boring bank job, marital troubles with Dad, family trouble—that's me—trouble with money, hopeless friends, and no sex life. Dad has: a boring job, marital troubles—my mom and his wife—family trouble—me again—money troubles—child support, meaning me—hopeless friends, and sex, which I'm sure there's none of that going on. I have

marital troubles—my folks; family troubles—Mama and
me, me and Dad; money troubles, which is logical; friends,
totally but totally hopeless; and sex, zilch. Zilch. My folks,
even if they live another hundred years, will be living more
or less the same life. But if I become some kind of analyst, or
something equally pointless, and live another two hundred
years, I'll have the same life, more or less, that I have now at
the age of ten. So, always the same. Well, I don't want that.
If I become a secret agent, I'd experience lots of stuff, I'd
be able to do lots of stuff, I'd travel everywhere; I'd have an
interesting job, no marital troubles, plenty of money, and
loads of sex, but not with Horvatica. No way. Because this
way, if you look at it closely, if it is always the same and boring, it turns out that it doesn't matter whether I live some
stupid ten, stupid fifty, or stupid two hundred years. There,
that's why I'll be a secret agent.

Earlier, when I was little, I didn't think about having to
learn something or become something, like a doctor, so
I'd have a cool life. I always wanted to do something more
interesting. I wanted to be a dragon or a sage or a wizard,
or at least understand the speech of animals. That's why I
liked those fairy tales, that's why I could imagine all sorts
of things, but not Mama's palaces and the golden slippers
and other stupid stuff.

Now that I'm getting older, when I think a little about
those fairy tales, I still think it's cool either to have wings,
or to be incredibly strong, or to understand the speech of
animals. Now, when I'm occasionally turning into just my
own head and I can hear myself breathing as if I'm inside a

big pot, I have the impression that I could hear an animal talking. Seriously. It's weird, but until you've tried it, don't say it's impossible. While I'm turning into a huge round head and breathing like in a big pot, I can't hear anything except for my breathing. But I think I could hear and understand animal language. Too bad that there probably aren't any animals around me and I can't try to see if I understand their language or not. Although it does seem to me that a little while ago, a tiny butterfly flew by. Who knows? Maybe I'll understand it if it speaks.

*     *     *

## At the window

The day was sunny and everybody was saying that the people of Zagreb would have fine weather this year for the All Saints' holidays. Damir and Our Little Lady, unfortunately, didn't dare contemplate taking another stroll. Cilika was frequently leaving the house, but she kept popping back in and was all excited about Ita's wedding, so things kept slipping her mind. Our Little Lady and Damir couldn't keep track of her ins and outs, so they chose to hide in Damir's room. Although they could talk without opening their mouths, Our Little Lady took the precaution of hiding behind the picture of the Blessed Virgin Mary, and from there she kept an eye on the door in case it might happen to open. Cilika finally called to Vilim to go help the girls *clean up the Zadruga and hang the curtains*. Both of them breathed a sigh of relief.

　　　　　　　　　　　　　　　　　　　　　　NADA GAŠIĆ

—Tell me, when you were little, younger, how should I put this, a boy, what did you want to become? You surely aspired to something.

—I did.

—Tell! Tell me!

He didn't speak right away. She began to fidget. He even had the impression that she was impatiently tapping on the picture frame glass.

—First, I wanted to become a cook.

—Ah, you'd be Little Muck and Dwarf Nose the Cook rolled into one! Now I understand why the gander bit you.

—Pardon?

—Oh, nothing, I was just talking, you know, to myself.

Damir pulled himself together.

—Later I wanted . . . I wanted to become a watchmaker.

—A watchmaker? How nice. But why?

He said nothing. He didn't like how she asked him questions the way he had heard grown-ups asking children. She felt it and tried to correct her mistake.

—I mean, that's a marvelous trade, but I'm interested in why *you* in particular chose it.

Damir checked her intonation. Now everything sounded okay.

—Because watchmakers had nice rooms where they worked. Because they worked with gears, tiny ones, barely visible. Because they had strong lights only for themselves. And you could hear tapping, ticktocking in their little rooms.

—Nice, yes. But why are you talking as if there aren't any watchmakers nowadays?

—There probably are, but it's as if there aren't any *here*. They're gone from the little streets. They used to be here. Lots of them.

—Yes, you're right. Just a moment while I check something.

Our Little Lady looked up, pondering, as if checking something.

—Soon in Zagreb you'll be bidding farewell to the last watchmaker. And not just the watchmakers. The rope makers, umbrella makers, duvet makers, knife sharpeners, cobblers. You'll need pharmacists the longest. And the health food stores.

Damir was alarmed.

—When? Why?

—Don't worry, not as soon as you think. But soon in terms of time as I see it.

—Time as you see it?

—Yes. My time.

—Of course. You know a lot about time. You're sort of like a watchmaker.

—No, but I do have a watchmaker in my immediate family. A very precise watchmaker indeed.

She gestured with her teensy hand.

—Enough about me. We're talking about you. Tell me, are those all the reasons why you wanted to be a watchmaker?

—No. I liked how people who came into the watchmaker's shop were worried, and when they left they were, mostly, satisfied.

—And?

—And because I imagined myself sitting on the watchmaker's chair—I've done all the work, everybody has left satisfied, I've taken off that device on my eye, and I slowly swivel on the revolving chair, the clocks around me ticking, ticking, ticking, and

I see people going by through the shop window. And they don't know that I'm measuring their time.

—Yes, a similar job to my son's . . .

She stopped and thought for a moment. Then she looked up, pointed with her teensy hand somewhere to the left, and calmly said:

—Over there, not so far from here, on Savska Road, at the time of the high waters, an old watchmaker drowned. His clocks accompanied him. With their ticktocking.

Both of them were quiet for a time, and with their regular breathing they joined the eternal sound of clocks that accompanied the old watchmaker.

Damir was the first to speak:

—So tell me, did you want to be something different, something different . . . from what you are?

—I don't know. All jobs seem difficult to me. Sometimes I have the impression that mine is not the most challenging.

—But you must have wanted something. I don't believe you never wished for anything.

—I didn't want to do something different, but I did wish hard for something. Never, never tell anyone this. It would be best that you forget it immediately, as soon as you hear it.

Damir became one huge ear.

—I wanted to hear high heels. And play with the jack-o'-lanterns during Halloween Night.

He opened his mouth. It was so silly that he effortlessly forgot both his question and her answer that very moment.

\*    \*    \*

Vidošić was sitting alone in his office, listening to his secretary's heels as they tapped on the floor of the adjacent room. The sound irritated him, but there was nothing he could do. Saying something against women's shoes . . . He'd be run out of the building.

The feeling that he hadn't budged even a centimeter forward in the investigation was eating at him. He felt the urge to ask somebody something and, in the end, he at least corrected the lie he'd served up to David's mother—he called his colleagues in the traffic department who were in charge of David's case. They had no new information about the black car, but they were working on it.

He got up. He felt like opening his lower desk drawer, but he decided not to. He went back to his desk, turned on his computer, and for the first time that day, finally, he beamed. The report from the forensic psychologist had arrived, under the heading:

### PROFILE OF PERPETRATOR OF THE SCHOLASTIC CASE MURDERER

Examination of the murder victim's body and evaluation of the place where the corpse was found may provide forensic insight into the psychological profile of the murderer.

Analysis of the autopsy findings indicates the following:

Because the victim was killed by manual strangulation, the size of the impressions from the fingers and the resulting injuries indicate that the perpetrator was a physically strong man, who committed the crime in a fit of rage. It is also possible to conclude that his is a personality that may present manifestations in an actual situation of an anxiety cycle, but one that results not in retreat, but in aggressive attack. As to the structure of the personality, this may be a person who is not inclined to attacks of rage in his everyday life. The death of the victim may indicate that the person is in a permanent state of suppressed, but controlled, rage that then erupted.

The bites of human origin located on areas of the neck, the breasts, and the inside of the thighs indicate that the person had an extremely negative and aggressive attitude toward women. Or this may be a man who was abused by his mother in childhood, or a person who grew up with someone who is not his biological mother (stepmother).

As there is no evidence of penetration and the sexual organs were not damaged, it is very likely that the man is impotent and is probably disgusted by a woman's body.

The removal of all body hair may indicate that the perpetrator has an attitude of repulsion toward the body of a sexually mature woman, and may suggest that he is a man with suppressed pedophilic proclivities.

Leaving the dead body in a public place indicates that the perpetrator is demonstrating his power or need for power. It also indicates that he has the need to publicly show what he is capable of doing. This is an exceptionally narcissistic personality, who has a constant need to be the center of attention. Such people follow the television reporting from the murder scene in the company of others and tend to comment publicly on the event. The murderer does not feel threatened, does not think about the consequences of his actions, because he does not experience the victim as a person. The perpetrator experiences the woman's body with no trace of body hair as if it were a doll.

It cannot be ruled out that the perpetrator has a family, and his impotence manifested in later years. It is also possible that his sexual habits and proclivities may be hidden by his wife.

Vidošić read through it once more and said, *Fuck, I already knew all of this. No movement forward.*

He called a meeting; there was debate, clamor, new ideas floated, suggestions, combinations, writing on the board. Simčić presented a list of the cars that had a tire profile that corresponded to the skid marks they'd photographed and preserved from the scene of the accident. Hundreds of automobiles and hundreds of owners.

Vidošić huffed:

—Go through them!

Zdilar said he had been digging to find everything he could about the people whose names had come up in the case; he had dug through everything he could dig through, and he'd even gone through real estate records online, and the only thing he saw was that something had recently been registered for the house where Irma Žiger was living, and that was all.

Regardless of Katarina's statement that Irma had spent the whole evening last Sunday with her sisters, Vidošić told Komšić:

—Call Žigerica for me. Have her come in straightaway.

Irma received the summons when she was already finished with teaching for the day and was on her way, with other teachers, from the school to the crematorium to pay her final respects to the ill-fated *young woman, daughter, sister, colleague, and friend.*

She kept her composure. The teachers chipped in for a wreath, but Irma also sent her own. She stood and sniffled into her handkerchief before briefly laying her hand on the coffin. The teachers who had come to pay their respects moved step by step in front of her, until her turn came to extend a hand in condolence to the family members, but as she wasn't close to any of them, she didn't kiss anyone. Then she waited out in front of the crematorium for them to *say their last goodbyes*. She only went in when the strains of Albinoni's music had already stirred everybody's tears, and she listened to the two eulogies by teachers and one from a pupil, in which there were repeated *from this day forward, the world without our loved one will never be the same; they swear to her on this hallowed ground that the criminal will be brought to justice, and they will never forget her, for she was good, generous, and expert at her job; she loved her students and fellow teachers, and they loved her.* Irma sobbed along with all her other colleagues while a talented student recited a love song in Spanish. Not once did she glance over at where the students were standing. She crossed herself and prayed like all the others, and in her heart she confirmed that the deceased was a sincere believer. She didn't stand apart in any way. She cried as much as was fitting. When everything was over, her colleagues suggested going out for coffee, *to recover*, but she apologized, saying she had to rush off to make arrangements for her younger sister's wedding.

She walked away at a brisk pace, was one of the first to reach the parking lot, got into her car, and adjusted her rearview mirror. In it she saw Švojić. He was standing still; he was not touching his ear, and he was not smiling. Irma started the car and shifted into reverse. Švojić jumped out of the way; Irma braked and smiled. It wasn't on purpose. Or so she thought. *Irma, you're lying.*

Vidošić was waiting for her with the same questions he'd already asked her. She was composed, but her face was different: she had put her red hair up and tamed it. It was wrong to attend a funeral and pay one's respects with one's everyday appearance. Indeed, she was relaxed and answered calmly. In the end, Vidošić decided he'd let her know that they knew everything about her, and he asked her whether she was aware of the notes registered to the deed for their property.

For the first time since he'd been talking with her, she reacted with her whole face.

—Probably the man my sister is marrying tomorrow saw to it that everything would be prepared before the wedding and her departure from our house. My younger sister sold me her part of the house. The place is tenant occupied, so she sold it to me for an almost symbolic amount.

The answer was straightforward. It couldn't have been more mundane, yet Vidošić wondered why she had stiffened and blinked, reacting to such a workaday question.

She was aware she had reacted the wrong way.

—Forgive me, I just came from the funeral; my nerves are frayed.

—Oh, I see. You can go. We'll see you again soon. You have only a very brief time left to recall the names of the friends you two had in common. Brief.

NADA GAŠIĆ

Irma left in silence. Vidošić reached for his bottom drawer. He took only a sip from the secret bottle, then removed everything from the drawer, and though he knew there was nothing left of the last pack he'd smoked two years before, he rummaged around and searched for cigarettes, until his sudden urge to inhale tobacco smoke subsided. He stood up and looked out the window.

—Who is this hairy, impotent, clandestine pedophile who hates women and who sees a living person as a doll, who has no first or last name or face? Who, Vidošić?

He said all this to the windowpane, leaving a circle of fog that quickly evaporated.

\* \* \*

At last, they were all together: Ita, Irma, Katarina, and Cilika. Katarina didn't say a word about them decorating the main house without her go-ahead. David was stable, the wedding was tomorrow; all she had to do was hold on a little longer, and everything would go as planned.

The glasses were set out and the cognac flask was making the rounds, but they'd decided each would only take a sip; they didn't want bags under their eyes the next day. Ita went first. Everything was ready: the wedding gown salon had been very helpful and sent their seamstress to measure Ita and adjust the train, which Katarina had tried, without success, to attach with straight pins. The makeup stylist was coming at the same time as the hairdresser and manicurist. Everything had been rehearsed and checked. Ita wouldn't see Lovro until the next day, as was the custom; Irma would go to the hairdresser in the morning; Cilika had scheduled her hairdo for noon. Her suit was already on the hanger, *ironed. Vilim can't button up his suit jacket, but who will be looking at him, anyway; he'll go as he is.*

And Katarina's outfit was ready. A longer bath tomorrow, bubbles, bath salts, the finest perfume, a little-more-careful combing of her hair, a squirt of hairspray—as soon as she got back from Dado's the next morning, she'd start getting ready. The house and Zadruga were *cute as a button*, the catering was coming on time, the arrangements were already in place. The rest to be delivered tomorrow. The drinks were already chilling outside.

—Katja, we're not going to be able to see Dadek tomorrow, but send him kisses from us. Will you?

Ita was on the verge of tears.

—Just as well, the nurses and doctors don't like the visitors. It's really only supposed to be me and his father. It is the ICU, after all.

Irma was watching her closely, so Katarina unwittingly brushed back her bangs.

—Katarina, your hair is a sight.

Irma said this without animus, without mockery, and Katarina agreed.

—I know, but I can't afford the two hours tomorrow to sit in a salon, I need to be with Dado.

—Why don't we spend a little time now on your hair and add toner? I have some dye left. Your face shows how tired you are—a lighter color will perk you up.

Even Cilika agreed.

Katarina slipped into household banter. As soon as you start tending to your body, the way you talked as a kid returns.

—Whatever's gotten into you? Where could we possibly do such a thing? Everything's been washed, put away.

—Right here, right now, in the Zadruga.

Irma ran to the house to get the hair dye, towels, a plastic sheet to protect Katarina and the floor around her; Cilika and Ita stepped back and made room, and Katarina gave in.

Irma did everything with practiced brushstrokes. As she spread the dye evenly, they laughed, chatted about ordinary things, thought of their mother. Ita's eyes filled with tears, and they finally forbade each other from dwelling on sad things or speaking of them until Sunday.

They each had more than just a single swig of the cognac. Soon Katarina was saying it was okay for Lovro to come with his band and friends, and they wouldn't have to give up on partying in the house, and Cilika agreed that *it's best that way.* She wanted to sing; they didn't let her. Cilika told Katarina the story about Lovro once more. *He had gravestone polish all over his head, shining like a light, like one of those police-car beacons.* They laughed and laughed. Katarina could feel the cognac mixing with the sedatives she had been taking ever since David's accident. She got dizzy and signaled to the girls to stop, that she needed a break.

They simmered down. There was a knocking at the shack's only window. Someone knocked, three times, at intervals.

They weren't merely quiet. They were silent. Ita got up.

—Girls, I'm scared.

The same knocking repeated at the door.

Katarina took a deep breath. She stood up with her hair all glued together; she was at the door in two steps and pulled on the handle with all her strength. The door didn't budge. Once more she rattled the handle, pulled: the door stayed shut. Cilika got up and she tried it.

—So what is this now?

Ita ducked behind the wardrobe.

—Someone has locked us in.

—Ita, don't panic, and don't be silly, the door has no key from the outside. The lock is ancient.

Irma went over to the door and jiggled the handle.

They stood there in silence. Again, there was a knock. Katarina grabbed the handle, kicked the door with all her strength, and finally it opened. She stood on the threshold and shouted into the dark:

—Hey! Get away from my house, whoever you are, this is my house, don't you dare come back!

She closed the door, and the women shot each other puzzled looks.

Cilika got up and kissed Katarina.

—You know, I had no idea you're so brave.

—Cilika, my dear, it's not that I'm brave, it's that everything I've been scared of has already happened. Nothing bad can happen to me anymore.

Irma stared into her glass. She tossed the drink back in one gulp.

They rinsed Katarina's hair out over the sink in the washroom, combed it, dried it, and admired her new look. Then it was time to disperse. A person needs their rest, and tomorrow was a day

NADA GAŠIĆ

when nothing could go wrong. They kissed at the door; after all, this was Ita's last night as a single woman.

The anxious white marshmallow watched them go.

Katarina went into the little house, lingered briefly in the bathroom, changed, saw to her ablutions, and checked her reflection in the mirror. She lowered her gaze immediately; she'd need some time to get used to the lighter hair. She went into David's room, ducked under the white garlands, and lay down on his bed. The clean sheets whispered to her, and Katarina froze. She turned on the light. The bedding had been changed. She lay down and burst into tears. *Bring me back the scent of my child, bring me back the scent.*

The alcohol and sedatives quieted her.

Only the sober little house wept till dawn.

# Seventh stone, seventh wave

—VIIILIM, VIILIM!

Cilika had been yelling at beleaguered Vilim since morning, panicking that *she wouldn't have time to see to everything*. She went to the bride's house and offered to help, but her help really wasn't needed; then Cilika asked for help, which nobody could provide, and she began getting on everybody's nerves, until Ita finally declared:

—Keep Cilika away from me.

Damir was familiar with Cilika's frenzied moods; he knew it was better to keep a low profile, so he hid in his room. Our Little Lady hid with him too. And though nobody could hear them, they whispered like coconspirators.

—Damir, will we see the bride?

—I don't know, maybe.

—I so want to see the wedding gown. I bet it's glorious.

Damir frowned.

—I don't know what the wedding gown looks like, but the groom comes to fetch the bride at noon. I heard them say that. If there's enough light, we can watch from the fence when they're getting into the car.

—Brilliant. I'll stand on your shoulder. I have to see the bride. Then she added:

—How I'd love to try on a white wedding gown!

Damir shook his head. He had no idea what to say.

*　　*　　*

Bustling around, Katarina and Irma had seen each other only in passing since morning. Irma, leaving the upstairs bathroom free so Ita could take care of her preparations in peace, used the downstairs one instead. Both of them were in good spirits; the preparations, regardless of all that had happened over the last few days, proceeded smoothly. Katarina didn't ask about the number of guests who would be coming over, whom Lovro would be bringing with him when he came to fetch the bride. They chatted about simple things. *No, that's okay, I'll wear the brooch a little lower, that way it won't pull at the silk; the color black looks terrific on you, the pearls are all you need at your throat; my high heels are too high, how will I manage with them, once the dancing begins you forget about everything else; your hair color turned out beautifully, you look five years younger, I'll help you brush it out; I'm off to my hairdresser, it takes ages, see you around noon, one o'clock at the latest, so I can help get Ita into her gown.*

Irma was dashing off to the hairdresser, Katarina dashing off to see Dado. Irma picked up her purse from the front-hall cupboard; she hadn't yet slipped it over her shoulder. Katarina reached to take her jacket from the coat hook, and the two sisters collided. Irma's bag and everything in it, all of it, spilled onto the floor.

—Jesus, sorry.

Katarina leaned over to help pick up everything. Her hand stiffened.

—Irma, this is Dado's phone. Why was it in your purse?

—No idea. I didn't even know I had it.

Irma didn't look up as she collected her things.

—Irma, I'm asking you: How come David's phone is in your purse?

Irma looked up, furious.

—I'm telling you, I have no idea. I don't check through this purse every day. Maybe David just happened to put it in there, maybe he was up to something. I don't know.

—Irma, my whole fight with Dado started because he'd lost his phone. How could you not have known? How could it not have rung at least once?

Irma picked up everything off the floor and stood up. They were alone on an empty stage, snarling at each other.

—Katarina, who knows, maybe Dado turned it off on purpose and left it there. He was probably trying to get a new phone, like all kids, and if it worked, it worked, if not, he knew where he'd left it, and all he'd say was that he found it. And besides, you know he liked to drag me into your fights. Come on, use that head of yours. Did you have to attack me like this right before the wedding?

Katarina retreated.

—Sorry, that's probably what happened. We'll see when he wakes up.

She took the phone and put it into her own purse. They didn't say goodbye.

*     *     *

I've been noticing that I'm alone a lot of the time. At first, probably the first days—though silly me wasn't counting, and couldn't because the light was always on, so I couldn't tell whether it was night or day—there was always, always, always somebody with me. But now, bit by bit, nobody's around. That's probably a good sign, because they're probably thinking, no, not thinking, they know I'm getting better and I'll wake up soon and go home, and that's why they aren't here with me all the time. And once I'm home, they'll be sick of me soon enough.

But am I fretting, as my grandpa would have said? Yes, I am. Why? Because I'm becoming a softie and I miss them. I don't feel like being alone.

There, that's me all over: I leave the house and ride around on trams and can be on my own until the day after tomorrow. Being alone doesn't bother me even a little, but here I'm not thrilled about being on my own. I'm totally becoming a girl. I've even gotten used to this one nurse; she has begun calling me *Miško*, and it's as if it hurts less now when she gives me shots. To be fair, it doesn't hurt at all, but she doesn't know that. There is one who is quicker than the one who calls me Miško, but I don't like her as much, maybe because she's quiet. And there's another one who laughs out in the corridor, so I can tell when she's coming, but she doesn't laugh when she's working around me. Instead, she keeps saying stuff like *the sun's out today, and soon we'll be up out of bed; now we're going to take this out, now we'll this, now we'll that*, which is good and it isn't. The bad part is that I can't see the sun, so that makes me feel crummy, but it's good that she's saying something, and later I can think about it.

It seems to me that a bug or little spider crawled across my face this morning. Or was it a butterfly? It tickled me a little, but I wasn't scared. I'm just sorry I couldn't see what was tickling me. When will Mama come? Here she is!

Katarina kissed him a lot, but she didn't cry. She opened her bag, took out his phone, and showed it to him. Now she was completely used to talking with him like she always had.
—Irma found it, but if you don't like it anymore, once you are out of bed, we'll buy you a new one. I don't dare go shopping for it without you for fear I'll buy the wrong one. Deal?

Then she went quiet, turned on the phone, and had a look at the recent calls. She took out her own phone, found Vidošić's number, and sent him a message.

Then she devoted herself to David. She told him that Aunt Ita was getting married today, that they were all sending him their love and kisses, and that she wouldn't be with him much more today, but tomorrow she'd be with him right away in the morning, right away, as soon as the doctors finished their rounds. She went quiet and remembered it was usually around this time that

Inspector Vidošić popped by. Not today. Saturday, tomorrow was All Saints', then after that it would be All Souls' Day. So she wouldn't be seeing him until Tuesday. If he came on Tuesday.

She looked over when the door opened. Boris Horak saw her face fall as she stood up.

—Listen, I can't be here any longer today. Ita's getting married. Can you stay with David a little longer?

—Yes, I'll stay longer—I need to be with my boy.

Katarina left without a goodbye.

Boris took off his jacket and sat by the bed. He patted David's hand, taking care not to bump any of the needles. He was quiet. Then he started in with *Daddy's big boy*, and told him some other secret words, like, *your Daddy-Dragon will watch over you.*

He remembered something, looked at the shelf by David's bed, opened the cupboard, and spotted the book of fairy tales that Katarina had left there.

He took out the book out and sniffed it. The scent of much-thumbed pages had soaked in the long-ago smell of David's fingers when he was old enough to leaf through books on his own and choose the story they'd read. There were chocolate smudges that smelled like David's stained fingers when he was still in preschool. There were a few drawings of cars and a few of David's signatures with a big backward D. Horak took a deep breath and finally began to cry. He stood up quickly, turned to the child's bed. *Pull it together, he can't see you, can't hear you, chill.* He calmed down and turned to David. He gazed at him briefly, then went to his jacket, took out his eyeglasses, returned to the chair, put on his glasses, turned the page, and began to read aloud:

# THE TALE OF THE LITTLE DRAGON
## AND THE MAGIC FISH

Long, long ago, in days of yore, while dragons and wizards still roamed the Earth, in a cave near a faraway kingdom there came into the world a remarkable little dragon. Its parents were powerful, terrible flying dragons who belched fire for fun, and as he was their first child, they were overjoyed with their little baby dragon. Both of them hoped the little dragon would soon grow up to become a terrible, horrible dragon. It was, of course, to be expected that the dragon was small to start with—all dragons are small at birth—but, soon enough, his parents began to fret and fume. Why? Because there were other dragon parents who had also been blessed with a bundle of joy, but all those other newborn dragon babies, also tiny at birth, quickly grew. As time passed, all of them, every single one, grew paunches, their tails developed an edge of sharp spines, they sprouted powerful wings, and they had the beginnings of magnificent nostrils from which the more precocious were already belching fire— all of them, every single one. But not our little dragon. He was the only one who failed to grow. While other dragons his age had already begun soaring through the skies, even amid terrible storms, the little dragon stayed small. His nostrils did grow a little, but they did not belch fire; his tail did, indeed, grow a tad, but it could not boast a sharp spine, and, what's worse, instead of reaching skyward, it curved down over his belly. But worst of all was that instead of his dragon wings, he sprouted a single small wing in the middle of his back, and his little legs . . . well, he hardly had any. In a word, dismal. Scarcely dragon-like.

Instead of flying with his peers and burning down at least one little village, his parents had to cart him around on their backs, or, to their even greater despair, bring him around in a dragon buggy. So, while they were flying with him perched on their backs or were taking him out for a drive in his buggy, the little dragon, instead of dreaming about fire and brimstone, watched the animals scampering through the meadows and the woods. Flying over romping horses and pristine rivers, he'd crow on and on about the pretty horses and swimming fish.

In vain, his mother told him that dragons steer clear of water because it can extinguish the fire in their nostrils, and that the speed of the horse is nothing compared to the lightning-fast flight of a dragon. In vain, because the little dragon went right on gazing at the horses and fish with love, and, I must admit, with a little envy.

His parents began to fret: out of her concern, his mother shed a vast tear that caused a flood so huge that it soaked all the shoes and gowns of the little princesses, and his father let loose a ponderous, troubled sigh that blew the roof clear off a neighboring palace, so the king himself had to sleep for a whole week under the stars, wearing a silly nightcap on his head.

That very king was a sage and canny sovereign who knew something had to be done at once, for if another dragon tear were to fall, it wouldn't only ruin the shoes and gowns of the pampered princesses, but the deluge might well wash away the entire imperial treasury. The sage king knew that a few more dragon sighs would not only blow the roof away but the entire palace, and with it, the king, the queen, princes, princesses, and dozens of courtiers. He puzzled and puzzled in his

NADA GAŠIĆ

royal bed under the stars, and finally thought of his royal wizard, who hadn't had much to do recently, though he knew all sorts of magic, and he'd probably conjure a way to deal with the remarkable little dragon child and his tearful mother and troubled father.

In the morning, the king doffed his nightcap that had preserved him from the nightly chill, donned his gold crown, and commanded his courtiers to summon the wizard. The courtiers made their way with great reluctance to the wizard's chambers, because one never knows what wizards are up to and what, if they are in a foul mood, they might change an ordinary person into. They stopped at the door to the wizard's chambers; from within came the sound of a hacking cough and sniffles, and, by God, thunderous sneezes. They longed to retreat, for they did not feel like going in to see a wizard with a bad cold, but then they remembered the punishment that would await them if they didn't do the king's bidding. So they knocked, and bravely they waited. With a terrible screech the door flew open, and the courtiers saw before them the wizard himself amid a cloud of smoke and soot. He wore a crimson cape, flickering with stars; on his head was a wizard's hat, in his right hand a wizard's wand, and in his left... in his left a cup of hot tea. And the wizard's nose? It was huge—swollen and sniffling, as if he'd need a hankie the size of a sheet to blow it properly. Oof! What a nasty cold!

The courtiers looked at one another but didn't utter a word; they just bowed and delivered the king's summons. The wizard snorted angrily, and even more angrily he marched off to the king's chambers. And from the threshold he shouted at the king:

—As you can see, I have caught an awful cold, thanks to wet feet and no roof over my head. This makes me feel like leaving the court once and for all.

The king heard him out and nodded with compassion.

—This is the very reason I called you, oh powerful wizard, to save us from even greater hardship. As you know, we have been living in peace with our local dragons, and we seldom have any major problems with them. But now our first dragon neighbors have birthed a dragon baby that is not getting bigger, and the distressed parents are the reason for the flood and lack of a roof. You are handsomely paid here, you live in silk and velvet, so please conjure a way to free us from these troubles.

The wizard sat on the bench he was offered; he sniffled and sneezed, and thought and thought. His runny nose and grating cough interrupted his thinking, but he knew something had to be done at once.

Should he cast a spell to chase away the dragons? That might help, but new dragons could move into their cave and could become very, very unpleasant. Should he dry the mother's tear? You can dry up one tear by force, but soon another could spill from her eye. Might he halt the father's sigh? You could halt one, but the next, sooner or later, would blow the kingdom clear away.

He thought and thought, thought and thought . . .

—I've got it! It is best if I help the little dragon grow like his peers. His parents will be overjoyed, and they will stop shedding tears and sighing.

The king leapt for joy with such vigor that he had to hold on to his gold crown with both hands.

NADA GAŠIĆ

—But how?

—Simple. I'll ask the little dragon what he'd like most of all, and he, I'm quite certain, will wish to be like all the other dragon children: a big, strong dragon who flies and belches fire. Magic always works best when a wish is very, very strong.

By now the king was bouncing around for joy, and he didn't mind at all when he splashed in a puddle.

—Oh, my faithful, mighty wizard, I'll give you carts full of ducats for your reward—just free us from this calamity!

Right as he was uttering these words, the mother dragon in their nearby cave was gazing at her freshly awakened little child, and, seeing how he was so puny and nothing to speak of, she shed another tear, which once more filled the hallways of the palace. The father sighed, and his sigh blew the court doors off their hinges.

Tripping over his gown, the wizard literally ran to the dragons' cave, with the king shouting after him:

—And on top of those carts full of ducats, you'll get yet another ducat—just please free us from this calamity!

Moments later, the wizard found himself standing before the entrance to the dragons' cave. He knocked politely, for one never knows with dragons. The door was opened by the fretful mother.

—Greetings, Mr. Wizard, what good brings you here?

The wizard entered and explained how matters stood: they had lived in peace until now, but their little one, he had heard, so charming at first, was maturing a little more slowly, and it was no surprise that the parents were anxious. But the point was that their tears and sighs had wreaked havoc on the royal palace, and he, the mighty wizard, was willing to help their only child.

Oh, how thrilled the parents were! And they, too, promised the wizard carts of ducats and, furthermore, a free flight on a dragon's back, and they'd gladly provide the sparks needed to start a little fire if the wizard was reluctant to get his hands sooty. Both of them were sure the little dragon would wish to be like his dragon peers: a big, mature, terrible dragon. They could hardly wait for the wizard to go to the dragon crib.

Though he had seen many things in his years as a magician, the wizard was astonished when he saw the little dragon: its sad little belly; its legs, hardly to be seen; its tail curled up toward its tummy; its little snout that looked more like the snout of a horse than of a dragon; and instead of dragon wings, there was something on its back like, like . . . like a stunted wing, a fish fin, what could that be? Oof.

But he said not a word; he just touched the little dragon with his magic wand and said:

—Oh, little dragon child, what is your fondest wish? What would you like to be when you grow up?

The little dragon came alive, jumped up, gazed with his wide eyes at the mighty wizard, and then very, very loudly, even a little too loudly for his size, declared:

—Oh, what I'd love to grow up to be more than anything is a little horse that can swim like a fish!

As soon as he uttered these words, lightning from the wizard's magic wand flashed and lit the entire cave. A thick wall of smoke rose up, and the wizard and parents began sneezing and coughing. They had to wait for the smoke to disperse so they could take a good look at what the wizard had wrought.

Oh no! Alas! Alack!

NADA GAŠIĆ

The wizard and the dragon parents were appalled to see that the cave was deserted. No little dragon. He had vanished! Where had he gone? Was he gone forever?

The mother burst into tears, and the sad father sighed. Powerful rivulets of water flowed from her tears, and his sighs became mighty gales of wind and blew away all the palaces and castles with all their kings, queens, princes, and beautiful princesses. The wizard himself disappeared, along with his cold.

The parents bitterly regretted having wished that their child should be larger and more powerful than he was, and off they flew, far, far away, inconsolable and tearstained, hoping that one day they'd find their little dragon child.

Sometimes, before major storms, a frightened child catches sight of the dragons' tails with the sharp spines and their terrible dragon wings as they wing their way over the city.

But for real?

Of course, there haven't been dragons on Earth for a very long time, nor have there been wizards plagued with head colds. Here and there, the occasional king and queen wonder, in amazement, at what they are still doing in this world of ruined palaces, which are visited by scantily clad, boorish tourists. In the deserted caves there are now electric trains instead of dragons and playful dragon children. So, what happened to the little dragon? Nobody knows. All that is known for sure is that in the deep blue sea there swims an amazing little fish that greatly resembles a tiny dragon. Its snout is tiny and looks as much like a dragon's snout as it looks like a horse's; its tail, like the tail of the little dragon, curves upward toward its belly; and on its back is a little wing, in fact a tiny fin, and that is what the odd little fish uses as it gaily plies the seas. Just like real fish. Some say this is what the little dragon child became. That fish is called a *seahorse.*

Boris closed the book and put it back where he'd found it.
—My little dragon, Daddy's little dragon, enough for today. Get some rest, and Daddy-Dragon will be back tomorrow. All Saints' Day is tomorrow, and I have to take flowers up to the cemetery at Mirogoj. But I'll come right afterward, okay? And how would it be for you to surprise me tomorrow and greet me wide awake?
He went out and slowly closed the door.

That wouldn't be so bad. But I don't know. I'm not sure I'll be getting up tomorrow. This wasn't bad, the story my dad read. Mama never read me that one, only Dad, but I don't know why they scheduled things this way. What's going on with Mama? Why does she look all funny, like she's lighter somehow? What's up with her? I can't see so well through this stupid curtain of mine, and besides she's being weird. Maybe tomorrow will be better. I don't like it that nobody will come to see me today. Not Dad or Mama. Fine, it's probably that I'm much, much better, so that's why they decided, but still, I don't like being here alone. I'm a little creeped out by it, though I know that's silly. If I were in bad shape, my dad would never have left, and Mama would be glued to the bed, sobbing. Now I'm beginning to feel as if I'd rather she was sitting here next to me, sobbing, than me being all alone, like this. Yuck. I'd even like it if that inspector guy showed up. That's how low I've fallen. And what's worse, I would really like to be at Ita's wedding, so I could hide all kinds of her stuff, then she rats me out to Mama, then Irma shouts at me, then I'm mixing the cakes and the ham together, then I switch around all the glasses and do all kinds of rascally stuff. I'd even let them put a bow tie on me; as if I didn't hear what they were up to. What ninnies. I'd even agree to that, if it meant I wouldn't have to lie around here anymore. By myself. Yes, and I'd bring them Big Boy Damir, to drive Cilika nuts. I'd really love that. I'm restless, I'm so jumpy inside, and I can't figure out why they don't see that on the outside. I keep think- ing I hear someone creeping around the door. But when I listen more closely, nobody's there. As if it's easier for me when I am a huge head, no hands, no feet, no neck. I lis- ten as if I'm breathing inside a big pot, and that helps me feel less scared. Then, when I go away somewhere, nobody can come after me. No dinosaurs, no sharks, no butter- flies, none of those bad guys from computer games or the movies, or criminals. Now I'd like it if I didn't have to duck deeper behind the curtain, and I wish Dad had stayed with me, and I wish I were the most important person in the world for him. I don't know. I probably am, I definitely am the most important. It's just the way he keeps things down inside himself. And only the devil knows what else. My Daddy-Dragon . . .

## Does the devil know what David's father keeps down inside himself?

*I see that I stopped when I was looking for someone to be close to.*

*My search for someone to be close to apparently started right after what, today, we're calling the Homeland War. I can't muster the feeling of bleak isolation that overwhelmed me right away after the war ended. I wasn't as surprised at losing my feel for community—I confess that in a way I'd had a premonition this could happen—as I was that my feel for the community evaporated so fast. Just as during the war, I felt a communal bond with every single person, I, literally, lost not only my communal bond, but every point of contact with others. Literally with every other person. Now when I remember the time before my isolation, it feels like it was a time with no apartness. A smooth surface of sameness. Like a lake that pools after a flood. Perhaps from the shore, from the safety of dry land, one can sense all the different things submerged under the water, possibly houses, roads, churches, but all one can see from dry land is water on all sides. A smooth surface. Nothing more. The only thing I don't remember from that time—silence. Things felt a lot like a wild football match, and our national team numbered in the millions. And I, who flatter myself that I tend to hold myself apart—with my background and my character—from the herd, I became an ecstatic, alcohol-fueled fan. That's how I now see myself when I think back on that time. If I do. The time of my bizarre congruence with everybody and everything. A time with no doubts. A time with no examining what ought to be examined, meanwhile questioning things that a sound mind would not doubt today. A time I have nothing to say about now. Nothing. Nothing good or bad. Simply put, a time with no apartness, and not only*

NADA GAŠIĆ

in publicly aired thinking, but in the very process by which thoughts were formed and shaped. A subtle process for which, I guess, everybody is responsible, and which should be as individual as a fingerprint. Exactly. Fingerprint-like. Thinking and the mysterious process of its formation ought to be unique. Yet during that time they weren't. And I, utterly aware with all my sober spirit, was a part of this singular moment, a part of this doubt-free time, this time for agreeing with everything and everybody. Even with my fellow passengers on trams. And this was me—me, who even before I went through puberty felt I was aloof, glad, in every situation and in every dialogue, to be the one who did not go along. That was my way of functioning among my friends and peers, the way I always had. Yes, even for me there came a time when I joined the crowd. The crowd of those who were mine. That's what it was like in my circle, to which I brought my wife, and in her circle, to which she brought me. Of course, I know full well, I really do now know that there were those who formed their own circles of skeptics, but I didn't find them, nor did they find me. And I don't know why I didn't come across a circle like that, why I didn't seek them out. Why did I give in, why didn't I go looking for those others who kept apart? Why was it easier for me to find kidney stones than people who kept their own counsel about things? I can't believe that certain vital hormones stifled my natural inclination to doubt and my position of resistance. Was I, the eternally cynical and aloof observer, afraid of standing apart in a dangerous time? Did I feel safer with the herd? I don't know. I am not capable of judging myself. I cannot believe today that the circle of my friends at the time did not diverge in a single articulated thought from hers. My God, the two of us were so different in background, education, social status—everything, absolutely everything. Yet we were the same. *Incomprehensible, but so it was. And even with her crowd, I felt good. This was in fact the only time when I felt good by the side of my ex-wife. Today I don't even like to run into the people I socialized with back then. I don't like to hear what they're thinking about. I don't like remembering what I thought then, if I thought at all, and I really don't want to remember what I was saying. When I add it all up, the only thing I seem unable to forgive myself for is that I accepted being part of the herd, not because the herd thought the way they thought, but because now, sobered, I see the herd as they are: bracing for each new disappointment, ready to seek new scapegoats, ready to go wild, flying in the face of their own decisions, their own actions, their attitudes, and their resolutions. There's the rub—I was at one with the herd. I feel this to be a humiliation, a humiliation I visited upon myself and bought into. I was everybody.*

*When the hostilities subsided, when things sorted themselves out in a different way, I was left alone. I could no longer tolerate being among the people who had surrounded me. And, frankly, I could hardly wait to move back to Vodnikova and return to the world my father had never left. I went to dig through what remained of his belongings. But, to be honest, I was digging in hopes of finding myself, the person I thought of myself as being. My sense of myself. A freethinker.*

*When I wasn't digging through old things, I was having a look at the books on the shelves and the paintings on the walls. Two paintings, to be exact. One a scene of antiquity, by which I can precisely trace my maturation: as a small boy, I was drawn to the little birds fluttering around the heads of the maidens; as a slightly older boy, I sought what lay beyond the distant, misty hills; while as a teenager, staring at the mons pubis of the maidens, I felt my first sexual thrills* with much greater intensity than from the pornography circulating in my classroom. The other painting enthralled me. It portrayed an odd tale, and I can't claim for certain that it was not part of my family lore, the sort of lore every family has, but I do know that it was evidence of a visit from a guest many years before, an officer of the Russian White Guard, who, in search of a happier country where he might settle, briefly enjoyed the hospitality of my apartment, which, in the mid-1930s, belonged to my grandfather. As a token of his gratitude, the visitor left this painting, one he had painted himself: oil on canvas, depicting a dramatic shipwreck, a towering wave about to engulf people who are clinging to the broken wreckage of the mast, soon to be swept away. From my childhood, I still remember how one of the castaways was waving a handkerchief, a scrap of some sort of cloth, but the rag was too pale, too light in color, and as a child I found this intensely irritating, because even as a child I knew that with this faded rag amid the churning sea, there was nobody who could possibly see the castaway. And I had the impression that the castaway with the rag also knew this. Now, as an adult, after all these years, standing again before the painting, the futile faded handkerchief again made me wince. Who could possibly see it, you sorry soul? While I was digging through things, I opened every book, hoping, of course, that I'd come upon a letter tucked away, or something else precious. I didn't know what. And so it was that I leafed through a large art book. In it I happened upon a reproduction of the original on which our guest of many years past had based his painting. The original painter, a man named Aivazovsky, had called the painting The Ninth Wave. I'm no connoisseur of fine arts, nor, I admit, had I ever heard of this painter, but the painting transfixed me. Our guest from so long ago had rendered, or copied, everything, every last detail, with remarkable mastery. But there was one thing that made our guest's work more than a mere copy. An intriguing detail. What had put me off the painting on the wall when I was growing up and made me wince was the faded handkerchief. While on Aivazovsky's oil in that art book, you see the handkerchief at once. The original is dominated by an obvious, bright, fluttering red kerchief in the hand of the castaway. The castaway probably knows that flourishing the little scrap of cloth will bring no help, but he is desperate. He doesn't give up, though the final, ninth wave is looming, soon to wash them all away. And yet still he hopes. He waves his red kerchief. He pours into it all his hopes. I cannot know whether the visitor who briefly found haven in my grandfather's apartment copied this painting from the art book or painted it from memory. This matters not at all. But even if he had been painting from memory, the red would have etched itself in his mind. You can see how much it dominates the reproduction in the book. The red kerchief would have done the same for him, regardless of when and where he'd seen the painting. Even if he hadn't seen the art book, or a tattered reproduction from an arts calendar, he would have had to note the red handkerchief. That color. He had to. Yet he refused to paint it. Perhaps he was depicting himself and his fellow sufferers, the broken and crushed forces of the Russian White Guard, an entire world, a civilization fading away. Perhaps he'd lost hope to the point that he could no longer identify with his desperate attempt at painting the castaway who was confronting his end with the flourish of the kerchief, or perhaps he simply refused to back off even a bit, not for the life of him, from his principles? Not even symbolically. Nor with this unhappy flaunt of the red kerchief. He did not wish to give in to the idea of the red. The essence of red. Now this was a man who was not of the herd. He may have risked a great deal—from the ridicule of passing critics excoriating his interpretation of the painting, to serious doubts that he might be color-blind. But he did not give in. He did not allow the reds to prevail. And I, the eternal skeptic, the doubter who was above the mob, here I was, wallowing with the herd. And once you do so, you can say goodbye to the words "never again." Leaving aside what color the herd was and whether the herd tomorrow might change the color of the handkerchief, I wallowed with them, and there can be no guarantee that I would never do so again.

Then, when I examined the painting with different eyes, I longed, as I had never longed for anything till then, for this vanished amateur painter, with no first or last name, this man with no face, to converse with me, to be a friend, a contemporary. To teach me how not to give in to the color of the herd. Regardless of what color that might be. This man, until I met my second wife, was the only person I felt close to.

Later I'll say something about her.


## And still, there by the window

They waited for time to pass, and finally the time came for Our Little Lady to see the bride. They warmed themselves by the window.

—May I ask you something, Our Little Lady?

—You are constantly asking me things. And even if I were to forbid it, you'd ask anyway.

—Yes, but this is very serious. Can you see David?

—I can.

—Is he alone?

—He's alone. I already explained that.

—I would like to ask you something very, very serious.

—Ask away.

She felt that this would be an unusual question. She was getting good at this, and she easily climbed up onto his sleeve.

—Do you know who killed the woman they threw behind the school?

—I do.

—Who?

—Unimportant. Many people know. But it is not up to me to disclose this.

—Do you know who scared David?

—I do.

—Who?

—I won't answer that either, because the answer for you would be meaningless. The name would mean nothing to you.

—Maybe it would. Try me.

—I don't play with things like that.

—Fine, but do you know whose *fault it is* that David was hit?

—I do.

—Whose?

—I won't answer that either. Because *that name would mean a whole lot to you,* so that is why I won't answer.

—You aren't . . . fair.

—Damir!

He huffed, blushed red. He knew he had gone too far, but he felt he had the right to protest.

—You think I don't know anything, that I'm stupid.

—I didn't say that. You know I didn't say that and I don't think that. But I'm protecting you.

—How?

—With ignorance.

—Ignorance is not protection.

—Oh yes, it is. It sure is!

—I don't want to be protected.

—I took responsibility for you . . . at least for a time.

The sun was barely breaking through, and a sunbeam licked the curtain in Damir's room. The beam looked as if it were trying to slip in.

Our Little Lady smiled.

—How cunning the sun is, looking for a cozy home.

She dropped her head as if she were tired.

—Everybody is looking for their own home, Damir, my friend.

—You're weaseling out of the conversation.

—I am weaseling out, yes, that's true.

—But I need answers.

—Don't worry. You'll hear them in time.

—Will everybody hear them?

—Everybody knows them. They just are trying not to hear them. Or say them.

—Does the identity of a murderer always come out?

—No, not always. But it is known.

—How?

—The murderer knows. The murderer is always the first witness.

—Not enough.

—Sometimes it isn't enough even when a thousand know. Tens, hundreds of thousands. The numbers are irrelevant. Especially to the murder victim.

—Does the murderer's conscience bother him?

—Rarely. The notion of conscience is overrated. Few have a conscience, and usually the ones who do aren't the ones who murder.

—I don't want to listen to you anymore. And I'll never ask you anything again.

—Damir, you're being childish.

—Well, you . . . you aren't as good as you pretend to be.

—Damir!

—Leave me. Go.

—Damir!

—Then I will go. Out into the yard.

—You will not. You'll be sad if you leave me.

Damir said nothing. Then he stood.

Our Little Lady teetered; she even had to spread her dress wide so the flounces could serve as wings and help her keep her balance.

Suddenly he took heart.

—Why are we always arguing?

She smiled at him. He liked this side of her. She was quick to forgive. Quick to forget. If she forgot . . .

—I'm calling from a pay phone. I'm off to the hairdresser, and I'll be there for a couple of hours. You know where the salon is. I need to ask you something.

Two hours later, near the salon:

—Listen, the agreement was that I would sell the house and land to that friend of yours, and through him to you. The agreement was that my older sister and I would each get our own apartment in the building to be built and a considerable sum of money in the bargain. Only yesterday did I have a good look at what I signed, and I can see that nothing is spelled out anywhere in the contract for me or my sister.

—Your problem. Contracts are read before they're signed.

—You were blackmailing me. I was half-crazed with fear.

—Also your problem.

—I want the money, now.

—You will get no money, and as to your apartment, talk with the new owner. For now, that's not me.

—I only saw him when we were signing at the notary. I don't know him. I agreed to do this with you, not him. You are the real owner of everything.

—Why didn't you pay attention? You can read and write, Little Miss Teacher.

—I'll end up with no money and no apartment. And my sister will be out on the street with her child.

—Your problem.

He laughed and tugged her hair a little. He was nearly gentle in the way he tugged it.

—There is always low-income housing. You'll be fine.

—I'm going to go public with this. I'll request protected witness status.

—No, my dear aider and abettor in covering up a murder. If things ever get hot and heavy, I'll be the one requesting that status. I'll know exactly when I need to. This is the last time you say such a thing. Understood? No more threats! Understood?

—You forced me to be in the car, that's what I'll say, and you think you chose that little street by chance? That you got stuck by chance? I know Trešnjevka better than you do. I recognized my David, and even if I hadn't, I wouldn't have let you run over a child. Beast!

He controlled himself; he was in perfect control. He relaxed his neck and shook the vertebrae loose.

—It wasn't just you who recognized him. I drove you home a few times and remembered him well. Anything more to say?

—No.

With one finger he turned her head to face him and sneered.

—Let me have a look at you. You're working tonight, Little Miss Teacher.

—No, I am not working, not this evening, and not ever again. We're done.

—Tonight, you'll be in the lounge of the Shellaton at 7 PM.

—My sister is getting married.

—7 PM.

—I need the white stuff. I won't be able to go without it.

—That, at least, is not a problem.

He reached into the inside pocket of his jacket and handed her a bundle.

—Give me the stronger pills. For later, not for tonight.

—For the white stuff and the stronger pills, your services are no longer sufficient. So we're hooked, are we?

He grabbed her by the breast and yanked it hard. She put out her hand and he dropped the packet into her palm.

—I need younger ones from your crowd. What about the woman you promised you'd bring? Us rednecks, we have this thing about schoolmarms.

She held the packets tightly in her fist as he laughed.

—I already promised her a trip to Milan. It will all be fine.

—See, you know how to be good.

Once more he pulled her hair. This time not gently. She went back into the salon for them to fix her hair. The hairdressers were surprised at how clumsy she'd been, mussing her hair when she got into her car.

*   *   *

The hair, makeup, and nail people all arrived on time. The Zadruga was ready to welcome the guests and the groom. They dressed Ita by the window in Katarina's room. And the white marshmallow was brought in. It hung on a hanger hooked to the wardrobe door. Katarina was in charge of it; she slipped her hands under the hoops, fluffed the puff of the sleeves, checked the train; it remembered her well, the reluctant little seamstress, how she callously pricked it last Sunday, and it quaked for the fate of its every thread, every piece of lace trim, every bead, fearful that she might reach for the straight pins again.

Then Katarina went off to get ready, slowly, no nerves. Irma was always late, but she'd come, she would definitely come.

Irma did get back to the house on time. She went up to the second floor and got ready. Her hair was splendid, her makeup discreet, her cleavage, adorned only by pearls, remarkable. The long sleeves of the black silk dress set it off even more.

Irma knew she looked stunning. She put on black patent-leather shoes with nine-centimeter heels and went down to check on Katarina. Not bad. Maybe her jewelry could have been a little fancier, but Katarina could not be dissuaded; she had to wear the crystal accordion player.

Katarina looked tenderly at her younger sister.

—Irma, you're so beautiful!

Irma shivered.

—Don't tell me that. I am not beautiful, Katarina, I am not.

This scared Katarina, and for the first time in years she offered Irma a drink.

—Should we have one for courage? Then we can go see how Ita is faring.

They each had a shot of rakija and then went to find the bride. But Ita found them first, already combed, dolled up, manicured, and dressed.

—Oh my God! Magnificent!

—Mother of god, you look like a princess!

The white marshmallow swelled with pride.

*    *    *

Cilika, poor woman, was fussing. It's not just that Vilim's sports coat was too tight, but she was barely able to do up her skirt, and her bra was *too tight, but everything fit last month. Gramps wandered off somewhere; that stupid hairdresser didn't get my perm right.* Everything looked wrong on her. The only good thing was that, thank God, Big Boy wasn't making a sound. *She had to give Gramps something to eat before they went; time flies, the groom will be here any minute with his groomsmen, and she, of all people, running late, she who was such a mainstay for this family, twice their kuma—once as Katarina's godmother and again as Ita's maid of honor. What a disgrace that would be.*

Carrying a dish with stewed leeks, she slowly opened the door to Gramps's little room. Empty. Forgetting to set the dish on the table, she could barely contain herself.

—Vilim, Vilim, find Gramps, who knows where he's gotten to.

Vilim, as always, had wandered off as well. Cilika set down the dish and began searching all over the house for Gramps. From one room to the next, from the pantry to the bathroom. She knocked on the bathroom door, then opened it gingerly, and when she saw that it, too, was empty, she panicked and began yelling again for Vilim. In the end, she had to take off her skirt so she could go upstairs to the attic. *It really is much too tight.* Gramps was perched up there on the bearing beam, and, firmly tied in place, he shone his flashlight at Cilika, announcing maliciously:

—I'll be safe, and the Sava is going to wash you all away. Damned bastards.

She couldn't untie him herself, and she didn't know where Vilim was. *Time is escaping, the groom will be here any minute, and I can't pop over to Katarina's to ask for help.*

Forgetting to put her skirt back on, she ran out of the house, and for the first time since people had moved into the new buildings, she spoke to a neighbor from one of them. The man was just on his way in.

—Dear neighbor, I'm praying you, I have nobody to ask for help—I have an elderly grandfather who is sick. He has tied himself up in the attic. Could you please lend me a hand?

The neighbor didn't quite understand; he was even worried that someone might have hanged themselves in the attic, but he saw that the poor woman was only half-dressed, and, of course, he jumped in to help. He was a robust forty-year-old man, agile in climbing and quite adept at untying, and strong enough that, with a little help from Cilika, they carried the old man down the steep attic stairs. When they finally finished the difficult task, having listened to how the Sava *would wash them all away, the bastards, but he'd be saved*, the helpful neighbor reassured Cilika.

—Come now, ma'am, no need to thank me. Who knows what we'll be like when we get old. If we live that long, the times being what they are. Come now, please, the old man needed help. It's not his fault.

And he smiled and thanked her politely but did not accept the drink she offered. Then off he went to close his garage door.

Cilika could not get over *how this very fine neighbor from that new building had helped her.* She fed Gramps, who quieted down and fell right to sleep; then she put back on her pathetic skirt, and, alone, with a big bouquet of pink roses, she went over to Katarina, Irma, and Ita's house.

The honking of horns could be heard in the distance.

She found Vilim in front of the Zadruga, standing with the guests who had already arrived from the closest family: aunts and uncles, in-laws, cousins, friends, godparents—there were more than fifty. He was drinking beer from a bottle.

—You'll get an earful when we get home.

That's what she told him.

The honking of horns was getting louder; the wedding party dashed around, alarmed, *Ita, where's Ita; watch out for the high heels, lift the train, don't touch anything till they come, and nobody can come out to greet the guests before Katarina does, as she is the oldest; Vilim, you go with Katarina, I'm her kuma; Katarina, be careful, your brooch came unclasped; Sir, please make sure everybody has glasses, so when the groom's party comes to the door we all sing the welcome song: Dobro mi došel prijatel vu skromni zagorski dom, all of us, all of us sing it.*

So maybe they'll change their mind after all and come. Mama too, and even stupid old Irma. The wedding will be going on all night long anyway.

The procession of cars led by the groom's best man and the other groomsmen pulled up in front of the house. The first to get out was the best man, and after him, hot-pink Lovro. He was wearing an elegant tuxedo, in his hand was a nosegay of calla lilies, but his head, oh Mother of God, his head.

Our Little Lady and Damir were already standing by the fence. Or rather Damir was standing by the fence, and Our Little Lady had twisted her teensy neck over his shoulder, so she wouldn't lose her chance to see the bride. She was flustered like an excited child, which amused Damir.

Nothing went according to plan. Vilim remembered to step forward to greet the groom, but he forgot that Katarina was the most important. He left her standing in front of the house and stepped forward himself, and nobody sang *Dobro mi došel prijatel*, because the groom arrived with an orchestra; tambura players struck up with *Tko te ima, taj te nema, tko te nema, taj te sanja,* and the groups commingled, offering one another glasses. Two of Ita's friends armed with straight pins and boutonniere pinned them to the groomsmen's lapels; the groom's mother was peeved at her husband; her husband was upset with his wife. In the end, they finally allowed hot-pink Lovro to enter the house.

The scene was exquisite, everybody said so later; Lovro couldn't take his eyes off of his queen, and she truly looked like a queen. Katarina, instead *of our parents who are no longer with us,* gave a welcome speech; then there was a toast. Everybody had glasses, thank God. Then the tambura players played their tune again, *Tko te ima, taj te nema, tko te nema, taj te sanja.* Cilika fought for them to play *Dobro mi došel prijatel vu skromni zagorski dom,* and when they did, she turned to Vilim, who smiled.

—Now, sing, when I tell you, sing! Can't you see they're trying to outdo us with their songs?

Vilim hugged his Cilika's goddaughter, Katarina, and together they sang so nicely. They sang sweetly.

Now I bet they're all singing. But Mama's probably not singing. She's probably thinking about me, feeling bad because I'm in the hospital, so she's not singing. I know her.

Quantities of alcohol were consumed at the bride's house, but hardly anything was eaten. Enough food was left over for another two weddings. That's what was said later. Cilika encouraged people to leave for the church, *better wait for her there, while they're still having their pictures taken, and it will do us no harm to be there by the church; it's not even cold, as if tomorrow were not All Saints'.*

The men discussed how to *organize the procession of cars to the church, these streets are narrow; you'll be driving into someone's bedroom when you meant to turn your car around. Who goes first, who goes second; Ita and Lovro in the second car, the best man leading the way; no, the best man is driving; not driving, the best man is with the tambura players; who is carrying the banner; he may be drunk, but he still has a firm hand.*

Finally they were ready to leave the house, and Katarina burst into tears. Ita was leaving their family home. Irma cried too; Katarina had never seen her like that.

*Tko te ima, taj te nema, tko te nema, taj te sanja.*

By the fence, Damir was worried that Our Little Lady might fall.

Ita came out; they were barely able to squeeze the terrified marshmallow through the yard gate. They went to the car that would take the bride and groom to the church, and Our Little Lady finally saw the wedding gown.

—My God, Jesus, it is magnificent. A heavenly queen!

Our Little Lady heard herself say this, and, just in case, she made a sign of the cross on her breast with her dainty hand.

The procession of cars left, and the fading sound of honking drew the neighbors from their windows. Damir went to his room and set euphoric Our Little Lady down on the table.

Katarina, Irma, and Ita's little house began to sing in a shaky voice:

*Tko te ima, taj te nema, tko te nema, taj te sanja...*

All its old neighbors joined in, and Mala Street rang with:

*Tko te ima, taj te nema, tko te nema, taj te sanja . . .*
They jumbled something with the verses. That's old age
for you.

So maybe it's better that I'm here till the wedding's over. I
know them—they'd want me to be the bearer for Ita's and
Lovro's rings. With a bow tie. Fat chance.

The wedding was nice and quiet, in the modest St. Joseph's
church. Long ago in the workers' neighborhood of Trešnjevka,
someone had designed and built this church; the interior looked
like a factory hall. But, fine, there were decorations, white bows
on the benches. Everybody was moved when Vilim delivered
Ita to Lovro. Lovro was no longer hot pink, but cardinal red; nobody noticed. Aside from Lovro's mom, of course. She glared
murderously at Queen Ita. The reverend said what he had to say,
their joint prayers were offered, and the newlyweds kissed, but
carefully, so the bride's makeup wouldn't smear.

Later, in front of the church, during the rice and rose petals
and confetti, someone waving a broom around shouted, *Who'll
be sweeping this up, who'll be sweeping this up*, as the tambura players played over it all—everything was fine.

The procession of cars drove off toward the Trade Fair grounds.

Our Little Lady and Damir were starting to get bored. She
would have talked about the gown, but Damir had no intention of joining her.
—Damir, do you want us to play Go?

NADA GAŠIĆ

—No. Maybe tomorrow.

—Good.

And that was all for that night.

I am as tired as if I had been at the wedding. I'll sleep a little.

*   *   *

They entered the white hall, bathed in white lights, with white slipcovers on the chairs, white tablecloths, white bouquets on the tables. There was commotion as people took their seats according to the seating plan.

The chair next to Katarina was empty. Irma was nowhere to be seen. Katarina, her face rigid, responded to the groom's mother, saying her sister would be there soon, shortly, any minute now.

Then the orchestra played a fanfare. A hush ensued. The bass guitar player was the emcee, and over the microphone he invited everyone to listen to the reverend, who had come to bless the evening. With the blessing came mild admonitions regarding extravagance and, in closing, a few verses by an unknown Catholic author. Bass guitar then suggested a round of applause for the serving of the appetizer. Heartfelt clapping followed for the platters that were dominated by Dalmatian-style Zagorje štrukli. With the rattling of dishes and the murmuring of conversation, the wedding dinner commenced. Waiters were soon clearing empty plates. Bass guitar bungled the order of events a little, but nobody minded. The appetizer had already been eaten when he called the assembled guests, before the soup was served, to listen to the Croatian anthem. The chairs scraped as the guests rose to their feet. Among the crowd of 178 members, only a few were already drunk, and the anthem was heard politely, hands on hearts, with humming. Singing aloud were Vilim and those from the farther tables, who, knowing that they were secondary both in terms of status and assigned seating, had already been guzzling before eleven o'clock that morning at the groom's apartment. Ita, now Mrs. Slaviček, abandoned the panicked stage-fright phase; her face showed no trace of the ecstatic blush that had heightened her complexion after the rites. But she was at a loss to explain how she could have failed to notice when one of the hoops of her crinoline caught on the chair and pushed it back when she stood to honor the anthem. The chair slid quite far back without a sound, ready to cause a catastrophe. To herself or others. But there it was; it happened. As everyone started in on the soup, Ita relaxed, prepared to take her seat. The white marshmallow shrieked, threatened, pleaded for someone to look down and prevent the inevitable; nobody heard. Ita later claimed that her whole body froze for a second, and then it realized that the support for its posterior was gone. She tried, poor thing, to stay on her feet. This is what sealed her fate. With her body imitating the shape of a chair, she staggered backward; her feet in twelve-centimeter high heels were able to take a step and a half, and then they adroitly took to the air, while her left hand clutched at Lovro's pocket and the right, desperately, reached for the tablecloth. The hoops of her crinoline prevented her from clambering back up, so Lovro pulled her by the hand with which she was clutching his ripped

NADA GAŠIĆ

pocket, and then he tried to lift her by taking hold of her silken corset that painfully whimpered as it tore. The marshmallow will confirm this statement. Everybody saw her breast pop out, no, not a breast, a titty, and Cilika's bulging thighs strained as Ita's maid of honor struggled to help her to her feet with invocations to the Blessed Virgin Mary and grunts.

Presented for the guests to admire, the gigantic six-layered wedding cake wobbled as Ita fell, and then it collapsed like an anxious, overweight old lady. Sadly and definitively. A tectonic scar zagged across the white marzipan icing; the cake split apart, and its chocolate innards poured out in an ugly heap, which half of the guests later said reminded them of manure. Lovro's mother said that as far as she was concerned, she had never seen manure. The figure of the bride and groom rolled off and under the plate of one of the bridesmaids' boyfriends. He grabbed it, not without pride, stood up, raised it toward the gobsmacked wedding party, and said over and over, *I've got it, I've got it, what do I do with it? I've got it, what do I do with it?* The women called on dear God, but the typical slapping of hands to the face in surprise was missing; a whisper of womanly instinct kept them attentive to their makeup. Then, a few men leaped to their feet and helped up poor Ita, who was no longer even trying to get up herself, nor was she in any shape to do so. Not to preserve her queenly dignity, nor the beauty of the gown, nor her elaborately fastened updo, nor her professional makeup. This last, of course, was the first to go: she sobbed, she wailed, her tears streamed down and trickled over the layers of powder and the mascara, which immediately dribbled into black rings; her bun loosened, and her hair flopped down over her left shoulder. No longer Queen Ita, her face was reminiscent of a manic panda. Katarina, with an unnatural burst of zeal, threw herself into scooping up the ruined cake and madly reshaping it, like a child with a crumbling sandcastle, striving in vain to rebuild it. Then, resigned, she unwittingly wiped her hands on her silk suit and burst into tears. With her wept the other women among their closest relatives, and all you could hear was *Oh Jesus, Jesus and Mary, here, here, come over here*. Summoned by this call, Lovro finally led Ita out. They were followed by Katarina, Ita's maid of honor, Cilika, and three friends that Cilika referred to as Ita's *krancle,* Cilika's word for flower girls. For a little while, there was still the buzz of excited voices; a child's cruel sneer was heard, then the sporadic sound of the cautious rattling of silverware, followed by comments such as *it'll be cooling off, the soup is getting cold*; then the sounds unified, coalesced, and the guests, tamed, began doing the job they had come to do. They dined.

Having left his new wife with her sisters and other close relatives, Lovro examined the remnant of his pocket and tucked it into the other one, still intact. Then he did something entirely natural yet so wrong: he went over to the bar. Just as the waiter was pouring him a whisky, a huffy Cilika appeared and, without a glance in Lovro's direction, commanded the young man behind the bar to bring a bottle of cognac and seven glasses to the women's washroom. Then she was gone.

Lovro responded to the waiter's cheery banter, but he did not, in fact, join in conversation. He was looking up at the mirror that covered the wall behind the bar, the way he'd looked three days before when he decided his head was too big and agreed to let his buddies shave him. The swelling from the allergy, with antihistamines and anti-allergens and a handful of aspirins, had come down a little, but now he had the impression that, what with all the excitement, the red had come back, so he decided he'd take an antihistamine. He had put them, just in case, in the pocket which was, luckily, intact. As this was an exceptional situation, he took two, and the waiter easily persuaded him to have another whisky. The women did not appear, and Lovro went for a third. Afterward he remembered nothing. Not how he slumped to the floor, or them lifting him up, or their attempts to wake him. He didn't see the drunken women emerge from the women's room, or how they came into the dining hall with Ita, who kept insisting that they put him, fast asleep, next to her. *No matter how he is doing, he's mine.* It was really as if he weren't there at his own wedding to hear the outrageous jokes on his account, which culminated before dawn when his groomsman poked him with a fork and shouted, *So, should I poke him harder?* and half of the men told Ita they'd happily replace the groom for the remainder of the wedding night. At about 3 AM, he was in their way while they were dancing the wedding train, so they decided to carry him out to the car and lock him in. In fact, this was quite a practical move. They even covered him. When Ita hoisted up her crinoline at daybreak, stripped off all the underskirts, pulled out the hoops, and clambered up on a chair to dance the cancan, the still-unwed guests and those who had forgotten about their wives clapped and clamored for her to take it all off. This did not happen, however, because Ita couldn't quite hear what they were saying.

Katarina was not there for that; she was sitting in the women's room, sobbing. She sobbed about everything: about Dado and drunken Ita and the ruined wedding cake and her smeared suit, and about Irma, who appeared only after midnight, and whose arrival was noted only by her and Lovro's mother.

At Katarina's *you are not in your right mind*, Irma said, *I know*.

And yes, there were melodies from the east—Bosnian and Serbian songs. And even Cilika joined in and *pranced* around to something she didn't know the words to, and couldn't quite keep up with, but she admitted to Vilim that it wormed its way into her ear and *she couldn't stop humming it*.

Day had broken by the time the Dinamo soccer club's anthem was sung, when the final snake dance started, and when one of those who had occupied one of the worst seats at the table realized that it was he, not the groom, who was stripping the blue garter from Ita's thigh with his teeth.

Morning chased the wedding guests from the hall. What had only a few hours before been a breathtaking scene with all its airy and elegant charm had been reduced to what all such parties come down to: a thick layer of trampled confetti, mouthfuls of cake left by plates of meat, mineral water in the red wine, sagging paper garlands, white and pink floral decorations that provoke a hungover grief, and limp balloons, which in the unsettled stomachs of the staggering wedding guests irresistibly stirred the urge to vomit. Some did just that, right next to the parked cars.

They were unable to wake Lovro, and Ita, who had abruptly sobered up, entered the phase of postparty depression and dully allowed herself to be placed next to sleeping Lovro and

NADA GAŠIĆ

driven to their apartment. While unwittingly kneading her pathetic veil that her friends had told her was as transparent and marvelous as a spiderweb, she turned and caught sight of a deflated white balloon that was wobbling by the entrance to the wedding hall. She burst into tears and couldn't stop crying until they returned home.

With her cried the marshmallow.

There, those were the visible consequences of the bride's fall and the groom's uncontrolled ingestion of antihistamines.

But there were less visible consequences as well. When the bride toppled backward onto the floor, Vilim held his breath. He could not look away; he could not avert his eyes. All he could look at, wordless, was Ita's bare ass. Although he might have assumed that the bride, in the spirit of the occasion and to honor the groom, was wearing a seductive thong, his untamable brain independently chose to believe that this ass had no panties on it at all, that it was totally naked, and all that was missing was a precious fraction of a second for it to cleave open before him. Clearly for Vilim this was not a *bottom, buttocks, a gluteus, a rear end*, or anything similar, but a luscious bare ass, a fat butt, whose image he would jealously treasure and remember to the end of his life. And how long that life would last? Now that's a different question.

# Eighth stone, eighth wave

## The holidays

NOBODY WAS CALLING out to anyone on Mala Street. That morning of 1 November was sunny, a time for solemn peace and quiet; for the scent of lavender, which had been preserving the fur coats over the last twelve months to protect them from moths; a day for washed cars and the finer hats; for walnut roll, turkey, duck, chicken, goose, candleholders in murky plastic bags, subdued radio and television broadcasts, music full of memory and sorrow, and special traffic regulations, as the radio stations were announcing from the early morning hours, *only cars with special permits and stickers are allowed near the cemeteries, while excellent bus transportation has been provided for all other people, leaving from the bus stop at Kaptol and going up to the Mirogoj Cemetery and the crematorium.* There were also announcements that all government representatives had already laid wreaths on the grave of the first Croatian president.

Katarina got up after 11am, crushed. She took a slow shower, slowly combed out her hair. She didn't even drink any coffee; her nausea kept her from the thought of opening her mouth. She didn't so much as cast a glance at their little house, or the Zadruga, or the yard. It was a horrible mess, and she knew she'd be needing help to return to it some semblance of order.

Ita would not be coming by today, and she was no longer counting on Irma, so she decided she'd go to the cemetery on her own and then go to see David later, when she was feeling a little more chipper. She shouldn't visit the boy like this. All she did, to keep bad luck at bay, was to move the crystal brooch from her beige silk suit to her jacket.

She went down the street, her head bowed, and when she turned onto the adjacent one, she shot a sideways glance at the window of the blue house: the white slats of the blinds were lowered, an ordinary new building. No jack-o'-lantern, no window shades like eyelids.

*You see, it was the nerves.*

For the first time since David's accident, she got onto a tram and took a seat. People weren't loud. They were talking on their phones, but politely and relatively softly; even if they'd been speaking more loudly, she wouldn't have heard them. Rather than looking out the window, she closed her eyes and listened to her heart.

PHONE, BELL:
Wait for me by the bookstore on the Square; I won't be able to carry the candleholders myself, okay? Fifteen minutes. We're already at the Cibona Tower.

NADA GAŠIĆ

A LADY, OUTGOING CALL:

Oh, thank God, I found you. Go into the kitchen to check to see if I turned off the oven. Did I? Thank God, thank you, we're passing by the theater now.

A MAN AND WOMAN WITHOUT PHONES:

Last year they were so well organized with the buses. We'll see how they've managed this year. Gorgeous weather. Gorgeous.

Most of the passengers got off the tram at Ban Jelačić Square and joined the line that stretched from the equestrian statue all the way to the first buses beyond the cathedral. The line moved along briskly, and everybody praised the organization and relatively short wait time. After all, the number of people going to Mirogoj and the other Zagreb cemeteries was in the thousands, if not hundreds of thousands. Impressive.

The bus ride was brief, and Katarina found herself out in front of the Mirogoj Arcades sooner than she'd expected.

She had been needing a day like this, crystal clear. The sun, the freshness, the red ivy growing up the arcades' walls shone as if it were of glass. There were many people; they walked by one another but didn't push or shove; they murmured but did not shout. She started toward the main entrance, but then she stopped.

Suddenly she could no longer see the entrance. Thick white smoke covered the iron railing, blurred her view of the chapel, and this confused Katarina. She turned to the left, and the smoke turned with her; she turned to the right, and the smoke followed her. There were even some little butterflies aflutter.

She saw them. *Nerves, Katarina, nerves.* She stood and waited to regain her composure. The smoke sank to her feet, and Katarina smiled.

Roasted chestnut vendors. By the entranceway to the arcades stood a vendor selling roasted chestnuts; he was scraping the red-hot surface with a black steel spatula, like a poker, turning the chestnuts. He separated the ones that were done and covered them, like babies, with a black cloth, to keep them warm. The woman next to him was fashioning cones from white paper, and the vendor was filling the cones and offering them to the passersby, who immediately began peeling the chestnuts and eating them, while their murky plastic bags with their candles for their graves swung in their busy hands. People peeled the chestnuts, blew on the peeled nuts, and little butterflies of sooty film, as thin as celluloid, fluttered up and, carried by the wind, flew, flew . . .

Katarina walked into the cemetery through the smoke. Their grave wasn't far, and she set off without a glance at the teeming crowds. Then she stopped. She looked. She should already have reached the grave. She turned randomly to the right. *Katarina, exhaustion, terrible exhaustion, sedatives, yesterday's excitement, worries. Nerves, Katarina, nerves. You took the wrong path. Here, to the left, it must be here somewhere.* Now she was breathing more deeply, trying to clear her lungs and thoughts; she felt she'd inhaled the chestnut vendor's smoke. She turned, left, right, *no, not here.* It would be best to go back to the entrance and start over again on the path she was familiar with. Good decision. She headed toward the entrance. Or so she thought. Again, she stopped. A golden cross. A cross that was far from their grave. Here it was in front of her. How had she managed to get turned around? *Nerves,*

*Katarina, nerves.* She moved away from the cross. Now to keep to the left, left; she'd recognize the old graves, just as she recognized the old houses in her neighborhood. But didn't recognize the new buildings. So many people, flowers, and candles. *Why are there so many children at the cemetery? Who brings children to a cemetery? Where is our grave? Where is the grave?*

She turned, heard a child laughing. She could even see him running among the graves. *Hey, a cemetery is no place for games.* The boy, dressed all in white, didn't even have a jacket on. God, it was as if he were in slippers, white cotton slippers.

—Ma'am, ma'am, are you feeling sick?

She realized she was sitting on someone else's grave, and two or three people had stopped. Yes, this really is a day when everybody is thoughtful. They helped her to her feet. On the day of All Saints', Katarina never did find her way to her parents' grave, the one they called *our grave,* in such a familiar way.

She set off for the hospital once she'd rested on a bench out in front of the arcades. When she reached the hospital, she didn't go down the corridor right away. She needed water. *Saved by water, saved by water.* She went over to the vending machine, and while she waited for it to drop her bottle, she heard an ambulance driver whom someone addressed as Tomica:

—Only an idiot could have come up with this. A total idiot. To build an old people's home right next door to a children's hospital? I'm bringing in a kid, time is of the essence, I need to drive up fast to the hospital entrance, and this old lady in her eighties ambles across the street, just because she feels like it. They're drinking our blood, mine and the children's, unbelievable. A totally abnormal city.

The one who had called him Tomica replied:
—A city like any city. We can't bear the sight of each other, and it's all the city's fault.

*     *     *

She entered David's room smiling, but she knew that after everything she'd been through, she wouldn't last even half an hour.

> Mama, at last. I hope she'll stay all day and tell me all about the wedding.

She didn't tell him about the wedding, she didn't even stay half an hour; she was on the verge of collapse. She kissed him, and while she was leaning over him, she touched him with her crystal brooch.

She did a double take. Had his hand moved? Was that possible? She undid the brooch and slowly put it into his hand.

His hand didn't move. She'd imagined it; she'd been seeing phantoms all day. But she saw and heard something happening with the apparatus . . . Steps were thudding down the corridor. The on-duty nurse and doctor were running. They gestured for her to leave the room. She leaned on the doorframe and waited.

*Hail Mary, full of grace, the Lord is with thee . . .*

Another younger doctor passed by without glancing at her.

*Hail Mary, full of grace, the Lord is with thee . . .*

She didn't know how much time had passed, but when they came out of the room, the on-duty doctor told her that she wouldn't be allowed in anymore today. Certain manifestations

NADA GAŠIĆ

had occurred and they didn't know the cause, but David would be given special treatment all day, all night, and it would be better if she called in to request information.

She took a cab back to her little house full of garlands, balloons, and floral arrangements.

She took a double dose of sedatives and vanished in an artificial dream. As she was falling asleep, she kept repeating:

*Hail Mary, full of grace, the Lord is with thee, blessed art thou among women...*

Something happened, but I don't know what exactly. I remembered something, but I don't know what. I was super scared. Like, I was scared silly, scared like a jerk, but I can't remember what I was scared of. I do know that after a hundred years I saw that butterfly, the big old bird, whatever, and I couldn't call to Dad and tell him to kick this butterfly, big old bird, whatever, with all his strength. I wanted to shout and call Dad in, but nobody heard me, so I fled far behind the curtain and became the head again. And I breathed, as if I'm inside a big pot, but harder and louder and faster. But it didn't seem to last long, though I can't know for sure. And Mama was here, but I don't know exactly when: before Dad or after Dad. I saw her and was scared. I was scared because she looks different—that's not her hair and she doesn't seem like herself. As if she had gray hair, a real old lady, and that's why she seemed sadder than she probably was. I remember she put something in my hand, something I was scared of. I got so scared that I turned right into my big head—no arms, no legs, no neck. That's how I know something happened, and maybe she knew that I was scared. For I long time I was way behind the curtain. Yes, I do remember, Mama was here before Dad.

*    *    *

## Seitan

The Horaks were having a holiday meal too. Nothing gory, nothing slaughtered, nothing skinned, nothing plucked, nothing killed, nothing dead.

But it was fragrant, yes, it was.

The table was attractively set, decorated with chestnuts in their shells to heighten the autumnal mood; the candles gave off a fragrance Boris couldn't name, and he didn't dare ask what, fearing an exhaustive explanation.

So, he started the conversation.

—I'm feeling like I'm coming down with a virus. Must be because I've acquired such robust immunity to your health food.

She didn't rise to the bait.

Dissatisfied, he went on.

—You know what the most amusing thing is about vegans?

—I don't, but I'm ready to laugh.

—The funniest thing is that you cannot forget the alluring smell of meat.

—Look, I don't find that so amusing. It's not amusing because it is not true.

—Oh, really? Why, then, do you eat this pathetic seitan? You fry it, bake it, sauté it—all of it to remind you of roasted meat. And you smoke tasteless tofu because it reminds you of the allure of bacon.

She didn't answer and didn't look up.

—My darling. You are all nostalgic carnivores. Just like those Yugonostalgia types who adore their past while listening to new covers of oldie goldie pop songs. You adore your carnivorous past, devouring these sorry imitations of meat.

She looked up.

—You are excused from the table.

—Have we finally become insulted?

—No, but you may go. I will not allow you to insult what I have sweated over.

—Why did you sweat? Supposedly you enjoy every moment you spend preparing these healthy dishes.

He brazenly bit off an impaled chunk of roasted seitan, then moved the fork away with the next bite and spun it provocatively.

He saw her lower lip shrink.

—You're excused. I told you to leave.

He put the rest of the seitan into his mouth.

—First, we will masticate this, using our canines and molars, in order to chew the food into small pieces, thereby making it more digestible. In so doing, it is our duty to taste all the tastiness of the dish, which in the hindbrain causes a vulpine craving for meat. Meat, my darling, meat.

She got up. He didn't feel like stopping.

—Where are you going? Is your beloved seitan so repulsive? It's not as awful as it seems. Sit down, enjoy. It actually does taste like meat.

At that point he did stop. He saw her lower lip disappear altogether. She was still holding her fork in her left hand and her knife in her right. She looked perplexed, as if she'd found herself in a strange place and couldn't remember where she'd put down her bags. Then he saw how she calmly placed her utensils next to her plate where her pathetic seitan was cooling. Then he watched her step away from the table, go over to the counter, open the drawer, and take out a long, sharp knife. A knife too large for her hand.

He looked down at his plate and began digging into the heap of brown rice, searching for a vagrant bit of shiitake.

—Sit down.

After the mushroom was swallowed:

—I'm exhausted, nothing is helping.

He could hear her putting the knife in the drawer, closing it, and, shuffling with her slippers, she sat.

—I'm tired, tired to death. And so, so hungry, my dear. So hungry. I'll go to my child hungry. David is alone.

*　　*　　*

Boris Horak went to David when there was nobody in the room. The boy's condition had stabilized, the apparatus was humming steadily, and nothing suggested that mere hours before there had been such a scramble. He didn't look for anyone to inquire about David's condition; what he saw seemed reassuring. The hospital was breathing with its holiday lungs. It was and it wasn't quiet. Fewer from the medical staff were there, but there were more visitors. The hospital made a holiday sound.

　　　　　　　　　　　　　　　　NADA GAŠIĆ

Boris sat by David, but he didn't read to him; he didn't even say much to his son. He was thinking about something of his own that had nothing to do with David. This wasn't usual for him, but he was mulling over the fact that even for the holiday, he hadn't been able to stop himself and had provoked his wife for no reason. What a shame the nice custom of written apologies has been lost; he'd have found it easier to apologize to her in a letter.

*    *    *

## What would David's father write about his second wife?

*As soon as I realized that all the things were missing without which life is impossible today, off I went to shopping centers to buy all the things I didn't know how to live without. I bought things. And I felt good. Like everybody, I was lacking air, but I stubbornly kept going on and on. All dehydrated, I drank water and coffee at the shopping-center cafés. And I felt physically depleted, but psychologically better. I was like everybody else then: a person who musters the strength to keep going after completing a task. Again, I was everybody. I know the comparison is strained, but this brought back to me the sense of community I'd had during the war. People at shopping malls are coperpetrators; all of them have the same goal, all are under the same lighting. I felt good in the shopping-mall lighting. As if I were at the beach. And on the beach, you can be alone as much as you like. You go about the business of sunning, just like everybody else, just like you do here after buying. And you soak up the light. If we were to mute the lights in the grand halls, even briefly, the number of shoppers would drop by half. I am convinced of that. I came for the light, to this city beach of ours; I bathed and cleaned myself with light as if I were under the sun, and I felt better. And as soon as I felt bad, and I was feeling worse and worse, instead of going to my family, which had already begun to forget me, I went to the shopping mall to soak up all the light I'd been missing my whole life, both in that gloomy apartment on Vodnikova and in the Trešnjevka house, where by noon you had to turn on a light in the hallway.*

*So it was that one day, four years ago, right after work, I went to a niceish shopping mall. I couldn't imagine going to my empty apartment, and even less to my ex-wife's for her glance from behind her bangs, or my look at the hand that would meekly offer me coffee and on which I'd see those white fingernail shovels.*

*That afternoon in the corridor of the shopping mall, for the first time I noticed, saw with my own eyes, became aware, that women now have their nails manicured in public. That was apparently the moment when I realized that the civilization of privacy and relative decency into which I was born had entered the final stage of its existence. Was it the loss of all intimacy, so publicly presented like this? Was this the invisible moment of transition to the new millennium that had propelled me forward? Was it this banal?*

*I turned my head away in disgust, and instead of continuing on to the atrium, I went into a leather goods store on the left. If this collision with my awareness about the demise of the civilization of relative privacy hadn't happened when I encountered the manicure counter, I probably never would have met my new wife. And if I'd met her only an hour earlier, her views on health food, on coexisting with snakes,* on companionship with fish, flowers, forests, and seawater would have held no meaning for me. Till then I was absolutely indifferent to these topics, and I lived with the world of nature at arm's length. But, it just so happens, I caught sight of her as she was trying to foist a brochure against the slaughtering and skinning of animals on the sales manager of leather coats. I didn't even hear what she was saying; I just stared at her hands, actually at her fingernails, which, as could be seen at a glance, had been cared for at home, in the intimacy of her bathroom, using simple nail scissors and an ordinary emery board. Unvarnished. Later, I'll admit to you straight-out, not without a tinge of shame, I recalled that I'd very nearly stroked her hair. She was someone I felt close to at that moment, someone like-minded, a vestige of the civilization of privacy and decency where I felt, more or less, at home.

I don't believe I have anything more to say about her. I don't know why I told you about the relationship. I did and didn't embrace her enthusiasm for a healthy way of life, healthy nutrition, who knows what all else. I did and didn't change my views. I did and didn't give up on myself. I accepted her tales of woe about the collapse of the carnivorous world, so I didn't notice when it was that I'd replaced these tales of woe about meat-eating savages with a more general tale of woe, with a general, again—shared—malaise. I didn't notice when this happened, but here I am, dear doctor, watching myself again in the herd. Surprise, surprise, here I am thinking like everybody again. But today—no euphoria, no solemn faces. Today doctors and waitresses and factory workers and professors and dirt movers and piano teachers and hairdressers and physicists all say the same, and, what's worse, they think the same. They think the same. And I do too, right along with them. Here we are in a community of malaise. Nowhere *any divergent thinking. If thinking could be portrayed artistically, it would look like the smooth surface of water. That we have replaced the satisfaction of a shared euphoria with the malaise of a shared deflated euphoria means nothing. Absolutely nothing. The only thing that matters is the permanent erasure of differences. And I, who so easily flatter myself that I am aloof, easily share the thinking of all those who are dissatisfied. Again, I'd return to the herd. Again, I'd be the herd. Yes, and my wife. She, too, is a part of that. Of course, for her, all of that is spiced with star anise, thyme, marjoram, and nutmeg, but she, too, is the herd. A herd through which there is nothing to see but movement, as if under the surface of the water there is a monstruous body moving.*

*And intimacy? Sex? Nothing spectacular. Like most couples who are afraid they'll be together their whole lives.*

*Oh, and yes, this too. I think she is skilled at conversation.*

Boris Horak did not apologize verbally or in writing to his wife. He kissed his dragon child and left, confident that the boy was doing well, and that he'd have more time to spend with him the next day.

*       *       *

I barely made it back to the edge of my curtain, but too late. Dad was already leaving and I couldn't call to him. I cried a little inside. I got so scared. And now, it's as if nobody is here. Dad left, I don't know if Mama's coming back, the corridors are deserted. From time to time someone can be heard walking, and those steps are what scare me the most. When someone comes to the door and stops, it's as if they're thinking about whether to come in or not. That's what I'm the most afraid of. Maybe someone will come? Ita? No, she won't. Irma? Even less likely. Damir would come, but they won't let him out. And if he were to come, he would sit here day and night by my side, and each time I woke up he'd wave to me.

Dad hurt my feelings because he didn't hear me and he wasn't around when the butterfly needed kicking. Aha, the butterfly came. I know it sounds silly that he hurt my feelings, but he did. I know it's funny that someone would be scared of a butterfly, but just try to imagine what a butterfly looks like that is a meter and a half tall. Wouldn't that be creepy? Now I'd be happiest turning my stupid head away and not saying or thinking anything for a long, long time. I'll just lie here.

And why won't they stop saying they love me.

*   *   *

*Cilika didn't give a fig about life*, or the cemetery or cooking. She was bone weary from the wedding, *more than words can tell.*

But, they went to the cemetery and had duck with mlinci and walnut roll. And the midday dinner and evening supper were *according to tradition.*

*She served Gramps and took Big Boy his.*

*Holidays are, while I'm around, to be honored.*

Damir ate a piece of the duck, he ate the mlinci, he ate the beets, and now he was about to eat the slice of walnut roll. But he couldn't bring himself to take a bite of the pastry. She wasn't there. And she hadn't been there all day. He got up a few times, peeked behind the picture; no, she wasn't there.

He was grumpy and restless; he didn't know how this could have happened. He turned to the window, and then he felt her come down onto the table.

—Where were you?

—First a proper greeting, then I'll tell you.

—Hello.

—Hello to you too. I was at the cemetery. Full of the living. Even the lively. It is quite cheery on your Day of the Dead. There were even children at the cemetery.

—Were all the people wearing black?

—Some were, but, as far as I can see, people in Zagreb wear black most of the time anyway, so there didn't seem to be much of a difference between the graveyard clothes and everyday clothes. All was black, in a way, but not widow's weeds. It was not a funeral, but a holiday.

—I was at a funeral once. It was all black. And sad.

—Yes, you were at Katarina's mother's funeral.

—When they grieve a lot, people wear black. And then everybody around them grieves for the person who died and for the person in black. They grieve sorely, sorely.

—Damir, dear, instead of wearing black dresses and suits, people who are truly grieving for someone should slap blinkers on their eyes so they can't see anyone who is living normally. The only thing to console a person is the illusion that everybody is suffering with them for their loss.

—That's not so. It shouldn't be like that. I was grieving for Katarina's mother.

—No, you were grieving for Katarina. But not for long.

—I still feel sad about it.

—Don't exaggerate. People, if they do grieve, do so only for a short while. A person doesn't feel the pain of others, beyond their own.

Damir bristled. He was seriously offended that Our Little Lady didn't believe him.

—I truly do feel sorry.

—Sorry? Feeling sorry is one of the most fleeting of emotions. It is much more fleeting than romantic or patriotic feelings. More fleeting than envy. If you start envying someone, you can be sure you'll envy them for the rest of your life. Feeling sorry lasts only as long as you are looking at the person you feel sorry for. I know all about this. Sometimes I see them in church, feeling sorry for me while they're looking at my statue. I follow them to the church door, and then I see that once they're there, they are already forgetting their sorrow. A few steps out the door, and they are no longer sorry for anyone anymore.

—Fine, you're the know-it-all. You're so smart.

Our Little Lady laughed.

—Now you really are being a child. Really truly.

He turned his head to the wall and found his point. He could not believe Our Little Lady could upset him so badly.

He was silent for too long, so she was the first to speak.

—Would you like me to leave?

This scared him.

—No, I was just thinking about something.

—Fine, what would you still like to know?

—Well . . . Were you right down there, on the paths, amid the graves?

—No, I didn't descend. There were a lot of candles burning. The flame from a candle can singe my wings.

—You used your wings to descend?

—I didn't descend.

—The question wasn't about whether you descended, but about did you have wings.

She turned her head away.

—How did you come back?

—Like everybody else.

—You didn't take the bus, did you?

—Oh yes. And the tram.

He was alarmed.

—Somebody could have seen you.

—No.

Damir perked up.

—Is Zagreb pretty?

—The hill above the city is charming.

—It's not a hill, it's a mountain.

—Okay, fine, the mountain. The city is like any city. I didn't check, but I have the impression that you're planning to demolish some streets soon.

—We aren't. Nobody is talking about that. Why did you think so?

—Well, in other cities, the store windows are smashed and the walls scribbled with graffiti either after or during demolition. I know that nothing dramatic has been happening recently, so I wondered if this might mean you're planning to demolish some of the streets. For instance, the one you call Tratinska. Where the water once poured down toward the center of town.

He was relieved.

—No, we don't have plans to demolish. It's for no particular reason that there is graffiti scribbled everywhere, and for no particular reason that the store windows are smashed.

—Damir, sometimes you really do seem infantile. Shop windows are never smashed for no reason, nor does graffiti appear for no reason, because people are never indifferent to disfigured things.

This upset him. These pointless conversations had begun to wear on him.

—I don't want to talk about that. I don't like talking about disfigured things.

Our Little Lady quieted him with her teensy hand and looked up.

—I checked. You won't be demolishing streets. Some houses will be collapsing entirely on their own.

Damir repeated the gesture with which she usually quieted him, but his bulky hand gave Our Little Lady an entirely different impression. She frowned.

—Damir, don't go waving your hands around. You made a breeze and it mussed my hair. Even when they are equal, big and small things are not the same. Little is little, big is big.

This hurt Damir's feelings. But then he thought about how it was a holiday, and because she was his guest, he really ought to offer her something.

—Our Little Lady, would you like me to open a sugar packet for you? I can have my walnut roll, and you can have your sugar, and that way we can dine together.

She bowed, and by the way she held her wide, velvety dress open, he could see that she knew how to be dignified.

—Thank you. I think a little sugar would do me good.

Damir carefully examined the bowl where he kept his sugar packets and chose one. He lay it on his hand, ran his thumb over the surface, had a look at the image of the elegant swan, then smoothed it once more on both sides and, only then, did he slowly tear open the packet. The contents spilled out onto the edge of his plate.

—Katarina gave me this packet.

Our Little Lady bowed again. She knew how to value sacrifice.

She perched on the edge of the plate and with her teensy hand, like a feeler, she delicately ferried the sugar to her mouth. Crystal by crystal.

The day was short, but night did not always mean sleep. They began to feel a little bored.

—Damir, would you like to play a round of Go?

—No.

—You promised.

—I know, but I can't.

—Why?

—I don't know how to place the stone the right way.

—You already did place the stone. More than one.

Damir turned away.

—Tell me, since you know everything, does it ever happen that people who are killed are sometimes buried along with the people who killed them?

Our Little Lady looked at him closely.

—Yes, it happens. But that is an ugly question.

—I know it's ugly. But I had to ask.

—You don't feel like playing, but you do feel like asking questions like that? Oh, Damir.

—Fine, let's play a round, but only if you answer more of my questions.

—Agreed.

She smoothed her gown over her knees and waited.

—Tell me, Our Little Lady, is there such a thing as a perfect crime?

—All crimes are perfect.

—Oh, no they aren't. You're wrong.

—I am not wrong.

—You are. Always, or almost always, the murderer is discovered. I'm just asking whether you know of a crime where the murderer was not discovered.

—The discovery of the murderer has nothing to do with the crime. The purpose of the crime is all that matters, not uncovering the murderer. Uncovering the murderer, that is . . . How can I put this? That's a technical process that is an end unto itself. It can serve something else as well, but it has nothing to do with the purpose of the crime.

—How can you say that? You're wrong. That is what matters most—the uncovering of the murderer.

—No, Damir, that is entirely unimportant. Crime is a pure, perfect, unadulterated act.

—What does that mean, unadulterated?

—Do you know what counterfeit means?

—I do. When someone copies a picture. Or a passport. Or money.

—A crime is never counterfeit. It is original, unique, because every victim is unique. You can't copy a victim, and for that reason, every crime is unique and perfect.

—That I can understand, that every victim is unique. The rest I don't get.

—Do you understand that crime always achieves its goal? Purpose?

—No. I don't.

He began to rock.

—Sooner or later you will understand, Damir.

He went on rocking.

Our Little Lady shook her head and signaled that they would not continue talking about crime. This decision calmed both him and her. Both of them focused on eating sugar. It calms the nerves.

Later she set up the board, and both of them placed their stones. They defended them the best that they knew how. They put the game on hold before there was a victor. A game of Go may last for years.

The two of them bored Cilika's house. It yawned, and after it all the others along Mala Street yawned, then they prayed their prayers for their dead and exchanged a few kind words. The newer buildings were mostly vacant; their tenants had gone off to visit their distant graves.

### All Souls' Day, the second day of the holiday

—Viiilim, Viiilim! I'm off to visit with Katarina. Irma says she's not feeling well.

Cilika was a practical woman, and she wasn't likely to be tricked into believing Katarina's stories about how she'd be fine: *All I need is a little more rest, tea, and another aspirin.*

—Don't you dare get up. Today, I'll be looking after you, no use from Irma, and now I'm going to call urgent care so they can give you something.

—Cilika, please, don't turn this into a circus; it's just that I'm too tired.

—That's what I said. But your exhaustion has brought you to the point that you won't be able to get up and go.

Cilika was practical and stubborn; she managed to convince them to come from urgent care. Katarina was a classic case of exhaustion and the doctor left, disgruntled that he had lost valuable time he could have given to a more important case. She was told not to leave the house that day.

—You're not going to see David today, that much is clear. His father will be with him. And you'll have some soup. Right? Now sleep.

On her way out, she shouted up to the attic rooms.

—Irma, don't you go getting on her nerves, hear me?

And to herself she said:

—I know you, you damned airhead. You came to your sister's wedding at midnight, shame on you.

\*　　\*　　\*

Boris Horak did come down with a virus. The apartment soon smelled like marigolds, four-o'clocks, bitter almond, black cumin, eucalyptus, wild thyme, lemon balm, and sage. Lying on his stomach, naked, Boris gave in to his wife's nimble fingers. She kneaded him as if she were shaping a totem of clay; she rolled the soles of his feet until they were fully softened, rubbed the muscles of his lower leg, fought with the firm muscles of his thighs, pressed to the point of pain the muscles of his buttocks, reminding him of his nonexistent tail. She played up his spine as if it were a clarinet, brought his shoulders to the point of liftoff, flipped him over like a child, and proceeded the same way along his front side. Pretending not to notice his erection, she primed his nipples to perk on his breasts as if he were a woman, she typed his face like a keyboard, and in the end she straddled him, but not for long, not long. Only as long as she needed; she remembered his insults from the day before. They panted briefly, Boris began to cough, and the essential oils had no more magic. Movement even less. All in all, this was a massage to remember. Mrs. Horak was not afraid of viruses; she had a robust immunity.

But Horak certainly couldn't go see David, at least for the next few days. The child needed to be protected from the virus.

I remembered what it was I was afraid of. In fact, I've remembered all sorts of things. Too many, really, but I won't think about that now.

Some doctors came. Mama hasn't been here. Dad will come later. He always comes a little later. Someone is always standing by the door; that is why it would be good for Dad to come as soon as possible. And Mama, if she comes, shouldn't wear that brooch.

\*     \*     \*

Katarina gave in to Cilika, who made her chicken soup, took down the garlands, and cleaned up David's room where Katarina was in bed. In the evening, Ita and Lovro stopped by, and even Irma was at home, and they all anxiously checked in to see how Katja was doing. Feeling better, she got up, took a shower, dressed, and went to the Zadruga, where all three were retelling the wedding. *Listen, nobody in the city of Zagreb has had a wedding like ours, half of Zagreb is talking about it, they all say they hadn't ever had so much fun, and no, that's not true, terrible, but in the end when you put it all together, it will be an event to remember our whole lives. And the grandkids will hear about it. Granddad slept through it all, and Granny did the cancan. Ha, ha, ha.*

There was a lot of food left over, so they all ate. Only Katarina withdrew into the corner; she couldn't bear the smell of the roast.

—Katja, are you okay?

—I'm fine, you and Lovro go ahead and eat. Your head looks better. You're not hot pink anymore.

They started helping themselves to food.

Katarina said:

—And please don't smoke, I couldn't bear smoke.

Ita reassured her.

—No, of course not, look at how low the ceilings are, you can't see through the smoke after three cigarettes.

Lovro joined in with his mouth full.

—Well, at least you two aren't going to be living in these shacks much longer. Right, Irma?

Irma bugged her eyes out to signal to him to stop. Too late. Katja heard.

—What do you mean by that? Irma, what does he mean?

—Nothing.

—Irma, I asked you nicely. Please answer me nicely.

Irma said nothing, and Ita broke the silence.

—Listen, sis . . .

Katarina got up; she knew something bad was coming as soon as they addressed her as sis.

—Sis, I hadn't gotten around to telling you because everything happened so fast. And then this thing with David—there really hasn't been time. Lovro and I needed money for the wedding and to redo his apartment, so I sold Irma my part of the house.

All that could be heard was the clock ticking over the door.

—I didn't offer it to you, because I know you're broke.

—Ita, what you sold was my patrimony handed down to me from my grandfather, not your part of the house. And we—you, Irma, and I, and the whole street—we know that.

Three of them lit cigarettes.

—This house belonged to my father, Zdravko Firman. My mother inherited it after he drowned some 5 meters from this same house. My mother and yours transferred the deed to your father so he could take out a loan to build this fucking shack, this fucking Zadruga. Your father left *his* daughters each a half of my inheritance, and my property. Yes, my patrimony, and my property. You two have now finished what he started.

—Sis, it's not like that.

—Ita, don't call me sis. You and Irma sold part of the house because she is your full sister and I'm only half. I am nobody and nothing to you.

—Katarina, wait till you hear the whole story!

NADA GAŠIĆ

—No, you listen to me! You took my father's house from me, the house of my father who drowned saving that same house. Are you listening? How can a person who is alive be left without their own home, without what their father and grandfather left them? How? Are you listening?

Katarina wasn't shouting, and this was the worst part. She was shaking. She tried to leave, but the door wouldn't open easily. Ita began to cry.

—Katja, wait for Irma to tell you, Irma will sort out everything. She found an investor. Everything will be sold. It will all be demolished. The investor is connecting our yard to the yard of the blue building, from the new blue building next door to ours. You and David will get the most beautiful apartment in the new building. Katja, no more living like the poorest of the poor in Trešnjevka. Look, look at the buildings that are going up around us! Irma, tell her.

Irma didn't tell her. Not then, not ever.

Katarina finally went out into the yard, ran back to her little house, and locked the front door behind her. Irma could sleep where she liked.

She lay down on David's bed, and in the light that shone through the slats of the blinds, she saw her arm fly up high in the air.

*Mama's little golden boy, they won't let me in to see you now. They won't let me in. Mama wants to, but they won't let me. David . . .*

I know now what it was that I was scared of. I know it all. Since I came here, I've been most afraid of the flashlights that the doctors shine into my eyes, because they are like the headlights of that car. And I know why the inspectors came. They think I saw someone and that I recognized someone. And it's true. I did. That is why I was scared of Lovro, because seeing him reminded me of the other man. Mama touched me with that stupid brooch. I know why I was scared. I recognized the man who threw the roll of plastic from the car.

I am going deeper behind the curtain, where nobody can touch me. Why aren't Dad and Mama here?

The little house couldn't come down to Katarina and pat her. It gave the top of the curtain a jolt, but nothing reached Katarina.

All the old-timers along the street learned what had happened, and they all knew what was in store for Katarina's house. And the rest of them soon enough. They kept their silence and quaked, appalled, till morning.

# Ninth stone, ninth wave

THE ROUNDS WERE over, the nurse had gone, my parents still hadn't come, so I spent some time thinking inside myself. I even thought about Mama's sea. Though not the way Mama would have liked me to be thinking about it. Much differently. Mama wasn't there at the sea, nor were Cilika, her kuma, or Ita or Irma. There weren't even any tourists there; it was just Mirta and me. Everything Mirta was wearing was light blue, and everything else on her, her hair and everything, was the way it was otherwise, because I like everything about her and it would never occur to me to change that. I was wearing real All Stars, not too old, not too new, because it's totally uncool when they're brand-new. And we were standing at the end of a dock. The sea was not smooth and it wasn't wavy. Just like it's supposed to be: there were little waves, so it was silvery and interesting, but the waves weren't splashing against the dock, because then they would have sprayed us and we wouldn't have been able to stand there. I told Mirta some things I usually only talk about inside myself, and that was normal for her, and she looked at me the same way she looked at me last year in the middle of PE when she asked me if the door to the playground was locked. It's just that I stupidly said nothing and then nodded my head—first up then down, then left and right—something only Soblić used to do, who was with us in our first grade class and later they moved him into special needs. She looked at me like I had never nodded my head in all directions and as if only she knew that inside I am smart, and that it was normal that I was telling her, particularly her, all sorts of things there on that dock. Then we looked at the fish in the sea, and I told her I often thought about how interesting it would be if a really, really clever animal trainer could train all the fish in all the seas to jump at the same time 5 meters into the air when he gave the signal. Then Mirta told me this would make a huge splash when they all fell back into the sea at the same time, and then we laughed. Then Mirta looked at the sea and I looked at Mirta and I didn't touch her, but I knew the next time I imagined us on the dock, I'd touch her. Yes, yes, I'll touch her. You heard me. And I am not sad that nobody is here, but I did cry a little on the inside anyway. I wanted to be with Mirta a little more on the dock, but somehow I couldn't picture it anymore. I was missing the face and I couldn't imagine that light-blue color, and that is why I didn't try more—so I wouldn't spoil it.

As soon as the room was quiet, and it was also quiet out in the corridor, I had the feeling again that there was somebody standing by the door. I totally lost it. Who could be standing by my door? I'm not the president, or someone who gets guards at his door. But still, somebody was standing there. I saw something like a shadow. Weird. I'll retreat way behind my curtain. Nobody will find me there. Nobody.

*    *    *

Katarina got up early, before six. She looked at herself in the bathroom mirror. With loathing.

She opened the cabinet and took out a packet of henna, a plastic spoon, a glass jar, old nylon stockings, and a plastic shower cap. She tore open the packet, poured the powder into the jar, and added enough hot water to make a thick paste. She stirred it with the plastic spoon and spread the paste evenly over her hair. With the nylon stockings, she covered her whole head, tied the legs up like a turban, and, finally, she covered it all with the shower cap. She tucked a little cotton batting under the cap's elastic band, supposedly to stop the dye from dripping down her face.

Irma, who had made do with the two-seater in the Zadruga that night, drummed on the door.

—Katarina, please let me in. I need to use the bathroom. Please, I have school.

Katarina opened it.

—What's that on your head?

—Henna. That wasn't my hair. David wouldn't recognize me looking like that.

Both of them decided not to speak of their fight the night before. Irma went into the bathroom. Katarina went to the kitchen, where there was the least chance of making a mess with the henna. If it did drip, the tiles could easily be wiped clean. She sat down and closed her eyes. She felt she had done something good. Feeling reassured, she soon dropped off for a brief snooze.

## Pavement mixed with mud

She saw herself hurrying toward David's school, concerned that she was wearing her work smock, which felt wrong for a conversation with the school counselor. Her feet weren't obeying her, and the school, instead of getting closer, was farther and farther away. Soon the building disappeared in underbrush and mud. She made her way toward a path she could barely see through the muddy bushes littered with torn rags, scraps of clothing, and shirts. Everything was gray; only the ragged shirts were white. She knew the dusk would soon fade to darkness. The mud was slowing her down, and she barely made it to Potok. The dark descended before she could reach Savska Road. And the pavement of Potok wasn't proper pavement. Mud. She was having trouble pulling her feet free. At the pedestrian underpass, bits of pavement mixed with mud began to shift, and Katarina stopped. She stood and listened to her teeth clicking ever so slightly against one another. The pavement was moving. Something terrible and alive began rippling. Katarina looked down in the gray gloom and saw hordes of rats scampering off in search of food.

She knew she was standing by the pedestrian underpass, and she knew this was the most frightening spot on Potok; she tried to move. Then something hit her back and slid down her smooth broadcloth smock. She froze. Before she could move, she felt with her whole body that what had hit her was alive, and that it slid down her smock of its own volition, not hers. A rat. It had leaped onto her from the wall of the underpass and darted down her smock. She couldn't scream; she couldn't make a sound. She could barely move, barely walk forward toward the light of Savska Road. She clambered up the eight steps and stopped. Instead of stepping onto the pavement of the street, she froze, seeing the terrifying yellow-brown torrent; it was sweeping along branches, tree trunks, and people. The people were on their bellies and she couldn't see their faces, but she saw how the current was swirling around carved pumpkins, which spun dizzily and cackled. She caught sight of a huge poster, a photograph actually, as the torrent swallowed the paper and the person came unglued from the photograph and extend his hand to her. She saw his face. Smiling. Her father. She reached forward to grab him, but the face mutated horribly, grinned, lost its hair, went totally bald, and she withdrew her hand. It wasn't her father. She heard David calling her. She forgot the face from the photograph and began searching for David's voice. She saw him being borne away by the torrent. Katarina plunged into the terrible water and reached for her child. With all her strength. Hands and teeth.

She started awake, began screaming and calling to Irma.

Irma flew down the stairs.

—Irma, drive me to the hospital, right now, right now!

—Katja, calm down, how can you go out looking like this?

—Drive me now!

\*    \*    \*

Damir didn't want Our Little Lady to appear; he was tired of talking with her. He went out to the fence, opened the gate, and came up to Katarina's house at the very moment when Irma and Katarina were leaving. Sometimes he was allowed to do that. Irma got into the car. Clutching a woolen cap she was pulling over all the dye she had slathered on her hair, Katarina waited for her sister to unlock the passenger door from the inside. Damir noticed a thin stream of something red dripping down her neck. He panicked. He went over to her and for the first time in his life he patted her sleeve.

Katarina winced, frightened and uneasy, and snarled:

—Let me go, Big Boy, you're all I need now!

Damir fled to his room. He curled up and focused on his serenity point.

\*    \*    \*

Josip Vidošić came back tired after the holidays. He and his wife and children had visited cemeteries, the graves of his family, her family, their own, ours. Herzegovina only feels close when you're in Zagreb. When you go there, while you are going, the drive kills you; when you arrive, your family and friends kill you. He'd had his fill of lighting candles; he literally stank of wicks and wax. His job was waiting. It hadn't let go of him while he was at all the graves—he kept thinking about what was clear in the case, what was hidden, and what had been missed. There were messages and messages on his phone. He'd have to go through them once more. Later. The only thing he was sure of was that Žigerica would be brought in and interviewed in such a way that she'd be wise to start talking. He looked at his watch. He'd called for a meeting only after noon to be on the safe side; people had dispersed for the holidays and there could be unintended delays, so he decided, after what had happened with Kasumić, to improve his image as boss a little. He had a little time. He decided to go first to the hospital and see whether the kid had woken up. Who knows? Maybe he'd remember something. Maybe Vidošić could bring sensational news to today's meeting. And he might see David's mother. Her hands.

I came right up to near the curtain. And then, all of a sudden, I got really scared, even behind the curtain. I have the feeling that during the first days here I was in better shape than I am now. Here I am, there's nobody around, and I can hear my heart jumping. It's not enough that I am listening to myself breathing, but now I have to listen to my heart too. There's nobody here, and instead of doing smarter things while I wait, the first thing I think about is whether there's somebody there by the door. Now I think there's nobody, but then again, what do I know?

I really am restless. It's weird how restless I am. Why haven't any of my peeps come? I'm totally out of it. I'd even like it if my folks came together and fought right next to my bed. That's how low I've fallen. I can't come up with anything to turn my mind to. I can't even imagine Mirta. But I've had to think about things like when I was a little kid. Some kind of fairy tale of my own. Like one where they're all together, and Little Red Riding Hood and all of the ones she was friends with and Sleeping Beauty with all her cooks and guests and good fairies and Cinderella with her doves and Little Muck and the lazy gardener and the fat king and Daddy-Dragon and Little Seamstress. They were, like, all on one side, having all kinds of fun, while the wolf from Little Red Riding Hood and the evil fairy from Sleeping Beauty and the stepmother from Snow White and the dim-witted princesses from all the fairy tales, they were across on the other side. While the ones in the first group are having a grand time, the creepy ones are in a horrible mess because they are doing horrible things to one another. For instance, the wolf is biting Snow White's stepmother on the leg; then the evil fairy from Sleeping Beauty casts a spell on the wolf, and it falls asleep for a hundred years; then the steel spider spins its web around the wolf. Lots of other stuff like that. I felt a little better, but I could tell I wasn't at my best, because I was happy when the nurse came in and it didn't bother me much that she was doing things to me. But I wasn't happy when she did her consolation thing, with *Mama's coming, be patient, sweetie,*

*Mama's coming.* As if I were crying inside, but I didn't want to be crying, so I was terribly restless. And I began to feel like my throat was choking. Like when I swallow too large a chunk of a palačinka. Now that too. Why is nobody here? I can hear the doctors laughing and the nurses giggling far away, but, actually, it is very quiet. All I can hear clearly are the apparatuses around me. Humming. The light doesn't bother me now. The light doesn't bother me at all. I'd even like for it to be lighter. Lightest of all. I'd like someone to come now. Even Big Boy Damir. I'd like to be hearing familiar footsteps. But now I can't hear anything. Only silence and my stupid breathing. I always feel like I'm choking when I am not crying on the outside, but on the inside, but that passes. Only now it won't, it won't at all. I have to pick up the pace with my big pot breathing.

I feel a little better, but not all the way better.

By now I'm pretty sure there is somebody lurking here outside my door.

Irma was a skillful driver, and she managed to fight her way to a parking space.

There was so little left to go, so little left until they'd get to David's room...

There is somebody outside my door. But it's not one of mine. None of mine...

I know my mom and dad will come, but somehow I don't have it in me to wait. I'll dip back behind the curtain. Deep, the deepest. Behind the curtain.

*So little left, so little left before they'd get to the room . . .*

There it is: I, the secret agent, finally admit that I want to become something ordinary. I want Mama and Dad to be here. I want them here. I want to not have to imagine anymore. I want to sleep, and when I wake up there will be no more curtain and there will be light, the right kind of light, the light of day. That's what I want. I want to be hungry, to feel like drinking a cola, to feel like eating cakes. I want Mirta to come, for half the class to come, no, let the whole class come. Even Horvatica and Kovačić, so he can talk about Gardaland and how he smoked. I want to go home, to my little room, to my street. I want Big Boy Damir to wave to me from the fence. I want to hear everything going on along our street: when somebody walks, when somebody runs, when somebody has to go home because they forgot something, when somebody stops because they changed their mind. I want to be where my head is its ordinary size, and not like I'm inside this stupid big pot. I want to hear the steps of people I know.

Steps? Who? Who is coming? Those are not the footsteps of my mom, or my dad, or the inspector, or anyone I know. Maybe a new doctor? Why did that person stop? Why are they standing in front of the door and breathing onto the glass? Doctors don't do that. Why am I so scared? It doesn't matter who comes in.

I see a shadow, purple, a purple shadow like ink on the door of the room. And huge butterfly wings.

That's why I'm scared. Dad, come right now and kick that purple shadow away so I never have to see it ever again. Why is the door opening so slowly? Foot, David's foot, move, get up, foot!

Hand, David's hand, move, get up! A shadow came in and didn't say hello. It has no smell. I'm scared, Mama, so scared! Dad, I'm so scared! Someone is coming over to me. Why is the person standing so near me and so quiet? Why is that person looking at the apparatus? Foot, get up, stupid foot! Hand, lift up, stupid hand! Speak, shout, stupid David! Shout, shout, stupid David! Mama, Dad, Grandpa! Have somebody come! Have somebody hear! No, not inside, shout out loud, stupid David! Out loud, stupid David! Stupid Daviiiid! Mama, somebody is turning out the light, tell them not to turn out the light.

Mama, tell them not to turn out my light.

Dad, someone is turning out my light.

Turn on my light.

Have somebody turn on my light.

Then David felt how he was retreating into his head, big and round. He saw the butterfly circling around his big, round head, sprinkling fine powder, like finely ground mother-of-pearl, like confectioners' sugar. He saw a thin, crystal spiderweb on his curtain, and in that spiderweb there was a big, smooth spider. As shiny as steel. The spider was busily pulling out a tender sugar thread from its shiny jaws while David, with no arms, no legs, no neck, no belly, watched how it carefully and steadily wrapped his huge head round like a classroom globe. Once more he heard his breath as if he were breathing inside a big pot. The spider was silent, and David couldn't tell whether or not he was able to understand the language of animals. He didn't feel the tear that slid down his peaceful face, nor did he know what he had cried about the last time. That way, from the inside.

They sprinted into the hospital. Katarina didn't turn to look at anyone, though people stopped and looked at the woman who had red stripes dripping down her neck.

She had so, so little left to go before she reached his room.

In the corridor in front of David's room, Katarina stopped.

She saw the on-duty doctor striding quickly to the door; the nurse was holding the door for him. Katarina heard voices and indistinct words. She went to the door. They didn't let her in. She turned and with her head, from which dripped a thin, red stream, she began banging the wall.

\*     \*     \*

Familiar with the rhythm of the hospital, when Vidošić arrived at the corridor that led to David's room, he stopped.

He *felt* the hurry and the unfamiliar bustle.

The on-duty nurse dashed past him and pushed open one of the double doors, not bothering to hold it. Vidošić froze. He didn't reach to grab the door, and it swung until it slowed of its own accord. Before it stopped swinging, Vidošić noticed the door jerk, as if in its own death throes. Only then did he push it and come into the corridor. He turned toward the room.

NADA GAŠIĆ

He *saw* the shock.

On the floor, by the door to David's room, her knees pulled up to her chin, shaking her red hair and madly tugging the sleeves of her sweater over her fingers—he barely recognized Irma.

A woman wearing a cap stood by the door—he did not recognize Katarina. She was standing with her face to the wall, her shoulders and arms hanging limply, swaying with her whole body which, dull and alien, banged on the wall. Down her neck slid a red drip.

He *heard* someone running. He turned.

Two doctors: they were not young; one was overweight, so the fact that they were running was notable.

A nurse flew out of the room and ran in the opposite direction down the hall.

He panicked. After a pause of four too-long seconds, he heard his own breath. As if he were breathing inside a big pot. He found it hard to move, but he moved. In a few steps, he reached the room.

He *smelled* the harsh chemicals which, three days before, hadn't been in this room. Someone tried to stop him at the door; someone had already called security. The doctor shouted, *You can't come in here, man, you've gone mad,* and the shouts of the people merged with the sounds of the apparatuses.

Two men in white coats doing something over David's bed. Over David.

Someone said, *There is nothing more we can do, it's over,* and then, aside from himself and David, there was nothing more he could hear, see, smell, or feel. He pushed aside one of the doctors, and the other, who grabbed him by the arm, him he may have punched. He leaned over, pulled the wires off of David's chest, and yanked the tube from his mouth, with which, he thought, they were deliberately smothering the child.

He glued his mouth to David's nose and mouth. And his hands and lips refused to feel the unnatural coldness of the child's body.

He blew air into David, pulled back, took a deep breath, then breathed air into David again.

Once.

A second time.

A third time.

He stopped.

He heard himself growling:

—Breathe, breathe with me, breathe, breathe with me!

Inhalation.

Exhalation.

Pause.

He rubbed the spot under which the heart should have been beating. Feeling that all he touched was smaller than his hand, he clenched his fingers to keep them from drifting into nothing.

—Breathe with me, breathe with me!

David did not obey him.

Inhalation.

Exhalation.

Pause.

—Breathe, breathe!

He no longer glued his lips to the boy's, but he knelt down by the bed, pressed his cheek to the boy's cheek, and concentrated on inhaling and exhaling air.

He was teaching David to breathe.

As if the child couldn't hear him because he wasn't looking into the boy's eyes, so he lifted his head.

—Breathe. Like this! David, like this!

He held the child, and the security officers who had arrived didn't know what kind of hold to use on him. The sounds of the people merged together and the room sobbed painfully, as if the premises were groaning, with the apparatuses, the people, and the walls. The guards only then dared place their hands on Vidošić's shoulders. And nothing more. One repeated, *Sir . . . Sir*, and this alien mantra brought Vidošić more or less to himself.

—David, don't give up.

David gave up.

Inspector Vidošić's shoulders softened; he laid David on the bed; he didn't turn to look at any of them and peaceably allowed the guards to escort him out. He didn't resist when one of them, just in case, laid his hand on Vidošić's back; he was not present when he provided his identification card and showed his police badge, nor for the agitated voices that kept saying *madman*, nor the sobs, nor the threats of reporting him.

The guard saw him to the hospital entrance.

He left the building. Out in front of the hospital, he was surprised by an unfamiliar voice asking him, *Boss, should I drive you to the police station?* and his *no, I'll walk a bit.*

\*     \*     \*

Irma more or less pulled herself together and managed to call Ita, telling her to come with Lovro.

—Don't ask. The worst, Ita, the worst.

Later, Katarina was given a shot of sedatives, though she wasn't crying, screaming, or doing anything one might expect her to be doing. Irma and Ita did the crying for her, and the hospital corridors sobbed too. Irma told Lovro to go fetch David's father. *Even he doesn't deserve to have a total stranger come and tell him his child has died. Now you're a member of the family; Ita, you go, you know where Boris lives. But first help me put Katja in the car.*

They led Katarina to Irma's car. *Cilika will be at home, call Cilika, tell her what happened; they said the sedatives will keep working for a while. And Ita and Lovro will come right away, after they go to David's father's.*

Irma buckled Katarina's seatbelt and wiped her neck with handkerchiefs. Katarina cringed, as if Irma had flayed her flesh.

Irma drove gingerly, though she didn't know why. She drove up to the house, stopped, and carefully helped Katarina out of the car. She opened the gate, and it moaned. Irma moaned with it. She brought Katarina into the kitchen, sat her on a chair.

Katarina didn't lift her head. She looked at the floor, if she was looking at all.

—Irma, you killed my child.

Irma was afraid not of the sentence but of Katarina's voice.

—Katja…

—Irma, it all started with his phone. The fight with David. You stole his phone so you could call your crew from a safe number.

The half-dead woman uttered coherent sentences in a steady voice.

—Irma, you killed my boy.

Irma wept with dry sobs as she hugged her sister. Katarina didn't fend her off, and seeing that her sister was not reacting to anything anymore, Irma went to her room to get towels and clean clothes to wash her up a little, before people started coming.

*     *     *

Katarina was still sitting as she had been when her sister left. Bolt upright, half on the chair, not reclining, not leaning back, her knees slightly apart, her feet firmly planted, her shoulders high as if she had no neck or arms, her wrists resting on her thighs. She looked down at her hands and saw how they were lying there, emptied to the extreme. Through her gaze, muddied by the sedatives, the life lines on her palms looked as if they had disappeared; the skin of her hands seemed to have been ironed smooth, and her fingers, like her hands, lay there like two placid udders. *Where is my life line? Where is my pain line?* She tried pulling her fingers together, but her brain refused to obey. Katarina was no longer looking at both of her hands; instead, she was only staring at her right palm.
—Pig, you slapped my David.

The hand said nothing back.

Katarina stood up. She went to the kitchen counter and from it she took a pot; then with movements that were not governed by reason, she took a bottle of oil off the shelf. In a thick stream she poured it into the pot, which, made heavier by the oil, shook in her left hand, while with her right Katarina switched on the gas burner and waited for the flames to catch. She lowered the pan onto the flickering blue flame. While staring fixedly at the bottom of the steel vessel in which the oil was gradually starting to bubble, she rolled up her sleeves with a soft womanly motion, and, together with the sleeves of her sweater, she pushed them up above her elbow. The oil gave off a typical kitchen smell, a smell attached to the unbearably simple memory of the smell of making palačinkas, and that is what finally spawned a moan inside her. She bit it off with her canines and stopped it before it left her throat. When the heavy oil boil first began, Katarina looked again at her right palm, as if she expected it to finally say something, and then, with no hurry or hesitation, she lowered it into the boiling hot oil. There was a terrible quantity of smoke. The stench of burning flesh flooded the kitchen, but Katarina couldn't smell it. And even if her hand had felt pain at first, the pain left the hand at once and moved to an utterly unknown place. It voiced in her brain, whimpered at the same time both inhumanly and extremely intimately, as if it weren't pain coming from the burned hand, but from somewhere in her gut, heart, and lungs. Though her breath was choppy, Katarina quite deliberately took her hand from the hot oil, and when she examined it, she knew this was no longer her hand, and that was why it hadn't told her anything. Then she noticed her left hand, which was cravenly curling its fingers.

—Pig, you held my David.

She lowered her left hand into the oil, and only then, swooning, did she slump to the floor.

Katarina Horak, née Firman, had departed from all pain.

*　　*　　*

Boris Horak's fever had gone down, but he had been foully fuming all morning. He climbed out of an idiotic bath that reeked of incense, dried off, and put on the kimono that his wife had hung for him on the door. She told him he shouldn't get dressed so she could give him a massage. A kimono is easier to take off.

The doorbell rang. Boris gave himself a full minute to think over whether or not to open it dressed like this. He opened the door. He did not recall closing it. He stood in the hallway and listened to the sound of his wife using the blender. The horror, pain, and incredulity hadn't yet begun. All he remembered was that he'd forgotten to ask Lovro and Ita to come in, and this oversight permanently fused in his brain with the feeling that he could have done something and that he'd missed this possibility forever.

The only thing he felt clearly was the silken kimono, which shivered instead of him and chilled his shins.

When his wife appeared at the door, he dropped his hand and stilled the swaying of the kimono.

—Who was that? Selling something?

She asked but didn't wait for his answer. She turned and went back into the kitchen, so though she'd been speaking to him, it was as if she'd been speaking to someone else.

—Will you come in? It has its best effect if you drink it right away.

He started moving and followed her.

His wife didn't look at him. Back she went to the kitchen counter and began plucking bunch by bunch from a heap of greens, dropping them into the blender.

She wielded the knife, swinging it like a pendulum; the blade caught the light, and for a time she followed it with her gaze. She didn't check to see if he, too, was eyeing the swing. Her left hand fingered the kiwis in the fruit bowl, seeking the softened ones;

she stopped and chose one. She palpated it longer than necessary. She smiled, now quite certain that he was watching her.

Then the knife went to work. The blade slid under the hairy skin; the ugly peel curled back, exposing the green body. She sliced it. Then she set the knife down in the sink. With a fork that had a long handle and sharp tines, she pierced the sliced kiwi.

Boris became aware that the egg-shaped fruit, when sliced lengthwise, was reminiscent of a miniature green melon.

His wife tossed the slices into the blender. She set the fork down on the counter. Then she added a bunch of parsley, pieces of ginger, a twig of thyme, and a pinch of cinnamon to the kiwi. She switched on the small, powerful device.

As if a huge dental drill had been turned on, Boris turned his head away to protect himself from the frightening sound.

His wife kept her eye on the machine; she lifted her finger from the switch, stopping it, tipped the blender lid, and stared at the thick, greenish-yellow liquid.

He felt his gorge rise, washing his mouth with nasty bile. He punished himself and, with clenched throat, he sent it back to his stomach in a gulp.

She poured the greenish-yellow contents of the blender into a tall glass. Pleased, her shoulders relaxed, and she picked up a long-handled spoon. She carefully stirred the thick potion.

He watched the spoon in her hand, and for a moment the handle looked bizarrely long.

Taking care not to let the juice spill over the edge, she stirred the liquid that had filled the glass right to the brim. While she was talking, she did not look up.

—It's vital to start drinking this while the liquid is still swirling, because that is how the energy that my hand has created pours into you. That's what you need.

She stopped stirring, then slowly and carefully proffered him the glass, watching her hand with fixed concentration.

—It's very important that you drink it down in nine gulps while the juice is still swirling with its energy.

She did not look up.

Had she looked up, perhaps she would have moved away in time. Perhaps she'd have seen the contorted face of her husband and his fist on which the tendons and bones had begun to assume the shape of the paw of a wild beast as it picked up the long-handled fork with sharp tines from the countertop. Maybe she'd have moved her head a millimeter away, and that would have been enough for her to dodge the sharply honed tines of the highly chromed, very fancy long-handled fork with which her husband, exerting very little effort, stabbed the artery in her neck. Before the meter-long stream of blood sprayed the kitchen wall, Mrs. Horak saw how the green eddy in the glass was threatening to stop its swirl of energy, and David's dad's hand felt that the tines of the fork passed through his wife's neck with minimal, almost negligible, resistance, as if piercing a deep-fried seitan steak.

*And in closing, Mr. Doctor, sir, please forgive me that I am not able to go into greater detail about the death of my second wife. I have no desire to justify myself, because there is no justification, or even reason, for her death. All I can say is that I would have been happiest stabbing that fork into my heart. But as it was, the hand chose a different direction. Perhaps I could have borne a little more, but my hand could no longer bear a single human movement, nor a single move of a human hand that was doing anything that would continue the process of nutrition and the struggle for a healthy and long life. I don't know. Maybe if she hadn't said that the person who'd rung the doorbell was selling something . . . I don't know. I'll never know. Nor will you.*

*No doubt, you, Mr. Doctor, sir, are wondering why I haven't mentioned my child.*

*Well, because, Mr. Doctor, sir, I think he would be bothered by someone he didn't know talking about him. He was irritated even when I spoke about him to people he knew, let alone those he'd never met.*

*And I owe it to him to say the truth: I knew it was him ringing the buzzer that afternoon, the same day the tragedy happened.*

*I didn't hear it? I didn't hear David ringing the doorbell? I knew it. I always knew it when he buzzed. I knew it. I just chose not to have to know it. Not to know, not to remember; this is not a lack of concentration or a loss of a talent for memory. It is my choice. A person chooses not to know and not to remember. I agreed to think that someone who was selling something had rung our doorbell. I preferred to bite my wife and sought her bites, played with the blade of a knife surrounded by dyed votive candles and inhaled the aromas of the essential oils produced in Sesvete. I let my wife knead my buttocks and pour macadamia oil from Konjščinska over my stumpy tail, and gave in to her blather about the transfer of energy, immunity, and stress. Yet I knew David was at the door. You can know people by how they ring the doorbell. Whole families ring doorbells the same way; they vanish from the face of earth, yet for years their neighbors, friends, and family remember them by the way they once* rang the doorbell. I knew David was standing at the door. I knew it was him, my David, who was buzzing. And I, I who am lesser than inhuman, I, who am worth less than the lowliest of beasts, let David stand there at the door and ring the doorbell. He didn't even ring for very long. Usually I had been concerned by how quickly he gave up on things. But then? No. I was overjoyed that he gave up so quickly and easily. I was overjoyed that my wife was rubbing my stumpy tail and both of us were waiting for an erection we'd remember. What mattered to me just then? Her hands with her clipped nails that didn't threaten to scratch me when she went from the invisible tail to ordinary jacking off, which we happily called massaging the life chakra. My life chakra was what mattered to me, and I let David's snuff out. Had I put a stop, literally, to the jacking off and opened the door, if I'd have seen him all upset, I'd have known that at least for that day, that night, he needed to be with his father. He told me everything—he would have told me everything. I wouldn't have left David alone even for a second. Not one second. There. That is what I should have done. Push her hand aside, stand up, and open the damn door. In time. Just open the door in time.

So, Mr. Doctor, sir, now I am thinking about the wandering painter. I have the impression that this steadfast man would never have left anyone, not even a pathetic Red wayfarer who was ringing the doorbell, to wait there at the door. Let alone his own child.

And me? My child. My very own child.

If I could be his father again, I would not have let a woman give birth to him. I would have carried him in my belly myself. I'd have become a seahorse; I'd have changed my gender, I'd have fertilized myself, I'd have done everything to be able to birth him. If I could be born again, I'd have sent the greedy females packing and become his

*father and his mother. I wouldn't have allowed anyone to touch him.
I wouldn't have allowed anyone to look at him up close. I wouldn't
have let them say his name when I was not present. I'd carry him; I
wouldn't even let him walk down the street. For him I'd have become
strong, I'd have become Spider-Man, I'd have become Superman,
I'd have become a child so we could hang out together and grow up
together. I'd have become his wise teacher and his peerless joker. I'd
be an authoritarian government, I'd be a tyrant, I'd drive off the
teachers who looked crossways at him, I'd be a licentious amusement
park, I'd be a playground slide so I could feel all of him, I'd be a dog,
a house pet willing to put up with beatings just to feel his touch on
my doggy snout. Everything—I'd be everything to my son, David, I
would be all of it and I'd be more than that, only so I could bring him
back, when he was just born, so tiny, all of 3 kilos and 400 grams, 52
centimeters in length, to hug him and never let him out of my arms.
But I can't do that, Mr. Doctor, sir. At least for now I can't. Momentarily I can't. What I definitely can do is to refuse any mention of
me being not in my right mind when what happened happened to
my second wife. I will have time in the prisons and asylums, with
no responsibility whatsoever, to dedicate myself utterly to my own
torment. I deserve nothing but that. I do not deserve peace, or sleep,
or death. I will stay alive and rational as long as I need to, so I can
terribly, immeasurably, grieve for my child, for my child, for my son,
David, for my David, until, counter to all the principles of God and
nature, I finally bring him back to life. I believe I can do this, and it's
up to you to judge whether or not I'm crazy, my dear Mr. Doctor, sir.
That's your job.*

\*     \*     \*

NADA GAŠIĆ

Just as the smell of oil and the stench of burning flesh spread through the house, Irma was picking up a pile of towels and clean laundry. Unaware of what had just happened, but with the instinct of someone wounded who knows that each unannounced change, even a surprising change of smells, portends only new misfortune, she raised the laundry to her face, as if shielding herself from a blow. Then she dropped it and ran to the kitchen. The moan that Katarina had swallowed finally found a throat from which to issue forth. Irma began baying like a dog. She came into the kitchen and froze. She dropped to her knees, and that was how, silenced, she crawled to her sister. A lock of hair, glued with henna, moved slowly, marking a red smudge on Katarina's neck. That smudge showed Irma that Katarina's body was still breathing. Horrified by the thought of waking her and bringing her back to so much pain, Irma touched the floor tiles with her lips and began, soundlessly, to kiss them, circling her sister's head.

To the tiles she whispered:

—I didn't mean to, Katja, deaaarest . . . Katja deareeeest . . . I didn't mean to.

Then the whispering stopped. Nothing more was heard.

On the light-colored tiles was left the banal, heart-shaped mark of her lipstick.


Lovro and Ita arrived a half hour later. The gate to the yard and the door to the house were ajar.

Everything was quiet; the sisters were making no sound. Ita instinctively hid behind Lovro and let him go in first. Lovro cautiously opened the kitchen door and then froze. Behind him, Ita burst into wracking sobs.

Lovro didn't realize at first that he was looking at Katarina's body, lying there with deformed, oozing stubs instead of
hands that were unnaturally thrust in the air, nor that around
that body was Irma's soundless body, crawling. He shook his
head hard, as if to shake free of the scene, and then he pulled
away from the door and pushed Ita back.
—Don't go in.

He could barely remember the number he had to dial for the
ambulance. He snarled at the operator and then started saying
over and over:
—But how are we going to bury that poor little child? Someone has to see the child off. Hey, people, we have to bury that
poor boy. Hey, people, what is this? Mother of God, help us now.
Mother of God!

\*       \*       \*

Tomica, the ambulance driver, waited for Katarina to be placed
in the back of his van.
—I'll beat the fucking daylights out of whoever is the first
to say the word *communication*. God damn it, all of you have
totally lost it, what the fuck is it with the sentence *you didn't
communicate this well*. Today, I heard some crazy lady on the
radio say we need to *substantiate our communication*. Substantiate your ass, why don't you, crazy monkey lady. As if I haven't
had it up to here with my job, and then she treats me like a
dumbass, instead of just playing music. As if it's easy driving
an ambulance, motherfuckers. This is a horror show, man,
sheer horror. I'd be better off driving a fucking hearse. You

know the deal, the mourners shed a few tears, say their good-byes to the dead person, but, basically, it's not so bad, easy street, really, peace and quiet. You can kick back and take it easy like a human being. But this, holy shit, recently all I've been doing is picking up kids off the street. Not alive, not dead. And you have to get the kid to the hospital in one piece. I drive like a madman. Nobody gets out of the way, as if I'm driving a load of cabbage; I can barely push my way through the Republic of Austria Square. I want to turn onto Klaićeva, and then some moron runs out in front of me. I'd be happi-est running him over, I shout, *Get the fuck out of my way, you fag, fuck you*, and he says I seem to be having a problem with communication. *You're the one with the problem with your fuck-ing limp dick, you fucking idiot*. A kid is nearly dying here, and this guy fucks with me about communication. The first one to say the word communication, I'll beat the fucking daylights out of him. A fist to the kisser is in the cards, and I mean that. And I'll beat the daylights out of anyone who dares say *how best to react*. And wellness, fuck you and your wellness. This, especially...

Did that little kid really die? And now this is his mom? The poor thing did something to herself. Where should we take her? Vinogradska? Fine. Vinogradska it is. What a mother-fucking job. I would be so much better off driving a truck from Žitnjak than doing this shit. And I was so sure the kid would pull through. I drove like a maniac. Formula 1 wouldn't have gotten him there any sooner. But the kid died. And now I'm driving his mother. Fuck this life. Turn off that radio, other-wise I'll smash it to pieces!

# An old folks' jamboree

Vidošić walked along Klaićeva. He noticed that the houses were getting smaller, and then they totally shrank. Slowly, he proceeded through a miniature version of the city, taking special care, as slowly as Gulliver, not to crush any of the pedestrians with his big shoes. For a moment, he stopped. Then his ears stirred. As if hearing sounds of distant waters and near waters, they summoned Vidošić to consciousness. He trembled from head to toe and stared, crazed, at his feet, unable to believe he was standing on dry pavement. The sounds he was hearing were no longer of distant waters, but it was as if he were approaching a factory where machinery was producing a rhythmic clatter, and, like a sleepy child, he clapped his hands over his ears. His subconscious was trying to grasp where his feet were taking him and to divert him to a place that would be farther from the maddening sound, but in this it did not succeed. He stopped at the spot where Ilica enters a delta, creating, with the other streets, Ban Jelačić Square. The unearthly sound reverberated off the buildings, creating a sort of *Rosamunde* performance, colliding with the eroded plaster facades that were succumbing before his very eyes to the vibrations, and a chunk of stucco broke off the facade of the Nama department store and dropped right at Vidošić's feet. He didn't step back and ignored the voices that were berating him, as if he were the one who pried loose the stucco flower. The bass line of the music punched him in the gut, and then with both hands he pressed his vibrating diaphragm. He looked out over the vast square. What with all the many-colored paper caps and bizarre, neon-hued T-shirts people had pulled on

NADA GAŠIĆ

over coats, he couldn't, at first, see any faces. As if they weren't people with the usual dimensions, but they also were not Lilliputians in comparison to him, the lugubrious Gulliver; instead, they appeared to be hunched-over adult figures. The first thing he noticed wasn't the rhythmic bouncing that accompanied the incessant and largely feigned gaiety of the poor folks on the square, already agitated by being moved from place to place. It was as if half of the people on the square had lost their bearings. The music stopped, and on the stage out in front of the bank building at the other end of the open space stood a barely visible emcee. Had Vidošić had the room to move, he would gladly have left the square. Standing there, trapped there, he didn't understand a thing: not who was being welcomed, nor whom the people were egging on, nor what they were applauding. The words were slow to reach him, ringing off the buildings and ricocheting around Vidošić, and, as if what the emcee was saying was suddenly of vital importance to him, Vidošić began pushing through the crowd toward the stage. The emcee shrieked, *The Majorettes*, music began thumping from the speakers again, and up onto the stage, with the help of the emcee, they hoisted the corpse of an elderly woman. Vidošić was frightened and anxiously drew in his shoulders; he wanted to shout something, call out a warning, but the corpse suddenly twitched, moved head and feet, gave a jumpy yelp, and waved, and the inspector clearly saw the cheeks streaked with makeup and the permed hairdo of the old woman who, tipsily, joyfully pranced around and kicked up her little plaid miniskirt. If anyone had asked him a few minutes before, Vidošić would have sworn there was nothing left on earth that could surprise him, but this hallucinatory scene truly crushed him. He managed a blush and averted his eyes, so he didn't see several more well-rehearsed old women, wearing little plaid skirts, skip out onto the stage; one of them coyly tossed her cane aside, planted her eager hands on her hips, and kicked up her legs. The inspector saw faces beaming all around. The whiskers on the faces of the women prevented their make-up from dripping off their chins, and the inspector looked up at the stage with disgust. It was far enough away, at least, that he didn't have to see all the details up close. By now, the emcee was shrieking in ecstasy. The square echoed with the resonant names of the successful homes for retirees and the infirm; cheers went up for the *Old Folks' Jamboree, Zagreb*, and then once again they dragged the entire group of old women, along with a few doddering men, onto the stage, across which they'd stretched a tennis net and placed deck chairs. An old woman with arthritic knees and a racket in hand, in a seductive tennis dress and thick brown woolen tights, began hitting a ball with erotic swings, aiming for an old man on a chaise lounge on the other side of the net. Vidošić had another look around and once more saw faces beaming. Then the siren of an ambulance rang out. Vidošić saw it cross slowly from the bank building toward the middle of the square. The music stopped. The mob slowly, like poured honey, closed the funnel that the ambulance left behind. They picked somebody up, the door closed, the blue alarm light went on, the faces very, very briefly expressed concern. Then the bass music thumped again. Vidošić came to and made his way, now quite steadily, toward Jurišićeva Street.

By the tourist information center, he pulled free of the crowd and leaned back, weakly, on their display window. The low sun glared in his eyes, it was cold; the steam from mouths obscured the faces, the paper caps bobbled, the neon-colored T-shirts for identifying the nursing home residents that they had pulled on over their winter coats, there under the sun, acquired a unique sheen of sulfurous fumes. The faces melted, and he caught his breath. The aggressive sound faded, and for a moment Vidošić thought he might be going deaf. Only then did he notice someone sitting on the ground, not a meter from him. He stared at the miniature chair, not quite 30 centimeters in height, and saw a man using the chair and enjoying the brief moment of quiet. The man stretched out his right leg, arranged the stump of his left leg by hugging it as if it were a doll, leaned back against the wall under the window, picked up his accordion off the ground, cradled it on his lap like a child, leaned his cheek and ear to the body of the instrument as if checking to see if it were still breathing, fingered the mother-of-pearl buttons, and finally stretched out the bellows. In the pause that suddenly yawned between the official sound system and this wall, the strains of the waltz "On the Hills of Manchuria" flowed toward him as if unglued from the pavement, and Inspector Josip Vidošić began to cry. He thrust his hands into his pants pockets, expecting that this gesture would stop his tears. Male, businesslike, he had to check whether others could see him sniffling. He looked for and found his reflection in the window of the tourist information center, among the little ornate red touristy hearts, the Dinamo soccer shirts, and the miniature replicas of the Baška Tablet, that medieval relic of Croatian literacy—his lips had formed an upside-down half-moon; his jutting chin trembled. He tried to gain control. *Be sensible*. This made his throat and chest ache in an ugly way. He thrust his hands even deeper into his pockets, rudely snorted, and tried to move. He couldn't. His body was stuck. The music began thundering from the speakers again, and the accordion quickly stopped. Vidošić was sure this would end his sobs. It didn't. He took a deep breath, threw back his head, shook it, dropped it to his chest, lifted it, took another deep breath, and, finally, felt he was done with crying. He could move. He glanced at the window once more to check his face. He couldn't find it right away, due to the interference of the flickering reflection of a television screen from the nearby bank's display window. He moved his head to avoid it. Then he turned, irritated. He stared at the screen across the way—a campaign ad was bouncing on it.

—What total assholes you are, you and the elections.

Vidošić must have said this out loud, because the accordion player looked up and shot him a toothless grin, pointing at the screen.

—Ah, that guy there, he is just holding that accordion. He is no accordion player. He does security for some big shot. If they'd asked me, I'd have played for them for a lousy 200 kunas. Or not even that much. I'd have done it for free. You know, for TV.

Vidošić looked, unblinking, at the accordion player. Unaccustomed to people stopping in front of him, let alone looking at him, the accordion player glanced down. He busied himself with packing his accordion.

—This will not be a good day for busking.

Vidošić ran down Jurišićeva all the way to the post office. There he stopped, as if he had finally grasped all the pointlessness of his behavior. He looked down the tram tracks toward the square. Because of the old folks' jamboree and the recent passage of the ambulance, the trams had been halted somewhere. He strode on at a fast pace. Finally, he remembered his phone.

—I need to get to Heinzelova fast. I'm near that fountain, you know, the one out in front of the bank... What's it called... the Croatian Nobles Square. Why twenty minutes? Turn on your siren! I'm walking toward Mosque Square; pick me up along the way.

Then he felt himself overcome by fatigue and an unpleasant sense of loss of trust in his own actions. Why had he run? It made no difference whether he got to the office a half hour earlier or later. At the corner of Smičiklasova and Račkoga, a police car pulled up.

He opened the door, and the driver asked whether he should turn on the siren. Vidošić held the door and didn't get in. The driver repeated the question a little louder.

—No, no need. Neither.


At the front desk at police headquarters, Vidošić asked to be shown the names of all those who had been registered over the last ten days and had asked to see Kasumić. He took out his notepad and wrote something down.

In the hallway in front of his office, he saw his men hanging around. Those who started to say hello stopped partway through the greeting—that's what he looked like.

He went into the office and first told the secretary to inform everybody that the meeting was being put off until later. Then he spent a long time looking at the first and last name of the man who'd been entered in the register as Kasumić's visitor. He turned on his computer and pored over the entire Scholastic Case from start to finish. He printed out several pages and stuffed them into the pocket of his jacket; then he summoned Simčić.

It didn't take more than a second for the officer to appear.

—Simčić, give me a cigarette and your lighter, whatever you've got.

—Boss, I don't smoke anymore; the doctor told me if I smoked I'd lose my job. It's my asthma.

—Don't give me that shit. Give me a cigarette.

Simčić took out his pack and lighter, left them on the desk, and left. Vidošić snatched up the pack, and, with a movement you never forget, he tapped out a cigarette, lit it, inhaled it deeply, dropped his arm onto the arm of the chair, and spun around to face the window. There was nothing to see outside—the city lights hadn't yet turned on, and the dark, overcast sky had hidden the city.

He turned, unlocked his bottom drawer, took out the bottle, and drank in long gulps. He returned the bottle and locked the drawer. From his landline he called his wife.

—Listen, I won't be coming home tonight. Maybe not tomorrow either. Something urgent has come up. I'll manage with the clothes I'm wearing. Don't you worry, I'll be fine. Listen, until I come, the kids are not to spend time out on the street. Did you hear me? Someone older should take them to school. I don't care how you do it. Wait, wait . . . You won't be able to reach me by my cell. Yes, it's that kind of job. Bye. Me too.

He first checked through all the rest of the messages on his phone. A shudder went through him when he saw Katarina's.

NADA GAŠIĆ

Then he got up, looked at the desk, looked at the drawers and wardrobe, and reached for his jacket. He entered the secretary's office and said, *I'll be away for a day or two.* She opened her mouth, but Vidošić was already walking away. He opened Simčić's door and dropped his lighter and cigarettes on the desk.

—Smoke!

When he left the police headquarters, the streetlights were already on. He went over to his car, stopped for a moment to think, and then went up to the parking lot guard.

—Listen, I'll be leaving my car here for a day or two. Okay? Just to let you know there's no cause for alarm.

He set off for the bus terminal on foot. He needed the fresh air to clear his head.

At the bar in the terminal, he downed a few grappas, then went on to beer, then back to grappa, smoking cigarette after cigarette all the while. His phone rang a few times, but Vidošić paid no attention, and finally he switched it off. He treated people to drinks with whom he hadn't exchanged a single word, missed two buses bound for Split, and got on the last one that was leaving Zagreb that night.

\*　　\*　　\*

—Viiiliim, Viilim, where have you gotten to? There's been an awful tragedy, our little David passed away, the angels have taken our Dado. Katarina has gone and done something to herself, Viilim, Viliilim, where are you, oh Blessed Mother of god?

Damir heard everything and ended up alone at the house. He waited for all sound to vanish from both the house and the street. Then he curled up, bent over his waist, inhaled with a loud, male gasp, straightened his back to the point of incredible pain, and strained to the point of fainting. He heard a snap in his breastbone. He waited for the flashing spots and circles before his eyes to subside, then he looked down. He saw his open chest, his lungs, his bare bones, his veins, swollen with dark blood, and his nerves as they madly throbbed. He saw his heart die of fear. He squinted once more, tucked his right hand in under his open ribs, and removed his heart. It crouched, instead of Our Little Lady, in his hand. All his pain drained away, and he began breathing normally. He looked down at his heart. It was small, the size of an egg, and Damir smiled. Until then he'd been sure his heart was big, not the size of a cow's, but roughly . . . like, well, pretty big. He scratched the surface of the thin membrane with his fingernail and opened his little heart. This made him sad; he took pity on the open heart and caressed it with his breath before looking inside it. He examined it, scratched it with his little finger, and with relief he ascertained that there was no longer anyone in there. He folded his heart over, squeezed it firmly to stop the bleeding, and once more he checked it and saw that it had closed seamlessly. He returned it to the cavity that was soundlessly yawning, then pressed in both lungs, then his ribs, then took a deep breath. Nothing hurt, nothing at all; his heart was finally made of ventricles and atria that pumped in oxygen; nothing more could fit inside, and Damir happily patted his chest. Light, light, light as a feather.

NADA GAŠIĆ

He sat and tested his breath. Air went into his lungs without impediment and exhaled without effort; his spine obeyed him, stretched, straightened, and supported his body and head. With his arms he could do whatever he felt like doing: raise and lower them, flap and fly with them, if that's what he wanted. But he didn't. There was still something to attend to.

He grinned malevolently, opened his right hand, and stretched the skin taut, as if wanting to iron smooth his life and love lines. He didn't have long to wait for her to land. Our Little Lady stood there and gawked in surprise at the smooth palm.

—Cup your hand, I'll find it more comfortable.

Damir obeyed. His palm softened, the lines reappeared, and Our Little Lady sat down, relaxed, holding the lapels of her soft little gown.

They were briefly quiet. Damir smiled.

—Your face changed, Damir.

—My face and my heart.

—I feel it. What are you smiling about?

—Freedom.

—Pardon?

—I'm smiling about freedom.

—Freedom is a difficult word. It's hard to utter, and harder yet to acquire.

—You're telling me.

Unsettled by his intonation, Our Little Lady crossed her arms on her chest. She snorted.

—You've done something. I can't yet see what, but you have done something.

—I cleaned my heart.

—Commendable. Only a person with a pure heart can open the door . . .

Worried that she was spouting trite phrases, she stopped halfway through the sentence, glanced sideways, and then into Damir's eyes.

—How did you clean your heart? With prayer?

—No. With my fingernail.

Our Little Lady reached for his Mount of Saturn with her dainty hand and nearly rose to her feet.

—The way you're speaking isn't nice. What did you do?

—I had a look into my heart, cleaned it with my fingernail, and that was how I acquired my freedom. There is nobody left in there, nothing but blood, and I am free.

—Am I not in there?

—Least of all you.

They fell silent.


—Oh oh oh! Mother of God, what has become of us in this world? Mother of God, please help us!

As she paced around the yard, Cilika wailed. Wails could be heard as well from the neighboring yards. But the new houses were silent.

Damir went stiff. Very slowly he curved his hand around Our Little Lady. He had the impression of wings fluttering in alarm.

As soon as she closed the front door behind her, Cilika stopped with her wailing. Damir knew her usual sequence of steps: she sets down her purse on the cabinet, takes off her shoes, puts on her slippers, takes off her jacket, hangs it up, goes to the kitchen, forgets to hang up her keys, goes back to the hallway, then back to the kitchen, where she stays for at least an hour.

That's why he wasn't prepared for this. Cilika suddenly burst into his little room.

—David's goooone!

She keened.

—Our David's gone—the angels have taken our sweet Dado...

She choked on the awful news.

—Our little Dado is gone.

Then, as if she'd bitten through her moan:

—What's that in your hand? Give it here.

Damir retreated to the wall. As fast as he possibly could, he tucked his hand behind his back. As fast as he could. He even tightened his fist so much that he felt the softness of her little dress.

With her meaty right hand, Cilika nabbed his elbow, while in her left she clutched her keys.

—Hand it over! That's an order! You old ape! Give it here!

Damir would have pushed away from her, but he focused all his might on controlling the clench of his fist so he wouldn't harm Our Little Lady. Left to himself, his elbow relaxed and Cilika managed to yank out his arm.

His arm shook.

Cilika looked at the fingers of the curled fist, concealing something.

—You brazen jackass, you've started bringing vermin into my house in your old age. Veeerrmiiin. Bugs. They'll be breeding. Let it go now. Let me see. Open your hand, you impudent fool!

Damir made not a sound, but he shot a sideways glance at how the wings slowly withdrew. *Go hide, go hide . . .*

—Did you hear what I said? Now you'll get yours! Now, now, now!

Gripping his elbow, Cilika first rapped Damir's fingers lightly with her keys.

The hand did not release.

She repeated the blow, now harder, meaner. The hand did not release, and Cilika became vicious; she snarled, yowled, gnawed at her prey. She beat his clenching fingers with the keys, and his knuckles began to bleed.

For a second Damir's mind wandered off, as if washed out, wrung dry. He felt his arm which, as if from an electric shock, sprang back from the elbow to the fingernails, and he barely was able to return to reality. He looked at his hand. It released. Opened. The traitorous fist. But . . . Empty.

Cilika, too, stared at the empty, bloody fist.

—Where'd it go? I was so sure you were holding something. I could've sworn on Our Lady, Mary, Mother of God that I spied something in there. A butterfly. All this is pushing me over the edge. Wait, hold your hand steady, I'll bring a bandage. Watch out that you don't go dripping blood anywhere.

Leaving the room, she invoked the Blessed Virgin Mary of Marija Bistrica and prayed for her to bring order to this world of ours.

Damir began to shake. He looked at his empty fist and the fingers that had suddenly stopped bleeding. The pain melted away.

Cilika came back with a roll of bandages.

—Well now, that's a sight better, I see I didn't hit you so hard after all. There's not even any blood. Where did you wipe it off?

　　　　　　　　　　　　　　　　　　NADA GAŠIĆ

You must have wiped it off somewhere, you foolish fool; you'll get everything dirty again.

But she didn't swing to hit him again. She even said the insults in a softer voice.

Damir shook.

Cilika sighed and turned to the door.

—Don't you be taxing my nerves today. Be quiet and don't set foot outside your room. I'll come in later, tidy up, and change your bedding. There's gotta be blood here somewhere.

Then she stopped. She turned to the table and saw the bowl full of packets of sugar.

—I won't have you luring the vermin with that sugar. I'm throwing it all out.

She picked up the dish, and by now she was addressing the door:

—He wiped away the blood somewhere, Mother of God, he must have wiped that idiot blood of his on something.

Damir felt his drool dripping onto his pants, and from his shirt pocket he took his handkerchiefs. He focused on wiping his mouth. When he put down the damp handkerchiefs, he lowered his softened hand to his leg and spotted Our Little Lady, who was settling down on his pain-free hand, fixing her hair.

—Well, well, now that was close.

Her voice was quite bright. Like after a lot of excitement.

Damir was silent.

—Don't you worry, Damir, nothing bad will happen to your hand. Maybe you'll have the teeniest little scar on one knuckle.

She looked at him with an impish grin.

—A teensy little cross. Nothing more.

He was silent.

—Why so quiet? You know what she's like. She'll be back in half an hour with cakes to comfort you. And herself.

He said nothing.

—Hey, Damir!

—Don't call me.

—Damir!

—Don't call me!

—Damir, talk with me. I'll help you.

—You'll help me? You?

—Well, me, yes, me.

Until that moment he'd been able to catch the changes in her voice. Everything, from anger, grief, concern, coyness, but now he didn't catch her confusion. She was sincerely confused:

—Yes, yes, I will help you.

—Will you, now? Like you helped push aside the mob of kids who peed on me when I fell, after they'd chased me down the street like a dog and howled Peter Pan at me? Like you helped Katarina love me? Like you helped David get better? Like you kept Cilika from beating my hand with her keys when I was defending you? I was defending you!

—Damir, we've already talked about this. There are many things that are not in my power. And besides, you, too, had to make sacrifices.

—Who did you learn those stories about sacrifice from?

—Me, learn? Me?

She didn't even notice she'd begun to harp. He said not a word. His breathing rasped. Feeling despondent, Our Little Lady reined in her confusion and backed off of her combative tone.

—I know you were expecting a great deal from me, but saving David was not in my power.

—So if it wasn't in your power, why did you even come?

—To help you.

—To help? How, in what way?

—I wanted you to be a witness. So you'd understand.

—What?

—I wanted to teach you to play Go well. If you'd finished a full game of Go, you'd have understood that the central stone is always defended. It must remain untouchable. It is protected and defended.

—Even now I don't understand what you're saying.

—Oh yes, you do.

—Do I? And what else did you want?

—I wanted you to be a witness, in place of David. Since you weren't an eyewitness.

—Me, a witness?

—Yes, you. I even told you the fairy tale to get you to see things around you a little more clearly. But you were sleeping!

—You found me, me, who's nonverbal, me, who's slow, you found me to be a witness? You're lying.

—Don't say such bad things.

—I'm saying bad things? You're spouting gibberish. I'm asking you: Why did you come?

—Among other things, so you'd be able to make it through everything.

—Well, you didn't help me make it through. You duped me.

—I did not dupe you. I never promised you I'd save David.

—You duped me. You kept telling me I had to hope. So I hoped.

—Well, hope is not a promise. It merely makes it easier for you to accept the inevitable.

—A kind of lie.

—According to your will and by your choice.

—I'd have known that fine without you. You needn't have come. Because of you, I pried Katarina out of my heart.

—That would have happened sooner or later. With me or without me.

—You're lying and you lied. You came to deceive me. Because of you, because of you I patted Katarina, because you told me I'm like other people. And better. It's because of your lies that all this happened.

—You're mistaken, Damir.

—Well, if I'm mistaken, why are you mistaken? You are the omnipotent one. Fix what you've done.

—I can't. What happened cannot be fixed. Miracles only happen in fairy tales.

—That's not true, it's that you don't want to.

—I can't.

—You can't? Then how can you do that thing where you shed bloody tears from wooden statues whenever you feel like it? How can you hover a few thousand times over the stony Herzegovinian landscape, every single day, and how can you promise stuff to all sorts of people, lift invalids from their wheelchairs, cure people's cancer, but this you can't do? Tell me! Well? Why are you looking at me like that?

—I can't fix what happened. That is not in my power. People see me the way you see me. When they need me. And things either fix themselves or they don't. For that I'm neither to blame nor am I responsible. I do not make choices guided by my own will.

—Then by whose?

—You know.

—I don't know anything, and I won't believe you anymore.

—How will you live like that?

—Lightly and easily. Free.

—Your freedom will be challenging.

—And with you I'd have an easier time of it? It will be what it is.

—I'll help you recover from your grief, Damir.

—You won't help me recover from my grief, because I am not sad. I am free.

—You are unhappy, you are not free. A free person never says hurtful things.

—I am free.

—How will you live with an empty heart?

—By breathing. How will you live when you know everything is your fault?

—It's my fault only if you want it to be. And besides, I can leave.

—No, you can't. You can't leave, because I won't let you. So you can't go off and find someone else to dupe with stories about hope and happy endings for people of a pure heart. You're not leaving.

—How will you stop me?

He said nothing. Then he smiled at her.

—You're not the Virgin Mary. You're a dippy butterfly.

—Damir!

With loathing he smiled at her.

—You're not going anywhere, crazy butterfly lady!

—How will you stop me, Damir? Damir! Damir!

He didn't say another word.

She spread herself out, gathered up her little gown, and, only barely managing to flap her velvety wings, she tried to take off and fly, but in confusion she dropped back down onto his hand. She was losing valuable time. Again, she spread her dress-wings, flapped them resolutely, but, somehow disappointed with herself, she fluttered aimlessly, heading straight for the lamp. She bumped into the glass, was dazed, began circling, and fell down. She tried once more; again she knocked against the lampshade and collapsed next to the lamp stand. Along the path of her flight and her fall there sifted a fine screen of dust motes, like finely ground mother-of-pearl. Finally that, too, settled. Then she shamefacedly tucked her little legs under her dress and waited. Only her arms were moving—she clasped her hands together in a prayer. She tried catching Damir's eye, but he wasn't watching her. Instead, he was watching his left thumb and finger as he shifted her to his right hand. Only when he'd set her down on his right hand did he look her in the eye. And in her eyes he did not see hope, or faith, or love. In her little eyes, as tiny as the head of one of Little Seamstress's pins, he saw nothing but a void that was filling with a timeless fear.

By then he was no longer looking into her little pinprick eyes but was staring at her tiny feet shod in leather straps, as she scooched them, anxiously, like a little girl, under her little gown. Then he looked at her dainty hands, with which she was covering her frightened face, and her fingers, on which he saw her pathetic little fingernails.

Then he glanced at the little cross, a bloody knuckle scab.

Only then did he focus on his own fingernails, watching them as his fingers tensed into a terrible male fist that unstoppably and irreparably squeezed and crushed Our Little Lady.

Squish...

He got up and went over to the empty window. Nobody was walking down the street; Damir kept his eyes on a mourning dove that had landed on the fence. It jerked its head, stretched its neck, showed him its dark, velvety necklace, then turned and off it flew. He wiped his hands on his corduroys, and his hands filled with the feel of the velvety nap. It wasn't the soft touch of Our Little Lady's dress, but the sensation was enough for tears to well up from his empty heart. He was surprised; he had not believed this would ever happen again. He had no thought of holding back—he let it mount from his throat to his nose, and then to his eyes. Everything began to ache; his spine tensed again, his back reclaimed its hunch, his arms got longer, and he had to sit. He sat down on the bed, as if perching on a wall, and felt how it wasn't just his tears that were flowing from his eyes and drool from his nose and the corners of his lips that were half-open, but he felt as if all of him were draining away, turning into a puddle, then into a terrible water that, as if pouring over rocks, was gushing down the bed on which he was sitting. He felt that even his hunchback had dewed up with pitiful tears that dribbled down into his trousers and underwear. Through his squinting, wet eyes, he hardly recognized Cilika when she appeared again at the door.

She threw her hands up and wailed:

—You jackass, you've wet yourself again! Jackass!

His bladder wouldn't listen, though he was trying with all his might to stop the wave of wetness. He pulled himself in, pressed his legs together, all in hopes that his body would obey him. But it didn't. Everything that was inside him poured out; the remnants of his urine poured into his slippers, and the only thing left for him to do was to raise his arms and protect his head.

Cilika came over quickly, spry for her age.

He expected blows; indeed, he hoped for them. All he wanted was for them to begin and end as soon as possible. As soon as the first one struck the top of his head, he was relieved. In a minute this would be over. He stopped crying.

The second to the back of his head.

The third to his hunchback.

The fourth—she was getting tired—didn't hurt.

—Take off all your clothes, Mother of God, what have I done to deserve this? All your clothes! Hear me?

She burst into tears, as if she were the one being beaten.

Damir went still and waited for Cilika to return, to hand him dry clothes and shut the door. He took off everything. He knew the procedure: wrap all the wet clothes into a ball, leave the ball by the door, put on the clean clothes, wait. Quiet. Head bowed, quiet. Wait.

He'd stopped crying a long time ago. Everything inside him had dried out. Cilika went in and out of the house, mumbled, opened up to neighbors, wept with them loudly, then went quiet, clattered with metal pots, made phone calls. Finally, aromas drifted from the kitchen, everything was stilled, the house settled down. The silence and peace had the fragrance of cinnamon. All traces of rage were gone.

Cilika came into the room, put the clean clothes on the bed; she collected the wrinkled, smelly clothes while mumbling, opened a window, and said softly to Damir:

—Big Boy, put these on and cover yourself with something so you don't catch cold. Strudel is coming. Just needs to cool.

She left the room. Damir got dressed, curled up on the bed, and pulled the blanket over him.

The open window gulped in the cold air and chased the smelly warmth from the room. The noise of the main street ebbed. With it came the sounds of the early evening: the careful closing of garden gates by the little houses and the automatic rolling out of the garage doors on the tall buildings. The doors of the smaller houses, Damir thought, were cautiously spreading the news about the terrible accident, and the garage doors didn't seem to care; they weren't even curious enough. As if they were repeating *vroom—open, vroom—closed, vroom—open, vroom—closed*... And the little garden gate, opened and closed by somebody's hand, cried out pitifully, *Aaa, aaa, aaa, aaa*. Or so it seemed to him.

He gave no thought to anything else.

The door to his room opened, and on the threshold shivered Cilika feverishly. In her left hand she held the plate of pastries, and with her right she turned on the ceiling light.

—Oops, did we forget to close the window? Oh well, that's okay, it can stay open a little longer, better to air out the room. Warming it up will be easier later.

She sat down on a chair by the bed and offered him the strudel. Damir accepted it and waited.

—Big Boy, don't be mad at me. Not for the way I chide you, or that sometimes... I smack you a little. I didn't mean to do that thing with the keys. They were in my hand, and that's how it happened that I hit you with them.

She stared shortsightedly at his hand.

—Will you look at that—nothing remains. Not a thing. Just that little cross, which will heal quickly. Soon enough there will be nothing left to see, not even the little cross.

Damir didn't eat. He waited for Cilika to finish.

—See, I'm sad.

She started to sob but quickly collected herself.

—I'm sad. David, our dear little angel, has gone to dear God. To the angels. Dear God took him, because he was such a wonderful child. Our beloved God takes all the finest home. You can see, he won't take Gramps, or you. You're already getting old. And I've grown old. I won't be able to look after you for much longer. And Vilim's no use. That's how dear God wanted it, and the Blessed Virgin, for you to live this long in the world. I will have to move you into care. The nuns. With people who are like you. I guess they'll take you in.

She took the strudel from Damir's dish and bit it.

—I could have added more cinnamon. But they aren't bad like this.

He didn't budge. The plate shook a little in his hand.

—Hey, set the plate on the table; you can eat them later. Better that than they end up on the floor.

She took the plate from Damir's hand and set it on the table. The pastries released more of their cinnamon aroma. Such peace reigned in the house.

—You are lucky, Damir, and the Holy Bible says so too. I was taught that *blessed are the poor in spirit, for theirs is the kingdom*

NADA GAŠIĆ

*of heaven*. You are lucky, because you don't feel a thing. Not sorrow or grief. Nothing. A place has been saved for you up in heaven, and the rest of us, we who are normal, we have to fight over that. And we're sinful. You're so lucky, you have no idea how lucky you are. The way I chastise you at times and yell at you, that's because you don't do what I say. There, see all the things that have happened to me—my kuma, my darling Katarina, our child has died. Dear God and Mary, give him . . .

Cilika began to cry.

—Come here, come here, dear Damir, Big Boy, pray with me. We'll pray together. Turn toward the cross and the picture of the Mother of God. Jesus! Did you knock over the picture?

Cilika leaned over and righted the picture of the Blessed Virgin. There smiled a plump, pale-faced woman in a dark-blue cloak, looking up at the heavens with a dull gaze, her hands clasped in prayer. Damir wouldn't look at her.

Cilika became impatient.

—Come here, up you get. Come over and kneel by me. It's hard for me to kneel too; my knees ache.

Cilika knelt slowly, holding on to the table with one hand and the chair with the other.

Damir got up from the bed. He too held on to the table with one hand, and, silently, he knelt by her side. He did not look up at the picture.

Cilika dropped her head onto her breast, knit her fingers together, and closed her eyes.

Damir dropped his head to his chest, knit his fingers together like Cilika, but did not close his eyes. He stared at his little cross, the scab on the back of his right hand.

There was a brief interlude of silence, and then from the room and through the night window onto the poorly lit street seeped their prayer:

—Hail Mary, full of grace . . .

—Aaaao, aaao, aaaaaa aaaa . . .

—The lord is with thee . . .

—Aaaaaaaa a aaaaaa . . .

—Blessed are thee among women . . .

—Aaaaaaaaaaa aa aaaaa aaaaaaa . . .

*   *   *

The doctor says to a young intern:

—The patient has been placed in an induced coma, something that is used in cases of serious burn injuries, to protect the body from going into shock.

Katarina saw the same yellowish-brown torrent on Savska Road and herself, swimming, carrying David in the crook of her arm. The water gave her a doglike nip, then a snakelike nip, and finally it whooped with laughter in her face. It gloried, gurgled, giggled, gargled with joy, and with its guffaws it chased from Katarina's head the effort to focus on her swimming; it greedily cozied up to the boy, grabbed him by the trousers and shirt, raised his limp arms to the surface, then took him by the fingers and drew him away from her. Katarina could feel herself giving up. She needed both her arms. To swim with all her might. She mustered her strength and began powerfully slicing through the water with her legs. With her right arm, while holding David's head above

NADA GAŠIĆ

water, she plastered his limp body along her breast, thrust out her neck to keep her own head above water, and, like a giant tortoise, she breathed in with a gasp that was briefly louder than the roar of the water. She dove down to grab the child's shirt. With her teeth she chomped the wet cloth and then, thrusting her jaw forward, she rose to the surface with David. She knew what the mouth is for, what the teeth are for: only for a bestially powerful clamp onto cloth, a clamp to hold the boy above the surface of the witch-face of the water. Her nostrils widened, and she breathed as evenly as she could. Finally freed, the right arm she'd been using till then to hold the boy could aid the left, and Katarina struck out swimming vigorously toward the riverbank. Now she could see people lined up along the water. They were standing on something, and this something was not dirt, but sandbags piled up to create a levee. She tried to call to the people and their faces. She felt as if she were shouting, but actually she was voicing throaty grunts that, clearly, weren't reaching very far. The people didn't move. They didn't see her. She swam even more vigorously. The riverbank was so close. But they didn't see her. Why didn't anyone try to help? Could it be that they couldn't see that she was carrying a child in her teeth? No, it's not true, don't lie, Katarina! They did move. They saw you. Now someone is taking action. Katarina sees a boy waving. People are going over to him. Why him? Why aren't they looking at her? Katarina, hold on a little longer, Katarina, wave, you idiot, you weakling, Katarina, you lazy old woman, accursed, wave with your left hand, wave with your right! They see you! Harder, Katarina, harder! Now someone will get into the water and lend a hand. Keep going. They took something from the boy's hand. Some black rocks and white rocks. The boy is screaming, crying, wailing. Who cares, Katarina, that someone else's child is crying! Who cares, Katarina, about other people's children! You hellish creature, shut up! My boy, David, would cry if he could. And I would if I could. I can't see David's face, but he's definitely smiling. Smile. Instead of shouting. Shout, David, wake up, David! And you, Katarina, swim! Why isn't the riverbank getting closer, why isn't anyone jumping into the water? Jump into the water, you brave men! Jump in and grab me. Me, not David, I wouldn't let you pick up David. I won't let him out of my grasp, nor teeth, ever again, ever again. To the end of my days. Finally, Katarina sees a man who lifts his hands and waves. Don't wave, come into the water, swim to me! Pull me out with David in my teeth, so the water won't drag us away. Don't wave! The water will wash us away.

Then she froze in hysterical panic. Something splashed. Something fell right near her. She stopped swimming. She wasn't paddling. Only her legs were still doing their automatic job of keeping her body afloat. She saw something flying toward her again. It splashed. A stone. She thought she'd seen a stone. And again, and again. One stone after another. White stone, black stone, white stone, black stone . . . She lowered her head to protect herself, to protect David. She commanded her feeble arms to row, to move. Damn them, move! Then she saw them, her hands, how they were slowly and surely turning into charred branches, and she refused to believe it. Then she saw her stumps of hands, how they were turning centimeter by centimeter into something that wasn't human. They were turning into . . . into dogs' paws, into dogs' paws . . . She felt as

NADA GAŠIĆ

if she were no longer swimming the breaststroke, but swimming a dog paddle. Then a shadow appeared below her eyes, and she looked down and saw how her mouth was elongating into a muzzle, a furry muzzle, and she saw she was not carrying David in her furry muzzle, but a puppy. The people on the riverbank weren't aiming at her. They were aiming at the bitch with the puppy in its muzzle. She could see their faces, and among the faces she saw two she recognized. The faces of David's father and David's grandfather. They were not throwing stones. They were just smiling. Someone was taking their picture.

The bitch veered away from the rain of stones and paddled toward the middle of the river.

So the water would wash her away.

*   *   *

Vidošić stepped off the bus, his legs numb from sitting, and instead of feeling solid ground underfoot, he felt empty space. About to fall, he grabbed the door of the bus, and, not sure his foot had met the ground, he froze, unable to move. His hand clung to the warm metal, and he trusted it. The driver bid him goodbye again; he heard the rousing passengers fidget in their seats, and he had to pull away his hand. The door shut and, recalling how to take a step, he stepped back. He heard the piteous whimper of a small, injured animal; this alarmed him, and he glanced down.

He was standing on a patch of ice that had formed over a shallow mud puddle and realized it wasn't a crushed animal he'd heard; the frozen dirt had squealed under the pressure of his foot.

Once he was aware of what he was looking at, he pulled his jacket tighter around him and struggled to do up the zipper. His hands were shaking and he couldn't manage it, so he flapped one half of his jacket over the other, tucked his hands under his arms, and turned to walk in the direction the bus driver had told him to go.

The darkness was ebbing, the light was changing, and it looked to Vidošić as if he'd caught the very moment, as fragile as cracked glass, when the light imprisoned by night is breaking out into day. Visibility was better, and he could already clearly discern the chain-link fence he would have to clamber over and the solitary bushes and narrow line of willow trees that followed the course of the rivulet. A path soon came into view, and Vidošić, without glancing to look back at the road, proceeded on his way down to the place where he'd been told there was a proper little bridge, or at least a log serving as a bridge.

Through night's lingering dribs and drabs, he sought the spots where he could already see the light of day. Soon the frost tightened his nostrils, and he exhaled through his mouth; the steam created a little cloud that reminded him of cigarette smoke, and irrepressible saliva began welling in his mouth. He stopped, looked around, and, seeing that he was coming close to the willows, he decided to first cross the waterway, and once across he'd reward himself with a smoke, the last in his pack. The water made no sound, but he could see that the ground was giving way and he was already standing on the very

NADA GAŠIĆ

riverbank. He peered ahead and finally caught sight of a small bridge, slapped together from an assortment of boards. Only on one side was there something like a railing. He took hold of the questionable railing and gave it a good shake. The little bridge shook, all 2 to 3 meters of it, but he could tell it wouldn't give way under his weight. Once more he peered down at the channel and stared at it without seeing much of anything for some fifteen seconds. He was looking for the water, and finally he spotted it. Then he shivered; it was if he weren't looking into the water, but the water was looking into him. Calm and steadfast, the rivulet was barely slithering through laconic water grasses. He watched them; they looked as if, rippling along, they'd pull free any moment from their roots and float off down the river. With long strides he crossed the bridge. The other bank was steep, and he had trouble scrambling up to the point where the terrain leveled off, where he could catch his breath and light up. He took out his last cigarette and the matches and remarked, with satisfaction, that his hands had all but stopped shaking. And there he stood for a time. To his left the dark was still lurking at the edges of the forest, but to his right he could already discern the outlines of houses. A dog piped up from somewhere with a whine, another barked in response, and Vidošić thought it might be wise to carry a branch with him. Then he laughed at himself for overthinking the need for caution. The sun rose, and now he began to see the scattered houses quite clearly at a distance of a hundred meters or so. Smoke was rising out of two of the single-story dwellings, and all he had left to do was decide which one more closely resembled what the bus driver had told him. He settled on one that was standing apart to the side. It had a Kasumić-like look about it. Stable.

He started walking, then after two or three steps he stopped. He was suddenly filled with acute distress, and the whole endeavor began to feel suspect. No decision broke through to his emptied brain. He turned toward the rivulet, as if expecting its advice, and noticed that along the steep bank the sun was shining through dewdrops on the bushes. Vidošić went over to the glistening bushes. A crystal spiderweb was mirrored an arm's length away, and he couldn't resist—he reached for the beady, glassy droplets of water, the spiderweb swayed, the droplets trickled off it, and the light of the magical bush was snuffed. He felt the wet web sticking to his hand; he pulled it back, the snuffed spiderweb stretched, and with irritation he wiped off the stickiness on his jeans. Where could this spiderweb have come from amid the frost? Then he turned and strode purposefully toward the house he had chosen at random.

He didn't turn, but a sideways glance took in the rest of the hamlet, a barely recognizable cluster of something that had, not so long ago, some fifteen years back, been a settlement. A shadow, a vestige of something that had been torched, devastated, voiceless, overgrown, and so dreadfully emptied that, without thinking, he covered his ears by raising the collar of his jacket. To avoid seeing the dead. On he went. The ruins of the roofless, headless, dead houses, with gouged-out eyes instead of windows, couldn't follow him. They stayed behind. Then there was a row of brand-new houses and some older ones where the roofs had been repaired and were bright red. Lit as they were by the

NADA GAŠIĆ

rising sun, they reminded him of the flames of these or other roofs, in the recent or not-so-recent wars, of nearer or farther neighbors, whichever.

He was already coming up on the house he'd been walking toward. He saw the fence and a dog that was fiercely charging at it. He stopped. The door to the house opened, and the dog ran over to the man who was standing on the threshold. The sun glared in the man's face, and he shielded his eyes with his hand. With his other hand he held the dog. Though Vidošić found it hard to believe that this man in rubber boots could possibly be Kasumić, he did recognize him. He didn't wave. Some 20 meters from the house, he felt himself short of breath, and he suddenly felt feeble and had to stop. If Kasumić had left him for another minute standing there, he would have slumped to the ground. Then he saw the man tell the dog something, let it go, and wave as if showing a driver how to park a truck. Vidošić scarcely made it to the door.

Kasumić didn't smile, but he also didn't look as if he were frowning or particularly surprised. Whatever . . . Like when a person has been expecting somebody for years, and has lost all hope, and when the long-awaited person finally does arrive, he is neither glad to see him nor disappointed. Whatever . . . Kasumić held the dog by the collar and led it over to Vidošić.

—Let it get used to you.

Only then did he look over Vidošić properly.

—Hey, Lika is not for the faint of heart.

—No, it is not.

Vidošić let the dog sniff his hands and pants legs, but when it turned its muzzle toward his groin, he covered himself with his hand. Kasumić tugged at the collar, and the dog raised its muzzle.

—Come on in. We don't waste indoor heat around here.

Kasumić crossed the front hall and went into the room where the warmth was emanating from. His guest also entered and took off his jacket.

With a glance, his host showed him which chair. Vidošić handed him his jacket. Kasumić took it, and for an instant they were caught in a moment of unwanted intimacy, when two people at odds with each other find themselves, inadvertently, holding the same object. They both let go of the jacket and it waved its sleeves, as if disappointed, while fluttering to the floor. Kasumić tossed it over a chair, turned, and took a bottle and two shot glasses from a cupboard. While he was handling the cupboard and dishes, Vidošić had the sense that Kasumić was not fully familiar with the furniture, as if his hand were still figuring out where things were kept. Vidošić had a look around the room. Every single thing there was brand-new. For whatever reason, the things did not bring with them the allure of new possessions and instead seemed out of place, even to themselves.

Kasumić set the bottle and shot glasses on the table and finally sat down. He poured carefully.

—Around here nobody asks what you'd like to drink. What we drink here is rakija.

Vidošić didn't know what was meant by *around here*, whether in this house or throughout the region, but he didn't ask.

They raised their glasses, then looked each other in the eye, and the guest felt as if he were not the only one blushing. He sloshed the rakija down his throat, as if punishing himself.

—Give me a little water.

—What about raspberry syrup and soda?

NADA GAŠIĆ

Vidošić couldn't believe his ears.

—Pardon?

—Like a cordial. People always used to treat guests to a drink of raspberry syrup mixed with water.

—No, just water, please.

Kasumić got up to pour a glass of water. He gave his guest the glass.

—Drink it slowly and watch your teeth, it's icy cold.

He was too late, and Vidošić dropped his head to his chest in pain and rubbed his jaw.

The host picked up his pack of cigarettes, stopped, shot his guest a questioning look, and turned the open end of the pack toward him. Both lit up. For a while they watched the smoke as it filled the room.

—How did you get here?

—Took the night bus for Split. The driver told me where to get off and the direction to take.

Again, they were silent.

—Hungry?

—No.

—When did you last eat?

—Dunno.

Kasumić poured and Vidošić downed.

—What about trying to eat a little something.

—No, thanks.

Avoiding the talk of food, Vidošić took another look around the room.

—Everything's new. You've done a nice job.

—Had to. From scratch. Nothing was left.

—I saw along the way that things have been repaired. But are most of the houses empty?

—Empty.

—Life will come back in time.

—No, it won't. Life does not come back.

—People will be back.

—The local Serbs won't.

—Maybe some of them will come back.

—The houses weren't emptied to be filled, nor cleansed so they'd come back.

—There will be life.

—There will. A new life, yes, but the old life will never be back. It's over and done with.

—Well, in time.

—Not in time or by force. Just like in nature when there is a . . . cataclysm.

He quickly tossed back the rest of his shot.

—Once life is gone, after a time newer forms happen, but the old ones never return.

Vidošić watched him, then looked down.

—Okay, but that is life.

—It depends. For somebody—life; for somebody—nothing.

Vidošić stopped talking and began sinking into his chair. His cigarette shook between his fingers. Kasumić noticed.

—Listen, I'm not your father or mother, but you should eat something; otherwise this will make you sick.

—No it won't.

—Did you sleep on the bus?

—No.

—Listen, the firewood won't chop itself, or the dog feed itself, or the food cook itself just because you came. I will take care of what I have to do, and you'd be best off lying down here on the sofa.

Kasumić went out, and Vidošić felt his host, with his sensitivity, knew his guest wouldn't have felt comfortable lying down in front of him. He sat down on the sofa, and he only had time to slip off his shoes before the room with its new furniture disappeared.

When he found himself there again, surrounded by sunlit things, a full hour had passed with no dreams or smells. Kasumić had his back turned and was fiddling with something around the stove. Vidošić sat at the empty table. He ran his fingers over his lower lip and had the impression that instead of caked saliva, he was fingering a spiderweb.

—Where can I splash my face?

Over his shoulder, Kasumić nodded toward the hall.

—The door right by the front door. There's a razor in there. Use the towel closer to the wall.

Vidošić entered the bathroom thinking all he'd do was splash his face, but when he saw in the mirror how dismal he looked, he decided on a more ambitious undertaking. He had a look at the room with the toilet bowl, sink, and plastic shower curtain. He stripped off his clothes and piled them on the toilet lid. He stared at the closed toilet and tried to remember when he'd last needed to go. As if he'd been cemented shut. Then he turned on the water, stood under the shower, and waited for the water to come pouring over him. He hadn't thought of whether to expect warm or cold water, but he couldn't believe that his body had completely forgotten how frigid water could be. He dried himself as if scraping off someone else's skin, and for fear of being disgusted, he put his underwear on without checking to see what it looked like. He felt his body suddenly warm up and lose its weight. The shave was not much of a success, but he did come out of the bathroom weightless, in a changed mood.

From the warm kitchen where he could hear the rattling of dishes, he smelled food being prepared. Vidošić turned his head away, and, still unprepared for the stimuli of food, he stepped outside.

He took a shallow breath. His lungs couldn't accept the chill of the bracing air right away; he coughed. He even felt slightly queasy. He hunched then dropped his shoulders, threw his head back, and forced himself to breathe in deeply through his nostrils. He wiggled his shoulders, shook his head, and listened to the thin voicing of the calcified vertebrae in his neck. He felt better. He looked toward the woods. They seemed closer. The trees were no longer silhouettes, and he felt he was no longer in the same landscape as he'd been in earlier that morning. The space had taken on its expected forms, and he no longer felt anxiety. He turned as Kasumić appeared at the door, and Vidošić spotted the pack of cigarettes in his hand. He even tried to be witty.
—Such a shame in this air, it shouldn't be tainted.

Kasumić took out a cigarette, licked it, and lit it, and, punishing Vidošić for those words, he didn't offer him the pack.
—I put some beans on, but they'll take at least another hour.
—I'm not hungry.
—You will be.

He puffed again on the cigarette and then, exhaling, watched the smoke travel toward Vidošić. The lonely puff was seeking the company of the man. They didn't talk.

—Heeeey there!

Both of them turned toward the voice that came from the woods.

A man dressed in a mismatched camouflage outfit was barely discernible against the dark background.

—Eeeeheya there, Teeslaaa! Whatcha got there, guests?

Kasumić cupped his free hand like a horn:

—Eeeeh, Josinaaa, someone from work.

—Got any raaakiiiijaaaa?

—Laaateeer. I'll caall youuu! Cooooking beeeeans!

The man waved, and off he went deeper into the woods.

— Don't you have phones?

—We do, but this is the way in Lika we chase off wild animals, the dark, the fog, the winter, the loneliness . . . Where's your phone? I haven't been hearing it.

—Muted. So as not to hear it.

Again, they stopped talking, until Vidošić suddenly turned to Kasumić.

—You haven't asked me why I'm here.

—Not asking. You'll tell me when you can.

He shot Vidošić a quick glance and had the impression that the man's face was sagging again and he'd started to tremble. Kasumić went into the house.

Vidošić was, indeed, trembling. It finally hit him that he was dressed all wrong for the climate, and the frigid air had him feeling a little hungry. He hopped up and down two or three times and then followed Kasumić in. He found him standing by the kitchen counter, spreading a fat layer of pâté on a slice of bread.

—The beans need more time. You have to eat something. Would you like this?

—Sure, I'll have some.

Kasumić set down his piece of bread and smoothed his pants leg. He took another can of the pâté and peeled back the lid. Then he reached for the round loaf of bread and curved his arm around it as if he were pulling a baby close. Vidošić was startled to think how easy it had been to forget that once, not so very long ago, this was the way bread was held when it was sliced. Only then did he truly feel hunger. Kasumić put down the loaf, took the piece he'd sliced off, scooped up pâté with the tip of his knife, spread it on the bread, and offered it to Vidošić. He did this with measured movements, reviving the gesture with which somebody in this house would have taken the responsibility of feeding a chance guest.

—So, I may have heard wrong, but it seems to me that somebody offered me raspberry syrup and soda this morning.

—You heard right. Like some?

—Yes, please.

Kasumić opened the cabinet where the bottles were.

Vidošić watched him take the bottle with both hands. He looked at Kasumić's hands when they lowered the bottle onto the table and saw that they were remembering a watchful childhood when people took great care to keep the bottle with the precious liquid from dropping to the floor. Kasumić turned to pour water into a glass carafe, and Vidošić used the moment to touch the bottle. Out of the corner of his eye, Kasumić saw his hand reach forward. It was as if Vidošić were patting the head of a child. Kasumić busied himself at the counter and left Vidošić

NADA GAŠIĆ

to pull back his hand. He put the glasses and carafe on the table and finally sat. The syrup in the bottle was thick and still, but the water in the carafe was still restless, unprepared for the mingling of the two liquids. Kasumić set the glasses one next to the other; with his right hand, he lifted the bottle of syrup and began pouring it carefully. The syrup inched slowly down the neck of the bottle; he was doing it closely, not allowing even the slightest interruption in his concentration to let loose a cascade of red. He ran his finger over the neck of the bottle and licked off the drip; then he poured in the water. As viscous as tar, a layer two fingers thick in each glass, this was no longer the same syrup from the bottle: its color had changed, had taken on a lighter shade, and there was a hint of a miraculous transformation to come. They were witness to the metamorphosis: the syrup rose, swirled through the water, and shyly declined to mix with the water, and the dark hue of the concentrate floated along the glass rim until Kasumić stirred the liquid with a spoon. The decisive moment, when both liquids succumbed, was something they couldn't see, but what they did see was that the transformation had come to an end: nowhere heavy syrup, nowhere pure water. The light hit the glass that Vidošić already knew would be his; he raised it, and, just when he was about to declare an ironic toast with the raspberry syrup and soda, his hand began to shake, quite unexpectedly, and a few droplets spattered across the table. He gave a dry sob. His chin trembled in agitation, a drizzle of invisible tears streamed down it, and his whole jaw, suddenly heavy, began to sag. Kasumić jumped up, turned to the wall to find a kitchen towel. The room was filled with the awkward sound of a man's sobs, inadvertently witnessed. Kasumić spent a long time looking for something, rummaging through drawers. He turned around only when the room was quiet again. Vidošić was calm; only his chin, mutilated by the unfamiliar razor, was still trembling. Kasumić sat down.

—Vidošić, is the kid . . . gone?

—Yes.

—Was it . . . complications, or . . . or did someone . . . ?

—Probably complications. These are not American procedurals.

—They aren't. They're so much worse. When will you know?

—Dunno. It hardly matters anyway.

Vidošić ran both hands over his face.

—I fucked up. I really did fuck up.

—Yes, yes, you did.

—I should have listened to you.

—You should have, but we can't know for certain that the kid saw something.

Vidošić looked Kasumić in the eye.

—He saw. I know what he saw.

Kasumić waited. Again Vidošić rubbed his face.

—Tell me, Kasumić, how well did you know Irma Žiger?

Kasumić took out a new cigarette. He took his time as he lit it. He inhaled the smoke and blew it under the kitchen table, between his legs.

—Four years ago, I spent two days with her. Or rather nights.

—And you failed to mention this?

—Failed.

—Did you catch on right away to what she was up to?

—I did and didn't. We didn't go to the Intercontinental on a proper raid, but to corroborate information. I didn't notice her and her friend at first. I turned when somebody, one of my, shall we call him old friends from around here, called me by name. He was one of those who, according to our local standards, had made it big in Zagreb. I sat with them. I thought maybe there were sparks between me and Irma. I was impressed; she was good-looking, smart, well educated. She knew foreign languages.

Again, he blew his smoke down between his legs and didn't look up right away. Vidošić had the impression that Kasumić was blushing.

—That evening we went to my place. And the next evening she came too, but there were no longer any sparks. It was like I was with a doll. And I had the distinct impression that he, the man from around here, had set me up. He'd served her to me, and I'd allowed myself to be hooked. Like a catfish. I extricated myself. She was relieved, and I can tell you I was too. And then when I ran into the two of them in Opatija, I could see, clear as day, what they were up to. She was escorting with a price, depending on the services rendered. There is nothing naive about it. They know exactly what they are getting into. Boosting their bottom line and spicing up their life. At least at first.

—And your local buddy?

—Without him and others like him, this doesn't work. There may be women who think they'll be able to play the rednecks with the shaved heads, the caterpillars who drive the big shots around and admire the women's sophistication, their smarts. No doubt they're hoping to land more than their fellow teachers at work can, but later it is all gimme, gimme, gimme. To keep up the tempo and stay ahead of the game, they try a little of the white stuff, *just this once*, but it's never *just this once*. With the help of the white stuff, nobody feels disgust about themselves. The yachts on the Adriatic are full of them. They arrive at the marinas with just their toilet kit in hand. The fancier ones go farther away, all the way to Italy, but Monday morning, there they are at their desks in their schools, clinics, offices. There are actual catalogs with the ladies, particularly the ones like this one who don't look like sluts. Well, you saw her.

—You're right, she doesn't look the part.

Kasumić stopped and looked at Vidošić. He was waiting for the question.

—So, what's the story with your . . . acquaintance?

—Nothing. He's just that. An acquaintance. A man I've met. I know a bit about him, but not all there is to know. There aren't many who know everything about him. All of us around here fought in the war, but he left his mark. That's what has been said. Who saw? Nobody? Who was with him? Nobody. Reports, if there were any, gone. Or somebody is keeping them in a drawer somewhere till they're needed. Where is he now? A driver and bodyguard for one of the big shots. He's not the first or last with a biography like his. How he lives, I don't know, but I'd say he has a hand in extortion, drugs, possibly weapons too, and I've heard that he is now getting involved in construction sites. But nobody has directly tied him to a case. His name is never aired in public, but he's everywhere, and he's always near the people in power. And that's all.

Vidošić took a notepad from his jacket pocket, along with some folded papers. He opened his notepad and showed it to Kasumić.

—Is this him?

—Yes.

—The top dogs keep him around?

—Silly question, Vidošić! The powerful people at the top like it if their subordinates have dirty laundry. A safety net. The police? The judiciary? The journalists? This is no octopus. An octopus is vulnerable. This is a spiderweb. The larvae are proliferating, but who are the spiders that sit there, spinning their web? Everybody sees them, but nobody knows.

Vidošić shrugged, dropped his shoulders, and looked at Kasumić, who was rolling the lit tip of his cigarette along the edge of the ashtray.

—It was him David saw. The bodyguard.

The ember on Kasumić's cigarette stopped; then he began knocking it on the edge of the ashtray.

—An assumption, but do you have proof?

—An assumption, but it will be proven. David's mother sent me an SMS that she needed to check some phone numbers on her child's phone. We were away on the holidays. I didn't see her message till yesterday. But the message is here. I still don't understand why that phone matters, but it may be part of the story. We'll see.

—How did you figure out that the bodyguard is in play here?

—Yesterday. After I left the hospital, when everything . . . was already over. I walked, I got to Jurišićeva. I stopped. I was terribly tired. Crazed. I leaned on the window by that tourist center, and a Roma man was busking, playing an accordion next to me. It was getting on my nerves. I stood there watching, and there was this big screen in the bank window across the way; that idiotic campaign ad was running, and the papers had all been writing that the people in the photograph are people who were dressed to look like supporters, but in fact they were on the payroll for the candidates—fake ordinary people, fake workers, fake farmers. There is one that everybody made jokes about, a little too heavyset for an accordion player, and his hairpiece looked all wrong. The Roma man said to me, this guy is just yanking the bellows around, he's not playing properly. That same second, I remembered that I'd seen the man with the shaved head at the police headquarters in the corridor, the day after you . . . left. He was looking for you.

—Looking for me?

—Yes, out in the corridor he was pretending to look for you, using your nickname, Tesla. So we'd remember he'd been there.

—And to let me know that because of my connection with Irma, he had me by the short hairs. He knew I'd hear he was looking for me sooner or later.

—Besides, he already knew you weren't around. We have a leak at the police station. He had come for information, to see how far we'd come along. Very clever, to go straight to the head. With no threat for whoever is leaking. They can't use the computer; that's traceable, and the same with printing things. They have to do their snitching directly, verbally, and it's the least dangerous to do so right there at the police station. He registered at the front desk that he was looking for Kasumić. The officer at the front desk was somebody who didn't know you'd left, so easy peasy. And he already knew there was somebody new at the front desk. I don't know whom he went to. I remembered that Žigerica, in her first conversation at the police station, mentioned the autopsy results, though we had only received the results a few hours earlier, and nobody but us knew about them. Who is snitching? Who is our Deep Throat? We don't know.

NADA GAŠIĆ

—And the kid?

—David must have seen him. I don't know how, but he saw him. We all gag over that campaign ad and the poster that shows the same group of little old ladies, workers, the accordion player— my kids can hardly wait, they sing along with it on TV. David is no different . . . He wasn't different. I remembered an incredible thing. I know it's a stretch . . . I remembered that while I was at the site where the body was found, my shoes got so muddy that I stood on a piece of paper. I looked down and saw that I was standing on a scrap of the poster, and somebody had scribbled on it. I had the impression that on the big guy with the accordion, a kid had drawn a cap with horns. Not exactly like Asterix, but similar. I remembered that David's mother said she watched *Asterix* with David. Everything came together in a second. I know it's a stretch, but maybe David was the one who drew that, maybe David recognized that the accordion player was your bodyguard, or driver, or whatever.

—A stretch, that's for sure.

—Really? And your story with the torn pocket and the backpack? If I'd believed your improbable story about the boy and the backpack, maybe David would be alive today. Not believing was easiest. It's so easy not to believe.

Kasumić didn't look up. He carefully slid the ember of his cigarette along the ashtray.

— Kasumić, it's him. It is. Somehow the kid saw him.

—We can't know. David's not here to tell us.

Vidošić scraped his hand along his jaw, and his teeth rattled. He closed his eyes and opened them abruptly. He was chasing an image.

—I know. David's mom, when she's able to, can tell me exactly where David was that night, when the body was dropped behind the school. I think she wasn't telling the truth. She was protecting her sister and didn't want to have David pulled in, so we wouldn't give him a hard time. Now she no longer has anyone to protect.

His voice trembled.

—Fuck this life. She was always wearing a brooch of an accordion player. If she'd known . . . How the hell am I going to face her?

Kasumić let him be for a moment. Vidošić opened the papers.

—I printed something out for you. Here, this is the profile of the murderer; we didn't have it earlier. I think it's pretty good.

—This doesn't mean a thing. All sorts of things are possible. Maybe this was just a plain old sex game that went awry, maybe she asked for more than the usual rate, or maybe she tried some sort of blackmail. They tend to take precautionary measures. They know a lot, and they are always a risk. Maybe this acquaintance of mine was, again, the second echelon. Maybe he was just handling a dirty job for someone else.

—Maybe. But Irma Žiger is here. She should be pressured. She will talk. She will talk, whether she likes it or not.

Vidošić took a sip of the raspberry syrup and soda and then pushed the glass toward the middle of the table.

—Give me the hard stuff. I can't drink this.

Kasumić opened the cabinet with the bottles.

\*       \*       \*

Irma opened the cabinet with the bottles.

She took out a bottle of cognac and drank from it with long gulps. Then she took out all the bottles and glasses and set them on the floor. She pushed the mirror to the side, and behind it there was a hollow space. She took out a box, and from the box took out a little bag. Again, she reached for the bottle and set it by the bed where she was sitting. She opened the bag, shook the contents into her hand. With her other hand she raised the bottle and, steadily, with a few brief pauses, swallowed the pills and washed them down with the cognac. She lay down. Soon all the sorrow and anxiety and fear went away. There was nothing. Irma's face looked weary even when it was no longer the face of a living person—the face of someone who was dead.

*     *     *

Kasumić reached for the shot glasses, then stopped and opted for wineglasses instead. He poured each of them half a glass, then, as if they were about to begin a game of Go, he set the rakija bottle down on the edge of the table. Without looking up for a toast, Vidošić downed two good gulps. He looked up and waited for Kasumić to look at him.

—I will never forgive myself for not protecting the boy. I really fucked up. Unforgivably.

—You will, you'll forgive yourself. But that you fucked up, yes, you did. And I fucked up big-time. Big-time. If I'd told you everything I knew about the teachers and the bodyguard, maybe everything would have gone differently.

—This can't be fixed.

—Everybody sooner or later produces shit that water can't wash away.

Both of them drank.

—Just so it doesn't look in the end as if the tram killed the child.

Kasumić finished his drink.

—Yes, it's possible that it will look as if the tram killed the child.

Vidošić also finished his drink.

—What do you think, who is leaking information from the department?

—I don't know. If someone is having their arm twisted, then Simčić, formerly Simić, would be the easiest to strong-arm. Those people who used to be Serbs are the most vulnerable. But then again, I think he'd be scared. He's a coward. I don't know. And Zdilar . . .

—He could. He's so sweet and always, sort of . . . so obliging.

—All of us are suspicious until something is proved.

—All of us are suspicious. They'll pressure you over Žigerica and the bodyguard. You'll have a lot of explaining to do.

Kasumić looked Vidošić in the eye.

—Who will pressure me? The same one who'll pressure you because you dismissed my information about David's backpack? Who is this, and who will tell him?

Vidošić looked down at the table and said nothing. Both of them felt that the silence had teeth.

Kasumić rubbed his neck and interrupted the silence.

—We don't know anything. Not where the murder happened, nor whether this will be pushed any further.

Vidošić pulled himself together.

—If someone needs for all of this to be exposed, it will be. We'll see how far they'll let us get. We'll see how tough the bodyguard will be and what he'll say. And what his car will show us. We have enough material for DNA. We have enough material to prove all of it.

—Did you tell anyone when you . . . left?

—My wife. And I said at work that I wouldn't be there for a day or two.

He smiled sourly and added:

—Do you want to come back with me? I wrote the proposal about your suspension and left it in my drawer.

Kasumić didn't answer with a smile.

—I don't know.

He got up, went over to the stove, and took the lid off the pot, from which a wisp of fragrant smoke rose. Vidošić watched the hand that steadily made at first bigger circles and then smaller and smaller ones, following a spiral forming in the thick stew. Suddenly he wanted to stand by the hot stove too.

—May I?

Kasumić didn't even turn.

—No. I cook beans alone.

Vidošić got up anyway and went over to the stove. He watched the steady hand that in the molasses-like stew tailored spiraling circles whose traces slower and slower filled in on the edges, and he felt a sudden pang of envy and an urge to mock the usurper of this precious task.

—What did your neighbor call you?

—Tesla.

—Where does that come from?

—I was always puttering around with things, so in elementary school that's what the kids called me. First I beat them up, then I got used to it.

—Ah, so that's why you studied Latin! Why didn't you say?

Kasumić was quietly focused.

—Fine, then, Tesla, do you put any heat in these beans of yours?

—I did, but I can always add more.

He reached for the lowest hot pepper on the red-pepper wreath, broke off its tip, and tossed it into the beans. He carefully scattered over the surface ground black pepper from a little paper packet, as if adding the powdered tail of a dried mouse. Like a seasoned herbalist, he did not taste his miracle-working dish. He stepped back from the stove.

—There. Now it should rest.

—Will that neighbor of yours come by?

—I haven't heard a mine go off, so he'll probably come by.

—Are there still a lot of mines out there?

—Quite a few have been disarmed, but there still are plenty. You can't go everywhere, and not everybody can deal with it.

He looked Vidošić in the eye.

—Would you like to come with me to my shed? I can show you something.

Vidošić nodded. They went out and stopped only to take a deep breath. They looked in the same direction and saw a man, bent over, wearing a mismatched camouflage outfit, coming toward them from the forest. Over his shoulder he had slung his gun.

*     *     *

From the forest in the north part of Zagreb there were no sounds. Well concealed, lying on his stomach, a sniper watched a man who closed the trunk of a brand-new light-gray BMW. Entranced by the beauty of the car, the man who'd closed the trunk stood still for a moment. Enough time for a precise shot to the head. The man was tall and strong, a real giant with a shaved head, dressed in a pristine suit and perfectly clean shoes whose size was not sold in shoe stores. He fell slowly, as if he'd thrown his arms around his new, light-gray BMW.

*     *     *

They knew it would take the neighbor a while to reach them, so they turned onto a path behind the house. Walking ahead, Kasumić led the way to a wooden hut some 20 meters away. Under the bared branches of an elderberry bush, the hut had been slapped together from brownish-gray boards that somebody had once thought might be put to good use but were forgotten and gradually deteriorated until they were closer to debris. Vidošić was genuinely surprised when he saw Kasumić approaching something he was able to recognize, only with effort, as a door. The door opened inward. Kasumić entered. Vidošić paused on the threshold and waited for his eyes to adjust to the gloom. He was surprised that inside the shed, which looked from the outside as if it were an integral part of its surroundings, the air was so different from the outside air. It even seemed warmer. He watched as Kasumić leaned over, as if checking to see whether a baby was breathing in a cradle. Vidošić came closer.

In front of Kasumić there was a small wooden device on a wooden stand. Vidošić didn't realize at first that the device was actually moving; unwittingly he reached toward it, but then jerked back his hand. Amazed, he stared at the miniature gears, pulleys, converters, receivers, and thin wires. Quietly, under layers of dust, everything was moving, moving ...

He watched the fanciful creation, avoiding the obligatory male gesture of crouching down and feeling under the base to check what it was plugged into.

Vidošić spoke only when he began to feel that the silence had reached the point when it ceased to express admiration and began to feel rude.

—Did you make this?

—Yes.

—What is it?

—I don't know.

—When did you make it?

—When I started fixing the house. The hut had been spared because it is nothing. Not a house, not a church. I stored things here, even slept here, and then bit by bit, I began fiddling with this. It relaxed me.

—It is always running?

—No. When it stops, I poke it, nudge it, and it starts again.

—And it makes no sound? It's as if it's built of silence.

—The wood has smoothed ... it slides.

—Looks like Tesla infected you Likans with technology.

—He didn't, he's one of theirs.

The two men straightened up, and though they hadn't touched anything, they wiped their hands on their legs. They were brushing off an invisible spiderweb.

—Let's go, so the beans don't get cold.

—So they don't get cold.

Kasumić waited by the door for Vidošić, who walked out backward.

They were accompanied by a monotonous sound.

They stopped outside the hut, protecting their eyes by squinting. The light was too strong. Then they separated and cautiously leaned each on their side of the doorway, leaving the door ajar between them. Kasumić took out his cigarettes and handed one, with the box of matches, to Vidošić. Seasoned smokers, aware of the pleasure of lighting up, they gave themselves over to the noble ritual of the birthing of the smoke. They inhaled and exhaled in unison.

They did not turn to one another, and they did not know that both were looking in the same direction, down the slope toward the river. Neither of them asked the other whether he'd picked up the smell of early snow, nor did they check to see, with look or gesture, whether both could see that above the unpopulated expanses of the region, like steam from the cracked crust of an overbaked cake, a sparse fog was rising through which the sun could barely shine. Little crystals of water glistened, and they couldn't decide whether what they were looking at was finely ground mother-of-pearl or confectioners' sugar dribbling from the baker's hand while they, despairing over their failure at the art of baking, pondered their unopened fist and mused whether to use up all the confection-ers' sugar filling in the cracks or to return the sugar, unused, to the paper bag. Weary.

# Water as coda

Only after the water receded was it possible to see what the Sava had left behind: the shacks that had been tumbledown before the flood, collapsed; where plaster had been damaged, it crumbled; bared brick caved in; what had been a road became a gully; what had been a garden was buried in mud.

Trešnjevka was ravaged.

Out of fear of more houses collapsing, and of outbreaks of infections from water polluted with waste and the carcasses of drowned animals and the sudden infestation of rats, none of which could be controlled, the authorities did not allow residents to return right away. There was no electricity for another full month, not even in the houses along the main thoroughfares, and some neighborhoods had to wait for months to have their streetlights restored. All the Trešnjevka schools closed for fifteen days, and after fifteen days, students were notified where their teachers and classroom desks would be waiting for them. The students of Kata Dumbović Elementary were transferred to Brotherhood–Unity

Elementary, and for a few months after that the classrooms served two classes; an hour-long class lasted for only twenty-five minutes. Students of Trešnjevka high school went to the Upper Town, and there, in dangerous mobs of sixty teenagers per classroom, they had a lively time of it for several months. Those who remember those days think back on them with nostalgia; never again was there so much fun to be had at school.

The afflicted residents of Trešnjevka stayed with relatives and friends for a time in the unflooded parts of the city, some in the outlying villages and some in hotels, until they wore out their welcome with their relatives and friends and the hotel staff. The Yugoslav People's Army soldiers banded together with fire-fighters, the police, all the workers whose factories had been flooded, employees whose establishments had been under water, and even the teachers and students whose schools had been flooded to clean the neighborhood, carting away the mud, the clutter from the ruins, the uprooted trees, the branches, and the layers of water-soaked furniture debris. But residents felt they were coming home only when they began cleaning their own houses, yards, and gardens and cleaned what remained of the intact furniture and dishes.

The houses were approached with caution, braving the stench of rot and the stink of the Sava waters, which Trešnjevka would reek from for another decade. One approached slowly, along the main streets. There were some side streets and byways that couldn't be broached at all. The inundation of sludge and the ruined buildings completely changed Trešnjevka's appearance. Not all the houses could be reached, and there were ones that never would. The water had brought them down.

Nobody remembers the houses that disappeared in the flood. Those who built them died, and those who lived in them as children forgot them. Nobody ever took photographs of those little houses, and even if they had, the photographs were washed away in the water. New houses were raised in their place, and the residents of those new houses remember the streets, the villages, and the towns where they grew up. And that's normal.

## About Ana, Katarina's mother

Ana Firman, Katarina's mother, was surrounded for several days after giving birth by people she didn't know, concern expressed by her doctors, and attention such as she'd never known; the foot of the bed buckled under the pile of presents, and volunteers from the Red Cross brought her a complete set, secondhand, of black mourning clothes. The funeral was prepared without her, and the doctor rejected the very thought that the young widow would be allowed to attend that sad event. Three days after giving birth and the news of the death of the father of her child, Ana's tears suddenly dried. The nurses praised her. The birthing mothers who came through their room one after another watched her in amazement, and then the amazement of the women and the approval of the support medical staff gradually stagnated, transforming into open intolerance, even a sort of envy for the gifts that now, it seemed, were there undeservedly at the foot of her bed. The women no longer addressed her in hushed tones, and the nurses stopped asking whether she needed anything.

The day before her husband's funeral, Ana, Katarina's mother, walked out of the maternity ward. Ignoring the advice of the doctors and the pleas of her sisters-in-law, on the seventh day after Katarina's birth, putting on her blue broadcloth smock over the clothes she'd received, she attended her husband's funeral. In response to a sister-in-law's incredulous *whatever moved you to wear that smock, when you were given good-as-new black clothes from the Red Cross*, Ana replied, more calmly than the situation might have warranted:

—This is the only thing I have that isn't someone else's or borrowed.

At her sister-in-law's apartment, the first two weeks passed in harmony, and then the first criticisms began, which ended in reconciliation and shared tears. After three weeks there was a fight that did not end in reconciliation, so Ana asked her other sister-in-law to look after the baby, and she went to Mala Street. Word had gotten out that there were brave souls who had begun the cleanup, and apparently it all wasn't quite as awful as it looked at first glance, and better to start cleaning before the mud dried. A light snow was falling that wasn't staying on the ground. She took the tram to the Museum of Technology; it didn't go any farther. The soil under the tram tracks had been washed out, so there were no tram lines to the Trešnjevka farmers market or to the car barns where the trams were stored. It took her another forty-five minutes to make her way through to her street.

Walking down Gvozdanska was almost impossible.

When she finally reached Mala Street, she felt a sickly lassitude come over her. She grabbed hold of a tilting lamppost and waited for her breathing to steady. She didn't look toward her house. In fact, she didn't look at anything. She just listened to the sound of the scraping of a shovel—measured, monotonous, as if someone were clearing morning snow from in front of their door. But snow, a real snowfall, still hadn't happened. She started seeing something white looking out in front of her house, and she knew this was an illusion, not a reflection off the surface of snow, and it meant that she was about to faint, so she gave her head a shake. The brownish view of the gloomy street returned and the sound of the shovel made more sense; someone in a nearby house was scraping mud. The shovel went quiet; a neighbor came out of his house and looked over to where the young woman was standing.

—Ana, is that you?

—Yes. Hello, Mr. Ožbolt.

—God be with you, Ana, but why did you come by yourself? I wouldn't have recognized you without the belly. What are you going to do here, in the frigid winter cold?

—I'm just here to have a look at whether the house is still standing.

—It's standing, oh yes, it's standing. Your old lady is not giving in. We're already scrubbing ours.

He felt his cheery tone was all wrong. Perplexed about whether to first convey his condolences or congratulate her on the baby, he decided that what made the most sense was to clean his hands, so he wiped them on his pants and went over to her.

—We haven't seen each other since . . . since then. Please accept my condolences. Such a strong, young man . . .

He teared up, moved by his own words. Caught short by Ana's dry eyes and icy face, he stopped his tears. How can one cry without company?

—I heard you had a little girl. My Cilika saw her at Vinogradska. You know that we sent Cilika that afternoon to my wife's sister in Trnje before the water reached us. We thought she'd be safer there. But the water reached them as well. They had to climb up on the roof. The rescuers had trouble finding them with a boat. And they, too, were taken to Vinogradska. Cilika says she saw the little one there. So it goes; we thought we were doing the best we could for her, but we nearly lost our girl.

Vilim caught himself and stopped, realizing that it wasn't kind of him to be speaking about his family, all of whom had survived the flood. Then he said:

—As long as the little one is alive and well, there will always be time for tears.

Ana said not a word. Vilim stood there awkwardly, and then, remembering his own first encounter with his flooded home, he dropped his head in sympathy and withdrew into his yard.

The regular sound of the scraping shovel resumed.

Her spell of lightheadedness had passed, and Ana walked over to her house. The wooden fence had tipped over; the once-white one-story building was filthy beyond belief from the muddy water; the accumulated sludge had eaten away at the windows; their upper edge was only 30 centimeters above the mud. Because of this, the house looked as if it had sunk. Ana glanced up at the roof and felt a surge of tenderness. It looked like their good old roof. Corroded, indeed, damaged, wounded, but their roof. She would have stroked it if she'd been able to reach that high. She smiled at it. She had a look around the yard and decided that *what happened* hadn't happen here. From that moment forward, until the end of her life, she never referred to the death of her husband as drowning, but always as *what happened*. She ventured one more step through the yard and had a look at the garden. Water-soaked heaps of all sorts of things prevented her from having a good look at it. She saw an unexpected open space and realized that the fruit trees were gone. They'd been uprooted. Then, the way a turtle pulls in its neck, she tipped her head and looked at the huge winter cherry tree. It stood there calmly, as if nothing had ever happened. Ana smiled at the tree, just as she'd smiled at the roof. There was nobody to whom she could make her promise, so she addressed the cherry tree.

—Tomorrow I'm coming home. I'll clean everything; my girl will have her home and her house, and nobody will ever drive her from it.

Before she left the street, she went over to say goodbye to Mr. Ožbolt. And after she'd said goodbye, she added:

—Mr. Ožbolt, Cilika was the first from our street who saw my Katarina. I am asking you, if you agree and Cilika is willing, for Cilika to be my Katarina's kuma for her baptism. Cilika is already a big girl, she has been confirmed.

Vilim said nothing, but he nodded. Nothing could stop his tears.

Later she couldn't recollect why, on her way back into town, near the Trešnjevka farmers market, she turned toward Potok, toward Savska Road. She never told anybody that she fought her way through the terrible mud and underbrush littered with remnants of clothing, that the dark caught up with her at Potok, that the pavement rippled, that she saw the vast shadows of rats and that she felt as if one of them had slid down her back.

Later, everything was regular life.

According to the taste and the opinions of the neighborhood, the street, that part of town, and her sisters-in-law, Ana Firman, who later took the name Žiger when she remarried, who was Katarina, Irma, and Ita's mother, had married too early, was widowed too early, remarried too early, had Katarina's sisters too late, and then died too early. After her, there remained the shadow of a doubt that for all that happened to her and her daughters in life, she was, at least partly, to blame.

## About Katarina's father

Zdravko Firman, Katarina's father, was found relatively quickly and relatively close to home by a search party aboard an army inflatable dinghy. Nobody could say with certainty how and why this powerful twenty-seven-year-old man had drowned, so the street and neighborhood made do with two versions: the first circled around Christmas, when people favored stories about goodness and personal sacrifice, and this version placed on a pedestal the torments of the selfless hero, who'd risked his young life and died trying to wake up the hard-of-hearing and cranky Zgorelecs, who were wide awake and didn't leave their attic until the waters receded. The other story made the rounds in late spring, when the fruits of the gardens still hadn't arrived, and the preserves in the pantry were dwindling, and there were rumors that Zdravko Firman's parents, during World War II, in the attic, had been watching over a chest of Jewish treasures, and as nobody ever came to retrieve it, Zdravko Firman tried

NADA GAŠIĆ

to carry out the heavy chest and drowned while clutching it. The rumors also alleged that the chest was later found by soldiers, and was robbed by officers of the Yugoslav People's Army. Nothing of this could be proved, and all that remained was the fact that Katarina's father was buried at the expense of the state one week after Katarina was born.

### About Gramps Zgorelec

Mr. Zgorelec had been proud his whole life that he, his wife, and his son, Vilim, *tied themselves up in the attic and saved themselves and their belongings from thieves*. While his wife was still alive, they took in, as guardians, a child from a home, a hunchbacked and mentally disabled seven-year-old boy; nobody knew who he was or where he was from. Funds to support the boy came regularly from the municipality, and Cilika got used to him when she, later, married quiet Vilim Zagorelec and moved next door to their house. Gramps Zgorelec in his ninety-second year not only didn't notice Big Boy, he had no recollection of him whatsoever. There were times when he no longer knew what to do, and, out of boredom and the feeling of despair that alternates, for nonagenarians, with a feeling of boundless joy that they are outliving people who were younger than them, Gramps Zgorelec would go up to the attic, tie himself to one of the beams, and shout at the top of his lungs, *The water will carry all of you away, damned bastards, and I'll survive and outlive you all*. His senility had chipped away at him, but it hadn't utterly undone him, and nobody could say for sure whether Gramps

was tying himself to the attic beam because of senile dementia or because he loved it when members of the household and helpful neighbors carried him down the attic stairs. And, soon enough, it happened that Cilika had *her hands full with work and would have to go to the farmers market*, and it was only at dinnertime when they noticed that the plate on which she'd served Gramps his doughnut had gone untouched. They stared at the decoration of faded flowers on the dish and called out:
—Gramps, Gramps, dear!

They found old Zgorelec up in the attic, dead, tied to the bearing beam with a smile on his lips and a flashlight in his stiffening hand. The flashlight was not on; old man Zgorelec was thrifty in this world. He'd need it for later.

## And quiet Vilim?

Nothing had ever happened so gorgeous or extravagant in Vilim's life as when Ita fell at her wedding and her legs went flying up into the air. He knew he'd remember this for the rest of his life, but what he didn't know was that his life wouldn't last for much longer, because after the splendid discovery of Ita's bare bottom, Vilim Zgorelec would live for only four more weeks. His impression of her magnificent bared buttocks significantly stoked his sexual appetites but shortened his biological life, something Vilim couldn't have chosen, nor repent in time. In this, in fact, Cilika colluded; she couldn't get over her astonishment when Vilim developed an insatiable sexual hunger in their otherwise long since dried-up sexual life, and wisely she decided to take advantage of it and chose not to challenge her husband or destiny with any heedless questions. She did wonder whether Vilim had a stash of pornography hidden away, but as the TV psychologists and the psychiatrists on the pages of magazines said, this was a normal, and, indeed, desirable form of sexual arousal; frankly, she was thrilled by her husband's sudden passionate advances. Had she known that before his eyes, while he was panting, slapping her on the bottom, and singing *cute little ass*, were flashing the white legs and cleaving buttocks of Ita Žiger, now Slaviček, Cilika would have behaved a little differently. As it was, all she did was breathe heavily and close her eyes, and she only sobered from the passion when, late one afternoon, four weeks after Ita's wedding, following an ample dinner and a long afternoon nap, she found herself on the sofa, pinioned by the heavy body of her husband, who had stopped panting and licking his lips and slapping her on her *cute little ass*. Although horrified, she kept a clear head and showed remarkable composure, and, though feeble, she managed to wriggle free from under her dead husband, because she hadn't allowed him to lie on top of her with his full weight, out of concern for her arthritic hip. As soon as she got up, she went to the bathroom to clean up, tend to her hair, and put on decent clothes. Tidied and already reconciled to the widow's fate, she went back into the room, and, with incredible effort, she dressed *Vilim, my cute little ass* in underwear, pajamas, thanking the Blessed Virgin Mary of Marija Bistrica that Vilim hadn't insisted on total nudity, and had simply dropped his pajama bottoms to his knees. The fact that her spouse had breathed his last on top of her was not entirely objectionable, and she sincerely wept and through her tears repeated, *Vilim was my love and I was his, what a cute little ass*. She repeated this at the dignified funeral, for which, just in case, she paid for an extra priest, and for another two months, right up to the moment when they held the probate hearing, at which her tears dried up the instant she was thunderstruck by the incredible fact that her beloved spouse, Vilim Zagorelec, in a legal and binding will, with no warning and without any publicly known reasons, had left half of his life savings, to the tune of 4,600 euros, to Ita Žiger, who took the married name of Slaviček.

It took two full days for widow Cecilija Zgorelec, née Ožbolt, known familiarly as Cilika, to come to her senses, and then she remembered that Ita had come to see them the day before the wedding to pick up the miraculous lotion for speedy hair growth. She remembered that she had popped out to the store and had left Ita alone with her late spouse, who, apparently, couldn't locate the beer bottle that held the lotion. She remembered that he had been confused and had given Ita the gravestone polish instead. She remembered that she had said goodbye to Ita that day at the door, and had noticed that she, the bitch, was red in the face. She got up, looked at herself in the mirror, straightened up; with her left hand she lifted her right breast, and with her right hand she lifted her left breast, and then loudly declared:

—Damned if you'll get a cent, you cursed whore—I bet you gave him pussy. That pussy will be coming out your ears.

With a surge of energy unusual for her age and the objective state of her hips, she marched directly off to the police station. Cilika never feared the authorities.

# And the others?

THE STUDENTS who waved from the roof of the student dormitory in Cvjetno naselje went their separate ways throughout Croatia and through the countries that emerged after Yugoslavia fell apart. Some of them went overseas. Today they are seventy-year-olds. Only a few of them remember the floods, but they have long since stopped trying to convince their offspring that they were surrounded by water in the middle of Zagreb. They no longer say that some of them took part in strenuous work brigades to build the embankments designed to protect Zagreb from the Sava River. Some of them think back on their shovels with nostalgia, some have forgotten, and some are ashamed that they worked for a month with no financial compensation. For the most part they aren't believed, some because of the weirdness of the story, others because of their advanced age.

THE OLD MAN who wept for his dog, died on an iron cot at the Red Cross shelter eleven days after the flood. His dog, Don, an unpedigreed German shepherd, survived the deluge of water and scrambled out onto dry land in the vicinity of Rudeš. He shivered for two days, there by a fence, and once he'd recovered, he made for the first small house where he could smell food. He was fed. The owner had a female dog whose hormones had been strained by the stress, and the odor of the bitch in heat kept Don by her fence for the next few days. The owner couldn't defend her dog. The call of love was stronger than all else, and

Don lost several precious days before he could return to the old dying man. When the dog regained his senses and returned to the Red Cross shelter, it was too late. He moped around for another year, barely surviving. People said they saw him near a small, devastated house on Bočačka, then in the vicinity of the train station, near the shelter, and someone even claimed to have seen him up at the Mirogoj Cemetery. The truth was different. Don couldn't forgive himself for his betrayal of the old man. Feeble, unable to accept a new master, he died near the tracks on Kranjčevićeva. The bitch he'd been courting whelped six puppies. From the litter, a soldier, on his way home, took one with him to Lika. Kasumić's dog descended from that puppy. Nobody would have had any reason to trace that dog's origins to Trešnjevka, or the flood, or even Zagreb.

THE SOLEMN MAN who was rowing along Savska Road was not from that part of town or the neighborhood. Some witnesses swore this had to be the state champion in white-water kayaking; others were prepared to swear by all that's holy that he was a mystery man who caught the thieves who, not long after the waters receded, showed up near houses where there was no owner present. Allegedly, he punished them mercilessly right there and then. No one ever found out who he was, not where he had embarked nor where the boat was going with its quiet oarsman.

THE BEDRAGGLED CHICKENS ON THE FENCE ON Drežnička Street are no longer there, so, therefore, they were taken up by the unresolved conundrum of the chicken and the egg.

THE TWO SEVENTH GRADERS who, after the news that the grading registers had been washed away in the building at #95/101A Savska Road, sang the song *Youuuu aaare myyyy destinyyyy*, met for the last time when they were eighteen-year-olds.

THE PEOPLE who were standing on the sandbag levee by the Student Center never saw the picture that was taken of them.

Their descendants are alive.

As are the descendants of the rats on the raft.

MURKY PLASTIC SHEETING

The man who hides behind the murky plastic sheeting is visible, but for now he is not recognizable. He doesn't like fast driving, so he may well live to a ripe old age. He is choosy about his drivers.

FOUR WOMEN, to put it politely, lost their lives. Someone will say they left this world; someone else will say they disappeared, or that they were taken from us, or done away with. Aside from these mundane phrases, and dozens of others, they all come down to the same thing: kill, kills, killed.

FOR ONE OF THE WOMEN, we don't know whether the name she was using was really hers, or whether she was the beloved illusion of a lonely man. If she was a late-season butterfly that hadn't felt the nip of the frosts in time, her time was passing; although, as she would be dying soon in any case, her death, no matter how sad it might be, could not be deemed murder. Of her it might have been said and written that her life extinguished.

THE SECOND: nothing was ever uncovered about her death; it wouldn't be known whether her putative executor gave her too many potent pills, or that her head rolled from the combination of opiates and alcohol. Of her there would be only a brief mention about how she died due to unexplained circumstances.

TWO OF THE WOMEN in this novel have no name.

About one, her husband-murderer said she was skilled at conversation, and that sufficed; both in this story and in life, this matters more than names and much more than last names. About her it would probably be said that she was the tragic victim of unfortunate circumstances.

SHE who was murdered, rolled up in murky plastic sheeting, and dumped from the trunk of a car had a first name, and she had a last name. But, as the face of a dead person is different from the face of a living person, so it is that the first and last name of the living person is different from the first and last name of someone who has been murdered, no matter how hard we try to keep this from being the case. It is therefore best to avoid using this victim's first and last name, just as it is best to avoid describing either her living face or her dead face.

Her face, like the face of water, is always changing and always unchanging, like the face of a river in southwestern Europe, which is 940 kilometers long, rises as Nadiža Creek in Tamar, then goes underground and emerges to the light of day in Zelenci, near Rateče, flowing in a southwesterly direction, given the name Dolinka, joins the Bohinjka and flows through Croatia as a river with its source between Triglav and the

Slovenian-Austrian border near Kranjska Gora, joins the Bohinjka at Lancovo and is our longest river, as it is in Bosnia and Herzegovina, where it forms the border between Bosnia and Herzegovina and Serbia, within which it is a southeastern European river with its source in Kranjska Gora and flows along the Karavanka Alps and the Julian Alps to the southeast; regardless of what the national Wikipedias say, wherever it springs, wherever it flows, all along its tributaries, this river has been named by all the members of the majority ethnic groups, the minority ethnic groups, the ethnic minorities, the name coming from the Greek *Saovios*, via the Latin *Savus*: the Sava.

*About Sandorf Passage*

SANDORF PASSAGE publishes work that creates a prismatic perspective on what it means to live in a globalized world. It is a home to writing inspired by both conflict zones and the dangers of complacency. All Sandorf Passage titles share in common how the biggest and most important ideas are best explored in the most personal and intimate of spaces.